Praise for Barbara Metzger

"Metzger's prose absolutely tickles the funny bone." —*L.A. Life Daily News*

"One of the genre's wittiest pens. Barbara Metzger deliciously mixes love and laughter." —*Romantic Times*

"Fresh, funny, touching, and romantic . . . one delicious read." —Edith Layton

"A doyen of humorous Regency-era romance writing, Metzger pens in the witty tradition of historical romance authors Marion Devon and Marion Chesney. . . . Regency romance at its finest and funniest." —*Publishers Weekly*

REGENCY ROMANCE
COMING IN FEBRUARY 2006

Rake's Ransom
and
A Loyal Companion

Barbara Metzger

A SIGNET BOOK

SIGNET
Published by New American Library, a division of
Penguin Group (USA) Inc., 375 Hudson Street,
New York, New York 10014, USA
Penguin Group (Canada), 90 Eglinton Avenue East, Suite 700, Toronto,
Ontario M4P 2Y3, Canada (a division of Pearson Penguin Canada Inc.)
Penguin Books Ltd., 80 Strand, London WC2R 0RL, England
Penguin Ireland, 25 St. Stephen's Green, Dublin 2,
Ireland (a division of Penguin Books Ltd.)
Penguin Group (Australia), 250 Camberwell Road, Camberwell, Victoria 3124,
Australia (a division of Pearson Australia Group Pty. Ltd.)
Penguin Books India Pvt. Ltd., 11 Community Centre, Panchsheel Park,
New Delhi - 110 017, India
Penguin Group (NZ), cnr Airborne and Rosedale Roads, Albany,
Auckland 1310, New Zealand (a division of Pearson New Zealand Ltd.)
Penguin Books (South Africa) (Pty.) Ltd., 24 Sturdee Avenue,
Rosebank, Johannesburg 2196, South Africa

Penguin Books Ltd., Registered Offices:
80 Strand, London WC2R 0RL, England

Published by Signet, an imprint of New American Library, a division of Penguin Group (USA) Inc. *Rake's Ransom* was previously published by Zebra
Books and Walker and Company. *A Loyal Companion* was previously published by Fawcett Crest, a division of Random House, Inc., New York.

First Signet Printing, January 2006
10   9   8   7   6   5   4   3   2   1

Rake's
Ransom

To Stacy and Jeri,
my two favorite nieces,
with love

1

"By all that is holy, Trevaine, you've got to do something about that daughter of yours!" If complexion were a barometer of feelings, Squire George Bottwick was in a raging gale of a mood. His round face as red as the scarlet hunt jacket he wore, he stomped into the library of Treverly Hall and pounded on his friend's desk. "It's unlawful, unladylike, and . . . and unEnglish," he sputtered, the last being the worst, in his view.

Lord Trevaine carefully placed a marker in the book he was reading, laid it gently on the side of the desk farthest from the Squire and, looking up, settled the spectacles on his nose. "Good day, George. I didn't hear you come in."

"Didn't hear me? Didn't hear me?" roared his guest. "And I suppose you didn't hear the riot and ruckus outside your front door, not an hour past?"

"Why no, I was studying this passage here. . . ." He waved a thin hand in the book's general direction. "Quite interesting. You see—"

"No, blast it, Elliot, it's your daughter you should

be seeing to, not some demned book. I know I ain't bookish, but anyone can tell you the chit can't keep haring around the countryside, riding astride like a boy—"

"She is only seventeen, and it's safer that way."

"That's what you said at fourteen, and fifteen, and sixteen. Man, she's not a child anymore, to be out with nary a groom."

"Come, George, nothing is going to happen to her in our own neighbourhood, and she does have her dog for companion."

"It's not *her* safety I'm concerned with! And you call that monster a dog! Hellhound more like. Misbegotten whelp of a—"

"Irish wolfhound, actually, for the most part."

"Aye, part Irish revenge on the English, and part devil. It's a pretty pair you've set loose on us, Trevaine, a ragtag hoyden and a barn-sized bristle brush with fangs. Do you know what they've done now? Do you even care? Look at me, Trevaine, just look!"

Squire was still storming around the small room, brandishing his riding whip at a bust of poor blind Homer and challenging the neat stacks of books. His face was still red and his waistcoat, already straining to meet across his more than ample girth, was in danger of surrendering the cause, with all his huffing and puffing. The whole ensemble, in fact, was mudspattered and wet, with spots, stains and scuff marks. Fox one, locals zero? No, there had to be more to it, Lord Trevaine ruefully acknowledged. There always was, when his daughter Jacelyn was involved. He gestured Squire to the leather seat facing his, while he reached for the cut-glass decanter of

8

fine French brandy he kept on the side table. This was not the first time he had entertained his friend in such a fashion, and he well knew the delaying tactics to let the storm of Squire's anger blow itself out. While his friend sipped and mopped at his damp brow with a handkerchief, Lord Trevaine steepled his fingers and considered how times like this made him miss his wife more than ever. She had been dead almost ten years now, leaving him the sole raising of their daughter, a sunbeam in his darkened life. Jacelyn was bright and happy and lively and loving, everything her mother would have approved. Perhaps she was a trifle high-spirited, her father admitted, but that was to be expected in a girl surrounded only by doting servants. The rough edges would smooth out in time, he was sure. After all, she was ever kind and tenderhearted. The last thought brought Lord Trevaine back to the present, and his present company.

He cleared his throat. "I take it this has something to do with, er, fox hunting?"

Squire Bottwick sputtered, choking on his swallow. "Were you even aware there was to be a hunt this morning, then?"

"Actually, no. But by your dress . . . and discomposure . . ." Lord Trevaine hurriedly refilled the squire's glass.

He sympathised with the Squire, truly he did, for he knew that what books were to him, fox hunting was to George Bottwick. Squire did not read much more than farming journals, and Lord Trevaine's uncertain health kept him from the saddle, yet they each respected the other's ways. Miss Jacelyn Trevaine, however, in the plainest of unvarnished truths, did not approve of fox hunting. Oh, she listened to the arguments of chicken farmers and gameskeepers, but countered with the foxes' depredations of the far more destructive rodent populations. If, in a rare moment of conciliation, Jacelyn was willing to concede the possible necessity of controlling the foxes' numbers, she would never, with her last breath if need be, agree to such a brutal, bloody, barbaric method as the hunt. So, with the single-minded dedication of youth and righteous morality, she set out to eradicate the gory sport, or at least make it dashed uncomfortable for the local Master of the Hunt, Squire Bottwick.

One of Jacelyn's earliest efforts employed a vast quantity of pepper, primitive but effective. Another involved most of the village lads and all the dead fish they could accumulate. Jacelyn strewed the latter over the deer paths and forest tracks, covering whatever scent a fox may have left. That cost many a stand-up supper for the boys, and lost Miss Trevaine her last of many governesses. Whether Miss Polk resigned due to the stench, or well-bred dismay at the deed, or simple acknowledgement that the task of making her charge into a lady was beyond her, her departure freed Jacelyn, at age fifteen, from whatever constraints society was wont to impose on young females. The following season someone managed to keep overfeeding Squire's hounds with good beef and mutton until they grew too fat and lazy to chase anything more than dream foxes. Bottwick had suspicions, of course, but could never prove them. Lord Trevaine quietly grew fond of omelettes.

Even her loving father felt that Jacelyn had used unfair tactics last year, bringing two orphaned fox kits over to Bottwick's where Squire's three little girls, still in the schoolroom, could help care for the "innocent victims" of their father's bloodlust and butchery. Such whining and weeping had to reach even the hardest heart; Squire discovered business in London.

For all that, Jacelyn never injured the dogs or the horses or their riders, which she could have, setting out traps or deadfalls or draglines across the ridings. No, it was only Squire's pride—and pleasure—which got hurt. Bottwick seemed relaxed by now, warmed by the fire in the grate and the good brandy, so, taking care to top the glass first, Lord Trevaine cautiously suggested, "I take it you and my daughter had another, ah, confrontation this morning?"

"Confrontation? No, I never saw her but, your daughter or not, if I'd had my hands on her—"

Trevaine cleared his throat.

"—what you should have seen to years ago." He stomped over to the window, pointed with his wineglass. "Look at it out. Cool, crisp, no rain for the first day this week. Everyone came out for the hunt—not the London crowd; they'll get here week's end—but all the local gentry. There we were, assembled in my drive for a stirrup cup to get the blood flowing. Horses pawing, the kennelmen barely holding the dogs, they're so eager. The trumpet sounds *Away*. Ah, Trevaine, there's no sweeter sight nor sound than the pack in voice on the trail, gorgeous horseflesh, fine riders. Then my Jasper, the best pack leader I've ever seen, starts belling. I can hear it now:

A-roo, A-roo. And we all follow, through the home wood, across the spinney, over the stream, then cut back through Granders' and over the bridge at Treverly. We lost the vicar at Four Corners. What a ride! No *View Halloo* though, just the dogs running like the wind . . . right up to your front door."

"Hold, George. I know Jacelyn's got no fox cubs here now, and she could not get your dogs to follow a dead pelt. So what—"

"It wasn't any damned fox! It was that infernal dog of hers, in season. Anyone with a ha'penny's worth of sense knows to keep a bitch like that inside, but is that what your daughter does? Oh, no. Miss Trevaine takes the dog, and its bedding, and marks every blasted trail in the neighbourhood, leading every jack dog in the county right to your doorstep and the biggest dogfight you've ever read a damned book through. It took all your people and all mine, and buckets of water, just to separate them. Now my Jasper is back in the kennels, howling like some curst Romeo. And there's nary hide nor hair of missy and the dog, of course." Squire realised his last bellows were rattling the windowpanes. He wiped his face again, turned and in a quieter voice asked, "What do you think of your sweet, tender-hearted girl now?"

Lord Trevaine coughed to hide his laugh, but he answered, "A trifle indelicate, but ingenious all the same. I'll make good on any damages, of course." He refilled the glass.

"You always do. When the dog steals a ham curing in the sun, or attacks some villager's washline as if it were a row of advancing Frenchies, or when missy talks the tenants' sons into letting her plough the fields. You've got to stop laughing, Elliot. It is different now. Oh, I'll recover m'dignity, and the dogs will be fit by the house party, and old Reynard can have a rest till then, but it is high time you took your nose out of your books and had a better look around. The tabbies are talking about Jacelyn, and it ain't good. This morning's escapade alone will keep them meowing for days."

"You know better than that, George. I don't care what the local matrons say, and neither does my daughter."

"That's just it, you don't care. But what's to become of your daughter, eh? She's not a little girl anymore. She cannot just stay in Cambridgeshire, sitting at your feet, making Maygames of the locals."

"Why not, if it suits her? You are just concerned with your own peace of mind," Trevaine said with a smile.

Squire was thoroughly at ease now—after four brandies anyone else would be comatose—and earnestly tried to make his friend see clear. "Nay, it's not my comfort, Elliot, but yours. Think on it. You won't be here to make good for her forever. What then?"

"Then she will be a wealthy young woman, free to make whatever decisions she wants."

"Free to fall prey to every loose screw with a sad story. You know she's got no more sense about men than a kitten."

"So what are you saying, that I should teach her not to trust anyone?"

"I'm suggesting that you try—try, mind you—to get her shaped up like a lady instead of a harum-scarum chit, get her launched into Society before she's blotted her copybook for good and all, and get her a good man to hold the reins when you're gone. Then we can all rest easy."

"A husband? But she's only—"

"Seventeen, I know. And how old was your Elizabeth when you met, hm? Remember, you are not going to make her into a butterfly overnight. Men don't want a gal with Greek and Latin; they want one with blushes and fluttery eyelashes. I bet my ten-year-old Amanda knows more about it than Jacelyn. And men *don't* want a wife their mothers won't invite to tea."

Lord Trevaine nodded. "You've given me a lot to think about, George, and I will this time, truly. Perhaps if I ask my sister again. . . . Yes, and I'll speak to Jacelyn too."

"And what about the hunt party for my house guests?"

Lord Trevaine pulled the bell cord near his desk.

If the adage about beauty being in the eye of the beholder needed any reinforcing, proof entered the library ten minutes later, along with Miss Jacelyn Trevaine and a footman carrying the tea tray. While the tea was being placed, Jacelyn gave the Squire her most demure curtsey, then dimpled at her father when she kissed his cheek and straightened a shawl around his shoulders.

What her adoring sire saw was a graceful sprite of a girl, not quite five foot three, with heavy·brown hair falling in graceful waves halfway down her back, held off her face by a yellow ribbon to match the cheerful colour of her dress. Her moves were all that was gentle and gracious, and her face exquisite, with her mother's dark brown eyes, now twinkling at him in shared humour. He saw a laughing, generous mouth, a serious, straight nose, and a healthy, sun-touched complexion that was all the more beautiful to him after his own indoor pallor.

What the Squire saw, on the other hand, was a skinny little dab of a chit in an outmoded gown, and way past the age not to put her hair up. Thank goodness his own little dumplings fit the mould of blonde, blue-eyed, rounded beauty. Oh, Jacelyn Trevaine was passable enough, he supposed, in an unfashionable way, but his eldest, Samantha, would have cried for weeks over the freckles, and even his youngest knew better than such public displays of affection. Why, if any of his girls gave him such a saucy look, he'd take a birch rod to her. If any of his girls, in fact, ever so much as hinted at causing him as much upset as this one, he'd drown the passel of them, see if he wouldn't. No amount of brandy was going to improve his opinion of Miss Trevaine. Squire was a firm believer in that other old saying: Pretty is as pretty does.

"Jacey, my dear, Squire and I have been talking," Lord Trevaine began.

"I'm sure you have," she agreed with an impish smile.

"Seriously, my dear, I begin to see his point. What would you think if I wrote to my sister in London about arranging a comeout for you?"

"Lady Parkhurst? I'd think you were wasting good

15

paper, Papa. You know she washed her hands of me the last time I visited when I—"

"Yes, yes, but that was two years ago. You are quite the young lady now, and perhaps it is time to consider your future."

"Do you mean marriage, Papa?" When he muttered something about that being what all girls dreamt of, he supposed, she saluted the Squire with her teacup, but said, "Oh no, Father, it's just the favoured method of ridding the neighbourhood of plaguey females. I'm quite content right here." Miss Trevaine then made a very pretty though incomplete apology to the Squire, with no prompting from her father. She apologised, that is, for causing him distress and for any injuries the dogs may have sustained, which she sincerely regretted, not having considered such a possibility. She did not, however, apologise for her behaviour or for disrupting the hunt. "I'll say the words if you think I should, Papa, but we all know I won't mean them."

What a good, honest child she is, thought her father. What a devious minx, thought George Bottwick.

"What about my hunt this Saturday, then? I've got a whole house party arriving, m'sister and her family. You remember m'nephew Arthur, don't you, Elliot? Fine boy, just back from Belgium now that the war's over. Mentioned in the despatches, don't you know. He's bringing some tonish friends, and my niece Priscilla is also. I've invited some other London acquaintances up too. Promised them fine sport, and I intend them to have it. Can I have your word on that, missy? If things go well, perhaps we could get up a

16

small dancing party so you could come meet all the young bucks. You'd like that, wouldn't you, puss, *if all goes well?*"

Jacelyn considered the nature of the offer, bribe actually, and the nature of the implied threat, and her own nature.

"Squire, what you like best about the hunt is the chase, the ride, the jumps, all the noise and excitement, true?" At his nod and the dreamy look that came over his face at the thought, she went on to ask, "Then why, after your glorious chase, don't you let the poor fox go?"

Bottwick chuckled at Jacelyn's naïveté. He did not usually have discussions with females, but perhaps he could humour her this time. "What, just tell the dogs good sport, let's go home? There is no calling them back once they've got their fox cornered, my dear."

"Then, sir, why don't you shoot the fox, to kill it cleanly and quickly, before the dogs get to it?" Jacelyn asked in what she thought was a reasonable tone of voice.

All the brandy, the tea and macaroons, the quiet talk and apologies, all went for naught as Bottwick thundered to his feet and roared: "Because that bloody well ain't the sporting way!"

It might have been a moral dilemma for Jacelyn, the hunt versus the ball which, she thought wistfully, would have been her first, even if she had no desire to dance with a bunch of London dandies, or to be held up as a rural frump by their feminine counterparts, including Squire's niece Priscilla, whom she had known—and disliked—for years. Whatever decisions Jacelyn might have made were scrapped when Squire took action of his own.

Failing to secure Miss Trevaine's cooperation, needless to say, Bottwick rode home in high dudgeon. His temper was not improved when he found his dog Jasper trying to dig a hole under the kennel fence, nor was his digestion aided by his daughters' prattle about the London guests, over luncheon. He left the table in mid-meal and retired to his study with his port, a cigar, and a grudge. He told himself no little chit was going to make a fool of him—again. Especially not in front of his uppity sister, the Town swells, and soldier-heroes he had coming. After all, he was the Squire; he was the Master of the Hunt; he was the magistrate.

Perhaps it was his solid body filled only with liquid nourishment that day, or perhaps all that fluid had washed away the cobwebs of his mind, but Squire had an idea, a strategy to deal with the troublesome Miss Trevaine and her pet. He was the local magistrate, wasn't he? He had the authority, the right, nay, the duty, to uphold the law and preserve the peace. The key to his peace of mind was simple: He would arrest the dog as a public nuisance, and hold it in gaol as surety for the girl's good behaviour. Simple!

"It's simple extortion, Papa," Miss Trevaine fumed. "Bribery didn't work, his efforts to get me shipped off would take too long, so he is resorting to blackmail! How could you let him take poor Pen?"

"I am not entirely certain Bottwick isn't within his

18

rights, my dear, and it is only for three days, after all. You know Penelope is being well cared for; Squire even said you could visit. Just think of her namesake, Ulysses' wife, waiting patiently all those years. You'll get through, both of you." He patted her hand. "Perhaps it is a good time to consider Squire's suggestion of a London Season, though."

"You know I would rather stay here with you, Papa, and it won't fadge anyway. Aunt Amabel vowed she would never have me back. . . . I wonder whatever happened to the monkey." Father and daughter both laughed. Jacelyn had been fifteen when she was last invited to visit her aunt in London, a good opportunity to widen her horizons, according to Lady Parkhurst, lest she think the whole world was made of Cambridge farmland. All had gone well, shopping, sedate teas with her aunt's cronies and other girls not yet "out," and carriage rides in the park. It was at the start of one of these drives, however, that disaster struck. Jacelyn and her aunt were seated in Lady Parkhurst's pink-satin-lined open coach for the afternoon "strut," when all the Beau Monde paraded down Hyde Park's Rotten Row for the daily spectacle. They were right at the entrance to the park when Jacelyn "rescued" an organ-grinder's monkey from its master's mistreatment. What a spectacle it turned out to be: grooms, guards, gypsies, high-strung horses and higher-strung ladies—and a monkey who did not like carriage rides! Aunt Amabel retired to Bath for the restorative waters, Jacelyn was banished home, the coach had to be sold.

Now it was time for another rescue, Jacelyn decided as she dressed for bed. It wasn't only the injustice of innocent Pen's capture, it was the whole idea of Squire's trying to dictate her behaviour, when he was the one who was so obviously wrong. Besides, Miss Trevaine simply did not like having her will crossed. As far as she was concerned, the gauntlet had been cast.

The plan she evolved by the next evening had all the derringdo appeal of the Minerva Press romances she read as avidly as the Greek and Latin she studied with her father. It had been an easy matter to find out from the servants that Squire's precious nephew Arthur was expected long after dinner. She would, therefore, waylay Arthur after her father's bedtime, stash him away in the old gardener's cottage with her friend Shoop, who would not be quite as easy to convince, then negotiate for a trade of hostages — and be home before her father missed her at breakfast! The plan wasn't a perfect drama, of course, for if Squire were the villain, and Penelope the damsel in distress, where did that leave her and Arthur? She remembered Squire's nephew from a visit at least ten years ago as a pouty, fleshy rudesby who had disdained the company of a mere girl on his country rambles, even though she knew all the fish holes and climbing trees. Since defeating Napoleon single-handedly, if one listened to Squire's boasts, Lord Arthur Ponsonby must be even more puffed up with his own conceit than ever. No, no tragic figure there. She would just have to portray the avenging hero herself. Jacey giggled as she drew on the old boots, breeches, and coat from the back of her closet, crammed her hair under a widebrimmed, low-crowned hat, and crept down the stairs, shielding her

20

candle. She looked more like a skulking stableboy than any kind of hero, which wasn't surprising, considering that her outfit's source was Lem, the apprentice groom. The lingering odour was less than epic too, and she wrinkled her nose as she tiptoed to her father's desk. His old pistols, even unloaded, made her feel more the part. The cold metal as she tucked them in her waistband sent a delicious shiver down her backbone. Maria Edgeworth and Mrs. Radcliffe would have been proud.

2

The beat of the horse's hooves was as steady as a clock, that and the creak of saddle leather the only sounds intruding on the night. The moon was reflected off the hard-packed dirt road, and the hedgerows shut out the rest of the world. The horse was sure-footed and tireless, the road was straight. Riding in the country after dark was a perfect time for thinking, if one's thoughts were good company. The thoughts of Leigh Merrill, Earl of Claibourne, were not.

Things were not universally gloomy, of course. At age thirty-two the earl still had his health, though the French had done their damnedest to change that during the last seven years. He still had his lands, mortgaged and marginally profitable that they were; he had rugged, fair-haired good looks enough for success in the petticoat line, and luck enough, combined with his army pay, to keep himself in a style his title and acreage could not. He had his brave charger, Baron, under him, and good friends like Arthur Ponsonby, for whose uncle's house party the earl was already late. What he didn't have was a future worth a groat.

Born to the land, coming to the title at a tragically early age, he should have been seeing to his estates, but he had managers far more capable than he, and what the land needed was not another mouth to feed, but money, for repairs, equipment, modernisation. Trained for war, rising to the well-decorated rank of major on Wellington's own staff, Claibourne could have stayed in uniform, but the battles were all fought, and he had lost his taste for vagabond army life. The war years had been hellish, costing him so many good friends, but at least they were full, and the command staff lived every day as if it were their last, which it well could have been. The victory was celebrated in Paris, Vienna, London, with almost enough hell-raising to deaden the pain of memories, or at least satisfy any hunger a soldier could name. Even that palled after a time.

And now? Now he was accepting invitations to provincial parties at strangers' houses for want of anything better to do. At least he and Baron would get some healthy exercise out of the visit. The earl had kept fit by sparring at Gentleman Jackson's, but the stallion was restricted to a few tame canters in the park. That was why the earl had come on alone, bringing his horse along in easy stages instead of driving up with Arthur and their baggage as they had originally planned. This way Arthur had not had to kick his heels while the earl kept his appointment with his man of business, which was all to the good, since after hearing Pettigrew's latest news of the current price of corn, Claibourne did not feel much like company.

Company. There would be plenty of that, besides exercise, at the gathering. The men were no problem; they would accept anyone who could ride hard, drink long, and gamble deep. The women were another . . . proposition. There would be the young widow or the married cousin whose husband was off in the diplomatic corps, or some such convenient errand. These ladies had an altogether different form of exercise in mind when they invited the tanned, well-muscled, elegantly dressed earl on a private chase. Even the younger ladies made much of a handsome war hero, giggling into their fans and blushing at his compliments, until they were warned off by their mamas.

The gabblemongers always had a picnic when Leigh Claibourne, as he was now called, so much as danced with a debutante. That he held a title supported by ancient tradition instead of wealth was no novelty among the ton, and no cause to strike his name from the invitation lists to come-out balls, even if the female's family was too hard pressed to consider an impecunious suitor. No, what kept him from being wholeheartedly welcome in these circles was a family closet so full of skeletons it was surprising the Claibourne crest still fit in.

What father of a wealthy girl — Claibourne's solicitor had just spent an hour impressing the earl that no other type of female would do — would give her hand, and dowry, in exchange for a name tainted with dishonourable duels, divorce, and the filthy blot of slave trading? Gads, they had it all, even near imbecility, in his cousin Percival. The scandals had been well aired ages ago, in Claibourne's childhood, and only the highest sticklers held his Uncle Fenton and Percy against him. Still, all of Society read the Claibourne wildness in his own richly deserved reputation as a rake. As Leigh had ruefully commented to his solicitor, if he could afford a wife or mistress of his own, perhaps other men's wouldn't have so much appeal.

Mr. Pettigrew's next suggestion for refilling the Claibourne coffers, if not reroofing Claibourne Abbey, was a marriage of convenience—dashed inconvenient, according to every tender feeling the earl still harboured—and to a cit, besides. Wealthy merchants were willing to overlook a lot in a son-in-law, Pettigrew explained, in order to see their daughters' names in Debrett's Peerage. Damme, that was how the family got landed with Fenton!

They were in Dun Territory even before Leigh's father Jonathan ran through most of his inheritance and then married a French noblewoman. The lady's family lost their lives and fortunes, including her *dot,* in the Terror. Jonathan rashly agreed to an arranged marriage between his sister Sydelle and Josiah Fenton, a man with no title but with considerable wealth and ambition. It was perfectly acceptable for a gentleman to make investments on 'Change or abroad, even gamble on trading ventures, as long as the gentleman refrained from soiling his own hands. Slave trade, however, soiled everyone connected with it. Fenton was no gentleman. The knowledge became public and Fenton was no longer accepted into tonish circles—or into Sydelle's bed. When he grew abusive, possibly due to another unsavoury product of his merchant trade, the opium pipe, Sydelle moved home. Furious, Fenton pressed for a divorce, claiming her unborn child was not his. Vowing he'd see Sydelle a widow before he'd let Fenton call her wanton, Leigh's father withdrew all of her marriage settlement from Claibourne holdings, mortgaging the property to establish a fund for her coming child. Then he challenged his brother-in-law to a duel. Duels were not outlawed yet, just discouraged.

Fenton shot early, making Leigh, at age five, the sixth Earl of Claibourne, with a French-speaking mother and an impoverished estate. Jonathan got off his own shot before he died, leaving Fenton crippled for life, although some said Fenton used the injury as an excuse for staying in his house instead of facing society's cuts and ridicule. Sydelle was forced to return to her despised husband, where she died shortly, and perhaps gladly, after bringing forth Percival, Leigh's cousin and heir.

If it weren't for that drunken fool Percy and his blackguard of a father, Leigh would have emigrated to America or journeyed to India to seek his fortune. He could even remain a carefree bachelor. But leave Claibourne Abbey to those two? Not on his life—or death!

Blast, if he stayed lost in his dreary thoughts, he'd soon be lost in Cambridgeshire. Where was that third Ryefield marker?

* * *

A light bobbed up ahead. The earl reined Baron in while still a way off, loosening the pistol from his saddle pack. Another gun rested in his greatcoat's inner pocket, and a very thin, very sharp pearl-handled stiletto reposed in a sheath carefully sewn into the seam of Claibourne's right high-top riding boot. He'd been a soldier too long and too recently to be easy game.

Baron took exception to the delay and the flickering light, sideskipping and snorting until Claibourne clucked him forward again. Soon the source of the light was discernible: a small man, no, a boy, from his high voice, dressed in rough, rustic garb and waving a lantern.

"Mister, hey mister," the boy was calling. "Please stop, sir. Please, sir, m'granfer's hurt somethin' awful, 'n needs help. Please, mister, won'tcha help me?"

"Aye, lad," the earl answered, "give me directions, and I'll ride for the doctor."

"No, no sir," came the desperate reply, hastily amended to "m'lord" when Leigh was close enough for the boy to see the obvious quality of the large grey horse, if not the elegance of the rider's clothing. "It'd be too late. He's took real bad, and . . . and I ain't knowin' what to do. Can't you follow me, please?" the youngster pleaded, wringing every drop of melodrama from the scene. Jacelyn was having a marvelous time.

Claibourne heard the near-tears tremour in the voice and instantly responded with an offer to take the boy up behind him, to make faster time. Jacelyn knew her disguise would never pass that kind of

27

close, tactile inspection, not when Lem's outgrown jacket already barely concealed her very feminine charms. She mumbled, "Faster'f I lead the way. Hurry," and took off down a side path before her quarry could change his mind.

As they turned off the main road, the taller trees blocked what moonlight fell, so Leigh was forced to slow Baron's pace, carefully picking his way on the turnings, the wavering light staying too far ahead for him to ask any more questions, like how much farther did they have to go, what would the lad have done if horse and rider had not chanced along, and what was the nature of the grandfather's illness? The earl hadn't seen any lights indicating habitation for ages, so why would the boy come *this* way, instead of ahead, which had to be getting closer to Ponsonby's uncle's place, or set off himself for the doctor? It occurred to Leigh that the old man might have been shot while out poaching, on Bottwick's land, perhaps, eliminating the Manor as a source of aid, as well as the doctor, since he would be bound to report a bullet wound. That would account for the boy's nervousness and reticence. He'd also said "hurt," not sick or ailing. Ah, well, Claibourne had seen enough of gunshots to know what to do as well as any surgeon, if it wasn't already too late. He hoped not, for the boy's sake.

After so many twistings that the earl knew he'd never find his way back to the main road by himself—at least not till morning—the lantern finally came to a standstill outside a small stone cottage. There was a fire's glow in the one facing window but the door was shut.

"Please, yer lordship, g'wan. I'll tie yer horse," the boy offered, stepping from the darkness of the clearing beyond the circle of light from the lantern, which he had hung by the door. He touched the floppy brim of his hat as an afterthought.

"There's no need, Baron will wait here. What's your name, lad?" the earl asked, quickly dismounting and looping the grey's reins back over the saddle so the horse couldn't trip on them. With a "Stay, Baron," Leigh followed the boy toward the door.

"Jace—Jason, m'lord," the youngster answered, scurrying on. At the doorway he stopped, as though adjusting the lantern, but urged the other in. "G 'wan, sir. It be unlatched."

A soldier is used to gathering impressions quickly; his life so often depends on assessing a situation in mere seconds. Ex-Major Merrill had the time between heartbeats to note a warm, tidy cottage scented with herbs hanging to dry; a cot, a table, a few log-hewn chairs and benches, some rough-fashioned shelves; a skinny old man with weathered skin crouched at the table, pointing a gun at him—and no back door. The next heartbeat added still another relevant impression: the unmistakable sensation of a gun being pressed into his back.

Lord Claibourne raised his hands slowly, not making any sudden moves which might jar unsteady fingers. The greybeard peered at him closely, as though he had difficulty seeing even the short distance, a fact the earl mentally filed, as well as the distance to either window.

"Please have a seat, m'lord," the boy said, coming around from behind. The hat still shielded most of the lad's face so Leigh could not read the intentions in his eyes, but the gun stayed firm. Leigh sat. He took the seat facing the old man, careful to place his hands in plain sight on the table. The grandfather nodded and, picking up some rags, started to clean the gun, his eyes still on the captive's. Any fool knows not to clean a loaded gun, Claibourne noted. What was going on here? The fine pair of bridle culls hadn't even searched him. Claibourne raised one eyebrow but the ancient only grunted, shrugged his boney shoulders and bent to his task. The earl relaxed, biding his time. Whatever huggery-muggery this was, it didn't seem to require drastic measures, like gunning down a smooth-faced youth or overpowering a wizened septuagenarian. The situation was beginning to appeal to his lordship's sense of humour, far more than dinner at the squire's would have. And here he'd thought civilian life was going to be dull!

Jacelyn was undergoing a few surprises herself. She'd never expected pudgy Arthur to turn out so . . . masculine, for one thing. Of course she'd not seen him for ten years, since he was just fifteen, and after all, what did she know about how boys developed into men? Still, he looked much older than his years—maybe that's what wars did, and living in tents—and so much more formidable than she could have dreamt of Arthur becoming. The boy she remembered was pudding-faced, sulky at being sent to visit relatives in the country when he'd rather have stayed in London with his own chums. He was a soft city child, singularly inept at the simple country pursuits which were the only available entertainment, and he had snidely refused to take advice from a mere moppet. The grown-up Arthur, however, looked to be all muscle, and all in command, all polite good humour as he sat there in captivity. She'd feared Arthur would throw a fit, just as he'd thrown rocks, fishing poles, and tantrums when frustrated. This man looked as though he could give a setdown with one golden eyebrow, never needing to raise his voice at all. If this was what the army did for young men's characters, Jacelyn heartily approved. As for his appearance, well, his hair was a lighter blond than she recalled — from the same sun that gave him such a bronzed look, she supposed — but neither the sun nor military discipline could explain the glow she felt just looking at him. Arthur was beautiful! With his wide brow, square chin, and strong, straight nose, he was positively the most attractive man she'd ever seen, and he didn't even recognize the know-it-all tomboy who'd followed him around, laughing at his mistakes. Goodness, she had to stop staring and get on with this.

"My lord, I am dreadfully sorry for any inconvenience you may have suffered," she began, too absorbed still in his lordship's features to remember her rustic accent. "It is just a small matter, really."

Shoop cleared his throat. "Methinks we'd best reconsider, Miss—"

"Missed his dinner?" Jacelyn broke in hastily. "Of course he did. I brought some wine and cheese,

31

remember? We have to take care of business first, though." She dropped the pistol on the table when she jumped up to fetch something, to Shoop's grumbled "Aargh." His lordship's lips quivered as the old man disgustedly reached over and switched guns, starting to dismantle the lad's for cleaning while the youngster set a bottle of ink and some paper on the table. The delicate white hand that offered the earl a pen certainly didn't match the oldster's workgnarled, knobby mitts, no more than that cultured accent matched this rough dwelling. The earl wished he could see the lad's face, but the hat's low brim still obscured all but a pointed chin and a full mouth which seemed on the verge of laughter.

The boy picked up the pistol, quite obviously unloaded, and determinedly pointed it at the prisoner. "Will you do as I request, write what I say?"

"You see me trembling with fear, ready to obey your every command," the earl drawled, which earned him a "Bah," from Shoop and a chuckle from Jacelyn.

"You're really being a good sport, Arthur. I should say Lord Ponsonby, shouldn't I?"

She began to pace, planning the words to use, so she missed his lordship's start of surprise. What would staid Arthur have to do with such a havey-cavey pair? Unless . . . no, the boy was too old to be a by-blow. Perhaps a young cousin, then. This was getting more and more amusing.

" 'Dear Squire,' " the boy dictated. "No, 'Dear Uncle.' No, 'My Dearest Uncle.' That's it."

That did sound more like Arthur, Claibourne acknowledged, writing, but how could the boy know Arthur's style and not recognise—

" 'I am being held hostage, my life is in dire peril, and I require your immediate assistance.' The earl had to laugh out loud at this. Not just at the threats as empty as the guns, but at the thought of his own uncle's reception of such a message. Fenton would be in such high gig he'd dance, crippled legs or no. And if, as Claibourne suspected, this missive was to be a ransom note, why, Fenton would rather see his nephew rot in hell than spend a brass farthing in his behalf.

"Please, my lord, this is serious. Continue: 'I will be freed as soon as you release the prisoner you now hold in . . . in durance vile. Your instant compliance is urgently requested!' Sign it, 'Your affectionate nephew, Arthur.'

"There," Jacelyn said triumphantly, sealing the note with a flourish and handing it to Shoop. "Remember to hand it to one of the grooms, as we discussed. Say some stranger gave it to you, a big, nasty looking brute with a scar down his face. Then you'd better play least-in-sight for a bit, in case Squire has questions."

Shoop made a last try at dissent, but gave it up when Jacelyn handed him a shilling for the local pub and herded him out the door. He shook his head resignedly and left, muttering about, " 'adn't oughta be 'ere atall, divil a bit alone. Niver could talk reason . . ."

Jacelyn called after, by way of reassuring her friend, "Don't worry, it's only Arthur." Then she

33

busied herself emptying a hamper onto the table. Bread, wine, cheese, mugs appeared, no utensils. Her "oh dear" changed to an "oh" of admiration as the gentleman withdrew a knife from his boot top. Wasn't Arthur complete to a shade?

Claibourne sliced off a wedge of cheese, pushed it toward the boy and said, "That's it? No names, no places, no times for exchange of prisoners? A most peculiar kidnapping, cawker. I take it the Squire, Uncle, that is, knows both you and your intentions?"

Jacelyn giggled around a mouthful. "You might say so."

"Then what's to keep him from coming after you, young Jason? Even if you succeed in obtaining your friend's release, you've still committed a crime. One cannot go around kidnapping people, you know, especially not a peer of the realm. You are obviously well-born, though, and young, so Squire might consider it a boyish prank. He mightn't send you up for hanging after all." Claibourne pensively sipped his wine, which, he noted incidentally, was excellent. "No, my guess is that he'll take a birch rod to your backside."

"I don't think so, my lord," Jacelyn answered as she removed the droopy hat, letting a heavy shower of dark brown waves cascade down past her shoulders. "I don't think so."

"Do you remember me now, Arthur? It's Jacey, Jacelyn Trevaine."

Remember her? The gentleman barely remembered

34

to breathe! No, if he'd seen this girl, he'd never have forgotten her. No girl, though, definitely a young woman, he could see now, especially as the shirt strained across her chest as she reached in a pocket for a ribbon to tie back her hair. He watched as she gathered the chestnut mass into a haphazard pony's tail, the rich brown colour catching the fire's light and reflecting its gold. Some of the waves strayed loose to frame her face delightfully.

"Don't ever cut it." He surprised himself by speaking his thoughts.

"No? Papa likes it too, but it's very unfashionable, you know."

"It's perfect." And it was, in a way, even trailing wisps, just as the girl herself was enchanting, in a warm, softly smiling way that was far from Society's standards. No china-blue eyes or rosebud mouth or porcelain complexion, or affectations. Miss Trevaine had pansy-brown eyes which sparkled with her enjoyment and a full, laughing mouth just made to be kissed! Claibourne cleared his throat and redirected his thoughts, with great effort. He carefully wiped the knife on a napkin and said, "Well, Miss Trevaine, I'd be mightily obliged to know just what rig you are running."

Jacelyn was a bit disappointed at the formal address; she much preferred "Arthur" to the sober "Lord Ponsonby," which did not seem to fit the gentleman now grinning as if ready to share her triumph. She compromised with, "Of course, my lord, you have every right. And I'd like to say that you're a regular Trojan, letting me play my game. I know I couldn't have kept you here against your will, even without the knife."

"You mean you wouldn't have pulled the trigger?"

The chit even had dimples—unfair! "But you didn't know the guns were empty, not at first, did you?"

"No, but I knew mine weren't. Come now, an explanation. And if it's not a good one, my girl, and honour-true, then I *shall* leave, and you'll really be in the suds." It was a silly threat; he could no more leave now than he could fly. He was already thinking ahead to what difficulties such a madcap might be in, to resort to kidnapping, and what strings he could pull to extricate her. First, however, what was such a little charmer doing in britches—he was trying not to stare—in a workman's cottage? "Now, ma'am, if you please," he ordered, severe with concern.

That voice had commanded whole battalions. Jacey started. "You see, my lord, Squire, your uncle, that is—and I'm sorry for that, not that he's your uncle, of course, else you'd not be here, but that it's your uncle that I'm referring to. Does that make sense?" Jacelyn was unaccountably flustered by her companion's look of disapproval. "Squire arrested Pen, and I kidnapped you in exchange," she hurried on, not choosing to discuss the reasons behind Squire's actions. "He will release Pen, I will, ah, let you go. You'll go on to the house party, I'll return home. Simple."

Her explanation wasn't simple, it was simple-minded, telling him nothing he didn't previously know except the other prisoner's name. If this friend

36

were a man, if this were all to free her lover . . .
"Who is Pen, and what are the charges?" he demanded.

Jacey shrank back in her seat. "There *were* no
charges, Arthur. Squire arrested Pen so I wouldn't
interfere with his fox hunt and . . . and Pen is my
dog, Penelope."

"A dog? Squire, er, Uncle, arrested your dog?"
Leigh had to laugh, partly at the idea, but mostly in
relief that a convict lover didn't wait in gaol for her.
He poured another glass of wine, then it struck him
as even funnier. "You are actually holding me hostage to ransom a dog? My dear, what a blow to my
pride! I'll have you know I was once traded for three
French prisoners of war, two officers and a spy; our
esteemed government thought I was that valuable.
Three Frenchmen, one dog. How the mighty are
fallen."

Jacelyn laughed with him. "But she's a very special
dog, my lord. She's named for Ulysses' wife, you
know, and she is every bit as faithful and wise."

"Wasn't Ulysses' dog named Argos? Why didn't
you name your dog after him?"

"Argos died when his master finally came home. It
was too sad."   .

"What a curious mix you are, Miss Trevaine. Swag-
gering highwayman one moment, sentimental schoolgirl the next. I don't even want to go into the
fox-hunting reference. I'm not quite ready for that
yet. Tell me about your grandfather."

"Oh, he's our gardener, Shoop. I thought you
would remember him for sure. He shouted at you for

37

practicing your cricket in the formal gardens."

"Did he? Will he find himself up on charges over this nonsense, or dismissed from his position?"

"Oh no. Squire only blames Papa. He'll turn all red and rage at my poor father to do something about me."

"And will he? Your father, I mean. You'd ought to be spanked, girl, for what I'm beginning to suspect is a long history of thoroughly disreputable behaviour. It's too much to hope, I'm sure, at this late date."

Jacelyn laughed at the idea of her dear sweet father even raising his voice in anger, much less his hand. "Papa is a scholar, remember?"

"Well, someone had ought to tan your sweet britches over this escapade, pet, for you've landed us both in the briars this time."

"You haven't changed so much, after all, Arthur. You always were a spoilsport. Too bad, I was beginning to like you. What, are you afraid of what Squire will say?"

"Aye, girl, Squire and the whole countryside, likely. Here you are in the middle of the night, in an isolated little cottage, improperly attired, alone with a man. Didn't you even think of your reputation?"

Jacelyn threw back her head and laughed, a sound which nearly melted the earl's heart for good and all. "But I don't have any reputation to speak of!" At his sudden scowl she hastily added, "Not for being a lightskirt, Arthur, just a hoyden, you know. And if you think Squire is going to storm in here, demanding you do the honourable thing by me, you're more paper-skulled than you used to be. Never fear, the last thing in the world Squire would want is to have me as part of the family."

She giggled at the very thought of it, till her companion quietly announced, "The only problem, sweetheart, is that I am not Arthur."

"George," Squire Bottwick told himself, hands crossed over his full belly, "life is sweet." Good wine, good food, good friends, and, for once, good riddance to the aggravating Miss Trevaine. He patted his inside pocket where reposed the most satisfying correspondence he'd had in years. He had received the note before dinner, and was still tickled pink at the idea of letting the interfering little wench cook in her own stewpot while he enjoyed his meal.

It was good English fare, none of those Frenchified dishes drowning in sauces that curdled Squire's digestive juices. It was good enough for the fine London folks, too, judging from all they ate and drank, even his sister Clothilda Ponsonby, who'd put on enough airs for a duchess after snabbling herself a title. In her widowhood she had grown positively stiff-rumped with pride. Plain missus was good enough for Mrs. Bottwick, Squire thought, glancing at his wife at the opposite end of the table. She had done him proud, just as though she set ten places with five courses and six removes every evening. Even his daughter Samantha, invited to leave the nursery party when they found themselves an odd number at table, was behaving just as she ought. The gal was young, but she could take a few lessons from her cousin Priscilla, who had been Out for two years and was considered last Season's Toast. Too bad Priscilla seemed to share her mama's top-lofty consequence. Still, she was a taking miss, judging from her partners' attentiveness. Colonel Highet, was it, and Lord Humboldt, or Captain Humboldt and Mr. Highet? Ah well, friends of Arthur's.

Arthur sat between Samantha and Priscilla's pretty friend Miss Marcella Chadwick, here at Squire's table, unthreatened, unfettered, uncaptured! Squire beamed. Top of the trees, young Arthur was, too, his shirtpoints nearly reaching his ears, his neckcloth done up in some pattern so intricate that it must have a name of its own. Personally, Bottwick thought it all a little overdone for a country dinner, but what did he know about fashion? He looked down regretfully at his own figured waistcoat, just a trifle redecorated with his dinner's spatters, and wished he could undo a few of the buttons. Ah well, a man couldn't have everything, he decided. It might spoil him.

By the time dinner was over and the men had shared port, cigars, and lies of their prowess on various hunting fields, Squire was fit to burst more than the seams of his jacket. A few more brandies, and the joke was just too good not to share.

"Arthur," he said when the tea tray was brought in, "do you recall Jacelyn Trevaine, m'neighbour's daughter?"

"You mean the nasty little tomboy with freckles? How could I forget? She pushed me in the lake once when I was searching for birds' nests."

"She's not changed much, I'll warrant. Oh, she's filled out some, but she still gets up to her mad starts. You'll never guess what she's done now!" He slapped his beefy hand down on his thigh, the sound drawing the attention of everyone except Lord Smedley, Clothilda's cisisbeo, who was snoring in the corner, a handkerchief over his face.

"I was just telling Arthur here about my neighbour," Bottwick informed his listeners. "The father's a good man. Not the sporting type, you understand, but good, for all that. The daughter, though, is an unprincipled baggage. Always was, always will be."

"You don't mean Jacey, do you, Father? You know she is the dearest, most good-natured girl. I—"

"You've said enough, girl. Past your bedtime anyway."

"Yes, Father." Aghast that she had disagreed with her father in front of all the fine London company and been reprimanded, Samantha made an awkward curtsey and fled the room, nearly in tears.

"That was unkind, George." His wife took Squire to task. "Jacelyn has been a good friend to Samantha, even though she is older." This last may have been quietly directed at Priscilla who, after a perfunctory kiss in the vicinity of Samantha's ear, had totally ignored her young cousin in favour of the gentlemen's company. "Miss Trevaine may be somewhat high-spirited, but even you, George, have admitted that she is pluck to the backbone, as you would say."

"Aye, the gel's got bottom, I'll grant you that. Just listen to the scheme she's concocted now." Squire read the note aloud, then guffawed so hard tears streamed down his red cheeks.

When he was able to speak again, Captain Highet pressed him for an explanation. "I do not understand, sir. Arthur's right here, and there is no mention in the letter of any Miss Trevaine. I say, could you let us in on the joke?"

So Squire sketched a background to the scenario, using such phrases as "like a boil on m'butt," and "a bitch in heat," to his wife's frown, his sister's pursed lips, and his niece's twitters. "And now she thinks to diddle me with this farrago of nonsense," Squire finished, "with Arthur right here!"

The young men up for the fox hunt were all sympathetic and now shared Squire's amusement. The lines of displeasure on Lady Ponsonby's face, though, deepened, until she recalled they might become permanent if held too long. "This is highly unseemly, George. I hope we are not to be subjected to more of this indignity. Kidnapping my Arthur, indeed."

"George," Mrs. Bottwick asked thoughtfully, "if Arthur is here, who do you think penned the note? Whatever Jacelyn might be, and I'll acknowledge that this does sound somewhat irregular, she is not foolish."

"Quite right, Uncle George. She always was a little hellion, but a downy one. She must have thought you'd go for it, but why?"

Squire was off in a laughing fit again when the

captain made the obvious deduction: "You mean the chit's held up some poor chap she thinks is Arthur here, and is holding him to ransom a dog?" He and Lord Humboldt pounded each other on the back, saying it served the pushy female right. Priscilla and Miss Chadwick, side by side on the sofa, shared haughty looks of feigned disinterest. *They'd* never be caught doing anything so ill-bred or vulgar, much less anything as silly as getting between a man and his sporting instincts. Mrs. Bottwick was murmuring about the "poor, motherless child" while Clothilda Ponsonby simply looked disgusted.

"Arthur," she addressed her son in an effort to change the topic, "I've told you not to wear that shade. It makes you look liverish. Or was it the food?"

Indeed, Arthur had paled to a greenish tint. He ran a finger under his suddenly too-tight collar. "Yes, Mother. That is, no, Mother. I'm quite the thing. A trifle weary. Um, Uncle, perhaps I might—"

"Dang," interrupted Squire, "I'd give my best mare to know who the chit's snagged."

Arthur choked. There was no hope of getting his uncle alone, not with everyone looking at him. "Do you remember when I arrived early I said there was another fellow who might come this evening, or else tomorrow, if it got too dark to ride? Another army friend?"

Mrs. Bottwick was relieved. "That's all right then, an officer friend of Arthur's. I'm sure he'll see that Jacelyn's just an impulsive child."

"Aunt Rosalie, ma'am." Arthur kept twisting his neckcloth. "It's not that I'd ever invite a here-and-thereian to your home. Leigh is a fine gentleman and officer, one of the best. Even Wellington's said so, hasn't he, Highet?" Highet's mouth was now hanging open, so Arthur got no support there. "It's just that, well, he's got a name with the ladies. I mean, I'd trust Claibourne with my life, Uncle George, ma'am, but I wouldn't leave him alone with my sister, and you know she's up to snuff. As for some unschooled country chit—"

"Claibourne?" Clothilda Ponsonby screamed, along with horrified gasps and exclamations from Priscilla and Miss Chadwick, a chorus of doom that would have done Macbeth's three witches proud. "You left a young woman alone for four hours with Rake Claibourne? George, how could you?"

Mrs. Bottwick dropped the teapot.

By the time Jacelyn heard the dog's woofs and whines, and then frantic scrapings on the door, she was beginning to doubt her wisdom. Not in the matter of Squire and his hounds, of course. Not even in the absurdity of capturing the wrong man, a natural error under the circumstances. No, Miss Trevaine was wondering if her own good sense could ever win over the new sensations shuddering through her. Perhaps Squire was right after all, that she did need some Town Bronze before facing such a nonpareil. Maybe then, when a tall, handsome gentleman gazed at her so warmly she would know where to look, instead of staring dreamily back into his blue eyes, mesmerised like some poor terrified mousekin waiting for the cat to pounce. Of course she wasn't precisely frightened, only trembly and breathless and, oh dear, what did one do with one's hands? Ah, she realised with a shock of clarity, that must be why ladies carry fans!

It was with a great deal of relief that Miss Trevaine opened the door and welcomed her pet, hiding her uncertainties in a fierce hug and having her burning face slobbered on.

"My lord, this is Penelope. Pen, meet your . . . your benefactor."

"Yes, hardly a rescuer," said Claibourne, coming forward with the heel of the bread loaf, which he offered to the big dog, making an instant friend. "She certainly is large," he said, looking for something good to say about an animal that stood as tall as his waist, with a miscellaneous assemblage of gangly parts covered with grizzled whiskers going every which way. The bread gone in a gulp, Pen looked up at him mournfully from under an over-hanging shag-rug brow. "And marvelously expressive eyes. You are certainly worth a king's ransom, old girl. Sorry you had to make do with a mere earl."

Blushing, Jacelyn began gathering things into her hamper. "We'd best be going, my lord. Squire will be looking for you, I'm sure, and I'd rather he not find me at all! Besides, if you keep petting Pen behind the ears like that, her tail will destroy Shoop's cottage, as if I weren't in bad enough straits with him already." She carefully wrapped the pistols in linen napkins before placing them in the hamper. Opening the door, she remembered to tell the earl, "Your direction is just to the rear of the cottage. You cannot miss the break in the hedge. The path there leads straight back to the main road, and Squire's gatehouse is only minutes ahead. I brought you 'round Robin's barn lest you—Arthur, that is—recognise Shoop's cottage too soon. My way cuts right across this clearing, my lord, so . . . so I wish to . . . to thank you and—"

"Not so fast, sweetings," drawled the earl, still looking perfectly at ease in Shoop's high-backed chair. He slipped his knife back into the boot, then slowly rose and came toward her. Jacelyn backed away until she was half in, half out of the doorway, feeling the cool night's breeze on her cheek. Then she was stopped by his hand at her neck, his thumb caressing that same cheek.

"No, I don't think I can let you go so easily." Leigh spoke almost regretfully. When Jacelyn glanced down to where her pistols lay on the top of the basket she held in her hand, he smiled, teeth white in the moonlight. "No more of your games, love, now it's my play. Or don't you think I deserve a reward for all I've been through, hm? Terrorised by highwaymen, threatened within an inch of my life, deprived of my dinner. Yes, I think I'm owed some restitution, wouldn't you say so, Miss Trevaine?"

"Yes, my lord," was Jacelyn's whispered response.

"What's that, my girl, not used to paying for your crimes?"

"No, my lord," meekly.

"Ah, in that case I won't demand too high a price. Perhaps just a kiss?" And he stood there, his arm negligently across her shoulder, waiting expectantly.

After a moment's indecision, Jacelyn stood on tiptoe and darted forward, quickly brushing the side of his mouth with hers. When she moved as if to leave, that strong hand firmed at the back of her neck.

"No, no, you'll have to do better than that. That was not even dustman's wages, much less an officer's. Come, little sparrow, let me show you."

He pulled her to him, his other arm pressing at her back, and bent his head to hers, his lips very soft and gentle on her mouth. She almost thought she was floating, till his hands started to move, to knead and caress. He raised his head briefly, to see a wondering look in her eyes, her mouth formed in a bemused "Oh." With a groan he covered her mouth again, this time with his lips opened, his tongue running over hers until she could taste the wine and his breath and his very soul, she supposed, as he must hers. Then she gave up what little rational thought was left to her. She had no frame of reference, nothing to compare these fiery new feelings to, to understand them better, so she stopped trying and joined wholeheartedly in her first real kiss. She raised her arms and held him as close as she was able, wanting to stir him the way his hands were rousing her, straying down her back to where a lady would have skirts and petticoats, so a gentleman couldn't take such liberties. Then his hand pushed aside Lem's jacket and stroked the side of her breast until she felt she'd faint if this went on much longer, and die if it ever ended.

It's one of those interesting observations that, whenever the cards are stacked against you, there are so very many jokers in the deck. Take now, for instance. Miss Trevaine had not only abducted the wrong gentleman, but she'd spent four hours alone with him. Furthermore, he'd turned out to be, by his own confession, one of the worst womanisers on two continents. And now, just when she was enthusiastically, devastatingly, definitively helping him prove that claim, who should come thundering into the clearing but Squire and half his house party.

It was Lord Arthur Ponsonby who, first spying the couple silhouetted in the open doorway, locked in a passionate embrace, gave the evening's most superfluous statement by shouting, "There she is!"

Jacelyn was right. Arthur always was a spoilsport.

4

She'd done it again. Squire Bottwick had no idea how the she-devil'd managed to bring off such a complicated, convoluted plot, but she'd done it. Here it was, a perfect Saturday morning in autumn. You could almost taste the crispness in the air as the thoroughbred trampled leaves under its hooves. Was Squire out riding neck-or-nothing on the heels of his hounds? Was he feeling the wind in his face as he took the jumps along with his friends, ridding England of one more vermin? No, he was plodding along, riding as slowly as the purebred under him would tolerate, on his way to Treverly Hall. Miss Trevaine had done it again, ruined another day's hunt. It was enough to make a grown man cry.

Bad enough he'd miss today's sport, Squire mourned; sure as hellfire his wife and sister would have him in church tomorrow, for all his sins. Monday morning the guests would be leaving, and he'd have to see them off. No hunting then either, but at least now there was something worth praying for. If his puffed-up sister sniffed down her nose at him one more time, he'd wipe it for her, see if he didn't.

Cloth-head Clothilda she'd always been. Cloth-head Clothilda she'd always be, complaining about country morals corrupting her precious Priscilla. As if Squire didn't have enough in his budget, that skitterwit had decided to faint in his sitting room, as though she'd been in any danger. More likely she resented not being the centre of attention. As for Arthur, the twiddlepoop, they might have squeaked through this if the nodcock hadn't rushed back to his mama with the news of Jacelyn's fall from grace. Squire could have hushed the servants, and Claibourne's fellow officers could have been trusted to hold their tongues, but Priscilla and that milk-and-water friend of hers, Miss Chadwick? They'd have the news broadcast throughout Cambridgeshire faster'n a cat could lick cream. As for Clothilda, she was most likely writing to her friends in London this very minute. She'd announced her connexion, via Ponsonby, to Sally Jersey often enough, and everyone knew Sally Jersey was the biggest gossip in London. Devil take it! Besides, fumed the Squire, feeling thoroughly put-upon, that blasted dog had nigh ruined his wine cellar before they'd freed it, excavating an escape route through some of Bottwick's best duty-free bottles.

This was all beside the point, and Squire well knew it. What was really gnawing at him was the look on Jacelyn's face, so pale there in the moonlight, when, without more than an "I'll see Miss Trevaine home," Claibourne had lifted her onto the back of a huge grey charger. He'd walked beside it out of the clearing, the dog on the other side. Squire'd silently dismissed the other men—he cursed himself again for not seeing they'd keep mum—and followed. Nothing else was said until they reached Treverly, when Jacelyn announced she would use the back door. She'd looked Squire straight in the eye, chin up, and told him there was no need to disturb her father until morning; he needed his rest. She'd slid off that great hulk of a horse before Claibourne could lift her down and, turning without another word, walked toward the house. No tears, no vapours, no recriminations, all of which Squire found waiting for him at home.

Dang, the chit had backbone. Yes, and class, he'd give her that too. Too bad she wasn't a boy. She wasn't though, and now Squire had to face his old friend and tell him—what? That he, George Bottwick, had found Trevaine's daughter the perfect husband? A nobleman of impeccable background and repute, with fortune to treat his only chick better than she was accustomed, who could be trusted to love and honour her for all of her days?

The truth was enough to break a father's heart.

At precisely eleven o'clock the Earl of Claibourne rode up to Treverly Hall, to the front door this time. It was a stately mansion of warm brickwork, not the rambling hodgepodge of Squire's manorhouse, where each generation had added its own style, whether it matched or not. Treverly was elegant and understated, bespeaking good taste and the wherewithal to maintain it. Evidence of Shoop's skill bloomed in perfect harmony, although the earl's knowing eye guessed Shoop must command a whole platoon of clippers, mowers, and pruners.

The boy who ran up to take Baron's reins before Claibourne could dismount smiled when Leigh warned him not to pull on the horse. "He'll walk with you if I tell him, but he'll raise Cain if he thinks you're making off with him. Cavalry horse, you know."

"Yessir," the groom said, grinning. "I'll stand right here with'm, if'n that's what he chooses."

The door was opened by a liveried footman who also took the earl's hat, gloves, and riding crop. Only then did the whitehaired butler step forward. "How may I help you, my lord?"

"Would you please tell Lord Trevaine that Leigh Claibourne wishes to see him."

"Certainly. I believe his lordship is expecting you, my lord."

You can bet your shiny brass buttons he's expecting me, Leigh thought, and likely the whole staff of servants knows it, from milkmaid to *monsieur* in the kitchen. Only his twitching lips betrayed Claibourne's urge to laugh at the butler, who had more dignity than the Prince Regent. Before he followed that stately personage down a hall hung with priceless masterpieces, however, he couldn't resist winking at the footman who, grinning, made a mock salute. Leigh also gave one last look to the riding crop. It had been a gift from Squire Bottwick, with the words, "You'll need it."

"I have to admit it's not what I wanted for my daughter," Lord Trevaine told his caller, although he liked what he saw well enough. Not the external trappings of a finely turned-out gentleman, in fawn knee breeches and muscle-moulded jacket of dark blue Bath superfine, but the firm handshake and the way this young nobleman sat at his ease in a stranger's library. The earl showed no nervous sense of guilt, nor yet any cocky self-assurance as he looked the older man straight in the eyes. Trevaine saw much to admire. It wasn't the earl's lack of capital which disturbed him, either; he himself had fortune enough to rebuild three abbeys, and no use for it beyond his books—and his daughter. He didn't worry that Claibourne would squander away Jacelyn's monies: from the earl's own account of his less than formidable prospects, his lands were of primary concern, and that was always a good investment.

Furthermore, Trevaine would make sure part of Jacelyn's wealth was held secure for her, no matter whom she married. Not even the young man's dicey reputation bothered Trevaine overmuch. Old family scandals could be instantly forgotten. Trevaine hoped he had more sense than to hold a boy responsible for his parents' misdeeds, much less those of an uncle by marriage, all carefully enumerated by George Bottwick. Claibourne's own tarnished name could be nearly as casually dismissed: restless youth, the brutal scars of war, and the fact that if people are predisposed to think the worst, it is often in the nature of spirited young men to live up—or down—

to their expectations. Even Squire, so determined to give an honest reckoning, had found no fault with the earl's personal integrity. All in all, this prospective son-in-law would have satisfied Jacelyn's father. And yet . . .

"She is so young. Not in years, as Bottwick keeps reminding me, but in spirit, so free and innocent. She always reminds me of a spring breeze, as sweet and pure, and in such a hurry to smell every budding flower, touch every newborn lamb." Trevaine's voice broke a little, and he removed his spectacles, wiping them with a handkerchief. "I would do anything to keep her that way. I don't care aught for gossip, my lord, but I'd not see her hurt." He blew his nose. "Mostly I'd hoped to have her here with me for a few more years."

What could Leigh say to this fine old gentleman in his library, surrounded by precious volumes and works of art when he, Claibourne, was stealing the most cherished treasure of all? The man was far from well, obviously, his blue-veined hands trembling. Was Trevaine's anguish to be laid in Claibourne's dish too? He had so little to offer in trade. . . .

"My lord, I swear to you on my mother's grave that I'll make Jacelyn a good husband, and have as much care for her happiness as you do. You have my word and my hand on it, if you'll accept."

Trevaine did, and shook the younger man's hand with a measure of relief. "I'll not force her, you know," he cautioned the earl, lest Claibourne think the deed was done. "If she won't have it, we'll weather through, no matter what the tabbies say.

Some new scandal will come along to set their tongues wagging."

"Aye, sir, but your daughter's just as apt to cause that one, too, from all I hear."

They smiled in shared understanding, removing the last tension from the room.

"I wonder what they'll find to natter on about when Jacelyn's in London?" Trevaine mused, only to be caught up by the earl's laugh.

"Do you think they won't find her name in the newspapers' gossip columns? Your daughter, sir, will likely set London on its ear. Rake Claibourne's betrothed?" At Trevaine's look of consternation, he held up his hands. "No need to worry, my lord, I'll keep her safe from overstepping the line, but I'll not bridle her," he said, finishing with a doubt-tinged "if any man could."

It was Trevaine's turn to be amused. "Not any easy task you've set yourself, my boy, but you'll do, you'll do. Tell me," he asked in a more thoughtful tone of voice, "do you think my girl is pretty?"

Claibourne considered for a moment, straightening the cuff of his shirtsleeve. "Pretty? No, I wouldn't call Miss Trevaine that. I've only seen her in boys' clothes, recall, with her hair undone, nothing anyone could label pretty. Yet there was a glow about her, a vibrant, entrancing appeal. A man would never grow tired of watching her face change with her thoughts. No, I think she'll be beautiful in time."

"Good," Trevaine said, rising slowly from his chair. "You've still got your wits about you. Hang on to them, lad. I'll be sending Jacelyn in to you."

After Trevaine left, the earl wiped his forehead. Gads, he'd rather face Boney's whole army than another such interview—and the battle hadn't even begun!

"I shan't marry you, my lord, and that's the end of it. All this fuss over one silly little kiss." When he cleared his throat she paused in her angry pacing, but he seemed merely to be examining his gold signet ring. Jacelyn had the grace to blush. "Well, one kiss, at any rate. It's not as though we were caught out at some inn, having an assignation or something. I see no reason why I should have to wed anybody."

"Will you stop moving about, sweetheart, you're looking like a disgruntled chicken."

"I look like a *what?*" This was too much! To be likened to some idiotic poultry after a harrowing morning watching her father grow paler and weaker. Even Mrs. Phipps, the housekeeper, had added her tuppence, practically scalping Miss Trevaine under the excuse of putting miss's hair up, as befitted a young lady "who wouldn't want to embarrass her poor, sweet mother's memory." The look on Mrs. Phipps's face added the unnecessary "more than you already have."

Jacelyn even had to change out of her plain round gown and into a sprigged muslin, "like a young lady receiving a gentleman caller," according to Mrs. Phipps. To Jacelyn it was more like dressing the sacrificial lamb! The whole thing was beyond reason, and she wasn't having any of it, nor any of his fine lordship, leaning so nonchalantly against the edge of her father's desk, looking superbly elegant and supremely relaxed for a condemned man.

"You should be gratified then, my lord, that this . . . this chicken refuses to marry you."

"More like a hornet now, poppet, but that's irrelevant," he told her, delighting in the sparks in her eyes, "for I haven't asked you to marry me."

Jacelyn's hand flew to her mouth. What a fool she must look now! "But Papa said, and Squire said, and —"

"Squire says a great deal too much and your father has rightfully left it to us to work out." He held up his hand. "No, that does not mean you can forget all about last night's ah, events, and go onto your next hey-go-mad scheme. I do have some honour, you know. I don't go around strewing the countryside with soiled doves." Her innocent confusion made him amend that: "I don't ruin a young lady's reputation and then leave her to face the censure of her friends and neighbours. So what I *am* proposing is that you come to London with me and my great-aunt, if I can arrange it. You'll like her, I know. Very much of the *Ancien Regime,* but a complete hand for all that, if you don't let her intimidate you. You cannot stay in my bachelor's quarters, of course, but your father spoke of an aunt of yours? . . ."

"Papa knows Aunt Amabel won't have me."

"He thought he could bring her 'round if she only had to give you house-room and an occasional introduction, if my great-aunt and I could act as chaperone and escort. Think of all the wonderful times we could have, just for a few months. You'd be home before Christmas. The theaters and bookstores, the parties and balls, all the sights and all the shops. *Belle-tante's* been longing to visit her old friends in London, fellow *emigrés,* you know, so she'll be thrilled to look after you. And it would get you away from Treverly, which might be uncomfortable right now, and out of Squire's sight, before he throttles you."

Jacelyn had to laugh at that, before reminding the earl that Lady Ponsonby and Priscilla would be in London, and Lady Ponsonby and Aunt Amabel were bosom bows. "If I am ruined here in Cambridgeshire, where everyone knows I'm always in some scrape or other, it will be a hundred times worse in London, where no one knows me. I won't be invited anywhere, and poor Aunt Amabel will have to go to Bath again."

Claibourne smiled at the girl's candour, and at all the shifting thoughts he could read on her so expressive face. You'd make a terrible cardplayer, Miss Trevaine, he thought. Right now he was pleased to see disappointment mixed with the restored good humour. "That's the other half of my proposal," he told her. "I'm suggesting we put it about that we have an understanding, a prebetrothal agreement, if you will. That way we can travel together, and no one can comment that I am too much in your company. Most important, your good name will be preserved."

Jacelyn shook her head. "I don't understand, Lord Claibourne. Squire said I was compromised and had to marry. How can a mere 'understanding' uncompromise me?"

"Ah, that's the glory of idle gossip. As I see it, the reason for protecting a maiden's name so well is that no man wants a wife who will, ah, kiss other men. And the wives don't want a woman in their midst who might kiss their husbands. So they have decided that a girl who kisses two men is no better than she should be and not acceptable. But if she kisses *one* man and appears to be close to marrying him, then that is love, and safe."

"What a bag of moonshine, my lord."

"Leigh."

"Leigh?"

"Or Claibourne, or Merrill, if you'd rather. Anything but Arthur. Then I can call you . . . Jacelyn?"

"Or Jacey. Anything but chicken!"

And they both laughed, the earl feeling they'd gotten over the heaviest ground, Jacelyn in delight that she seemed to have made a friend of this paragon.

"But, my lo—Leigh, if it is just a private, unannounced engagement, who is to know? I mean, how will that stop all the rumours?"

"Oh, I might drop a hint or two to Lady Ponsonby, *entre nous* of course. That should take care of Cambridgeshire, London, and all of the counties in between, if not the Outer Hebrides."

Jacelyn's dimples appeared. "What happens then? We can't just keep on having an understanding, can we?"

"Not forever, no. But we can say it's for your first Little Season. That way if young Lochinvar rides up and sweeps you off your feet, I can bow out grace-fully, a wounded but wiser man. If there is no one you'd rather have who will put up with you, brat, and you still don't want me, well then, I'll parade a few opera dancers in front of your aunt's house, so you can throw me over because of my rakehell ways. No one will blame you, I'm sure."

"And if . . . if . . . ," she began shyly.

"If we should decide we'd suit after we get to know each other better? Then I will get down on one knee and ask if you would do me the great honour, and you, you minx, will reply that the honour and plea-sure are all yours."

"Yes, my lord," she replied with a chuckle.

"Unless, of course, you've reconsidered and wish to marry me now," he teased. "Then if we didn't suit, I could always find a war somewhere."

"That is not funny, Leigh." Nor was the idea of marrying a man—albeit he was everything she'd ever dreamed of in a husband—who offered simply to save her reputation.

He touched her suddenly serious mouth with one finger. "No, sweetheart, it isn't funny. Besides, it would just give the scandal brewers more broth if we married now, as if we were rushing to consecrate the union before the confinement. So shall we agree on our 'gentlemen's agreement'?"

Jacelyn knew she'd gone too far this time, abduct-ing a gentleman, and she knew how upset her father was. She also knew how her heart yearned for her to say yes, because her body knew he would kiss her, to seal the bargain. How she wished to be held in his arms again! For once, however, possibly because her last calamity was so recent, Miss Trevaine was determined to think before she acted. Her father would be pleased to see her reputation intact, and Squire of course would be delighted to see her gone, even if just for the fall hunt season. And there was an undeniable, unnameable something within her that was dancing right now, at the thought of even those few months with this man. But what about Leigh?

If he didn't see to her name, his own reputation would be tarnished, yet from what Squire'd told her father, a rake did not worry overmuch about honour or what others thought. So why should this hero, this Nonesuch, wish to be saddled with a ragmannered brat like herself? Self-confidence? Jacelyn didn't even have enough self-*awareness* to think for a moment that his lordship could find her attractive. So, "Why, my lord? Why would you do all this for me?" she asked.

Now it was Leigh's turn for self-doubts. Would she believe him that it was because he found her adorable? That it was the only way he could think of not to frighten her or put her back up like an angry kitten's? Would she laugh if he proposed love-in-a-cottage to her, all he had to offer? He picked one of Baron's grey hairs from his jacket's sleeve, not looking at her face, at the hurt he might see there. "There is the money, you know," he drawled.

"Oh, that's all right, then." Jacelyn was surprisingly content. This made sense, and satisfied her own sense of honour. After all, the whole escapade was entirely her fault — except for the kiss she tried not to remember—so why should the earl have to suffer? It was only fair he gain something in exchange for his freedom. Besides, the story Bottwick had told of Leigh's struggles to bring his estates back from ruin had touched her with the same instinct that made her heart go out to motherless kittens. If her dowry could ease his way, it should be his, unless . . .

"Leigh, you didn't kiss me to ensure I'd be compromised, did you?"

He raised one thick golden eyebrow. "Do you mean did I know Squire and his house party were coming, or do you mean did I know you were wealthy? The former was obvious, I suppose, that sooner or later someone would come after you. As for the latter, an easy deduction. Any fool could recognise you for an heiress by your elegant dress, your fine manners, the table you set. On the other hand, perhaps I just kiss every pretty girl who holds me at pistol-point. You'll never know." He raised one of her hands to his mouth and gently kissed the palm. "Poppet, you'll just have to trust me. You'll hear many stories about me—some of them will be true—but I swear I won't do anything to shame you, or cause you upset. Do you believe that?" At her nod he softly kissed each finger before saying, "Good, because if this doesn't look like a love match, we'll never pull it off. Settled, then?" he asked, ready to pull her into his arms for the kiss he'd been long awaiting and felt he richly deserved for not simply throwing the chit over his shoulder and riding off to Gretna Green with her.

Jacelyn still had some reservations, despite the tingle in the hand he was nuzzling. She withdrew it and stood looking down, fiddling with the folds of her dress. "My lord," she said awkwardly, "I need a . . . a promise from you."

Claibourne groaned inwardly. Here it comes, he thought. She'll ask me to swear off ladybirds. He'd do it, of course, but it would be a dashed short engagement, no matter what he'd said before. "Anything, my love."

"Please, Leigh, swear you won't ever go hunting with Squire Bottwick? I couldn't bear him thinking he won, after all."

Claibourne laughed out loud and agreed, "But only if you promise to have a care for your reputation in return, if not for my sake, then at least for my poor aunt's, and your unborn children."

"My children?"

"Of course. You wouldn't want all those freckle-faced darlings to come crying home because Priscilla Ponsonby wouldn't let them play with her brats, would you?"

How wonderful a kiss felt, when you were already smiling!

Lord Trevaine invited Leigh to stay for dinner, but the earl refused, citing all he had to accomplish in the fortnight he'd be gone. He mentioned seeing Lady Parkhurst and fetching his great-aunt; he didn't mention trying to regain his sanity. He wished to be on the road to London well before dark, if Trevaine's letter to his sister was ready, since he was sure that Lady Ponsonby would not approve of travel on the morrow, a Sunday.

"And I am sure the good Lord sleeps better at night, knowing Clothilda Ponsonby is doing His work," Lord Trevaine added. "Godspeed, son."

Jacelyn only whispered: " 'Ware of highwaymen."

5

What a difference a few hours made in a man's life! Just the night before, Claibourne had been on this same road, his good horse under him, and not much ahead of him. Now his future looked interesting, at least, if not bright, and he rode a chestnut gelding from Squire's stable. His honour wouldn't let him touch a groat of Jacelyn's money before they were wed, although her father had trustingly and touchingly offered. The earl was not nearly so under the hatches as to be tempted to accept, nor to take Arthur's guilt-ridden suggestion of a loan for travelling expenses. Squire's offer, however, was harder to refuse: a tidy sum of money and the use of a mount, in exchange for Baron's service with the broodmares for the two weeks Claibourne would be gone. The brute would be hell to ride after, but he'd only be eating his head off in a London stable while Claibourne went north to fetch his aunt. Besides, they all had to make some sacrifices for the cause.

If his horse was back there in Cambridgeshire, so were a great many of my lord's thoughts. Gads, what had he gotten himself into? She was so young and so appealing, so honest in her nature, and so deliciously devious in her methods. She had the innocence of a loving child, yet her kisses were those of a seductive woman. What a conundrum, and what a delight! The high-born debutantes he'd known, admittedly few and those only slightly, had exactly three public facial expressions: smirk when they were being complimented, sneer when they weren't, and simper when they couldn't tell which. Each expression used the minimum of effort, as if they feared any movement of their lips might ruin the perfect china-doll look they struggled to achieve. His Jacelyn, though—already he thought of her with the possessive—held her emotions right in the eyes, in her full mouth, in the straight little nose which crinkled adorably. He was certain he'd not seen half the combinations the changeable little creature possessed. He only hoped London didn't teach her to cloak all her thoughts and feelings with the mask of ennui that Society deemed necessary.

His first chore, though, was to see that Jacelyn got to London. He had the letter to her Aunt Amabel, along with Lord Trevaine's hints toward obtaining her compliance. Trevaine had told Leigh that his letter appealed to Lady Parkhurst's strong familial instincts as well as her mercenary ones, the latter fed by the extremely generous sum put aside for incidental expenses beyond Jacelyn's clothes, servants, horses, and come-out ball. That and the fact of Claibourne and his great-aunt undertaking the day-to-day responsibilities for a debutante ought to convince his flighty, lazy, but generally agreeable sister, confided Trevaine. As for Lord Parkhurst, his seat in the

House, his dinner, and a good game of whist were the only things he considered worthwhile, and he disliked having any of them disturbed. Therefore, cautioned Jacelyn's own loving father, revealing whence she'd derived some of her circuitous logic, Claibourne was to play the trump card as a last resort only. Unwritten in the letter, but to be implied by the earl in person, was the precarious nature of both Trevaine's health and the proposed betrothal. If the engagement and Trevaine's heart both failed, the Parkhursts would have the sole responsibility for their impetuous, unconventional, problematic niece. Yes, the threat ought to clinch the invitation.

Lady Parkhurst's letter arrived at Treverly three days later, along with Leigh's note that he was now en route to Littleton at Stockton-on-Tees in Durham, to convey Lady Parkhurst's invitation to his own great-aunt. Lord Claibourne saw no difficulties there. He was finally offering *Tante* Simone a sojourn in London near many of her friends, along with the chance of a great-grandbaby to spoil. She had been after him to wed for years now, and a wife whose dowry would help restore the Abbey could only thrill her. Leigh could see no reason to mention any irregularities about the betrothal — or the bride!

Miss Trevaine, meanwhile, was finally acting in anything but an unusual manner for a seventeen-year-old girl. She was thinking about her future, clothes, and men.

It took all of one day for Jacelyn to discover the changes Claibourne had made in her life, outwardly, at any rate. At church that Sunday, she was no longer Miss Jacey to the villagers she'd known all her years, nor that wild Trevaine girl to the matrons who had barely given her a nod previously. Now her old friends bowed and tugged their forelocks, and even the gentrywomen graciously bent their heads in her direction, smiling. Of course now she was a few steps down the aisle and two short words away from being a countess, no matter how she'd done it. She, Jacelyn Trevaine, a countess! Even Priscilla Ponsonby and her mother would have to curtsey to her. That was a heady notion for a young girl, so she practiced her best *grande dame* looks, sitting in the Treverly pew between her father and Mrs. Phipps. She even tried raising one eyebrow as she'd seen his lordship do, to such majestic effect, until Mrs. Phipps pinched her arm.

Looking around, she caught Samantha's wink, across the aisle in Squire's pew. Her air dreams came back to earth with a painful thump. For there, next to Arthur in his high collar and nipped-in waist, sat Priscilla, in high-waisted primrose muslin, with matching ribbons holding silk roses to her bonnet. Her friend Miss Chadwick wore a sky-blue jaconet gown with an ermine tippet, and a white satin bonnet with blue ruching and a large blue bow tied off to one side of her heart-shaped face. Even Squire's daughters, dressed alike in pale pink pinafores, were better attired than the countess-to-be.

Jacelyn wore the shapeless navy kerseymere with the white fichu she'd worn to church every Sunday.

That was what Mrs. Phipps thought suitable, and since Mrs. Phipps made most of Jacelyn's clothes, cleaned them, pressed them, and laid them out for her, Jacey had never given it another thought. Her chipstraw bonnet was nearly new, but the ribbons were tangled, and Jacelyn had been in a hurry, late as usual, so they hung in a bedraggled knot somewhere under her chin. She had also been too late, exercising Pen, on a lead, at her father's insistence, to change her heavy wool tartan for a paisley shawl, and she'd only pinned it with a tin brooch from the last fair, lopsided besides. Why, she looked more like a ragpicker than an heiress! They'd all laugh at her in London. Worse, they would laugh at Lord Claibourne, with his reputation for beautiful women, being saddled with such a fright. No one would believe for an instant that he was attracted to her. Why should they, when she didn't?

After the service, when the congregation clustered in the churchyard, Jacelyn impatiently stood by her father, accepting best wishes and ignoring innuendoes as best she could, until Squire's party came near.

Lady Ponsonby wouldn't offer her hand to shake, sniffing that "it's a long way 'twixt St. David's and Dover," which Jacelyn took to mean my lady wouldn't acknowledge her till she had a ring on her finger. Priscilla took her cue from her mother: "Congratulations are in order, I suppose, Miss Trevaine, though I wish you well of your bargain. Heaven knows, *I* wouldn't have him.

"Oh," Jacelyn inquired sweetly, "has he asked you?"

Priscilla flounced off, leaving Miss Chadwick to titter, "I think you are very brave, Miss Trevaine. I couldn't even think of being alone with such a rake."

To which Jacelyn replied, "And I, Miss Chadwick, would never think of wearing some poor dead animal around my neck." It was the little beady glass eyes on the other girl's fur wrap that did it. Jacelyn excused herself to her father when she finally saw Mrs. Bottwick leaving the vicar's side.

"Ma'am, could I please ask a favour of you? It's terribly important, you see, and there's no one else."

"Of course, Jacelyn dear. I know you must miss your mother at times like this. I thought Mrs. Phipps would explain to you . . ."

"Explain? Oh no, Mrs. Bottwick, I know all about that." At the look of horror on Mrs. Bottwick's round face, Jacelyn hurriedly added, "The farm animals, you know. This is more important! I . . . I can't go to London like such a frump. I'd die. Mrs. Phipps can only make one kind of dress, short sleeves for summer, long sleeves for winter. And if Aunt Amabel has the dressing of me, I'll end up looking like a . . . silly debutante."

"But you are a debutante, Jacelyn. I'm sure your aunt knows what's best."

"No, Mrs. Bottwick. She only sees a hobbledehoy little girl she has to hide in ruffles and frills so no one will notice I'm different. And I'm not just a girl in her first Season, I'm nearly engaged, and to a top-of-the-trees Corinthian besides!"

Mrs. Bottwick was beginning to see Jacelyn's problem, more perhaps than Jacelyn did, and her natural motherly feelings were stirring, but it wasn't for her to interfere.

"How can I make you see?" Jacelyn wondered, desperate to be understood. Her eye caught Samantha Bottwick, standing next to Arthur. "There. Look at Sam." She didn't notice Mrs. Bottwick's wince, which changed to a proud smile with Jacelyn's next words: "She'll always look beautiful, just standing still, no matter what she wears. She's tall and blonde; she'll be exquisite in all the pastels and white lace. I'll get lost in them! A poor little brown dab of a thing!"

"What do you want then, my dear? You cannot dress in red satin like some opera dancer, and you cannot damp your petticoats like Caro Lamb. I won't hear of it, and I'm sure your aunt won't either."

"Is Jacey going to damp her petticoats then, Mama?"

"Samantha!"

"Hello, Sam," Jacey said, grinning at her friend. "I am trying to convince your mother to help me find some *style*. I need to cut a dash, as Arthur would say. You know you have *La Belle Assemblée* the same week it's out in London."

Samantha looked at her consideringly. "She's right, Mama. Everyone is going to stare at her anyway, you know. And it's not like there's ever been anything exactly ordinary about Jacey either, so maybe she does need a look of her own. Besides, if we don't go shopping with her, she's liable to go off to London looking like Cambridgeshire girls make their clothes from horse blankets."

"Now, Samantha. Jacelyn, if your father gives his permission, we'll all go into Ryefield. Perhaps I could have my aunt in Kensington send some fabrics. I recall some dark green shot-silk at the Emporium Arcade. . . ."

So Jacelyn's next few weeks, and most of her thoughts, were taken up with clothes. There were trips to Ryefield and even an excursion to Royston, consultations with the *Ladies' Journal* and Mrs. Bottwick's aunt. And fitting after fitting. Jacelyn had never stood still for so long in her whole life.

She had an evening gown made of the emerald silk, with gold braid and gold slippers to match, and gold ribbons to thread through her newly styled hair, brushed back smooth except for a few curls at either temple, then piled on her head in twisted coils. Also for evening there was a cream satin embroidered with gold butterflies, and a gold tissue with a lace overskirt. Her day dresses were of peach and apricot and amber, with simple lines to grace her figure, and only simple trims, nothing fussy to overwhelm her.

This was only the start of her wardrobe. The rest would be selected in London by a much more knowledgeable Jacelyn, but it was all the local seamstresses could accomplish in the time. Amazing how "young miss" would have had to wait for weeks, after being served by the lowest apprentice. Miss Trevaine, after a few words from Mrs. Bottwick, could have her gowns fashioned in days, assured Madame d'Journet (née Nellie Jones) herself, nearly forgetting her French accent in calculating her income from this windfall. With the chance of dressing Squire's three daughters if she pleased the ladies now, Madame would sew the seams herself, if she had to.

There were two items of disagreement in the new wardrobe. The first was a deep rose velvet gown with a décolletage Mrs. Bottwick thought far too daring. Jacelyn adored it, and Samantha labelled it regal. They compromised with a lace insert, which Jacelyn determined wouldn't reach London.

There was no compromise on the other outfit Squire's wife considered in dubious taste. Jacelyn saw the fashion plate in *La Belle Assemblée* and couldn't rest until she had one made: a riding habit with a scarlet Hussar-style jacket with black buttons, and a black split skirt.

"But, dearest, you cannot mean to ride astride in London!" Mrs. Bottwick was aghast.

"Of course not," Jacelyn assured her, wondering if she could find a way. "But think about my present habit!"

Jacelyn's bombazine riding outfit was serviceable, Mrs. Bottwick had to give it that. Otherwise it was a mud-coloured brown that was always dirt-streaked. The girl never seemed to remember to pick up the extra width so the train either dragged behind her or tripped her up. It was remarkable how such a graceful rider looked like such a clumsy waif on the ground. Mrs. Bottwick relented. They even found a tiny scarlet cap to match, with a white feather to curl down the side of Jacelyn's cheek, highlighting the white lace she'd have at collar and cuffs.

All in all, Jacelyn was satisfied that her clothes were out of the ordinary without being outlandish. If she looked special, maybe, just maybe, Lord Claibourne would think she was special. Mrs. Bottwick, on the other hand, acknowledged that the new styles gave Jacelyn a more dignified, mature air, which should, the good Lord willing, make her act that way!

Luckily for Jacey, the new concern for her clothes took up a lot of time, time she'd otherwise have spent wondering about that other new discovery she'd made: men. Not men as in her father or Squire or Shoop or even Arthur. Men as in Lord Claibourne, as in all she didn't know about farm animals despite what she'd told Mrs. Bottwick, and all her father's books didn't tell her. These wonderings she hugged closely to herself at night, and dreamt of blue eyes and lazy smiles.

"But what if his aunt is a dragon, Papa?"

"Then tell Antoine not to overcook the beef," Lord Trevaine answered wearily, having lost his place in the Suetonius again. "Jacelyn, it's just a small dinner party for a few of our closest friends, stop fretting so. After three days in a carriage, Madame Aubonier won't wish anything more. Now go help Mrs. Phipps set the table, and leave me in peace!"

Miss Trevaine could face Squire's wrath and think nothing of taking hedges higher than her horse, but tonight's dinner had her quaking: her new gown, her new hair style, her new role—and to be putting them on for the first time at such a gathering! Most of the guests had known her forever. What if they laughed? No, as her father said, they were all friends. These people, her father had insisted, were the ones he wished to share his pride with, so the county would see this was no hole-in-corner affair. The alternative was worse, the evening alone with Claibourne and his aunt, so Jacelyn hurried to get ready.

Squire was fidgety too, ruining his second cravat. " 'Can't see what your daughter needed a new dress for. She's too young to be dining out in company anyway."

"Jacelyn particularly asked that Samantha attend. I'm sure she'll feel easier having another young lady there. Besides, it will be good for our Samantha to get out more before her own presentation. Those young girls pitchforked into Society all at once often make a mull of it."

"Well, I won't have a gal of mine picking up any froward behaviour from that Trevaine chit. Deuce take this linen!"

"Hush, George, let me. Though why your valet has to be in the stables is beyond me."

"He knows a lot more about physicking, humans and animals, than any stableman I've ever had, that's why, and that new gelding Raindancer's a deuced sight more important than all this dandification."

"Anyway, dear, think of how nice it will be for Samantha in her own Season next year, if one of her best friends is a countess. I'm considering bringing Samantha to London for Jacelyn's come-out ball next month. There, your neckcloth is tied. Don't tug at it so."

"What, another dress for the chit? Next you'll be expecting me to leave the country to go to London and do the pretty. No, madam, I tell you the girl is too young.

"Just as Jacelyn Trevaine is too young to face all of this without her friends nearby."

"Gammon. If you mean by that what I've heard all week, that the chit's too young to deal with a man of Claibourne's stamp, why, I say it again, he could be the making of her."

"He could break her heart. If it weren't for you and your—"

Samantha was going to London.

Bien. Everything seemed to be going *bien*. Mme. Aubonier had arrived on schedule, a tall, rigidly erect, thin-faced woman dressed all in black. She had raised her lorgnette to survey the house and its occupants, and declared them all *"Bien, bien."*

"How was your journey, Madame?"

"Bien, bien."

"May I show you to your room? Would you care to rest before dinner? Shall I have tea sent to you?" All received the same answer, till Jacelyn wondered if perhaps Madame didn't speak English. Hesitant to practice her schoolgirl French, she was relieved when Madame surveyed her chintz-papered room, fire well lit, fall asters in a Meissen pitcher, and declared it all "Lovely, lovely." What a peculiar chaperone this would be!

At least her presence saved Jacelyn from the awkwardness she'd been dreading, that first meeting with Claibourne who was, incredibly, as handsome as she'd remembered. She curtseyed, he bowed, a few polite words were exchanged between the *biens*. Then she'd gone off to see to his aunt's comfort, her own toilette, the rest of the guests, and finally the dinner, all without having to face that first private moment. Madame, seated between Jacelyn's father and Vicar Shankman, seemed to have found her vocabulary, English or French, Jacey could not tell from her place at the opposite end of the table. Claibourne's scarecrow of an aunt also seemed to have found her appetite; she appeared to be a trencherwoman of Squire's caliber. And for all his grumbling, Squire seemed to enjoy the turbot in oyster sauce and the veal *marselaisse* as well as he did the plain rack of lamb Jacelyn had Antoine include for his benefit. Even Samantha was managing well, between the vicar and Admiral Hopkinton, who was an old dear, even if he was nearly deaf and persisted in refighting the Peninsular Campaign across the table to Claibourne, in a voice booming enough to stir the autumn leaves Jacelyn had arranged for a centerpiece.

Claibourne was all poise and polish, making his replies to the admiral through Jacelyn, so she was the one forced to shout out Wellington's strategy, while Leigh conversed quietly with Mrs. Bottwick on his other side. Claibourne looked even more elegant in evening clothes, Jacelyn noted during a lull in the admiral's wargames, and she was quite sure his shoulders weren't padded, as Arthur's undoubtedly were.

All in all, she thought, the evening was going quite well, with only one adverse comment about her new looks. When Samantha had exclaimed over the green gown, Squire had commented to the admiral, in a necessarily carrying voice, "Well, I suppose it's an improvement, but I wouldn't let any daughter of

mine go out in public without her stays."
Claibourne's lips twitched, but he didn't miss a word
in his description of the road conditions to the vicar's
wife. Thank goodness no one mentioned the episode
behind this whole celebration, not even Squire, who
was still feeling guilty over his part in it, according to
Sam. *Bien.*

Dinner was finally over; the men had their port.
Madame retired to her bedchamber to rest for the
next day's journey, and the vicar, Squire, and Admiral Hopkinton joined Jacelyn's father for a round of
whist while the vicar's wife and Mrs. Bottwick discussed winter floral arrangements for the church and
Samantha softly played the pianoforte.

"Do you play?" he asked—the only *he* in the room,
as far as Jacelyn was concerned. He sat beside her on
the sofa.

"About as well as I do watercolours," she said,
laughing.

"Ah, that's the first time in two weeks I've heard
that sound. I thought you must have packed it away
with your britches."

Jacelyn was fingering the silk of her gown. "Do
you . . . do you like it, my lord?"

"Fishing for compliments, are you, dewdrop?
'Well, I suppose it's an improvement,' he teased,
quoting Squire and looking where Squire hadn't
found any corset. He smiled at Jacelyn's furious
blush, then let his hand between them softly brush
her thigh. "And here I was looking forward to strolling down Rotten Row with you in Lem's castoffs.
N'importe, you'll make just as big a stir now, poppet.
You look quite beautiful."

She laughed again. "Stuff! It's only the dress! I just didn't want your friends to think I was a sha-brag. I didn't need the whole butterboat poured on me!"

He gave her a quizzical look. "Then you are the first woman I've ever met who didn't love flattery. How do you feel about diamonds?" he asked, taking a little box from his pocket. The ring he held out for her inspection was gold with a round diamond set in a circlet of tiny rubies.

"It's beautiful, Leigh, but—"

"But what, rosebud?" he asked, trying to see which of her fingers it fit best, while she sat benumbed.

"But I thought we didn't have to have a real engagement. You said we could just put it about that we had some kind of understanding."

"And so we do, don't we? Never fear, that's not the Claibourne diamond, just a little piece from the family collection. We'll have to fatten you considerably in London if you're to wear the real thing, else you'd not have strength to hold up your arm. There's a tiara and a bracelet, besides the wedding set. I simply thought you might like this."

"Oh, I do, Leigh. It's just that, well, if we're not really engaged, is it proper for me to accept such a gift?" Regretful, she looked over to the facing sofa, where the older ladies sat, pretending they weren't watching her every move.

"What, are you going all prunes and prisms on me? Fancy gowns, elegant hairdos, the perfect host-ess, and now the picture of respectability! You must be a changeling; I'll wager you're some other brat Lord Trevaine's trying to foist off on me so he can

80

keep the real thing to himself." He drew out his eyepiece and surveyed her slowly through it with all the affectation of a Bond Street Beau. From her side, of course, his eye looked like a distorted blue billiard ball.

"Silly, I suppose you'd prefer it if I still set frogs loose in the dining room."

" 'Still'?"

"Only once. I put some frogs under the covers of the serving dishes so when Phipps opened them to serve . . ."

"No wonder the man has white hair! And no, pet, I don't mean to encourage you to such pranks. Just know that I like the bandit as well as the belle, so you don't have to playact for me."

"Since you are being so agreeable, Leigh, there is something we should discuss."

"Oh-oh, I'm beginning to recognise a particular golden flicker in your eyes that betokens some deviltry or other, and I misdoubt that tone of voice. What horrible scheme are you concocting?"

"I want to take Pen to London with us. She'll be unhappy here without me and won't get enough exercise, so I've decided she has to come along. Either she comes or I don't," Jacey ended militantly.

Smiling, Claibourne raised Jacelyn's hand, the one with the ring, to his mouth for a sweet salute. "Of course, Jay-bird, it's all part of the deal."

"What deal?" suspiciously.

"Why, the deal I made with your father and Bottwick, of course. Your father agreed not to call me out if I took you off his hands, and Squire agreed not to challenge me if I agreed to take the dog out of the county."

"Do be serious," she told him, meanwhile very aware that he had not released her hand.

"Serious? Then listen, Jacelyn, I'm not your father, nor even the squire, to call you to account for your actions. I want us to be friends, not keep coming to cuffs over foolish things. Agreed?"

Jacelyn nodded, though she couldn't help wonder if he meant she should be as complacent about his behaviour as he seemed prepared to be over hers. What if he meant he'd overlook a huge dog in the drawing room, in exchange for her turning a blind eye to . . . to a fancy piece in his flat! They didn't have a real engagement, of course, but even the idea sat like a lead weight in her chest. Many men had mistresses, she knew, yet how could she bear the earl's ever touching another woman's hand the way his thumb was stroking hers? Or smile that warm, slightly lopsided grin at someone else? She'd toss her in the Thames, decided Jacelyn, and see how easygoing his lordship was at *that* foolishness!

"About the ring." Jacelyn thought it best to change the subject lest she blurt out her intentions. "I don't understand why you've kept all these beautiful pieces in a vault somewhere gathering dust, when you needed money so badly. You could have sold them long ago and reinvested the money in the estates, or whatever, couldn't you?"

"The diamonds were handed down from countess to countess for centuries, part of the Merrill clan's history. They weren't mine to sell."

"But you can give this one away?"

"Yes," he told her, squeezing her hand but gesturing around the room with his other. "You see your home, your friends, your father? I wanted to bring you a bit of my heritage, to have you meet the family, so to speak. I wanted the pleasure of making you smile, and I wanted something of mine to be special to you. Do you understand?"

Bien. Bien.

6

The heavy old coach had new black paint and the Claibourne family crest. It had four hired horses and two hired postillions with weapons. On the box it had Clive, Madame's old coachman from the Abbey in Durham, and a huge, scraggly dog sitting beside him, to Clive's disgust. His first trip to London in twelve years, and to arrive looking like a travelling road show. *Pah*. Enough to throw a man off his feed, it was, especially when the beast had enough of feeling the wind in its face and stretched out across the box seat — all across it, so those big cow eyes looked up from Clive's own lap, and hairs were clinging all over his new uniform. "I wouldna do this for nobbut the young master," Clive told the animal as he watched the road ahead, where Claibourne led the way on his grey stallion. Clive spat tobacco juice over the side of the coach. "You're my paying off a debt, belikes, for all them easy years a-driving madam to the village 'n church on Sundays while Master Leigh was off to war. 'Sides, if gettin' you and young miss to London is going to settle 'is lordship down 'n right things at the Abbey, guess I'd tote a bear up here."

The situation inside the coach was very similar. Mme. Simone would rather have stayed in Stockton-on-Tees than spend another day being jostled across the length of England, but she also dearly wished to see Claibourne happy and the Abbey restored to a semblance of grandeur, if not glory. The little heiress seemed to suit on both counts. In her day the deed would have been done: a scandal, a wedding. Simple, no? Names and funds would already be transferred, and the bride and groom would be left to find love and affection later, inside the marriage, it was to be hoped. But these young English, they wanted it all. Leigh wanted to woo the *fille* and show her a good time in London. His Aunt Simone would do her part.

"So," she said to her charge when they were finally on their way and silence had lasted long enough. "We go to make you a success, no?"

Jacelyn laughed. "Oh no, Madame, we're not attempting the impossible, only the improbable, getting the ton to accept me."

"Why should it not? You have the birth, the breeding, I see. My nephew gives his ring. What is to interfere? You have manners, no?"

"Well, not always, Madame." Jacelyn was looking self-conscious in her new navy wool spenser and light blue travelling dress. She'd placed her new bonnet on the seat opposite almost reverently, to protect the blue silk flowers which peeped from under the brim. His lordship had called it a lovely cross between innocence and allure. Just like Jacelyn, he'd said, giving her a great deal to think about, beyond how she was going to miss her father and all she held dear. What a confused muddle her emotions were in altogether!

She was sad to leave Treverly, of course, but eager to explore London's attractions, including the exclusive shops, now that she had a taste of fashion. She was excited over Claibourne's company, yet anxious that she wouldn't please him. Mostly Jacelyn was uncertain she *could* remain a lady under such conditions as Mrs. Bottwick and Mrs. Phipps tried to drum into her up to the last minute: A lady never goes anywhere alone, a lady never walks on Bond Street in the morning. A lady may not waltz until approved, may not speak to a man unless introduced, may not—not—not! So many senseless and stupid restrictions, yet the slightest breach of this etiquette would see her sent home in disgrace. His lordship certainly wouldn't want a wife who was laughed at, no matter what he claimed.

"Its more than just my manners and breeding, Madame. Samantha says that Priscilla says that it will take a great push to get me into Almack's—it's this exclusive club attended by everyone who is anyone. My aunt, Lady Parkhurst, won't make the effort to get me vouchers. She doesn't quite approve of me, you see, and doesn't wish to jeopardise her own good standing. And Samantha says that Priscilla says I'll be ignored totally if I'm not accepted at Almack's. You know, not invited to balls and parties, not recognised by other young ladies."

"This Samantha I met, but who is this Priscilla who has so much to say?"

"She's Squire's niece Priscilla Ponsonby, and she's an Incomparable. That's what they call the most admired women. She had five offers in her first Season, but no one was good enough for her. Besides, she's tall and pretty and never has stains on her gloves or a single hair out of its pins."

"Ah, so we shall steal all of her beaux, yes?"

"Oh, Madame, I wouldn't want any of them, just . . . just . . ."

"Just to show this *chat* that Mademoiselle Trevaine can shine in the first circles also?"

"Yes, but I don't see how."

"Didn't my grand-nephew ask me to see about your debut? Today is what, Friday, and this Almack's meets when?"

"Wednesday."

"*Oui*, plenty of time. Don't worry, *petite*. I'll see it done."

Jacelyn did not want to offend the older woman, though she couldn't see how Mme. Aubonier could have any influence whatsoever in London, having been isolated in Durham for so long. She hesitantly mentioned, "Vouchers are extremely hard to come by, ma'am. Samantha says one must know the patronesses who run Almack's. Priscilla's mother is close with Lady Jersey, which means we couldn't ask her."

"Enough of this Priscilla, child. I am tired of her already. And that Jersey *chien* is a scandal unto herself, *l'affaire* with your prince. No, I would not let her invite us. Princess Esterhazy is still a patroness, no? She is a connexion of Claibourne's grandfather, my father *le Duc*. And Lady Drummond-Burrell, her husband brought her to *la maison* on their wedding trip, many years ago. *Il fait.* It is done."

"I am sorry, Mme. Aubonier, for doubting you. I did not realise you had such connexions in London."

"Call me *tante, petite,* as Leigh does. I like you. And *non,* how could you know I would still have good friends and good correspondents, so long since I have seen them?"

"But, *tante,* if you have all these friends, why did you stay alone all those years while Leigh was away? Weren't you lonely?"

"Child, I had lost my home, my husband, my son. The last of my family was Mignon-Marie, Leigh's mother. Then she too was taken, and the boy went off to fight to save my country, too late. How could I be anything but lonely, wherever I went?"

"I understood there were many other French men and women in London. Perhaps you could have stayed with them?"

"Ah, I could have stayed French, and stayed lost in memories, *n'est-ce pas?* But Claibourne Abbey had no mistress, and the boy had no one else to come home to. So I stayed and made a new life and new friends. It was still sad, *triste.* But listen, Jacelyn, and remember, you can be lonely among the largest crowds, without your own loved ones. They are who matter, not people like this Priscilla, whose opinions are worth cabbage, yes?"

"Yes, *belle-tante,*" Jacelyn said, impulsively reaching over to kiss the other woman. "Thank you."

After a relaxed luncheon at the Crowned Drake, about halfway to London, Leigh handed Baron's reins to one of the outriders and settled in the coach with the women. He took the corner opposite Jacey, his back to the horses, his long legs in tight buckskins and now-dusty Hessians resting on the other side of hers.

"So, ladies, time for a council of war. What plans have you made?"

"Clothes first," his aunt proclaimed. "The dressmakers can be working while we see to introductions."

"But I have plenty of clothes. They were sent ahead to Aunt Amabel's."

"A lady never has enough clothes. *Tiens,* styles change overnight in London. Now you two make your arrangements. I rest."

Jacelyn looked at the figure of Claibourne's aunt in her corner, all in black again, a high-necked stuff gown, and was dubious about the lady's taste, much less her knowledge of the current fashions. Aunt Amabel, however, would have the vapours over the styles and colours Jacelyn chose. She wasn't even in London, and already there were difficulties.

As if reading her thoughts, Mme. Aubonier opened her eyes briefly and fixed Jacey in her glance. "Not to fear, *petite.* I go to visit these *grande dames* of your English ton. They talk more frankly without a *jeune fille* present. *He* goes with you to the shops," she decreed, nodding in Claibourne's direction before shutting her eyes again.

"You, my lord, trailing after me in the dress shops?"

"And the milliners and booteries; I'll wait outside the corsetière, of course." He caught Jacelyn's look in his aunt's direction. "All very proper: an open carriage, your maid for chaperone."

"I haven't got a maid," Jacelyn contradicted. "I don't want one, fussing about me and telling me what to wear, like a child."

The earl inspected his sleeve for lint. "I'd be your abigail myself, pet, doing up all those little buttons and combing out your hair, but I draw the line at mending and pressing."

"Mrs. Phipps always did that for me. I see that I cannot expect Aunt Amabel's London housekeeper to sew new ribbons on my gowns. How does one arrange to hire a lady's maid in Town? At home Mrs. Phipps would have promoted the second housemaid, or found a cousin who was good with a needle."

"I'm certain your aunt has already seen to it, once your clothes arrived." He held his hand up when he saw her brow start to lower. "You needn't keep her, whoever your aunt selects, if she doesn't suit you. Remember, your father sent funds of your own, so you can hire any amount of fancy dressers, or second housemaids, if you'd rather."

That satisfied her but, curious, she asked, "Do you have a valet?"

"Arthur and I share a man-of-all-trades. Haggerty was my batman in the army. He can remove stains from a cravat and poultice a horse's hock and cook a fine rabbit stew, if need be. Mostly he makes certain I'm tricked out *à la mode*."

"Do you know a lot about ladies' fashions?" Jacelyn wanted to know, getting back to the subject at hand, though she was fairly sure of the answer.

That speck of lint seemed most tenacious. Claibourne cleared his throat. "I have had a, er, deal of experience in such matters."

"I'm sure you have, if half the rumours are correct!"

"Hold your claws, little kitten. I never said I was a monk. One mustn't listen to rumours, anyway."

"Sometimes one cannot help it. People think they should tell you, for your own good. One story has it that you have an uncle"—she lowered her voice to a near whisper—"who is a slave trader."

"Didn't your father explain about all that? I was sure he would."

"No. He said you had an unfortunate family history which had no reflexion on you. Is it true?"

"Yes, Fenton did own ships in the black trade; I don't believe he does any longer. You needn't worry about seeing him, however, he never goes out and I certainly never visit him. You won't meet up with my cousin Percival either. He is not received in polite circles, thank goodness. A greater nodcock you'll never see."

Then, under Jacelyn's interested questioning, he explained how his family tree got so infested, how his Aunt Sydelle was pushed into a hastily arranged marriage when a crop failure threatened the family with bankruptcy. The talk of divorce, the duel, Leigh covered it all. "So now you'll know the whole of it, instead of the half-truths people will dredge up for your benefit. Now you'll also see why I'm not top-drawer elite. Will it bother you?"

In one sense it bothered her very much: what if she obtained those prized vouchers for Almack's and he couldn't go? Suddenly her desire to attend that pinnacle of snobbery evaporated.

"What is it, Jacelyn? Does my background upset you so much?" Leigh was concerned at the look on her face.

"Not at all, you gudgeon. It's just that your aunt is seeing to invitations to Almack's, and I wasn't sure if you . . ."

"Were granted permission to enter the sacred portals? Lord, yes, I've never been blackballed anywhere. Why in heaven's name do you want to go there, though? It's dull as ditchwater. It's hot and crowded, and the cakes are stale. The dowagers sit around like gargoyles making hideous faces at anyone requesting a dance with one of their charges, when everyone knows they only bring the chits there to get rid of them. The Marriage Mart, they call it. Dreadful place." He shuddered, making Jacey laugh.

"Well, you are going to have to attend, my lord, because I'm to be all the crack!"

"Are you now, my fancy lady? Then *avaunt,* let's go. Besides, if I'm to be seen with you, perhaps I won't get those gimlet stares. See how much good you are doing me already?"

"Don't be goosish. I have nothing to do with your ancient history."

"History, no, but there is, ah, a more recent past"—one eyebrow raised—"which we shall not discuss, save that it makes it impolitic for me to be judging your behaviour. Suffice it to say I was not an eligible *parti,* nor even a particularly desirable dancing partner for a young lady."

"What, did they think you would ravish them, right there on the dance floor?"

"You'd best watch your tongue, my girl, if Almack's is your goal," he teased. "One such remark and your next invitation will be when Satan goes sleigh riding. And no, I never stayed long enough among the debutante set to find out what their mamas feared worst: a flirt or a fortune hunter. Now, pet, thanks to you, they won't have to worry about the big bad wolf turning their daughters' heads. As long as you are on my arm, I'll be as safe as a lamb."

"You better be," Jacelyn muttered under her breath.

"What was that, my love?"

The next miles passed quickly, with a deck of cards. The earl played leisurely, relaxed as always, yet seeming to know where every card was in the pack. Jacelyn would begin a hand with great determination, vowing to concentrate on the discards, until she was distracted by a passing wagon loaded with baskets, or the need to know what dramas were showing at Drury Lane. After two hours Leigh put the cards away and consulted the tally sheet.

"You owe me five hairpins, two feathers and—

what was this last stake? The button from your gloves. I think I'll defer collecting, as it wouldn't do to arrive at your aunt's doorstep all undone. Don't ever consider making a career of the pasteboards, dear heart, you'd starve."

"Perhaps I'll go on the stage, then. I can't sing but I can handle the breeches parts well enough. Can you see me as Portia?"

"As well as I can picture you in hoops and head-dress for the Queen's drawing-room presentation. By the bye, have you considered at all what you'll do after Christmas, pet, if no one else catches your fancy and you decide not to have me?" Over my dead body, he vowed to himself, but his noncommittal, jesting attitude stilled any assurance Jacelyn might have given. How could she speak of her newborn feelings when he still considered this a temporary liaison at best, a bothersome debt of honour at worst?

Her pride answered for her: "Oh, I'll simply return home to Treverly. I never wanted a husband, or thought to need one. Most girls see marriage as a means to independence, a home of their own without chaperones and all the restrictions. I already have that, at home."

"What about children?" he asked.

"Oh, puppies are more appealing," she replied, "and a great deal easier to come by, from what I hear. Now that you mention it, however," she added, with that look of mischief which set off sirens in Leigh's head, "there are some things considered unsuitable for a maiden's ears, which I wish to understand.

94

Since we are nearly engaged, and this might be my only opportunity in life, perhaps you could explain them to me when we're in London."

The earl pulled his hat down over his eyes, crossed his arms over his chest, and pretended to go to sleep.

7

It's strange how spiders have such a bad name, even among the insect groups. Go outside on an early spring morning when the dew is still on the grass, or a late summer afternoon when fog settles down, and there, by the trellis or under the eave, you'll see one of the world's priceless treasures, gleaming with diamonds. The spider is not remembered as the master craftsman, however, only as the villainous nighttime schemer. Perhaps the spider's poisonous bite adds to such ill repute, coupled with the creature's methods. Not for the spider honourable face-to-face combat; he spins art into artful, then lurks in shadows by his trap, waiting for unwary victims.

Now picture Josiah Fenton, hook-nosed, shrunken of frame, huddled in his spoke-wheeled Bath chair, spewing his hatred like venom into a dank, ill-lit, cluttered room. With apologies to arachnids, he resembled nothing so much as an evil spider, weaving treachery.

"Wars," he muttered, tapping his long fingernails

on the *London Gazette* in his lap. "Years of wars. Countless dead. Why couldn't he be one of them? Hare-brained heroics ought to have done for him long ago. Blast his curst luck!"

The last exclamation did not manage to stir the dreary room's other occupant, who was sprawled on the loveseat: Fenton's son Percival, if son he was. Fenton was the only one to disparage Percy's lineage because, at twenty-five, tall, skinny, and stoop-shouldered, with an enormous, boney, bobbing Adam's apple presently unconcealed by the soiled neckcloth draped across his knobby shoulders, and that same hook nose, Percy was his father's image—and despair. The only feature Percy didn't share with Fenton was his hair; the younger man's dank dishwater blond was proof enough for Fenton of Sydelle's infidelity. Ignoring the memory of his wife's shining gold curls, he swore she'd played him false. She had to have; Josiah Fenton could not have sired such an infernally stupid son! Percy was so stupid she must have mated with a tailor's dummy. Percy was so stupid that he halfway, or hopefully, believed Fenton's claims himself.

"Wake up, you comatose clunch-head, you inebriated imbecile," Fenton raged. "Your lickspit life is being ruined. Get up and do something about it!"

Bloodshot eyes opened in their pouches. Stringy fingers groped among the debris on a nearby table for a glass, a bottle, anything liquid to irrigate the desert in his throat. "Aargh. It's water."

Fenton threw the folded newspaper at Percy's head. "Read this, you wantwit, if you can. Lord knows if you stayed at any school long enough to learn how."

Percy bent to pick up the paper. A monocle, a fob watch, two keys, and assorted seals fell out of his pockets, all dangling by gold chains and ribands, now hopelessly tangled across his puce waistcoat, which was embroidered with green and red cabbage roses. Percy managed to gather up the paper and read: " 'The Upper House voted today in favour of—' "

"Not that, you feebleminded fribble. The *on dits* column."

"Oh. 'During last night's rout at Lady E.B.'s, a certain Miss G. W. was seen returning from the garden with a Spanish dignitary. Could it be—' "

"Lower."

" 'It is rumoured that a certain hero of the past campaigns, known to love 'em and Leigh-ve 'em, will shortly be escorting to Town for the Season an unknown deb, announcement to follow.' That was what has you in such a taking?"

"Are your attics to let, boy? Do you know what this means?"

"M'cousin Leigh's getting leg-shackled after all this time, right? It is about Leigh, ain't it, Da?"

"It means that damned Claibourne cub made it through the bloodbath, and now he's looking to marry and fill his nursery."

"Well, he is thirty-something, ain't he? Time he saw about his posterior."

"His posterity, you gap-toothed gudgeon! You're his heir!"

" 'Druther be yours, gov, more money, don't you know."

Fenton grasped his head in his hands and moaned. "Whatever I may have done in my life, I never deserved this." He took a deep breath. "Listen, Percy. Shut your mouth if it will help. With my money and his title, you could be anything, go anywhere. Parliament, Carlton House, you name it. Any woman, any government post, whatever you want. Don't you see? That's what they promised me, those Claibournes. They promised me, and then they stole it away and put me here in this chair. But it's yours, boy, yours. They owe you. Don't let some unbreeched bastard rob you of it!"

"He won't be a bastard, Da, if Leigh marries the girl."

"Then see that he doesn't, you addle-pated ass!" With a final roar, Fenton shouted "Jensen!" and a small-sized mountain lumbered into the room. Little-headed, beef-broad, and as mad as his master, Jensen picked up Fenton, wheelchair and all, and carried him from the room.

Alone, Percy gathered all his chains, fobs, and ribbon pendants back into their more or less appropriate places, and stumbled over his boots on his way to a bottle and a glass. He poured himself a generous portion while he tried to set the problem in perspective.

There was his cousin, Leigh Merrill, Earl of Claibourne. Handsome, heroic, handy with sword, pistols, fists. A devil with the ladies and accepted everywhere.

Then there was himself, Percival possibly-Fenton. Handy with nothing, accepted nowhere. But a fine dresser, if he had to say so. According to the governor, somehow it was Percy's job to prevent Claibourne's marriage.

No one was *that* stupid. Percy had another drink.

Meanwhile, across town in her Portman Square mansion, Lady Amabel Parkhurst was sipping a glass of ratafia to settle *her* nerves. Two weeks to prepare and she was still not easy about her niece's coming. She'd had plenty of notice: her brother's letter, Claibourne's visit, the arrival of Mme. Aubonier's baggage via post chaise. The baggage was attended by a homely shrew of a maid named Hammersmith who'd set Parkhurst House at sixes and sevens, ordering everyone about, redecorating Madame's room, informing the chef of her mistress's tastes. Then a carriage had arrived from Treverly with trunks full of Jacelyn's belongings, whose unpacking Hammersmith insisted on overseeing, while a newly hired, very pricey lady's maid had tea in the housekeeper's pantry. The Treverly chaise was accompanied by an impudent boy by name of Lem, in charge of two riding horses. According to Trevaine's message, Lem was to act as groom to Jacelyn, see to her mounts, etc. The *et cetera* had Lady Parkhurst trembling with memories of apes in little red jackets. How bad could it be? Lady Parkhurst wondered. The girl had a groom, a chaperone, a maid, a chaperone's maid, and a near-fiancé. Surely her aunt had nothing to worry about.

The butler, Marcus, opened the front door when the carriage pulled up. Through the entryway proceeded her niece, certainly looking much more presentable than Amabel had hoped. On one side of her, however, stalked a veritable vulture of a black-clad crone, and on the other side, smiling wolfishly down at the girl as if she were a tender game pullet, strode one of the most notorious womanisers in all of London. Worst of all—she'd strangle that brother of hers—was a creature so immense its wagging tail threatened the Chinese vase on the hall table. The outrageous girl was still trying to turn Parkhurst House into a menagerie!

The butler's lapsed "My stars" was shortly followed by Amabel's "My salts! My vinaigrette!"

Vapours cannot be hurried, but eventually matters sorted themselves out. Lem was called to take Penelope for a walk in the park and an introduction to the stables. Hammersmith was summoned to escort her elderly mistress to her rooms, after a few mindless "lovely's" and "*bien*'s." The earl forfeited his reputation for bravery by hastily bowing his way out of Lady Parkhurst's baleful stare. On his exit he reminded Jacelyn of their early morning ride, assuring her aunt he was at her service, if she required his presence sooner. She didn't, not even for the quiet dinner *en famille*, which would have been courteous, so he left the ladies to become reacquainted. It did not take long.

"Why isn't it a formal announcement, Jacelyn? Your father wrote that Claibourne offered. Let me tell you what a feather that is in your cap. But you cannot dangle a man like him forever, you know. He'll not stay still for your shilly-shallying. Or do you think you'll do better, and that's why you're holding off?"

"Oh no, Aunt Amabel. Leigh is everything that a girl could want. It's just that . . ."

"Just what, for heaven's sake?"

Jacelyn looked away. "He doesn't love me."

"Hogwash! What's that to the point? He offered for you, didn't he? You like him, it seems from that foolish grin on your face whenever you mention him, and he looks at you as if you are some bonbon to be snapped up. So what's the difficulty? You'll lose him, girl!"

"He'd marry me for his honour, and be pleased with the money. Oh yes, I know all about that, and his reputation, too. That's just it: we'd be wed, and I'd lose him anyway, if he didn't love me. Oh, he'd show me respect, Aunt Amabel, but it's not enough, so I have to wait, and try."

"Jacey, you and your crusades and hopeless causes! Why do you always take the long way 'round? This fox-hunt business, that absurd chaperone no one's ever heard of, now trying to win the heart of a man who may not even have one! Ridiculous, child. Do you remember that visit some years ago when Cook promised you one of her tabby's kittens to take home?"

"I was only ten, Aunt Amabel. You can't compare—"

"And she let you choose. There was a fluffy white one I admired, I remember that. But you couldn't pick the pretty one, or the biggest one, not you. You had to choose the one that wouldn't nurse, the puny one that kept getting stepped on by

102

the others."

"He needed the most love."

"Yes, and you cried for days when he died. You even climbed down the tree outside your bedroom, to sit by his grave so he wouldn't be alone at night. Thank goodness you're too old for that, my dear. You wouldn't listen then, though, and I'm sure you won't listen now, but I'm afraid you'll still cry over this new foolishness of yours."

Before going to her own room after dinner, Jacelyn scratched on Mme. Aubonier's door. It was opened by the hatchet-faced Hammersmith.

"*Belle-tante*, I just wished to see if you were comfortable."

The old woman was reclining among a flotilla of pillows, a glass of warm milk by her side, a book in her hand. "Fine, *petite*, lovely."

"*Tante* Simone, I don't wish to be impertinent, but why do you just say things are fine, even when my aunt was too busy having the vapours to offer us tea, and Pen tried to get the butler to play with her by stealing his gloves?"

Blue eyes twinkled back at her. "Why should I waste my breath, child, with useless chatter? This way I tell people what they want to hear, I smile and nod, and *alors*, I am free to read my book, see?"

Jacelyn laughed. "I see I am dismissed, Aunt." She went over to the bed and kissed the elderly woman's cheek. "Good night. Thank you."

Her own room was the neatest a room of hers had ever been. No clothes lying about, no stack of unfinished books, no dog hairs, only a very proper lady's maid in dark grey with a black apron and a black lace cap. Not a wrinkle, not a smile, not a first name. Just "Vincent, miss." Jacelyn dismissed her as soon as her gown was unbuttoned. She wanted to be alone with her thoughts, especially those that Aunt Amabel had termed her fool's missions.

She pulled her lawn nightgown over her head and unpinned her hair before she realised how silly she'd been to send the maid away. There was no Mrs. Phipps to put her long hair into a braid, and she'd only make her usual rats' nest of it, leaving it in knots by morning. Besides, she hadn't told anyone to call her early for her ride. This was only her first night in London. How many more mistakes would she make?

Maybe the whole trip was a mistake, maybe Aunt Amabel was right. Her father would know, but he was very far away. The bed was warmed by a brick; still, it was big and strange. The night sounds were different too, all carriage wheels and clatter instead of crickets and bird calls. It was her first night in London, and she could not sleep. Worries gnawed at her like gnats. There was only one thing to do. She opened her window—yes, the plane tree still almost touched the sill—and climbed down. Stopping a moment to locate the kitten's grave, she picked her way across the rear courtyard's gardens to the stable. She whistled softly and soon had Pen smuggled back up to her room via the back door, setting a great many worry bugs to buzz around the second footman Eugene and the under cook, enjoying an illicit after-hours cuddle.

Jacelyn's bed was a lot smaller now, and a lot more like home.

Jacelyn needn't have worried over waking at her usual early hour. If the sun didn't do it, the baker's boy would. Or the egg man, knife sharpener, or herb vendour. Milk didn't even arrive in its usual fashion, from beast to bucket. This was London; milk came in great clanking tins aboard creaking drays.

Jacey washed hurriedly and scrambled into her new habit. There wasn't much time to fuss with her hair, so she left it in the ragged braid she'd managed for bed, just pinning the whole into a crown on her head, and setting the red cap atop it. She and Pen went out by the kitchen door, winking at that same cook, whose job it was to serve breakfast, a chore considered beneath the French chef's dignity. The cook grinned back and offered a pan of still-warm, crusty rolls. Jacey helped Pen to two, then wrapped more in a napkin, to share later.

At least Claibourne had thought to notify the stables, for Lem was waiting with both the chestnut gelding and the little bay mare from Treverly, neither saddled.

"Didn't know which you'd prefer this mornin', Miss Jacey. Both be rested from the trip, but the gelding's not used to city traffic yet."

"Why don't you put the sidesaddle on the mare then," advised Claibourne, riding up on Baron, "since Miss Trevaine isn't familiar with Town congestion either." Just as she was about to bristle at his high-handedness, Leigh dismounted and disarmed her with: "Good morning, my love. I hope you don't mind my fretting over you. That outfit is much too grand to land in the gutters." With a smile he added, "You *were* intending to ride sidesaddle, weren't you?"

"Wretch. Only if I must."

"Almack's?"

"I must."

Hyde Park was blanketed by fog. The only figures to be seen were exercise grooms trotting horses up and down the paths. After a few such tame canters, the earl led his little party down a different path, headed farther into the park where there were more trees, less people. Pen took off after some geese, then seemed to decide that London squirrels could be gotten down from trees to chase, by barking at them. Jacelyn handed out the rolls.

Claibourne looked at Jacey, sparkling with animation and humour, and knew that, no matter what else, keeping her happy was all that mattered to him. "Lem," he called out, dismounting, "I think Miss Trevaine's horse picked up a pebble." When the groom came near, holding the gelding's reins, they both bent over the mare's hind leg.

"Nothin' there, sir."

"Sure there is, Lem. The gelding just won't hold

still enough for you to look properly. Why don't you make sure the mare is all right while we, ah, keep the chestnut from getting nerved up by the traffic?"

"Pardon me, m'lord, there ain't no traffic."

Jacelyn was already sliding off the mare, a delighted smile on her face. "May I really, my lord?"

"I won't tell if you won't, pet," Claibourne told her, giving her a leg up onto the gelding, her split skirts to either side. Before the earl could remount she was off at a gallop, her silvery laughter floating back to him.

Lem pointedly turned his back. "I don't see no traffic, I don't see no pebble, 'n I don't see whatever's goin' on back there."

"What will your maid think?" Claibourne teased as they rode home in perfect decorum. "Your hair is all undone, and you look decidedly windblown. Quite different from the lady she sent out."

"She won't think anything, because I dressed myself. I couldn't think of waking her at daybreak."

"But you are the mistress, poppet."

"Yes, but I'm sure it takes her longer to dress. She's so starchy she only needs one name!"

Later that morning Lord Claibourne was to see how seriously my lady's maid took her position. When they reached Madame Bertin's, the premier modiste of London, Vincent examined every bolt of fabric and scrutinised every design modelled.

"If I may be permitted, Miss Trevaine, knowing London ways as I do, the pink sarcenet, *not* the emerald lutestring," and, "With your pardon, miss, all debutantes must wear white for their comeouts."

The earl, lounging in one of the showroom's comfortable seats, wondered how long it would take for the fireworks. He wasn't in the fitting room, of course, when the superior dresser felt it was her duty, in accordance with Lady Parkhurst's wishes, to adjust upward the neckline of an azure blue crêpe. Vincent had to step over the little fitter's apprentice, making the girl drop all her pins, which earned her a scolding from Madame Bertin herself, coming into the draped cubicle to make sure all was going smoothly with this new, favoured customer.

Madame had had her doubts, at first, that the girl in the chic orange muslin mightn't just be Claibourne's latest convenient, a proper maid—and one mustn't discount all the rumours. Madame was always happy to have the dressing of a future countess, and this one would only add to her already high standing, if Miss Trevaine didn't fold under the maid's pressure to dress as demurely as any other debutante.

In her haste to take Miss Trevaine's side, figuratively and literally, the dressmaker also tripped over the apprentice, who was kneeling to gather up the pins she'd lost. There followed a lot of French words that would have made *Tante* Simone blush. Although none of the audience understood entirely, the gist of the modiste's angry speech was obvious: the little red-headed Marguerite was ham-handed and hen-witted, more suitable for milking cows than for serving in a fine shop.

"Forgive me, Mademoiselle, I only took on such a one as a favour to my coachman. Farm girls, *pah.* This one shall bother us no more. About the neckline . . ."

The 'prentice sobbed quietly, still trying to collect the pins into her apron, and the fitter scowled, and the dressmaker gave Jacelyn a toadeater's smile, and Vincent gave the neckline another tug.

"With all due respect, Miss Trevaine, please recall that my previous employer was the Duchess of Richmond's daughter, so I know whereof I speak. That amount of cleavage is quite, quite common-looking. Not at all the thing for—"

"Mademoiselle sets her own fashion. Any imbecile can see she is not of the usual mould."

Jacelyn had had enough. She stamped her foot. "I shall ask Claibourne." At the cluckings, she added, "I'm sure he knows more about ladies' bosoms than any of us," scandalising two avidly listening dowagers in the next cubicle.

Trailing yards of blue crêpe and a shower of silver pins, along with the fitting room entourage and the interested matrons, Jacelyn stomped out to the showroom and demanded of Claibourne, "My lord, will you tell these peahens where a lady's gown must start and end."

Fireworks indeed. Not twelve hours in Town and she was putting on a show for Lady Rivington. Leigh recrossed his legs and raised that one expressive eyebrow.

Flushing, Jacelyn amended her request: "Forgive

109

me, my lord. Would you please give us your opinion of this gown? Is the décolletage suitable?"

Leigh almost ached to show her just what that creamy expanse now tinged with pink was suitable *for*. Instead he told her, "You'll have to decide, Miss Trevaine. You'll be the one drawing attention. I can tell you that many ladies"—he emphasised the last word—"wear theirs even lower, though not usually such young ladies. Then again, many young women wouldn't look as attractive. You have to consider whether you wish to be approved or admired."

That was all very noncommittal, Jacelyn felt, when what she really wanted was *his* approval and *his* admiration, without having to ask. "As you will be the one escorting me, my lord, I thought my choice would affect you."

"Quite right, my dear. Tell me when you are going to wear it so I can buckle on my sabre to fight off all the smitten mooncalves. Proud to be of service, ma'am."

"Gudgeon. Well, I can always wear a shawl. Thank you, Lord Claibourne, ladies." She turned to go back to the fitting room when the abigail tried one last time.

"Lady Parkhurst is sure to object, miss, and I regret that I must agree."

"Lady Parkhurst isn't paying your wages, Vincent, and I regret that I am. As a matter of fact, I don't think we will suit at all, so if you will return to Portman Square and pack your things, I'm certain Lady Parkhurst will write you a glowing reference. Lord Parkhurst's secretary is handling my accounts, so you may discuss your wages with him.

That will be all."

Scarlet-faced, Vincent rushed out the door. When it closed on a stunned silence, Claibourne softly applauded. "To the manner born, my lady. What a countess you'll make! Why, Princess Caroline couldn't have done it better."

Grinning, Jacelyn lifted her straight little nose in the air, pronounced "Quite," and glided regally out of the room.

Mme. Bertin was not amused. Such a scene in her showroom was bad for business. Still, she smiled at Jacelyn, guaranteeing that, yes, the gown could be hemmed by the next day, the others made up within the week. She expressed her annoyance again on her way out by berating the apprentice.

When she was gone and Jacelyn was being helped out of the pinned gown, she asked the red-eyed girl why she stayed in such a place.

"It's m'mum, m'lady. I send her the wages, so my little brothers won't have to go to the mills. I was happy to get this position, ma'am."

Jacelyn took a good look at the girl, a little younger than herself, and liked what she saw: curly red hair and wide, honest green eyes, and many more freckles than Jacey had. She appeared country-clean, healthy, and unhappy. Impulsively, Jacey asked, "Tell me, um, Marguerite—"

"Margaret, ma'am," the girl said, bobbing a curtsey as she fastened Jacelyn's buttons, "but my brothers call me Pinkie."

"Pinkie, tell me, what did you think of me in the blue dress?"

"I thought you looked a treat, ma'am, 'n the way

you held your head, why, no one would mistake you for anything but a real lady. I been working here a month, nearly, and seen all the young ladies and their mums. Not a one could hold a candle to you."

Jacelyn hired herself a maid.

It took a very short time, while Pinkie gathered her few belongings, to settle the girl's contract. Jacelyn had only to voice her doubts over the almond-coloured cambric for Madame to lower her outrageous demands. Claibourne's reminder that Miss Trevaine still had to consider a presentation gown, while Jacelyn herself fingered the lace of a bridal doll, had madame toss in the girl's grey and white uniform, and good riddance!

A very well-satisfied threesome, four if you counted Lem in his fine new livery on the footman's ledge at the back of the carriage, proceeded to every fashionable shop on Bond Street, and a few not so well known down side streets. As is often the case, Jacelyn found more courtesy and cooperation in the smaller shops, so she was able to ignore the fact that Claibourne seemed known by name in each establishment. Busy with cottage bonnets and kid slippers, she didn't need to disturb herself over his knowledge of women's fashions or his remarkable patience. She simply accepted, and enjoyed, both.

When the carriage was nearly filled with boxes and tissue-wrapped parcels, they proceeded to Gunther's, for ices, then drove around some, showing Jacelyn the sights.

"There is so much I want to do and see, like the Tower and Hatchard's bookstore and the Pantheon Bazaar and—"

"Hold, my dear. Enough for one day! I promised your aunt to have you returned in time for tea. We have months to do the town, unless you were planning on becoming a couch-kitten, sitting at home looking pretty, entertaining all the beaux."

Miss Trevaine just gurgled delightedly.

8

Fashionable London was like a sharp-beaked dowager in a purple turban: nosey. Miss Trevaine's appearance in Hyde Park that afternoon in Claibourne's curricle made the ton twitch with curiosity.

"There's that girl Claibourne escorted to the shops. Sophrina Rivington saw them at Bertin's. Said she bought out the place."

"They say it's a match; she'd better be rich."

"But who *is* she?"

Or, "Merrill's been driving around all day with that chit. Never known him to be so obvious before. Milbrooke told me they were laughing together at Gunther's. Handsome girl, but who *is* she?"

Speculation continued whenever two riders stopped for conversation, and in nearly every carriage. In one satin-lined brougham, however, a little girl, dressed as a precious miniature of her mother, was heard to ask: "Mama, why may that lady have her dog in the carriage and I cannot take Tippy?"

London also had a long memory. When Claibourne's curricle pulled up next to Amabel

Parkhurst's, enough people recalled she was expecting her niece; others could identify Lady Parkhurst's black-clad companion as Claibourne's great-aunt, so they made the same deduction. Either way, the question now was: "Wasn't that the chit with the monkey?"

If the *belle monde* had caught a glimpse of Miss Trevaine in the afternoon, that night they were to get an eyeful. Since Jacelyn wasn't officially Out, she couldn't attend large parties until her presentation at court, a formal come-out ball or, at the very least, an appearance at Almack's. Of course, without the last, she'd still not receive many invitations. In any event, Lady Parkhurst had chosen the Royal Opera House for the evening's entertainment, and had invited some young people to share their box.

"How kind of you, Aunt Amabel. What is the programme?"

"I'm sure I don't know. No one goes to listen, at any rate."

"Oh. And who else is coming?"

"Claibourne of course, though his aunt would rather stay home, and his friend Ponsonby, and Ponsonby's sister. She's all the crack, you know. You can take some pointers from how she goes on."

"But Aunt Amabel, I don't like Priscilla Ponsonby."

"What's that to the point? It will do you good to be seen with her."

"Is Priscilla's mother coming too?"

"Yes, so see that you do nothing exceptional. She

115

has agreed to forget the Treverly incident, for my sake."

"Has the blue dress been delivered, Pinkie? Yes, it should be perfect for this evening. . . ." The azure was not a hide-in-the-woodwork colour, even if the gown's low cut didn't cry for attention. It had silver ribbons at the high waist, and Pinkie threaded a silver ribbon through the curls she'd arranged atop Jacelyn's head, and wove another into the one long ringlet allowed to trail down across Jacelyn's shoulder. Nothing exceptional, indeed.

"Better take a shawl, ma'am, in case it gets chilly," the maid advised, draping a Norwich silk with silver fringe around Jacey's bare shoulders.

Contrarily, the theatre box grew more chilly after she removed the shawl. Lady Parkhurst's mouth hung open like a flounder on ice, while Lady Ponsonby sniffed her frigid disdain. Priscilla turned her back entirely, to survey the rest of the audience. It was Arthur, though, who thought he'd give Miss Trevaine a set-down by staring at her exposed parts through his monocle. She cured him of that with one raised eyebrow so much in Claibourne's manner that the earl applauded.

"How long have you been practicing, brat?" he asked, smiling and very casually placing his arm across the back of her seat where his hand could just touch the top of her neck. If that didn't put the seal of approval—and possession—on her, nothing would. Lady Parkhurst started chattering to Priscilla and her mother, while Leigh directed Arthur to point out the notables to Jacelyn. Lord Parkhurst, who arrived late with his young aide, Mr. Carter Sprague, kissed his wife's hand absently, but told Jacelyn, twice, that she looked fine as fivepence. Ignoring the other ladies, he and Mr. Sprague took the rearmost seats and began discussing the day's Parliamentary debates.

A soprano seemed intent on shattering the prisms of the huge crystal chandelier with her piercing notes, yet no one except Jacelyn gave her a moment's notice. Jacey gave up trying to decipher the warbled Italian over the din in the boxes, and gave in to enjoying the spectacle. All the women were in their finest, many trying to fit much larger girths into much less material than made up her own gown, to Miss Trevaine's satisfaction. What they lacked in fabric, they made up in jewels, rivalling the same chandelier for glitter. The men were only slightly less gaudy, with their diamond stickpins and striped waistcoats. Many, like Claibourne, wore the dark evening shades decreed by Brummel, their intricately tied white neckcloths more gleaming by contrast. The Tulips in the pits were another matter. Wearing every hue imaginable, every ring or ruffle they could manage, they made a kaleidoscope of colour, especially since they never sat still. Despite the ongoing performance, the fops and bucks in the pit constantly moved around, calling to friends, teasing the orange girls, making arrangements with the women who plied their trade at other entertainment, and ogling the ladies in the boxes. Jacelyn drew her fair share of their attention, even laughing back when one of the blades bowed in her direction, blowing kisses.

117

Intermission brought even more noise and movement, as though the audience needed a break from their concentration. Leigh and Arthur left to fetch lemonade, and the older women joined Lord Parkhurst for a brief turn about the corridors. Priscilla preened. She smoothed her cornsilk curls and adjusted the folds of her shell-pink skirts, ignored the hungry-pup gaze of Mr. Sprague, and smirked at Jacelyn. Now I'll show you, Miss Nobody, her expression clearly read, what it means to be an Incomparable.

Gentleman after gentleman entered the box, as Priscilla knew they would. Lord This and Sir That, here was her devoted court. For the first time in Miss Ponsonby's reign as an accredited beauty, however, the callers had not come to worship at her throne. Instead of poetic tributes to her face and form, instead of invitations to late suppers and carriage rides, instead of pleas for a dance at the next ball, the gentlemen all wanted introductions to that underbred, overblown Jacey Trevaine! It was too much for a delicate—and not so generously endowed—female to bear.

"It's so very close in here, I fear I might faint," she lisped to the only gentleman who was paying her any attention, Lord Malcolm Anton-Fredricks. "Do you think you could accompany me to the hall for some fresh air?"

"My very heart's desire." The well-oiled nobleman's reply fairly oozed.

Priscilla departed, making a great to-do over her incipient swoon, which no one noticed, shamefully leaving Jacelyn alone with a box full of strangers and only a mortified Mr. Sprague to play chaperone.

The situation didn't faze Miss Trevaine an iota. Goodness, if she could deal with the worldly earl, what were a few boys, more or less? Laughing, showing her dimples, she treated them all alike, even a Spanish count and the son of a duke, all the same way she treated Lem or her neighbours' schoolboy sons—like friends. Soon they were all laughing over some of Pen's exploits, for the big dog had certainly not gone unnoticed in Hyde Park, and dogs were such an easy, comfortable topic of conversation. No one had to think up flowery compliments or discuss the weather when an item like Pen was around.

Talk soon flowed from the subject of one four-footed creature to another, the major interest of the sporting gentlemen.

"I say, Miss Trevaine, do you ride?"

"You forget I'm a country cousin, Lord Milbrooke. Of course I ride, if you call your Hyde Park trails much of a course."

"My groom mentioned a lady riding with Claibourne this morning. That must have been you, then. He said you were a real goer, your pardon, ma'am."

Jacelyn chuckled. "No apologies needed, and thank him for the compliment. I like riding above all things."

There followed suggestions for day rides to Richmond and Surrey, so many conflicting invitations that Jacelyn had to smile and mention that her aunt may have plans. Then Viscount Farthingale had such a splendid idea he had to raise his voice to make sure that Jacelyn heard: "What about a fox hunt, Miss

Trevaine? I know Ponsonby's uncle keeps a pack. We could—"

"My lord." Jacelyn's voice rang out in the quiet following the viscount's shout. "I do not hunt. My friends do not hunt. If you choose to pursue such a grisly hobby—note I do not say sport—then I think you should consider something less gruesome, like bashing each other's heads in at your Gentleman Jackson's. Either way, I must request that you not discuss this topic with me, as it distresses me greatly."

The shocked silence was broken by Arthur's gagging. He and Claibourne had returned with the lemonade, which Arthur swilled at the first mention of a fox. Claibourne was about to come forward when the *Conde* de Silva, a polished fellow more interested in his clothes than his horses, put in, "No one would think of distressing such a charming *señorita, si?* Not when your laughter has more music than the *periquitas* on the stage. Who needs such exertion anyway, when just seeing you in your magnificent blue gown is enough for mortal man?"

Jacelyn's dimples returned. "*Gracias, señor,*" she said, "but I am sure you exerted more effort on your costume than any of us!" bringing the laughter back.

Priscilla was not taking chances with the second intermission. She commandeered Arthur to escort her to the vestibule. Since a mere brother added nothing to her consequence, she lowered herself to invite the secretary, Sprague, along too. Aunt Amabel stayed put, having been unpleasantly reminded of her duties by Lady Ponsonby's: "I see the chit's behaviour is still as common as her dress. My sympathy, of course."

120

In this *entr'acte,* however, curiosity overcame diffidence, as many of the mothers of the previous visitors called at Lady Parkhurst's box. This time Aunt Amabel performed the introductions, and Jacelyn answered prettily, not even bristling when quizzed about her pedigree by the Duchess of Hockney.

"Ah, Trevaine's daughter. I'm sorry to hear of his ill health. Yes, you have your mother's look. What a cheerful girl she was; we all miss her. Glad to see you've got her liveliness too, instead of your father's bookish ways. Not to say a girl should have more hair than wit, but we can use a little lightheartedness. This place has gotten so proper"—with an eye on Clothilda Ponsonby—"a lady dasn't belch. Why, in my day . . ."

Jacelyn and Claibourne were still chuckling when Her Grace and the others left and Priscilla returned to the box.

"I suppose that old dragon warned you away from her son, Farthingale," Miss Ponsonby hissed as she took her seat next to Jacelyn.

"Why no, she invited me to tea."

The Ponsonbys did not stay for the third act.

The next day being Sunday, everyone went to church, St. George's in Hanover Square, naturally, where everyone who mattered could be seen at prayers. Everyone except Mme. Aubonier, that is, who announced she would rather attend St. Francis d'Assisi, a Roman church popular with the French emigrés.

"I have been a loyal and devoted member of the

121

Anglican church at Littleton in Durham, the *only* church in Littleton, *n'est-ce-pas?* for nearly thirty years. Today, when I have the chance, I would like to visit a church of my younger days. Perhaps I shall renew some old acquaintances, who knows?"

"Of course, Aunt Simone," Jacelyn agreed, immediately calling for another carriage to be brought 'round. "But doesn't it matter? I mean, I thought one was either a Catholic or an Anglican or a Methodist or whatever."

"It is the same God, no? *Le bon Dieu* can find me when He wants me, I am sure."

Lady Parkhurst was still fussing about it on the carriage ride home from church. "A Papist, Jacelyn, of all things! She barely speaks English, she dresses as if she's in mourning for the whole French aristocracy, and now this. How your father thought she'd lend you countenance, much less make a respectable lady out of you, I'll never understand. Your behaviour last night was so bold, and that dress! Where was your chaperone then, miss? I don't know what I'm to tell your father."

Jacelyn was nodding and saying, "Yes, Aunt," having learned a great deal from Mme. Aubonier, and wondering what she should wear for the afternoon's carriage ride with Leigh.

Her aunt's tune changed abruptly when they entered the house. Resting on a silver platter, on the Sheraton table, in the marbled hall, was a thick cream envelope addressed to Miss Trevaine. Hand-delivered, according to the butler, who was grinning almost as widely as Lady Parkhurst. Marcus had won two shillings; Aunt Amabel would be able to show her face. Miss Trevaine was invited to Almack's.

Then it was "Perhaps you should take dear Mrs. Aubonier for a drive in the park, or maybe she would like to invite some of her friends for tea. I did mention the yellow parlour was at her disposal, didn't I? I'll have to write to your father immediately after luncheon; so proud, my dear. I knew you'd be a success. We'd better make plans for your come-out ball before all the dates are booked. I hadn't wanted to make anything definite until . . . that is, in case . . . you know."

"Yes, Aunt." Jacelyn went off to tell Madame the happy news. The old lady had her shoes off, her feet up, and a book in her hand. "This is what you wanted, yes? Now it is up to you."

Pinkie more than made up for Madame's lack of enthusiasm, dancing around with Jacelyn's pelisse in her excitement, then tearing open the clothespress for a hasty inspection. "We'll show them us country girls know a thing or two. My own lady goin' to Almack's! Won't mum be proud."

"If you want to write and tell her, I'll ask Uncle Parkhurst to frank the letter for you."

"Thank you, ma'am, but my writing's not so good, and mum's got no reading at all."

"Would you like me to help you with some lessons? Maybe your mother could find a neighbour or a curate to read her your letters, so she'll feel easier about you being so far from home. I taught Lem to read and write, you know."

123

Pinkie's face was scarlet as she stammered her gratitude. Jacey didn't think the girl could be embarrassed over her poor education, since most servants had even less. "Lem? Has he been teasing you, Pinkie? You tell me if he has, and I'll talk to him. He's a great one for pranks, but he means no harm."

"No, ma'am, he's been real kind." The girl's eyes still didn't meet Jacelyn's.

"I see. Well, just stay away from that second footman Eugene. He's a real flirt."

Pinkie giggled. "Yes'm. I already put him in his place. But Miss Jacey, about Almack's, if it's all right with you, maybe I could ask Hammersmith for some suggestions about your hair, since you won't hear of cutting it."

"Hammersmith, Mme. Aubonier's maid?" Jacelyn was mystified. Aunt Simone certainly did not show off her dresser's skill, and besides, everyone in the household seemed intimidated by the sharp-featured maid. "Why not Lady Parkhurst's abigail?'

"Your pardon, ma'am, but Miss Hammersmith's been teachin' me all manner of things. She knows all about what's proper for when, and she takes a real interest in your success, she does. Lady Parkhurst's abigail only worries that we won't do the house proud. We'll show her, won't we, miss?"

Jacelyn just shook her head. It seemed she still had a lot to learn about London ways, front stairs and back.

Arthur Ponsonby rode up to the landau where it was positioned near a tree. Mme. Aubonier was speaking French with an elderly gentleman on foot who wore his hair powdered in the old style; Jacelyn was talking to Claibourne, alongside on Baron.

"Miss Trevaine, Leigh, just the people I wished to see. My mother's getting up a party for this evening. No cards or dancing; Sunday, don't you know. A musicale, she calls it. I think that means Marcella Chadwick is going to play the harp and m'sister the pianoforte. Will you help a fellow out and attend?"

"It sounds dreadfully dull, Arthur. Why don't you just beg off?" Jacelyn couldn't bring herself to call him Lord Ponsonby, not when he looked so much like a squat old bulldog, bow-legged and testy.

He gave her the look he'd always given her: contempt mixed with conceit. You are impertinent, it seemed to say, but I am older and wiser, so I will ignore it, and you. He leaned past an amused Jacelyn to extend the invitation to Claibourne's aunt, who had finished her own conversation.

"Nothing very deep, ma'am, family commitment, don't you know," he added for Jacey's benefit.

Madame flatly refused. Jacelyn might go, she said, if Lady Parkhurst would attend with her, though why anyone would inflict such an evening on their friends was beyond her comprehension.

Jacelyn read the message in Claibourne's slight nod and told Arthur she would ask her aunt. Then she warned Arthur to get down and check his saddle's girth; she'd heard a strange creaking noise when he bent near. His bottom jaw shot out, and his brows lowered, reminding her even more of a bulldog—and of the pouty child he used to be, though she couldn't understand why the nodcock would be in such a swivet, nor why his face was turning the colour of his waistcoat, a bilious purple. She said she'd go, didn't she? Then Claibourne leaned over and whispered, "He's wearing stays."

Instead of looking contrite and apologising for drawing attention to such a personal matter, Jacey went into the whoops. Claibourne joined her, and even his aunt smiled, until Arthur had to grin too.

"Oh Arthur," Jacelyn said when she could talk again, "wouldn't it be easier just to leave the second cream puff? I know, you'll have to come riding with us in the morning."

Lady Parkhurst did not really want to attend—no one did; Parkhurst claimed a speech to memorise—until she recalled the invitation to Almack's. What was one more boring evening against the chance to gloat?

As the audience of twenty or so sufferers politely applauded the final duet, both Miss Chadwick and Miss Ponsonby having done solo turns previously, Jacelyn turned to Claibourne. "There, that wasn't as bad as I thought."

"That was only the first half, puss. We get to find some nourishment to sustain us through the second half."

Aunt Amabel's groan confirmed it, but encouraged Jacelyn to enquire, hopefully, if her aunt had a headache. "I am sure La Ponsonby would understand if we had to take our leave early.

"No, she wouldn't. Clothilda is one of my closest friends, but she can be somewhat overbearing. Claibourne, take my niece and find her some refreshment."

The supper room was crowded; the table was not. Lady Ponsonby was heard to comment that since it was such an informal gathering, and Sunday besides, they must all have had their fill at dinner. Fruit punch and little honey cakes were the only offerings.

"Get used to it, Jay-bird, the Almack's patronesses are just as nipcheese."

"What, are you going to Almack's?" Arthur asked, coming toward them with a plate full of the thin slices. "Lord, they must have relaxed their standards. Don't let the patronesses catch you in britches!"

Jacey looked around quickly to make sure no one else heard. "At least my britches don't need a tent's worth of fabric!"

"Children, children." Claibourne held a cup to Jacelyn's mouth, effectively blocking her next comments, and reminding Arthur that they were here only as a favour to him. "By the bye," he added, changing the subject, "your sister's over there with that Anton-Fredricks fellow again. He turned her pages for her too. Do you look for a match in that direction?"

"Dashed if I know. I thought m'mother was looking toward Farthingale, Hockney's heir, you know. I hope they don't choose Anton-Fredricks, at any rate; chap's all flash, no bottom, if you get my drift. I don't know if he's dropped the handkerchief yet, nor if m'sister would have him. Not my place to pry, you know, until he comes asking me if he can pay his addresses."

Jacelyn didn't agree with him, as usual. "How can you say that, Arthur, when she's your own—Why, good evening again, Priscilla. I must congratulate you on your performance. It was, um, edifying. Your interpretation of Vivaldi would certainly have delighted the composer." If he could have recognised it, she wanted to say, but didn't.

Claibourne and Arthur added their praise to Jacey's and the others' who were now gathered around. Very well satisfied with herself, Priscilla decided to appear gracious, offering to share the limelight with Miss Trevaine, especially since she was very well aware that Jacelyn had no drawing-room accomplishments whatsoever.

"Surely you'll oblige my guests," Miss Ponsonby pressed after Jacey's first, laughing, refusal to sing or play. "Everyone has some talent."

"I'm afraid mine remains undiscovered then," Jacey said, still smiling, until Priscilla smugly informed the group, "How odd. I thought all young ladies of breeding could entertain company."

"Now that you mention it," Jacelyn heard herself saying, "I do have one small talent. I can imitate frog calls."

Arthur was looking as pop-eyed as any lilypad dweller, and Miss Chadwick was tee-heeing. There was no backing down. She didn't dare look at Claibourne. She just shut her eyes and gave her best bullfrog croak, throwing in a few peepers for good measure.

Priscilla's mouth could have caught flies, but some of the young gentlemen, laughing merrily, took up Jacey's dare to do better, Lord Farthingale challenging anyone to best his chuckwillow. A whole stream of boisterous birdcalls and guffaws followed.

"That niece of yours is turning my parlour into a

barnyard, Amabel. Do something!" Lady Ponsonby ordered. Lady Parkhurst searched her reticule for her smelling salts.

Jacelyn, however, was no longer participating in the romp. This was *not* how she'd planned on behaving, not in front of Claibourne's friends. Now he'd never see her as other than a headstrong, rag-mannered child. Fancy clothes and elegant hairstyles weren't enough to show him that she was a mature, sophisticated woman, worthy of his attention—and his love.

Embarrassed, upset, not wanting to face the earl, she slipped back into the nearly deserted music room. A few older gentlemen were dozing in the back row, and a few young matrons boasted of their children in one of the sofas along the side wall. A single young lady, looking as dejected as Jacey felt, sat by herself at the pianoforte, her hands folded in her lap, her lower lip trembling.

"Do you mind if I sit by you for a few minutes?" Jacelyn asked. "If I sit by myself my aunt will find me, or Lady Ponsonby, and there will be the devil to pay."

Silently the other girl pulled the billows of her white tulle dress closer around her, making room on the bench.

"Are you to play next?" It wasn't a hard guess. "You *can* play, can't you?"

"And sing. A little."

"Well, a little would be a great deal more than we've heard. At least you have some talent," she added ruefully, thinking of her own shortcomings. "What could be the problem? Do forgive me, I know it's none of my affair. Here I was just scolding myself for my last indiscretion. My tongue seems to have a mind of its own."

"No, no, don't apologise. I wish I had some of your . . . your . . ."

"Brass? I'd gladly lend it, Miss . . .?"

"Endicott. I already know you as Miss Trevaine." Jacelyn grinned. "Fame travels fast. I'd be pleased if you'd call me Jacelyn, or Jacey, if you wish."

The other girl finally smiled back. "Rhodine." She let her fingers trail over the keys; the smile faded.

"Are you nervous? You could say your throat is scratchy or something?"

"No, it's just that—Oh, listen to all the fun they're having out there. And . . . and they'll come back and take their seats and put on polite smiles. Their eyes will go all glassy, like mannequins'! They'll be bored again. Then they'll clap and tell me how charming my voice is. It isn't! My music instructor said my voice was pleasant, no more."

"*My* music instructor said the barn door needed oiling, and left!"

Both girls were laughing when the rest of the company drifted in and took their places. Catching sight of Leigh and Arthur coming their way, Jacelyn said, "I have an idea. Do you know 'I Met Him in Spring'? Why don't you do the opening and then ask everyone to join in for the chorus. Everyone knows it, and they'll be happy to participate, rather than sitting like logs."

"Oh, but I couldn't ask them—"

"Arthur could! They're his guests, after all. Besides, I think he'd like nothing better than to sit turning your pages and directing us all. I promise to mouth the words! Then you could do some rounds or whatever. Arthur will know."

Everyone complimented Lady Ponsonby on the evening's entertainment. Most enjoyable night they'd had in ages, they told her, wondering why more hostesses didn't follow her lead. Of course, the departing guests sympathised, it was too bad Priscilla had developed the headache and couldn't enjoy the lively half of the party.

Jacelyn was pleased also, and not just with her new friend. Claibourne had a lovely rich baritone voice—and he held her hand during the entire second half.

"I've been hearing things, Percy."

"I told you to cut down on the pipe, Da."

"You blithering bacon-brain, I've been hearing things from my man Jensen."

It was after noon, but you'd never know it by the darkened room nor Percy's attire, his skin-and-bones, six-foot-plus frame covered by a dragon-embellished silk dressing gown and stubble.

He poured his breakfast. His shaking hand only spilled a little down the glass's side. "And here I thought he could only grunt, not speak."

"You have all the humour of a hangman, fool. I've been hearing from Jensen what they're saying in the taverns; I've been hearing from Cook what they're saying at the market. I've been reading what they're saying in the blasted papers." He brushed the *Gazette* off the table with one angry arm-sweep. "All about Claibourne's chit. How she dresses, where she goes, who her people are, how he's in her pocket. What I don't hear"—he smashed his fist down on the mahogany—"is what you've done about it."

As proud as an old man with a young bride, Percy announced that he was dealing with the situation. "I have a plan."

Silence.

"Oh, do you want to hear it, then?"

"You misbegotten mutton-head, why do you think I called you here?"

"You didn't call. I live here, remember? You really better watch the—"

"Your plan!"

An even more idiotic grin than usual swept over Percy's face. His Adam's apple convulsed in excitement as he solemnly intoned: "La Fleur, the Flower. Remember her? She's the high flyer Claibourne used to keep. Actually, talk was someone else always paid the rent and he sublet, so to speak. Then Fortenham bought her a place of her own out in Islington, so she's fairly independent about who she entertains. They say Claibourne stayed there to recuperate on one medical leave."

"So? She was in the Ballet Corps over fifteen years ago. What's some faded demirep got to do with anything?"

"That's my plan. I've been going out to Islington waiting for cousin Leigh to show. He will. He never stayed away from a willing woman yet, that I heard of. Then I've got him! No green girl's going to like seeing her beau with such a dasher."

"You've got him? What did you think, you stilt-legged sapskull, that he'd trot out his middle-aged mistress to impress his bride?"

Triumphantly: "I thought of that! I figure to write

a note to the girl telling her all about it. She'll turn tail back to Cambridgeshire 'fore the ink's dry."

"Percy, you have all the wit of three men: two fools and a lunatic! Why should she believe you? Claibourne would only deny it, of course. Besides, the chit may be an innocent, but even two days in London will show her that most *real* men have a bit of muslin in keeping."

The stress on "real," needless to say, was for Percy's benefit. He started working on his lunch. "Got another part to my plan. A good general has more than one strategy. Didn't Wellington always say that?"

"Yes, when he was in retreat. I'm almost afraid to ask, what's the rest of the brainstorm?"

Percy's face wore its usual nobody-home look, only more so. "I talk to La Fleur. Get her to see the girl in person. You know, by chance in the park or at some fancy shop. Then Claibourne can't weasel out of it."

"Ah, I begin to see a glimmer of hope for you. The old mare confronts the filly, for a price, naturally. Well worth it, if Miss Trevaine was hoping for a love match. Maybe there is some Fenton blood in you after all. What did La Fleur say? How much does she want?"

Red splotches spread out on Percy's cheeks. "I, ah, haven't asked her yet. Sent m'card up, but the maid came back, said her mistress wasn't taking on any new 'callers.' But I'm working on it."

" 'Working on it'?" Fenton sputtered. "What are you doing, passing out in front of her house so her carriage has to run over you? I cannot believe it!

She's a paid doxy, for heaven's sake, and she won't even *talk* to you!" He looked upward. "Are you happy now, wife? Are you enjoying your revenge?"

Wearily, he reached down for the newspaper on the floor. "Listen, you lobcock. The *Gazette* says Miss Trevaine's an animal lover, a real fanatic, she sounds. All the gossip about her says the same. Must be one of those do-gooders who preach about kindness to dumb creatures, meanwhile sitting down to their mutton and capon and turtle soup, wearing their fur hats. Where do they think their kid gloves and egret plumes come from, some beast that died of old age? No, they don't mind the killing as long as they don't have to see it. I know the type. Your mother, blast her soul, was one of them. Wept over the slaves while stirring sugar into her tea, as though that sugar hadn't taken African sweat to make. Soft-hearted and cloth-headed. London's a rough place for such a one, and you're about to make it rougher for Miss Trevaine."

"I am? I don't—"

"You are going to do two things: One, you'll wait outside the aunt's house and follow the chit so you know what she looks like. Don't let Claibourne see you; I don't want him to get suspicious. Two, you'll make certain she sees London's harsher side: starving cats, mangy dogs, you know, what would upset a vapourish female. Enough of that and either she'll go home, as your mother did, or Claibourne will have his fill of caterwauling watering pots. Again, don't let Claibourne see you. Don't tip our hand."

Percy wouldn't let Claibourne see him, not if his life depended on it, which it most likely did.

Jacelyn had a new plan for that day, too, which she put into effect early that Monday morning. No more fripperies, no more hoydenish behaviour. (She would start right after the mad gallop that had her cheeks flushed and her eyes sparkling.) Today she would show Leigh her love of learning, her aesthetic sensitivity, her cultured poise. When he asked what she wanted to do that day, she reeled off a list of attractions that would have impressed Marco Polo. She needed to take out her subscription to the lending library. She had promised her father a first-hand description of the Parthenon exhibit at the British Museum, and Lord Parkhurst had recommended a visit to the Royal Academy. There were also Westminster Abbey, Pall Mall, the Royal Exchange, and the Tower of London, for a start.

"What, all in one day, pet?" Leigh asked, flecks in his blue eyes dancing as he took in the picture she made, slightly tousled and out of breath from the ride. He knew what *he'd* rather do that day. All he could manage properly, though, was to hold her longer than necessary when he lifted her down from her horse. "Besides, you're doing it much too brown. You've already got the vouchers, and the dragons won't take them away until you have been there once at least. Wouldn't you rather visit the Arcade or Ranelagh Gardens?"

It was hard enough being a bluestocking for one day. He didn't have to test her resolve before breakfast!

"Another day? I told Papa I'd search out a new

copy of Longinus for him, and I promised Pinkie we'd go sightseeing. Can you believe, she's been in London a whole month and hasn't even seen London Bridge?"

Arthur, incidentally, was not with them in the park, having mumbled, "Good idea. I'll get to it right after breakfast," before rolling over and pulling the covers around his ears.

Pinkie got to see the famous bridge, which wasn't anything she'd have to write her mum about, when her penmanship improved. Westminster Cathedral echoed as if all the saints knew her mind was on Lem, not on the sacred. Things got better after that, when Jacey told her she could wait in the carriage outside the bookshop. Lem was up as footman.

Jacelyn found the Longinus with no trouble, and a primer for instructing Pinkie. She was having difficulty selecting a book for herself though, since buying the Minerva Press novels would have been like framing a Rembrandt with kindling wood. They didn't match the picture she was trying to paint today. Besides, Aunt Amabel was sure to have the latest purple-jacketed volumes, and Jacelyn was, in fact, a voracious reader with wide tastes. Unlike the tiny library in Ryefield or even the bookseller in Royston, one could get lost in these London bookstores, with shelf after shelf of titles to explore. While the earl was involved in a conversation with a man in a brown stuff jacket, near what seemed to be tracts on farming methods, Jacelyn wandered to the rear of the building. She thought she'd seek out that new author everyone was talking about. The Prince himself had requested the author to dedicate her next volume to him, it was said. A Miss Austen, Jacelyn believed.

A stunning auburn-haired lady a little older than Jacelyn recommended her favourite of the author's works and, smiling, some other titles she thought Jacey might like.

"The strangest thing," Jacelyn told Claibourne later, after she'd paid for her purchases and he'd handed her back into the carriage. "That lady told me not to worry, the game was worth the candle. What do you think she meant?"

"I am not sure, my sweet, but that was Lady Cheyne, one of the premier younger hostesses. Her husband, incidentally, was one of the greatest scape-graces I've ever known, until the army and then Lady Cheyne tamed him down."

"I wonder if—Oh, there was another odd thing at the bookstore. While I was looking over the shelves, I kept thinking someone else was there, only I didn't see anyone. I smelled something peculiar, like peach flambe, only with horse liniment mixed in. Then I took a book from the top shelf, and a man *was* looking at me through the empty space! He ducked away but kept popping out from behind stacks and around the corners of the aisles. I was quite relieved to see Lady Cheyne come toward me."

Leigh frowned. "You should have come for me."

"I was going to, if no one had come along. The creature seemed harmless enough."

"Still. What did he look like?"

"I never saw much of him, but he was very tall, with spindly legs. And he had a large nose."

"Sounds like my cousin Percival, but it couldn't have been. Not in Hatchard's. He's allergic to the printed word. No, must have been some lovesick suitor, rosebud."

The Royal Academy was not meant to be seen in an hour, or even two, although most of the well-dressed connoisseurs had no trouble ambling through the major exhibit halls deep in conversation, occasionally pausing in front of a Lawrence portrait to discuss the subject, not the art. For Jacelyn, the place was overwhelming. So many paintings and sculptures in such a small space, and displayed so poorly! Why, one of Claude Lorrain's landscapes in his new style was hung so high, on top of a cavalry-charge scene distinguished only by its immense size, that Jacelyn had to crane her neck nearly backward. Even then, she could only make out the wavery haze. The noisy, jostling crowds disturbed her, too.

"Why do they come, if not to see the art?" she asked. "They aren't paying any attention to the paintings at all, only to each other."

"That's why they come, my dear," Claibourne said, hurrying her past an undraped statue to which she was giving more than enough attention. "It's the same as Hyde Park and the Opera and the endless teas. They wish to be seen in the right places, with the right people."

"Is that what you want, Leigh?"

He turned her toward him, away from yet another full-length Apollo on a pedestal, and straightened the bow tied against her left cheek. "Today I only want what pleases you, pet, and the rest of the world can go hang."

"Well, it might please me to study those Greek sculptures, but I won't embarrass you, Leigh, so shall we admire the Gainsborough over there? Did you notice the portrait of my mother at Treverly? It's very similar in style. . . ."

Still, Jacelyn glanced over her shoulder. Yes, it was the same tall, gawky man from the bookstore, acting just as peculiarly. Now he seemed to disappear in back of one of the Greek gods, beakish nose emerging seconds later from a marble armpit.

"Leigh, do you see that strange person behind us?"

When Claibourne turned, there was no sign of anyone following, of course, just the naked statue in its full glory, without even the decency of a fig leaf. He shrugged. "Odd lot, those Greeks. Didn't care much for clothes."

Jacey shook her head and walked on. She couldn't resist one final look backward, though, so she just glimpsed boney fingers clutched around Apollo's derrière, as if for support. The Greeks weren't the only odd lot, it seemed.

"Why didn't Lord Elgin just leave them in Greece? Papa says they really belong there." They were in the vast exhibition hall, in a group of twelve, following a bald-headed guide. The lurker didn't seem to be on the premises, so Jacey could relax, sharing her impressions with Claibourne.

The guide, overhearing, frowned in her direction. He interrupted his discourse on frieze-work bas-relief and impedimental statuary to announce that Lord Elgin had shipped the pieces of sculpture from the previously destroyed Parthenon temple to protect them from further vandalism, with the approval of the Greek government. Souvenir hunters, he said, thought nothing of bringing home a bust or a horsehead to put in a stairwell niche or in their gardens. In addition, he declaimed, the political climate was such that the ancient buildings had frequently been used as battlegrounds, and could be again. Finally, with an especially hostile look at Jacelyn, daring her to refute him, the guide cited Lord Elgin's nobility, bringing these treasures home at great expense, "for the enrichment of the British peoples."

"I believe he made a bit of profit, too," the earl said in an undertone.

Without taking a moral stand, Jacelyn was free to absorb the grandeur of the pieces themselves, ignoring the guide's lecture about Pericles and the Phidean style. Her first impression was depressing: all those noses gone, hands, feet, even heads missing, like a rose browning on the edges, a reminder of mortality. Seeing beyond that, especially in the larger-than-life piece of the three headless women, she could feel the grace and flow of their draperies, their perfect composition for the triangular cornice. They and the large reclining male figure were supposed to be gods and goddesses watching the birth of Venus from the head of Zeus, the guide was droning. They seemed fairly casual about such a remarkable event, a small portion of Jacelyn's mind irreverently noted, while the rest stared in awe at the sheer majesty. Together with the less three-dimensional horsemen from the frieze and smaller pieces displayed on tables and in cabinets, the statues created a sense of the wondrous artistry achieved. One could not look on such masterpieces without wanting to touch an edge. They were cold, hard marble, not clay, which could be shaped, moulded, *moved*. There was no adding to stone, no repairing errors. Each fold of the gowns, each sinew of the god, had to be chiselled and hammered and honed.

"I'm sorry, but I'm selfishly glad these pieces are in London, right or wrong. At least until I get to Greece."

Claibourne was holding her pelisse out for her. "Would you like to go to Greece someday, pet?" he asked, thinking bridal trip, warm beaches, long boat rides.

"Only if the men wear breeches," she answered, grinning.

Her heart smiled too, at the sound of their shared laughter.

Next stop was the Tower of London: shuddering past the dungeons and torture chambers, eyes turned from the room where the young princes died, a quick peek at the Crown Jewels in their dusty closet.

"Don't they ever polish them?" Jacelyn wanted to

know.

Then they moved on to view the Royal Menagerie. Claibourne tried to warn Jacelyn beforehand, that the animals were in small, dirty enclosures, and the air was nigh unbreathable. She had to see them anyway, naturally.

Now here was a moral dilemma a lot worse than the Elgin Marbles represented. After all, the Greeks hadn't been taking such wonderful care of their treasures, while the British were building a whole museum around them, for an admiring public. The Menagerie, however, had captured animals content where they'd been, she supposed, bringing them to live in deplorable conditions, for public amusement. She'd get to Greece sooner than she'd see India or Africa, most likely, and heaven knew when she'd see another giraffe, but oh, its big eyes looked so sad. Her first elephant, reaching that fire-hose appendage in her direction —

"Best step back, ma'am, the elephant be mean," a uniformed guard warned her.

"You'd be mean too, standing in your own filth! Why aren't these poor creatures given bigger areas and fresh air to breathe? We paid out admission; why isn't the money used for the animals' upkeep?" she demanded.

The attendant grimaced. Another bloomin' do-gooder. "We do the best we can, ma'am. There ain't enough money collected, 'n what there is goes for food. Prodigal eater, a elephant."

Claibourne was trying his best to soothe her. His best wasn't good enough, especially since it seemed to consist of reminders that he'd tried to warn her, which had nothing whatsoever to do with remedying the situation, as she told him.

"Do you mean to tell me the British government cannot afford to feed and house these unfortunate beasts, when there is a fortune in diamonds turning back into coal up there? When the Prince can fill Carlton House with every gilded geegaw that catches his eye? When the poor, mad king—"

"Watch the seditious talk, love," Claibourne teased. "Remember the dungeons." He was enjoying this hugely. Not her upset, of course, nor the gawping crowds, but Miss Trevaine on her uppers was better than Kemble doing King Lear.

"I doesn't make those decisions, ma'am," the guard was saying. "Its not in me wage contract. You want to take it up with His Highness, be my guest."

"If he'll be at Almack's Wednesday night I just may." Ignoring Claibourne's muffled snort and the guard's bulging eyes, she turned away and marched out of the room.

She was still ruffled when the earl's long strides brought him to her side. "Tell me now," he said in the slow tones he used for play, "if I should join the Royal Navy tomorrow. Save Prinny the trouble of transporting me on Wednesday."

She spared him a ha'penny's worth of dimple, called him a gudgeon, and resumed her angry monologue. "It's a disgrace, that's what it is. I'll bet the Prince spends more on one jacket than those animals get in care. Not enough money to go around, hah! I've a good mind to—"

She rushed off, back the way they'd just come.

The earl took his time following, having a good laugh, which was not entirely *at* Jacelyn, but couldn't be *with* her since she wasn't laughing. He doubted she'd appreciate his humour this time.

Surprisingly, however, Jacey was all smiles when she returned. "There," she announced.

"There? In two minutes you have paid off the war debt so the government can afford muckers for the Menagerie?"

"No, silly. I gave that man—his name is Lewis, incidentally—a crown to see to improving the conditions here. And I told him I would be back shortly with another, and so on."

"Well at least Lewis's family will eat better, my little innocent."

"Not on my crown, they won't," Jacey said, giggling. "I told him that if the pens weren't clean when we get here the next time, I'll have you use him for a mop."

"Its growing late, your aunt will worry. Perhaps we should ride home through the park so she'll see I haven't ridden off to Gretna Green with you."

"If she weren't afraid of the scandal, I'm sure she'd be relieved if you did!" At Leigh's questioning glance, she explained: "She's positively quaking that I'll do something outrageous and give you a disgust of me. Then she'd have me on her hands forever. She'd rather be boiled in oil."

Leigh vowed to tell Lady Parkhurst what a perfect lady her niece had been all day. Exemplary, in fact, if one omitted only a few minor details. "Indeed, you played propriety so well, I think you deserve a treat. I know I do. Would you like to go to Astley's Amphitheatre this evening? There is an early performance, so your aunt won't have to send the Bow Street Runners after us."

Brown eyes shining, Jacey nearly danced in her seat. "To see the fancy riding? I'd like it better than anything!" Then she remembered her dignity. "That is, how kind of you, my lord. I would be delighted to attend if you feel it won't be too, um, common."

"Come down from your ropes, poppet. You look like you smell something bad. Astley's isn't too plebeian for my taste. There will be a lot of cits there, and youngsters, of course, but I've always enjoyed it. Perhaps I'll ask Arthur to accompany us if you don't mind."

"Of course not. Do you think I might invite Miss Endicott? You know, the young lady who led the singing so prettily last night. She didn't appear to be friends with the other girls there, or to be having a good time. I promised her I would call soon."

"Invite whomever you wish, sweetheart, but you ought to be aware that your shy little Miss Endicott is properly called Lady Rhodine. She's Spenborough's granddaughter."

"The Golden Duke?" His nod affirmed it. "But Rhodine—Lady Rhodine—is not at all high in the instep. She never even mentioned a title. She didn't put on airs like some of the other girls, either."

"Her father's the third son, so there's no hope of the succession. Not much money there either, they say. Endicott gambles."

"But her gown last night—"

"A fortune in fabric, a groat in glamour, right? Lady Tina Endicott is bringing the chit out this Season. That's Endicott's second wife. She's less than ten years older than the daughter, and doesn't want any comparisons, so she overdresses the girl in frills like an infant. The girl is too quiet to complain, or doesn't have the sense to realise she's done up like a wedding cake to make Lady Tina look better. Endicott only sees that the bills are high."

"But if there is no wealth, why should they spend so much on her clothes?"

"First off, no one said Endicott's actually been paying the bills. Second, it's called baiting the trap. Your Miss Endicott is to be married off this year, no matter what it takes. They say she is to go to the highest bidder. Her father's debts, you know."

"How terrible! Won't her grandfather help?"

"That's the icing on the cake: Spenborough won't tow his son out of River Rick, but he's let drop hints that the girl is named in his will. No amounts mentioned, of course. The betting book at White's is full of speculation. Anyway, that's why the other young ladies stay away from Lady Rhodine. The competition."

"It can't be that awful, Leigh, so . . . so cold-blooded and conniving."

"Wake up, dewdrop, that's what the debutante Season is all about: finding the richest husband or the highest title. At least now the girls have some choice, and the fellow gets to see what he's buying before he steps into parson's mousetrap. Not so long ago these things were arranged from the cradle."

"Poor, poor Rhodine. It will have to be Arthur, after all."

"Arthur and Rhodine? What notion are you hatching in that pretty little brainbox of yours?"

"At first I thought Mr. Sprague would do. He's so very polite and refined, you know."

"Carter Sprague, Lord Parkhurst's aide? He's a good man, serious type. They say he has a fine future in the government. What has he to do with anything?"

"Well, Mr. Sprague is infatuated with Priscilla Ponsonby. It cannot be anything more, for she doesn't even notice he's around. So I thought to wean him away from such a hopeless *amour* and point him in Rhodine's direction. Now I see it won't fadge. He isn't wealthy enough for her family, is he?"

"No, but Arthur is. Is that what you're aiming at, vixen?"

"Its only a possibility, mind," she admitted happily. "But think of how proud Arthur would be with a titled wife. Especially one so sweet and unassuming. As for Rhodine, she needs someone to look out for her, to give her confidence. Arthur is so sure of himself, some of his pride would be bound to rub off on her. And consider how pleased he'd be to have someone to be important *for.*"

"But Jacelyn, Arthur's not anxious for leg shackles. Besides, you can't move people around like some giant chess set."

"Can't I, even if it's for their own good? Just watch me!"

The park was thinning of coaches and riders, but they did spot Arthur on horseback near a stopped chaise, which, to Jacelyn's irritation, contained his sister Priscilla and what Jacey was dubbing the shadow twins, Miss Chadwick and Captain Highet. Why was the man still in uniform, she wondered, if all he did was peacock around Town in Marcella's wake? No wonder the country was in financial difficulty!

Surrounding the carriage were a few pedestrians and a knot of riders, from which Lord Farthingale's voice called out: "There they are now. Miss Trevaine, Lord Claibourne, good day. We've been planning a picnic ride out to Richmond tomorrow, while the weather still holds. I know you might have previous plans for the evening, and you ladies need time to make yourselves even more beautiful"—Miss Ponsonby simpered—"but if we leave at ten we'll be home by four or five. My mother's going along, and she particularly asked that I extend the invitation to you. Would have done so myself anyway," he told Jacey, somewhat flustered. "Be pleased if you'd accept."

Judging from her scowl, Miss Ponsonby wasn't pleased at all. She had assumed the excursion was devised for her amusement, not the farouche Miss Trevaine's. Viscount Farthingale had been the biggest fish on Priscilla's line since her come-out. Just because she hadn't decided whether to keep him or not didn't mean she was ready to toss him back.

"I'm sure Miss Trevaine would find it much too tame," she advised Farthingale and the rest of the company. "We *ladies* do have to ride sidesaddle of course. Oh." She put her hand up to her mouth in mock dismay. "I wasn't supposed to say anything about that, was I?"

Arthur hissed, "Bad ton, old girl," at his sister, but Claibourne cleared his throat, deflecting the daggers in Jacey's eyes and the sharp words on her tongue.

"Quite all right, Miss Ponsonby." He addressed Priscilla but made sure they all heard: "Everyone knows Miss Trevaine rode astride on the privacy of her father's estates. It's the only way to break and train your own yearlings. From what I gather, riding astride is something all younger ladies of spirit try. When they are among family and friends, of course, who wouldn't betray them to censure. Miss Jacelyn, further, is a superb rider in either mode."

Bravo. Jacey wanted to clap! All she'd been able to think of, for wiping that smirk off Priscilla's face, was hurling her reticule at it. Instead, Claibourne had smoothly, gently, implied that Priss was old, dull, bad-mannered, and had a seat like a sack of turnips. Jacelyn rewarded him with her most brilliant smile.

" 'Faith, did you really train your own mounts?" Lord Farthingale was excited. He'd never understood women — just look at how Priscilla Ponsonby was turning from a purring housecat into a clawing tiger — but horses he knew. "Are they in London with you? Do you race them? Please do come tomorrow."

With just a quick glance at the earl, Jacelyn accepted, pending her aunt's approval, naturally.

"No need to worry about that, with m'mother along for chaperone," Farthingale reminded.

"Right, Priscilla," Arthur goaded his sister, "if Miss Trevaine sets too bruising a pace for you, sidesaddle, of course, you can always ride in the carriage with Her Grace."

Arthur rode alongside their coach on the way out of the park, still apologising for the odious Priscilla. "Bacon-brained thing to do anyway. Made her look no-account in front of her friends."

"Why don't you mention that fact to her, Arthur," Claibourne said, "in case she's tempted to make any more fuss about the Treverly happenings. No one else seems to care about the gossip at all."

"Wait until tomorrow night before you bet your watch on it," Jacelyn told him. "*Tante* Simone says the chaperones' corner at Almack's is the cruellest battlefield of any war."

The earl patted her hand reassuringly. "You'll do fine. You'll be so busy dancing, you won't have time to go near the dragon's den."

Even Arthur forgot himself into promising to stand up with her for the maximum two dances allowed, when he saw Jacey's big-eyed, woebegone look. A moment later he recollected. Gads, he'd offered to dance with little Jacey Trevaine! He better go home and physick himself.

Instead he agreed to go to Astley's with them after an early dinner. He always enjoyed the riding, especially the ladies in sequined tights. The last time he took his young cousins, there was a redhead

. . . He looked at Pinkie, sitting demurely with her back to the horses, studying her primer.

Claibourne coughed, almost as if he could read his friend's thought. Colouring, Arthur agreed that Miss Endicott just might appreciate the simple pleasures of roasted chestnuts and sliced oranges. She seemed like a quiet kind of girl, from what he remembered. "She didn't have a lot to say, which isn't bad, mind you." He glared at Jacelyn. Two dances! "In fact, I may as well toddle off there now to invite her in person. Quicker than waiting for you to get home to send a message. It may be too late anyway; I'll let you know."

Jacelyn gave Leigh a look of triumph, but he wasn't ready to concede. "Early days, my girl. I don't think your Lady Rhodine can hold a candle to silver sequins. I heard about *that* dasher for a month. By the way, my sweet, if Lady Rhodine does accept for tonight, we'll have to do something about a chaperone."

"Pinkie would love to see the horses too, I'm sure."

"Then Pinkie shall go on her afternoon off. No, my dear, she did admirably all day, trailing behind you like a grey-striped duckling, or sitting prim as can be on a bench studying her lessons. She'd be ample dogsberry if it were daytime, or just the two of us, since we have the supposed blessing of your father. But it will be night, and a closed carriage, and two gentlemen. Think of Lady Rhodine's reputation, if she comes along. You wouldn't want her to be called fast, would you?"

"Who would ever believe Rhodine capable of anything untoward, in her angelic white dress?"

"Still, those tabbies can talk, and I think she'd find it painful."

"Heavens yes, but are you positive Pinkie wouldn't be adequate? Lem could come too."

"Pinkie is just sixteen. She's much too young. Besides, she has no control over your behaviour, as a proper chaperone should. It's obvious she believes you can walk on water. As for Lem, he'd stand on the riverbank cheering. And that's supposing the two of them had eyes for anything but each other. Lady Endicott would never lower herself to anything so unstylish, so we'll just have to ask the aunts."

Mme. Aubonier acted like they'd asked her to go to China on a camel. She'd agreed to escort Jacelyn to social events, she said, not harum-scarum nursery parties. Lady Parkhurst, on the other hand, was too distracted to pay attention to Jacelyn's problem. The dowager Lady Parkhurst had sent a message that she would be arriving tomorrow, to attend Almack's with them. Her mother-in-law, according to Aunt Amabel, was the fussiest, snoopiest, sharpest-tongued woman she knew. On top of that, if that wasn't enough, besides worrying over Jacelyn's debut, some Bedlamite kept tossing cats over the courtyard wall and tying half-starved dogs to the front gates. The whole house was in an uproar, not at all aided by Jacey's dog. Pen, it seemed, disapproved of scruffy cats landing inches from her nose, to say nothing of the cats' thoughts on the matter.

As for the dogs, Marcus the butler was nearly in

tears. Not for their sad, undernourished, insect-populated conditions, but for the calling cards they left. Each had been untied and presented with a lamb chop, as Marcus saw his Christian duty, then sent on its way. Any fool could have told him that a hungry dog is less likely to depart such an hospitable neighbourhood than a pig is to fly. Finally the watch was called to bring a cart and fetch the whole barking, whining, growling herd of mutts away. Where to, Lady Parkhurst neither knew nor cared.

One silver lining shone out through this whole day of clouds, as far as Aunt Amabel was concerned: Jacelyn wasn't home. Otherwise, Lady Parkhurst was certain, every one of the mangy beasts would be sitting down to dinner with them and sleeping in the guest chambers—leaving fleas to bedevil her persnickety mother-in-law!

Such palpitations she had, and Jacey wanted her to play duenna at a circus! Devil a bit!

Aunt Simone finally unbent a little when Rhodine's note of acceptance arrived, delegating Hammersmith as chaperone. No one could remotely imagine anything havey-cavey going on in her austere presence. They wouldn't dare.

Before going upstairs to change for dinner and the evening, Jacelyn went to the stables to retrieve Pen. She went out through the kitchen door, hurriedly. Chef was throwing saucepans and skillets and Gallic curses, furious at having to replan his menu, without lamb chops.

Pen was exhausted, but content. Lem and a stableboy were trying to splint a pigeon's broken wing with a shaved stick and some string.

"What in the world has been going on here, Zack?" she asked the groom. "My aunt is nearly incoherent, and Marcus has locked himself in the butler's pantry."

"Coo, ma'am, you sure missed a rare sight. 'Twere rainin' cats 'n dogs in Portman Square. Sick pigeons too. Your dog took care o' the cats, all right n' tight, though she don't bother with the stable tom none. Then that Clive what drives for 'is lordship's aunt 'n Henesley, the head groom, they sent us out on patrol. A regular militia, we was, miss, only we had pitchforks 'n broom handles 'stead of pistols. We didn't see nothin' either, more's the pity, but what a peculiar day!"

10

"What a peculiar day," Jacelyn told Pinkie later, after her bath.

"Yes'm, it sure was. To think I've been in London all this time 'n never knew there were so many big buildings. 'N all those statues. Some were older nor London itself, his lordship says. I can't think of years in all those thousands, not when I'm used to hearin' about m'granfer's times. Those Greeks were dead 'fore even St. George was slayin' dragons. Bet m'mum won't never believe it."

"We did see a lot today, didn't we?"

Pinkie was towelling Jacey's hair. "Yes, miss. But if I'd had my druthers, I'd have seen the ruckus here. Or was that what you meant by peculiar?"

Jacelyn hadn't been thinking of the day's marvels at all, actually. She'd been considering his lordship, and not comprehending him any better than Pinkie did Greek history. He'd been so kind and attentive, laughing and teasing, even coming to her defense when needed, almost like an older brother—too much like an older brother! Then he'd carefully listened to her opinions, as though they were worth tuppence. Yet tonight they were going to Astley's, at his suggestion. Half the time he treated her like a real lady, as with the chaperone nonsense; the other half he encouraged the tomboy in her.

"Drat, what does the man want of me?" she said out loud, used to confiding her thoughts to the dog. Pen, lying near the open fireplace grate, perked her ears and wagged her tail, sending a cloud of soot into the room. Pinkie, though, was more helpful, correctly interpreting her mistress's question, if not all the uncertainty behind it.

"You know that second footman Eugene?" she asked, grinning. " 'N you know what he wants?"

Tossing a damp towel at the impish carrot-top, Jacelyn said, "That's all you know, Miss Margaret, with all your years of experience! Why, his lordship hasn't even tried to see me alone since we've been in London." She wondered, to herself this time, if maybe that's what had her so suddenly blue-devilled. Maybe if she wore that new peach muslin, with the brown velvet ribbons crisscrossed under her breasts . . .

"Pinkie, what gown have you laid out?"

"Miss Hammersmith says the dark blue merino, miss. The one with the long sleeves and the lace insert, or she won't go. She says it's dignified 'n won't draw unwanted attention."

Hammersmith sat as rigid as a ship's figurehead at the end of their row. Laughter, gasps, and applause parted like waves around her. Claibourne sat next to her, casually elegant in dark pantaloons and a fitted jacket. Jacelyn was next in the row, with Lady Rhodine on her other side. Overdressed for a dinner at Carlton House, Rhodine looked even more out of place next to Jacey in her conservative dark gown. At first Rhodine was noticeably uncomfortable with all the attention she was receiving from the rest of the audience, a very eclectic group indeed. There were rich merchants and their families, shopgirls and their beaux, a pickpocket and his decoy celebrating a good day's work. No one was dressed as richly as Rhodine, with four flounces to her pink gown and her hair prinked into ringlets. Jacey tried to set the other girl at ease by describing all the wonders she'd seen that day, even mentioning the ride planned for tomorrow.

"Why don't you come along? I'm sure Lord Farthingale won't mind."

Colouring up, which made her seem more like a strawberry meringue than ever, and lowering her eyes and her voice, Rhodine declined. "I'm not that good a rider. I would only slow you down."

Arthur, on Rhodine's other side, reassured her. "Quite all right, Lady Rhodine, not every woman can ride like a red Indian, and not every woman can sing as prettily as you did last night. Meant to tell you."

"That's true, Rhodine," Jacey told her, ignoring the gibe, "but no matter. You can still come. You can ride in the carriage with Lady Hockney, Farthingale's mother."

Now the blush fled from Miss Endicott's face, leaving her the colour of milk spilled on brick floors. "I lied," she gasped. "I'm not just a poor rider. I'm frightened of horses but . . . but the duchess scares me more!"

Luckily, the lights dimmed, shifting everyone's regard away from Rhodine to the center of the dirt enclosure. Jacelyn did consider how terrible things must be at Endicott House, for the horse-shy Rhodine to visit Astley's with them—to see the trick riding!

A tall man came out then, wearing a red coat and satin britches tucked into high white boots. He welcomed them, and Jacey forgot all about Rhodine and her problems.

There were tumblers and jugglers and groups who did both. There was a bear in a little skirt, which danced on two legs while the orchestra played a waltz. There was a lady whose gown was so covered with sequins she looked like silver-polishing day at Versailles. She had four little white dogs who danced and twirled and jumped through paper hoops. On their last turn around the enclosure and through the hoops, another performer entered the ring and joined the circuit: a tiny pink pig with a red collar. The audience whooped and whistled. Arthur stamped his feet. Farthest away from Miss Hammersmith, he was naturally the least inhibited. The others applauded.

Then there were the horses. Drill team horses, dancing horses, horses that could count—all with neither rein nor rider. The man in the scarlet coat directed them with only his whip and his voice.

The earl whispered to Jacelyn, "And here I was so proud that Baron would stay on command." She didn't answer, too intent on a trio of white horses moving in precise formations, long white manes and tails flowing as they cantered into figure eights, three across. From the sides you could see only one set of legs, so evenly matched were they.

The orchestra played a fanfare, and the man in red introduced the first rider, a man called Jesse. Wearing white sequined tights and an open-necked shirt, Jesse rode out on a black horse—but standing on the horse's back, not sitting at all! A few turns later, he jumped down, landing lightly on his feet. After that he was a blur of motion, as the black horse kept to its steady gait around the ring. Jesse somersaulted over the horse, did handsprings to its rump, tumbled under its pounding hooves, and came up astride without using his hands. For a finale, Jesse dismounted in a roll and bowed while the horse also lowered its head and right foreleg.

The lights came on, to a great gust of noisy appreciation. Clapping fiercely, Jacey felt like weeping because it was over.

"Don't worry, sweets, it's only the intermission."

Arthur eagerly chipped in: "The women riders come out in the next act," earning him a frown from Hammersmith. He turned to Rhodine to find out if she was enjoying the entertainment, despite her lack of affection for horses. She was, immensely, though her particularly favourite act was the little dogs. Before either Jacelyn or Arthur could comment on this heresy, she added, "That and the remarkable man on the black horse." Turning to Jacelyn, she asked, "Wasn't he handsome?" Arthur sucked in his stomach when he and Leigh went to find refreshments. Claibourne looked back and winked at Jacey.

The girls couldn't go much further with talk of the virile rider, not within the bounds of propriety and Hammersmith's hearing, so they turned to other topics.

"You're going to Almack's Wednesday, aren't you?

I suppose you've been before." Jacelyn chattered, not waiting for answers. "I'm going to wear the gold tissue gown I had made in Ryefield. Aunt Amabel doesn't know it yet, that I'm not wearing white or a pastel. She'll have the vapours, but it's the prettiest gown I've ever owned, and I'm sure to need it, facing all the owl eyes and raised lorgnettes. *Belle-tante* approved anyway, didn't she, Hammersmith? What are you wearing, Rhodine?"

It was the wrong question. Losing her cheerful animation, Rhodine became a limp rag.

"Oh." Jacey delivered a vast understatement: "You don't like it?"

It seemed that Miss Endicott not only disliked her dress for Almack's, a pink and white confection with every froth, furbelow and flower a berserk—or greedy—dressmaker could attach, she hated it. Moreover, she hated all her dresses, how they made her look childishly silly, how they made people stare. She hated having her stepmother Tina select them for her, and she hated all the money the gowns cost, when everyone knew they were only window dressing. The Endicotts' pockets were to let, but her father insisted she be gowned like a duke's granddaughter, lest anyone forget.

No one ever forgot her clothes, she wailed, but no one remembered the girl in them!

Another injured pigeon, and Jacey vowed to do her best to fix it. It wasn't long before she'd convinced Rhodine that between them—them being Jacey, Pinkie, and, with a slight nod, even Hammersmith—they could improve any gown. It would have to wait for Wednesday, since Jacelyn was committed to the daylong ride on Tuesday, but they

161

could work miracles. Pinkie was such a hand with the needle, and Hammersmith had a way with curls, and maybe Jacey wouldn't have time to get so nervous, if she was helping her friend.

The gentlemen, meanwhile, were making their way back through the crowds. Arthur couldn't believe the earl had spent the day sightseeing, much less taking in the cultural highlights.

"Zounds, you really went to the Parthenon exhibit and the Royal Academy in the same day? With all the attractions London has to offer, you chose those? Incredible. Why, I'd rather go to the tooth drawer. I can't believe it, Rake Claibourne bear-leading a brat in and out of museums!"

"Actually, old son, I can't recall enjoying a day more. You should try it."

"Now I know you're dicked in the nob."

The earl just smiled. "Your day will come, Arthur."

"Me a benedict? Not on your life."

As they reached their seats, however, the earl noticed his friend's face was red and his brow furrowed, from the concentrated deep breaths he took to flatten that paunch!

The second half began with four riders cantering into the ring: two women in silver tights and short sequined tunics on black horses, two men in black tights and black vests on white horses. The quartet proceeded to change horses in midair, sometimes doubling up on one mount, sometimes with the women being tossed back and forth, and all while they stood, barefooted and upright, on the horses' backs. It was like juggling with people!

Four different riders came out next and began to juggle in earnest: oranges, plates, top hats, hoops, still standing, not sitting astride. While their horses circled the ring, then changed direction, each kept his three or four items in the air. It was hard to count, they moved so fast. Two more turns and the men started throwing to each other. Colours blurred and objects flew, and the horses kept going 'round. Jacey clutched the earl's hand. The jugglers didn't drop even one orange, and each rider ended with his own matched set, and the thunder roared.

The lady with the dogs came back. This time the dogs rode the horses. The horses didn't seem to mind, but the dogs had their tails tucked firmly between their legs, so Jacelyn wasn't as impressed with this act. She whispered to Claibourne that she'd once tried to convince Pen to ride a horse. Jacelyn had been scolded for the claw marks on the saddle. Worse, Pen hadn't gone near the stable yard with her for days.

Six women in sequined stockings and barely decent dresses did some graceful ballet steps atop their mounts. Hammersmith snorted loudly. Arthur joined the whistlers.

Jesse came back, dressed as a red Indian this time, complete with war paint and feather headdress. He did the same routine as before, but with loud whoops and warbles.

The orchestra played a long, dramatic drumroll. This was the finale, the announcer intoned, the Magnificent, the Marvellous, the Mysterious Miss Moira herself.

The horse was an enormous grey, almost as tall as

Baron, and Miss Moira stood posed on its back like a Joshua Reynolds portrait. All draped in multicoloured layers of gauze, you'd never know she was standing on a moving animal. As the orchestra, then the horse, picked up tempo, Moira began to move. She tossed at least an el of gauze to the announcer, while Hammersmith clucked, to reveal white tights and a brief white top which resembled a corset. Jacey and Rhodine shared a scandalised giggle. Heaven knew what Hammersmith did. Jacey couldn't look over, too fascinated by the equestrienne's actions. Moira was standing on one foot, kneeling on one knee. She was twirling at the horse's side, only one hand on the bridle. She was spinning in the air, grasping the horse's tail! It was the most wonderful exhibition Jacey had ever seen; not just the woman but the horse also won her exuberant applause. The big grey seemed to anticipate the girl's every move, to increase or lessen the stride to be in the perfect place for her landings on its back. Of course it helped that the horse's back was wide and flat, like Baron's. . . .

She stopped clapping. It was as if the sun had just come out—the moon and the stars too! Eyes wide and shining, face lit up with near-religious inspiration, she turned to Claibourne.

"No." Lord why hadn't he thought of this! Why? Because it was a long time since he was ten and tried standing on his pony. Luckily, the pony had short little legs or he'd have broken his skull instead of just his arm. Jacelyn? If ever there was a stunt more calculated to appeal to the minx, he didn't know it. He cursed himself for being three kinds of a fool, bringing her to Astley's.

"No," he said again as they waited for the carriage.

Making certain that Hammersmith was with the others, she pleaded: "Not my gelding. He's too skittish. I wouldn't be that caper-witted. And the mare's too narrow. But Baron is broad, and well mannered, and he'd do anything you asked of him."

"No."

Nothing more was said about it in the carriage, of course, not in front of Hammersmith, and not until they had dropped Rhodine at her door and Arthur at his club.

His lordship escorted Jacelyn and the maid to the door of Parkhurst House. Hammersmith went in first, but stood in the open doorway next to Marcus, her arms crossed over her boney chest, daring Claibourne to dawdle over his good nights.

"I'll call for you at the regular time tomorrow, for our ride," Leigh said clearly, for the servants' benefit. "Unless you'd rather forgo it, since we'll be all day in the saddle out to Richmond?"

Jacelyn shook her head, not really paying attention.

Then: "No promises, scamp," he whispered, "but bring your britches. I'll see what I can do."

She gave him a quick peck on the cheek before scurrying inside. Claibourne could swear Hammersmith slammed the door on him. It couldn't be Marcus, not with all the *douceurs* Leigh'd been handing him for just such occasions.

"This is against my better judgement, pet, and I am only doing it to keep one jump ahead of you."

"I don't know what you mean."

"Don't you? Tell me you weren't figuring a way to

bribe the people at Astley's for a chance to ride! Maybe it would have been better. I understand they use ropes and pulleys to train."

"But Leigh, that would spoil all the fun!"

"Fun? Remind me how much fun we had when I have to explain your black-and-blue body to your aunt, my aunt, and more devoted servants than the heir to the throne has!"

The foursome—Claibourne, Jacelyn, Lem with a small satchel, and Pen loping alongside—were on their way to the stable where Baron had his stall, which happened to have an indoor schooling ring. Jacelyn was bubbling with excitement; the earl was grim. She had on two layers of clothes, Lem's outgrown britches under her heavy riding skirt; if she had as many layers as he had worries, they'd have to roll her to the stable.

Leigh's first concern, though not necessarily his greatest, was that she'd break her damnfool neck. If no one had done it for her yet, though, he decided, she must lead a charmed life. Besides, he had enough confidence in her natural grace, Baron's steady gait, and his own ability to catch her if she fell, to rest easier on that score. For insurance, he'd dickered with Lawrence, the stable owner, for a fresh load of sand to be put down.

There lay his next botheration, the expense of this venture. The money for the sand and silence wasn't important; his skill at cards held even when luck wasn't with him. If worse came to worst, there was always the challenge book at Jackson's Boxing Parlour, and side wagers. The cost Leigh regretted most was Baron's services for two days, Lawrence's fee for one half hour's private use of the indoor ring. The grizzled old veteran had justified such extortion of his ex-officer by pleading honesty. He could have used the stallion any night Claibourne wasn't watching, couldn't he? Not if he wanted papers on the foals, he couldn't, the earl had countered uselessly. Good thing he was better at sparring than at haggling, else he'd be under the hatches *and* horseless. The worst of it wasn't even having to ride one of Lawrence's hacks for two days; it was how surly Baron would be later, going on rocking-horse rides in the park.

Claibourne's main worry, however, was one he'd least expected when he woke at dawn this morning. He'd discounted Jacelyn's claims of being followed yesterday, and the garbled account of stray dogs and pigeons made no sense at all. Yet this morning, when he arrived at Parkhurst Mews early to give Lem his instructions—and bribe—the stable yard was abuzz with talk of a horse left there overnight. The poor brute was still tethered to a crosstie where, it was assumed, someone had tied it after the stablemen had gone to sleep. Obviously mistreated, with great weals and scars across its back, the horse was standing three-legged, head down.

"By Jupiter, man, what are you waiting for? Put the poor nag out of its misery—and do it before Miss Jacelyn gets here, for goodness' sake!" Claibourne felt his own stomach wrench at the horse's condition; he could only imagine Jacelyn's reaction.

"Yessir," Henesley answered, "we're waitin' on the knackers' cart. Misdoubt the beast could make it that far on's own."

They decided to get the wretched horse into a stall, as quickly as they could move it. Henesley brought a bucket of grain. "Least we can do is let 'im go with a full belly, sorry bastard. I'd like to have my hands on the devil what done this."

"Have you any idea who it could have been, or why?"

"Talked to the night watch, just afore you came. He was goin' off. Says he saw a tall, skinny gent leadin' a horse, around three or so. Thought it was some nob whose horse'd cast a shoe."

"A gentleman, you say?"

Henesley spat. "No gentleman did this. The watch says the swell was all over jewelry. Noted it particular, he says, 'cause the toff was lookin' out for dark alleys 'n such."

"And tall?"

"Real tall, he says, 'n skinny as a fireplace poker."

Lem told Jacey that the shot she heard as they rode away was a rat in the hayloft Henesley'd been after. So big it was, it near ate the old tom.

Her floppy hat kept falling off. Lem would leave Baron's side and chase after it, until Pen decided this was a new game.

"Leave the blasted hat, and come back to your place," Claibourne called. "No one is going to come in anyway." He was riding a gelding on Baron's inner side, and he was exasperated.

Jacelyn didn't even notice, having such a grand time in her britches and stockinged feet. She could go from her seat to a kneeling position easily now; Leigh only had to steady her arm once. She could rise to a standing position without much trouble, with Baron at a walk. It was the canter that was eluding her. She sat down, hard, on Baron's bare back, doing neither of them much good. She did better the next time, standing for a few paces after Claibourne clucked Baron into the faster pace.

The earl caught her, grasping anything he could. For a second he had her feminine softness pressed all over him, till he could deposit her back on the stallion's withers. Lord, he thought, if she didn't manage to stand soon, he'd lay her down right there in the sand.

"Let's try the whole thing at a canter, instead of changing gaits while you're balancing," he suggested, and it worked. He paced Baron around the ring, saying, "On boy, steady there," keeping the gelding as even as he could.

Jacey soon got the rhythm. She rose slowly until she was finally erect, her arms spread out, and a huge grin on her face.

"I did it! Now you back away."

Claibourne pulled over a bit, so her glory was complete, until he called, "How are you going to get down?"

Disconcerted, she looked down, and found herself sailing over Baron's rear end. She landed in a whoosh of sand and dirt. The earl was beside her in an instant, gathering her into his arms, cradling her.

"Are you hurt? Did you twist anything?"

"Is our time up, or can I try again?" she asked, hugging him back, proving the ground hadn't knocked any sense into her.

That clinched it. Lifting her to her feet and brushing off the seat of her britches as delicately as he could, Leigh decided to forgo the ride to Richmond. He just didn't feel right about going without Baron, without finding out what Percy was up to, without a cold bath — or whatever it took to get Miss Trevaine's perfect little body off his mind.

11

"Nonsense, Jacelyn, of course you'll go. His lord-ship's note said he had urgent business. You have none. It's much too late to cancel; Lord Farthingale would be offended, to say nothing of his mother, Lady Hockney. Oh dear, Lady Hockney. You sim-ply must go, Jacelyn, I insist."

Jacelyn did not want to ride out to Richmond, not without the earl. She couldn't even take Pen, not having asked Lady Hockney. There was no rea-son to take Lem, and Pinkie didn't ride. She would be all alone, just like on her first night in London, lonely in a crowd.

"What foolishness! Claibourne wrote that Arthur would take care of you."

"Arthur? Aunt Amabel, Arthur couldn't even take care of his toes, if they weren't attached." Jacey thought of asking Mr. Sprague, who was indoors so much he could use the ride. Except that he'd be tortured by Priscilla's flirting all day. No, it was just Arthur, till they met the others at Hyde Park, then she'd be the odd, extra female. Blast.

"Come, Jacelyn. This isn't like you. You'll go,

meet new friends. You don't want to sit in the earl's pocket, do you? He's older, you know, and . . . and used to certain freedoms. I'm sure you'll find it more convenient, after you're married." Lady Parkhurst blundered on: "If you don't make mice-feet out of it now."

Leigh would dislike a wispy, weak clinging vine above all things, Jacelyn silently agreed as she left her aunt's bedchamber and trudged to her own room for a much needed bath. Sitting in a hard saddle didn't seem like a pleasure right now, whatever the company, but yes, she would attend. She'd go to be polite, and to show the earl that she could manage without him, no matter how precious his companionship was becoming to her, whenever he tired of debutante do's. Urgent business, in a pig's eye! But, and it was a very big *but,* she'd thought they were friends. She wouldn't have let one of her friends down this way.

Pinkie wasn't any help. "At least you'll get to wear your pretty new habit," she said, lifting the heavy brown velvet over Jacey's head. "It's a pity his lordship won't be there to see it." The new outfit had baby-blue braid, and a full, shorter skirt instead of an awkward train. When she sat in the saddle a bit of her ankle would show, an ankle encased in a sturdy black leather riding boot. If that scandalised Lady Hockney, so be it. It would be better than tripping all over. The waist was tightly fitted, but the sleeves were loose, giving her freedom of movement. On her head she wore a brown hat shaped like a man's, with a brim to protect her face from the sun. Its masculine severity was broken by a wisp of a blue gauze veil, held on with a nosegay of silk forget-me-nots. Jacey agreed with her maid: the outfit was pretty. And it was wasted.

There were more people waiting at the park than she could remember the names and faces of, and more than a few she'd rather forget. As they rode out behind Lady Hockney and her companion in the carriage, the group split into twos and threes. When they left the city traffic and reached country roads, a strange quadrille began. Riders kept shifting positions, partners, even steps — in this case gaits. Some would gallop ahead in a private race, others would drop back to chat with stragglers, or jog up to reintroduce themselves to strangers. The rules of this dance seemed to include talking with every member of the party.

Lord Farthingale rode up to her and Arthur. He was enthusiastic about Jacelyn's mare, wanting to know her parentage, her times on the flat, if Miss Trevaine would care to try her paces against his gelding while they were still fresh. Arthur moved away to join Miss Chadwick and Captain Highet. He didn't stay there long, riding ahead to the next pairing. Priscilla Ponsonby, meanwhile, joined Farthingale and Jacelyn before they could determine the length of their gallop. Jacelyn had the pattern of the peculiar dance, but not the protocol. Was she supposed to ride off, or was Priscilla? Or even

Farthingale?

Priscilla hadn't improved with daylight, time, or closer acquaintance. In fact, Jacelyn reflected, Priscilla would only improve with distance, so Jacey set her mare to a gallop. As she rode she recalled her father's estimation of Napoleon: he was one of the few men of all time who could so benefit the world—by leaving it. Jacey wanted to let the mare out; Farthingale wanted to look good in her eyes, so met her challenge and took off after her; Priscilla wanted Farthingale and knew she'd never catch them. She therefore made a remark about how unbecoming hot, dusty females looked.

Happier after the race, which she graciously conceded to the viscount, since she had had a head start, Jacey decided to avoid his company if she could. She just wasn't comfortable with Farthingale's high-flown praise of everything she said or did, especially without Claibourne there to smile at the absurdity. She had no desire to speak with Priscilla, Chadwick/Highet, or—Lords, was that Humboldt from Squire's house party? It must be; he was staring at her all goggle-eyed. No, not him either.

Two blonde ladies, sisters or twins, she couldn't tell, rode with a blushing young man who wore yellow breeches, a green jacket, and a large red rose in his buttonhole. Lord Tayson, he stammered. The ladies were Miss Brynne and Miss Beryl Roth, but Tayson's nervous stutter did not make clear which was which. The sisters made no effort to help him. They did, however, ask if Jacelyn had been at the last Devonshire House ball. Jacey moved on.

Oops, Lord Anton-Fredricks was part of the next couple. If Farthingale's compliments were effusive, at least they seemed sincere. Anton-Fredricks proceeded to declaim his joy at riding with two such heavenly examples of feminine grace. Jacelyn immediately decided she liked the older woman riding with him when that lady's first words were: "Poppycock, sir. Save your breath to cool your soup." In truth, the kindest thing one could say about the lady's looks was that her horse wasn't *much* prettier. Anton-Fredricks tipped his hat and rode away, affronted. The lady grinned, held out her hand for a firm grasp, and said, "Smarmy caper-merchant. I'm Riva Montmorency. We met earlier, in the crowd."

"I'm Jacelyn Trevaine, Miss Montmorency, and I *do* like your style!"

Farthingale interrupted. As usual in his presence, talk turned to horseflesh. Miss Montmorency was knowledgeable and interested. Jacey excused herself and galloped briefly toward Arthur, who was riding with the last unknown member of the group. She was a tall, handsome woman with a superb seat, and the two seemed engrossed in their conversation. Jacelyn hesitated about approaching them, and was even considering revising her plans for Arthur and Rhodine when she noticed that Arthur was doing no talking, only nodding his head. He looked relieved to see Jacey.

"Miss Kinbeck was telling me about a book you might find interesting, Jacelyn. Miss Trevaine's father is quite a scholar, Miss Kinbeck, I'm sure he's

heard of it: *Indication of the Rights of Women.*"
He rode off as quickly as he could when both
women corrected him to *Vindication.*

"Were you really discussing Miss Wollstonecraft's
book with Lord Ponsonby, Miss Kinbeck?"

The other woman was indignant. "Why not? All
women should be well-informed and well-read."

"Of course. I meant *Arthur!*"

So it went until they finally reached the gardens
at Richmond, where servants in blue and gold
Hockney livery were waiting to take the horses and
lead the party to refreshments. Jacelyn's idea of a
picnic was what she'd experienced at Treverly: Cook
packed some bread and some fruit and whatever
was left from last night's dinner, you found a comfortable spot, put down a cloth, and opened the
hamper. The only thing similar here was the comfortable spot.

Tables, chairs, blankets, cushions were laid out
under some trees overlooking the ornamental lake.
Two tables held the huge buffet, and uniformed
footmen served. They also poured from a selection
of wines, fruit drinks, and even hot tea.

"What," Jacey asked Miss Montmorency, with
whom she was quickly on such terms, "no finger
bowls?"

The ride may have been merely an excuse to
overeat in pretty scenery, but Jacelyn had been
looking forward to seeing the topiary gardens and
the famous man-high yew-hedge maze. Most of the

party, though, seemed content to relax on the cushions after the heavy luncheon. The ladies fanned themselves, if they couldn't find a flunky like Highet to do it for them. Arthur had a cloth over his face and was wuffling into it. Miss Montmorency assured Jacey it was permissible to wander about, since this was a very informal party, but Jacey wasn't sure the other woman could be accounted a proper social arbiter, not with her outspoken views. She was relieved, therefore, some minutes later, when Farthingale asked to escort her to the maze. Other groups were taking his lead and bestirring themselves to stroll around the lake or through the formal gardens. Priscilla looked as if she'd eaten a bad oyster, hearing Farthingale's offer, and drafted Lord Humboldt to show her the rose gardens.

"Arthur," Jacelyn gently prodded, "I'm going to the maze with Lord Farthingale. I didn't want to leave without telling you."

"What's that? What in blazes do I care what—Oh." He remembered his sworn obligation, and Claibourne's handy fives. "Quite all right, I'll be there in a moment. Meet you at the centre." He nodded off again, confident it would take her awhile to find her way in. He, of course, would purchase a guide from the maze keeper.

"You needn't worry about getting lost, my dear Miss Trevaine," the viscount was saying as they approached the entrance. "I have the route by heart."

"But, my lord, one is supposed to get lost in a

177

maze! That's why they let the shrubbery get so high, to make it harder!"

The silly pup was so proud of his cleverness, Jacelyn couldn't give him the set-down he deserved. It was her own fault, she acknowledged, for forgetting her resolve to avoid him. He only wanted to coddle her, but, "I must insist on going in alone, my lord. You are much too downy, but I think I'll enjoy the challenge."

Crestfallen, he asked, "May I at least wait in the centre for you?"

"Oh no, the fun is trying to remember the way out, once you're in! Here come the Misses Roth. I'm sure they'd be delighted to find the heart of the maze without all the effort. I'll just wait here a moment so your voices don't give me any clues, and don't worry, if I get too lost, I can always call out."

The maze's interior was like tall green corridors, very hushed, cool, and shaded. Some of the blind alleys ended in pocket-sized flower gardens, or rosebushes, or benches. Some other paths just wound back on themselves till Jacey had to giggle, passing the same birdbath the third time—unless the maze's designers were so diabolical as to repeat landmarks. She didn't think that was the case, just that she'd missed a turning. The next path had a lot of gaps leading to other alleys, whose ends she couldn't see. She decided to try the straight course first, then backtrack to each corridor in turn, if need be. Her way ended at a small dolphin fountain, just like the one at Treverly. She could hear Farthingale's proud voice on the other side of the hedge, so she must be close to the centre, even if she couldn't get to it from here. She stayed at the fountain, listening to its quiet babble for a few moments till the voices faded, and she missed her father and her home all over again.

The second pathway back from the fountain brought her to the centre, after only one dead-end bluff. The heart of the maze was larger than she'd suspected, from all the outer rings. It had stone benches surrounding a garden where the sun could more fully penetrate, and in whose centre was a sundial. Jacelyn took off her gloves and sat on one of the benches, lifting her face to the warmth.

"Ah, like one of Nature's petalled beauties, lifting toward golden Sol's caress, and I, the wandering bee, to sip its nectar."

Phoo. Anton-Fredricks was taking a seat next to her on the bench. He was lifting her bare hand to his wet mouth—and what was that drivel about nectar, anyway? She stood up, ready to curtsey and leave, but Anton-Fredricks still held her hand.

"Please, sir, I must be going. The others . . ."

"Not so fast, lovely lady. I saw you delay until I approached the maze, and I know you were waiting here in the centre for me, clever puss. Now you shall have your reward."

Of all the idiocy! "I did not do any of those things, and I insist—"

He pulled her to him and was kissing her! This slicked-back shabster was actually drooling on her face, very much against her will. With one well-coordinated effort, necessary due to the disparity in their sizes, she brought her hard, wooden-heeled riding boot into contact with his right shin, and her open palm into contact with his left cheek.

"How dare you!" she hissed, not wanting a raised voice to bring anyone to witness this. Lord, what this could do to her reputation! She wiped her mouth on her sleeve, in disgust.

"Very pretty act, ma'am, but I heard you weren't quite so clutch-fisted with your kisses." He reached for her again. She slapped him again.

"Oh God. I knew it. I take my eyes off the chit for ten minutes, and look what happens. Damn you, Jacey Trevaine, can't you ever stay out of trouble?"

"No trouble at all, Arthur, I was just leaving." She took his arm and hurried him out. He didn't even have time to consult his map. At the fountain, Jacey drew him to a halt.

"I didn't do anything, Arthur. Really I didn't. I was just sitting there when he came along."

"Cut line, Jacey. I know that. You don't even know how to flirt. You may be flighty, but you ain't a high flier. Still and all, Claibourne's not going to like it."

"But there's no reason to mention it, Arthur. I'm sure Lord Anton-Fredricks won't bother me again, and I'll certainly keep out of his vicinity."

"Tain't that so much, as Claibourne's the man to teach you. Here, look. You don't hit a bounder with your hand. Make a good tight fist and throw it from the shoulder. Leigh'll show you.

"Why, thank you, Arthur!"

Shoop had once tried to teach a very young Miss Trevaine about topiaries, how you have to train the shrub with wires, and trim it as it grew, for years and years. Years were bogey men to Missy, then: when you grow up; your next birthday; in two years. So she took a shears and a likely looking privet bush, and started clipping. At first it was going to be a rabbit, but one ear disappeared by mistake. Fine, a duck would be—oh-oh, a double globe. A small heart?

The result was that Miss Trevaine had great admiration for topiary and its sculptors. Richmond had some of the finest of both. Knights on horseback, jousting. Dragons and unicorns and griffins. A mother goose and three little goslings. All in thick green shrubbery. Jacelyn was enjoying the display with Miss Montmorency and Miss Kinbeck, and enjoying their company.

Miss Mary-Margaret Kinbeck had all manner of irrelevant information, which she cheerfully shared, and which Miss Riva Montmorency just as cheerfully called tomfoolery, pifile, and tommyrot. Soon the three women were happily using first names and making plans to meet again.

"Shall you be at Almack's tomorrow night?" Jacelyn asked.

Riva answered: "Mary-Margaret's too much of a bluestocking to enjoy the social chitchat, but I always attend. I love to dance." Jacelyn was surprised. She would have thought the graceful and truly exquisite Mary-Margaret would be the party-goer, not the less-favoured, rough-tongued Riva. The world was a strange place.

"Drat! I must have left my gloves in the maze! Will you accompany me back there?" Jacelyn said.

As they walked, the conversation drifted into deeper waters: "I understand you're to make a match with Claibourne," Riva said.

"It's . . . it's not definite yet," was all Jacey could think of to answer. She didn't want to mention any of the circumstances around her problematic betrothal, nor did she want to sound evasive to such a straightforward individual.

"Good," Mary-Margaret put in. "Take your time, make sure. It's always a mistake, the way they rush young women into decisions, as if marriage were like a new bonnet."

"Listen to her, Jacelyn. She's had six years of offers to consider, and she hasn't accepted any."

"Don't you want to get married, Mary-Margaret?"

Miss Kinbeck reflected on the question as though she'd never heard it before. Refusing eligibles for six years, she'd heard it aplenty. "I am not certain," she finally admitted. "I have recently been considering Mr. Fabian Holmes's kind offer. He is in orders, you know. I feel I could be of great service as a prelate's wife. Alternatively, I have wondered if founding a school for indigent children wouldn't be more worthwhile than having just one or two of my own."

"Couldn't you do both? Start a school and marry

your cleric?"

"Capital!" Riva teased. "The best of both worlds."

"And what about you, Miss Montmorency, Riva? Have you plans for matrimony? That is, if I am not being impertinent?"

"Impertinent? How could you be when I've just asked about you and Claibourne? It's a question, incidentally, all London is itching to ask. My future doesn't merit the tiniest scratch, I've been so long on the shelf. But yes, Ferddie Milbrooke and I have decided we might as well have the banns read next spring. The music's good."

Mary-Margaret snorted. "About time." But Jacey asked about the music.

"Pianoforte, you know. We play together a great deal, even try composing some new material. We may not have stars and cymbals and the earth opening at our feet, but there are some very pretty duets."

"I met Lord Milbrooke at the Ponsonby musicale, but he didn't play. Why didn't you attend if you—"

"Do you think Priscilla Ponsonby would invite anyone to her affair who could play better than she can? Not half likely. The only reason she saw that I was invited today—and Mary-Margaret too—was that she knew we wouldn't steal any of her beaux. How you got invited is another matter."

Jacey giggled. "Lord Farthingale and his mama wanted me. If Priscilla's nose was any more out of joint, she'd be wearing it as an earmuff."

There were so many pictures of matrimony in

Jacey's mind—and none of them a masterpiece. She had Claibourne's description of the hunt for money and prestige, then her aunt's ill-concealed hints that a wife might find it convenient to ignore a husband's lapses in fidelity. Miss Chadwick and Captain Highet were engaged, inseparable, and insipid. Now Miss Montmorency would marry someone who shared her hobby, and Miss Kinbeck would wed to do good works! Whatever happened to true love?

When they were finally at the maze Jacelyn stopped her musings to concentrate on the proper pathways. This was no time to get lost, when the servants were starting to resaddle the horses. She'd been through last, even though she'd exited by instinct rather than memory, so the other women followed her lead, right to the little fountain.

"How foolish of me, but no matter. The centre is just two turns back. Here, through this gap and left. There! See, my gloves are right on the bench where I left them."

And right on the other side of the sundial, on another bench, were Priscilla Ponsonby and Lord Anton-Fredricks. Springing apart. Red-faced. Mussed.

Miss Kinbeck *tsk*ed; Miss Montmorency muttered something about dirty dishes and demireps, but Jacelyn simply said: "How nice for you, my lord. You found what you were looking for also!"

She rode home in the coach with Lady Hockney.

* * *

The Earl of Claibourne was hoping Jacelyn's day had gone better than his. He should have gone with her; he shouldn't have left her among strangers while he chased his tail around London all day. He'd been in every gaming hall he could think of, most of the taverns a well-heeled man could walk into—and safely out of—and a few bawdy houses. The afternoon was wasted, he'd thrown a small fortune to boys to hold a dumb horse, and more to butlers, barkeeps, and abesses, all for nothing. He'd found neither hide or hair of his cousin Percy, nor anyone who'd seen him in days. Nothing. Two places he didn't think to make enquiries: the house of his own one-time mistress La Fleur, née Flora Cobb, and Josiah Fenton's residence on Mount Street. His wildest imaginings couldn't have made any connexions to the first. His worst nightmares wouldn't have taken him one inch near the second, where, unfortunately, Percival was still retching from the horrid sights he'd encountered at the knackers, and all the Blue Ruin he'd drunk to erase them.

When Arthur returned with the tale of Anton-Fredricks's lechery, Claibourne wanted to rush to Jacelyn's side and beg her forgiveness for not being there to protect her. It was dinner time, though, Arthur reminded him, and he'd not been invited to Parkhurst House until nine. He settled on pulling the libertine's cork then, but Arthur didn't think much of that idea, either. There was no need, he said, since Jacelyn had handled the loose screw like a trooper.

"Not much science, but plenty of pluck. Besides, if you call him out or anything, it'll be all over Town. That would put paid to any hopes of keeping Jacey's name clear."

Claibourne sat down again. "I can't just ignore it, you know."

"Actually, since Miss Trevaine was in my care, it's my obligation. I'm thinking of having a few words with the rum touch anyway. I think he's trifling with m'sister too, though heaven knows she asks for it. Something else went on in that maze, but nobody's talking. Jacey and her friends came out giggling like schoolgirls. Priss left, like a storm cloud. So het up she was, she didn't watch her skirt. Tripped right into m'arms. Not like Priss. A few minutes later Anton-Fredricks came out. Going to talk to m'mother about it, if she'll listen to me."

"Very well, I won't do anything rash until we see who gets to flatten him first. Now tell me, who are Jacelyn's new friends? Do I have to worry they'll lead her into more scrapes?"

"That girl doesn't need *anyone* to find mischief! Do you remember a Miss Kinbeck? She's been out for ages, devilish handsome woman, but a real bluestocking. Couldn't understand three words in ten she said. The other's Riva Montmorency. You know, the platter-faced female who talks like an artillery gunner and dances like an angel? Nothing to worry about there. But young Farthingale . . ."

Leigh was at Parkhurst House at the ninth chime,

with a huge bouquet of flowers and a prayer that Lady Luck would be at the faro table later tonight. First, though, he and Jacelyn played piquet for bonbons, under the not-so-watchful eye of his great-aunt Simone. Mme. Aubonier had her book, but she'd much rather be abed and her throat clearing made her opinion plain: whatever damnfool *pas d'fous* he'd started now, he'd better end it soon.

"I'm sorry I couldn't go with you today, Jacelyn, especially when Arthur told me about—"

"My point again. You're not concentrating, my lord. I have all the bonbons."

"You've been eating some of mine, Captain Sharp. Seriously, I feel badly, when I promised you and your father."

"Was your business really urgent, or did you just not want to go?"

"Is that what you think? I wouldn't have accepted in that case. You should know by now I almost never do what I don't wish. Life is too short for that. I did think my business was important, although it turned out not to be."

"It . . . it wasn't to do with 'certain freedoms,' was it?"

"Freedoms? What maggot have you got in your head now?"

Jacelyn couldn't meet his searching blue eyes. "A woman?"

Leigh leaned back in his chair and laughed. "Cads, sweetheart, neither Baron nor I could handle another woman!"

Assuming he meant the bareback ride that morning, Jacelyn was convinced as much by his smile as by his words. "And we're friends?"

"Friends . . ." He turned the word over like a new taste. "Yes, I suppose we are. Good friends." He popped a bonbon into her mouth and said good night.

12

"Where's Baron? He wasn't hurt by my ride yesterday, was he?"

"Quite the contrary,. Ah, that is, he's back at the livery. I'm exercising this new hack for Lawrence, as a return favour. I'm thinking of purchasing him."

"Why would you? He has a surly disposition, and he doesn't like dogs."

"True. Shall we get down and walk? I'm enjoying this as little as the horse."

They left both horses tied to a tree, in Lem's care. Now the earl could relax, and Pen could race around without fear of being kicked if she came too near the bad-tempered gelding. Jacelyn was happy enough to dismount. What was tender yesterday was sore today, despite hot soaks. Not intending to gallop, she had worn the brown velvet habit again, only incidentally hoping for his lordship's warm approval. She only had to fluff out the skirt once or twice with her crop, and adjust the blue veil on her hat before he noticed.

Grinning, he said, "Very becoming outfit, by the way. I meant to tell you at the mews, but I was so

189

overcome I couldn't get the words out."

"Gammon! I suppose Spanish coin is my reward for fishing for compliments."

"Pet, you don't need to fish. Why, I'd be singing your praises right now, if I didn't fear it would turn your head." When she laughed he realized that one of her greatest charms lay in her not believing quite how beautiful she was. He doubted even the acclamations of the Polite World would turn her into a spoiled Diamond, thank goodness.

"Seriously," he went on, "aside from what's in it, the style is very attractive, and practical. Not all that ungainly yardage to be tossed over your arm like a dishcloth."

Since Jacelyn was now using both arms to tug a stick away from the dog, she agreed wholeheartedly. "Isn't it silly what some women will do for fashion's sake?"

"I'll wager more will be adopting this style. I, ah, understand Miss Ponsonby had a bit of difficulty with *her* train yesterday," he said, doing some fishing himself.

Jacey chuckled. "Miss Ponsonby was a tad overset. Would you believe Miss Perfection herself acting so unladylike? Tripping over her skirts and"—she looked back at Lem, in the distance—"being found in a compromising position. I wouldn't say anything to Arthur or anyone else, but I know you'll appreciate the jest."

"Anton-Fredricks?"

"Of course, though how she could—"

"And how compromising?"

"Not fatally, I suppose. It would be enough to

give Aunt Ambel kitten-fits if I did it, but they were only embracing in the center of Richmond Garden's maze."

"That's bad enough. Tell me something: Why didn't you tell Arthur or Lady Hockney or any of the others? You can be sure Priscilla would have been the town crier, if it were you."

"I know, and I thought of all the satisfaction it would have given me to tell. I even thought it wouldn't be a bad thing if she and Anton-Fredricks had to marry. They deserve each other. I couldn't do it though, and Miss Kinbeck and Miss Montmorency agreed: no woman should be forced to marry against her will."

"Miss Trevaine, I compliment you as that rarest of women. Not only beautiful, but kind and wise beyond your years — and your deuced ox of a dog has its muddy feet on my new Hessians!"

"If Cinderella's godmother could make a coach out of a pumpkin, I'm certain we can do *some*thing with this gown."

Pinkie wasn't so sure. "But Miss Jacey, ma'am, Cinderella's godmother had a magic wand!"

They were in Rhodine's bedchamber, where the drapes were threadbare and the ceilings had water stains, and where one of the ugliest dresses in creation hung from the wardrobe door. Pinkie just stared, dumbfounded, Hammersmith sniffed, and Jacelyn tried to keep Rhodine from weeping, though her own confidence was shaken at the task confronting them. If this gown were an infant, she thought, its own mother would disown it. Getting some cheerful conviction into her voice took an effort, but she did it. "We'll have more of an idea when we see it on. It will look better, I'm sure. Do you want Pinkie to help you, or shall you call for your maid?"

Lady Rhodine did not have a maid of her own, sharing her stepmother's abigail. Tina did not stir until noon, and the dresser, taking her cue from her mistress, played least-in-sight for Rhodine's needs. The girl was pitifully grateful for Pinkie's help. All in black as usual, Hammersmith looked like a judge finding the whole ménage guilty of a severe breach of propriety. Such goings on in a gentleman's house!

The house, the maid, the selfish stepmama, nothing was to the point, only the Dress. Jacey was wrong. It didn't look better on. Now it looked as if a berserking tent had dragged itself across Araby, through an oasis of roses, to savagely attack poor Miss Endicott. There was a pale pink satin underdress, totally unstructured on top, except for a loose waist, puffed-out sleeves, and a neckline that did just that, with a stranglehold on Rhodine's throat. Fashion dictated a fitted bosom and no waist, tiny cap sleeves and, if not cleavage, at least a collarbone!

"Tina said I mustn't look fast."

"You don't even look human, much less fast."

On top of the underdress was a white tulle overskirt consisting of four tiers of gathered ruffles which stood out so stiffly Rhodine could have sailed to Calais in a strong breeze. More of the gauzy stuff was gathered at the collar, and trickled out of the sleeves, halfway down her arms. More? Roses. Pale pink satin roses made out of the underdress material, with green silk leaves and stems, with a white satin bow around each stem. The flowers were strewn haphazardly, so the white ribbon streamers dangled everywhere. The matching headpiece, a mixture of all of the above ingredients, was laid out on the dressing table like a casket wreath.

"Do you have a long cape? Oh Rhodine, I'm sorry. Don't cry! We'll fix it . . . won't we, Pinkie? Hammersmith?"

Pinkie was soon rummaging through her workbasket, while Hammersmith was poking and prodding, trying to find if Rhodine actually had some shape in there. She also pulled at the girl's prinked curls. Too bad it wasn't a wig, the maid's expression said.

Then they got to work. Gown off, hair washed. The entire overdress was soon in a pile on the floor; Rhodine's hair had a soft wave to its pale, streaky blonde. Underdress back on. Damp hair gathered up into a knot. Another conference.

The women, Jacey adding encouragement as well as creativity, decided it was better already. At least there was less of it. Now all they had to do was make it fit like a gown, not a sack. Pinkie pinned and basted and cut and sewed. There was no time for perfect edges with tiny little stitches, so the new neckline would have to be camouflaged. Jacey's job was cutting the roses off the netting, then undoing the white ribbons. She found a housemaid willing

193

to press them, for a coin. Hammersmith worked on Rhodine's hair, using ingredients from her tapestry satchel. They worked straight through the luncheon no one offered them. When the maid came back with the ribbons, Rhodine ordered her to fetch something from the kitchens. The girl stood staring wide-eyed at the room in chaos and at the step-daughter who had never demanded anything, and was now requesting meals for servants.

"Go on, girl, get." Hammersmith flicked a towel at her. "You heard your mistress. Gawking like a bumpkin at a two-headed chicken won't get your work done. And mind your tongue in the kitchen."

"Yes'm." It was Hammersmith who received the curtsey. Pinkie giggled, but kept on sewing.

It was nearly four o'clock when they finished. Jacelyn would be late for tea with the dowager Lady Parkhurst if she didn't hurry. That, according to Aunt Amabel, would be enough to set the old girl off on her high horse. But it was worth it.

"Remember, don't go down to supper; have it in your room. And call for that other maid to help with the buttons, not Lady Endicott's dresser. And don't lie down, it'll muss your hair. Put your wrap on upstairs so by the time Lady Tina sees you it will be too late to change."

"Yes, yes, Aunti Jacelyn, I'll remember! Now you'd better go, or you won't be ready on time yourself. Pinkie, will you please help me out of the gown?"

Jacey took one last look at her friend's glowing smile and knew it would be worth it, even if she missed Almack's altogether. No, she amended, she had to get there early, to see Lady Tina's face—and Arthur's! Rhodine was lovely, the gown was superb. The slip dress was now gathered under the bust with long streaming white ribbons. The collar, cut down to a modest décolletage, was edged with a thin rolled layer of the white gauze, with one of the pink satin roses at the V. The gauze also formed tiny strap sleeves and small flounced insets at the sides of the swagged hemline, held by two more roses. The rest of the roses were twined together to make a caplet for Rhodine's hair, now a shining soft-wheat crown with loose curls at the back. Even her cheeks had a delicate blush, thanks to Hammersmith's satchel. The sparkle in her eyes, though, came from the heart, not a bottle.

Jacelyn burst through the rear entrance of Parkhurst House, Pen bouncing around her in welcome, and called a hallo down the long corridor to Marcus at the front door. Her hair was undone, her gown was creased and had threads and snippets of gauze clinging to it, and she was late. She made a turn for the stairs, and nearly bowled over a tiny, plump old lady just coming out of the west parlour. Aunt Amabel was behind her, shredding her handkerchief.

"Doesn't look much like a countess to me," the dowager grumbled. "Nor even like a lady."

Jacelyn was far from a Long Meg herself, but she looked down on the round little figure, not many inches over four feet, and said, "Good, we're even. You don't look much like Satan's stepsister either, but we'll both manage, won't we?" She curtsied, kissed her aunt's trembling cheek, and fled up the stairs.

She wasn't born a tall, willowy blonde with a peaches-and-cream complexion. She hadn't turned into one recently, and it didn't appear that she soon would. She didn't have Rhodine's pale, fragile prettiness, nor Priscilla Ponsonby's stately golden aura, nor even a magic wand. She'd done the best she could, though, with Pinkie and Miss Hammersmith's assistance. It wasn't half bad, she told herself, for a little brown wren. The gown from Ryefield was deceptively simple: a deep gold slip dress of sheerest silk, with four lighter gold, spiderweb-soft Valenciennes-lace panels falling straight to the floor from the underbust waistline. When she moved, the panels flared loosely around her, letting the underdress cling to her hips. The top was entirely unadorned, what there was of it. Not indecently low, it still managed a rounded softness and an expanse of honey-warm skin, broken only by a large topaz on a gold chain, one of her mother's jewels. She also wore a gold tiara from the Treverly vault, confining the thick coils of chestnut hair. The few tiny wavelets around her face, seeming to be there by artless chance, had taken Hammersmith forty-five minutes to accomplish. Tiny gold satin slippers with ribbon laces and long cream-coloured gloves completed the effort, with a light dusting of powder to conceal the last of the freckles. Not china-doll pretty, but regal, elegant, exquisite. Or so

196

everyone said when she went down to dinner.

"Fine as fivepence, my dear," Lord Parkhurst declared. "I might be tempted to dance with you m'self."

His mother answered Jacey's demure curtsey with a muttered, "And I always thought you couldn't make a silk purse out of a sow's ear."

Aunt Amabel was still uncertain about the gown's colour. The whole evening was so fraught with tension, though, she ignored this minor issue and said, "Charming."

It was Leigh Claibourne whom Jacelyn looked to, however, not the smiling Mr. Sprague nor the "Bien" of Mme. Aubonier.

His lordship was looking bang up to the mark himself, Jacelyn noted, with muscle-contoured black satin knee-breeches, wellfitted midnight-blue coat, sparkling white linens, a small black pearl in his intricate neckcloth, and blond curls casually brushed. Right now his blue eyes were gleaming as he told her simply: "I'll be the proudest man there." It was enough. Then he handed her a tissue-wrapped parcel. "Here, little princess, for your first dance."

His gift was an ivory filigree fan in a gold holder, with a tiny pencil attached. He showed her how her dance partners' names could be written on the delicate spokes, by entering his own on the first and another toward the end.

"Only two?" she asked, disappointed.

"That's all the patronesses will approve, dewdrop, otherwise I'd be tempted to claim them all."

Mr. Sprague wrote his name, and then Marcus

was announcing the arrival of the dinner guests.

They were fourteen to table in all, with Jacelyn, Claibourne, and Sprague the only young people. After Aunt and Uncle Parkhurst, in fact, no one was much under sixty. These were the dowager's friends, the Old Guard of London Society, when men wore powdered wigs and high-heeled shoes and the ladies wore patches and paint. The dowager now sported purple bunting and a red turban with an enormous diamond in the front. The turban was nearly all you could see of the elder Lady Parkhurst as she sat to her son's right at the long mahogany table. Her chin barely crested the tabletop, and how she could reach her glass was a mystery to Jacelyn, who was trying not to embarrass herself by giggling.

Lord Parkhurst tapped his glass with his spoon, raised the glass, said, "Health," and they all drank, starting the meal—and giving Jacelyn an idea.

She caught Marcus's eye at the sideboard and, when he approached her, whispered her idea to him. Claibourne, at her side, raised that sardonic eyebrow but Jacelyn turned her attention back to her soup. Marcus disappeared. When he returned, concealing something behind his wide girth, he nodded to Jacey. As the soup bowls were removed and the wine was changed for the next course, Jacelyn tapped her own glass and stood up.

With a lady standing, every gentleman in the room had to rise also, but with this group, it took some time, and some canes and footmen's aid.

"I'd like to propose a toast to my aunt," Jacelyn said in a clear voice. "Will you all rise?"

Now this was unusual. Ladies rarely proposed

toasts, hardly ever stood to do it, and never demanded that other ladies rise, especially not whitehaired matrons in turbans. She turned to Mme. Aubonier in silent appeal. Madame shrugged, but stood. The others followed, again with effort. When they were all erect except Aunt Amabel, Jacelyn turned in her direction, all attention on her, and said, "For all your kindnesses, ma'am, in being like a mother to me at this important time, I wish to thank you most sincerely. To my aunt."

Everyone sipped and sat down to the next course, prawns in drawn butter. Aunt Amabel was bewildered; she hadn't had two conversations with the pesky girl in the week she'd been here. The dowager, however, now perched on the sofa cushion Marcus had slipped onto her chair while she was standing, smiled and raised her own glass to Jacelyn.

Not much got past Claibourne, despite his casual air. "I wonder how many other hearts you'll win tonight, sweetheart," he said.

He would never see the inside of Almack's Assembly Rooms, not in this twisted lifetime, but Josiah Fenton spent the afternoon getting ready for it all the same.

His unfocussed eyes gazed on the future, and he didn't like it. The poison of his hatred writhed around him in smokey black tendrils. His right hand contracted, and his head fell forward on his scrawny neck, then jerked upright again.

"Percy!" he shouted.

The loud noise startled Percy, who was in the midst of his usual occupation: pouring fluid from one container to another, so it went more smoothly into the third. His hand twitched, and the liquid spilled, so he dispensed with the intermediary step, lifting the bottle of brandy straight to his mouth.

"Damn you for a simple-minded sot, Percy. How many have you had?"

"Bottles or glasses?"

"Oh God. Put it down and listen. What have you done about the Trevaine girl?"

Percy set the bottle on the table, but dabbled his fingers in the puddle there. "Trevaine? Oh, Claibourne's chit. I followed her around one day, like you said."

"Stop sucking your fingers, lumpkin. You're not a child, you only think like one. What was she like?"

"Small. Dark. Drab except for an orange dress so I could spot her easily in the crowds. Blue-nosed. Seemed to like the bookstores and the galleries. I couldn't see what Claibourne would want with her."

"Only wealth, a willing wife, and heirs, nothing you'd understand, you raw-boned rattlepate. So what have you done about getting rid of her?"

Percy did not want to remind himself of the whole terrible incident of the horse—or the dogs or the cats—so he searched for some cheerier information to relate. Beaming like a baby who's just found his toes, he uttered: "She smiled at me."

Fenton's glassy eyes grew round, his mouth dropped open. "It couldn't be. I cannot believe it's true. Percy, tell me, do you really think to end

Claibourne's engagement by stealing his bride's affections? *You?*"

"Miss Trevaine's got nothing to do with it, Da. Brown dab of a female. I told you I'd talk to La Fleur. Today she looked right at me . . . and smiled." Percy was in love.

"At least there is some limit to your stupidity. Do you know what today is?"

"Wednesday."

"See? And tonight?"

"Uh, Wednesday night?"

"It's Almack's, you cup-shot cabbage head! Where the aristocracy goes to play. The French may have had the right idea after all."

"Smart people, the French. They make damn good brandy." Percy eyed the bottle longingly. His father ignored him.

"They go to their private club to show each other how exclusive they are, as if they needed to be reminded of their social standing once a week. You're not invited to Almack's, you're nobody. You get accepted there, you're Somebody. Claibourne's little nobody will be going tonight, and you've got to see she doesn't become a Somebody."

"Huh?"

Fenton pounded his fist on his wasted legs. "You see these, shrivelled and shrunk from lack of use? That's what your brain must look like! I'm telling you, you've got to stop that woman from being a success tonight. Once she's recognised by the social set, Claibourne can never back off; it wouldn't suit his notion of honour. Nor would having a bride who's a social outcast. Those Merrills and their fancy family pride! You've got to stop it, Percy!"

"Me? I mean, how? You need somebody to go inside and make the girl look no-account, and you just said I'm a nobody, gov, I think."

"Don't think, boy, save your effort for breathing. I have a plan that may work."

"I ain't going back to the butcher."

"I pay a cook to do that, you fool. Besides, they don't serve meat at Almack's, only cake, tea, and orgeat."

"No liquor? I'm glad I'm a nobody. Now Fat Mona's place is kind of private, but *any*body can—"

"Shut up, Percy! From the *on dits* pages and what Jensen picks up, the girl's a high-strung hoyden. So far she's not gone in over her head, but a scene outside Almack's ought to put her beyond the pale. Here's my idea: You and Jensen will hire an old broken-down horse and cart. Buy it, if you have to; it'll be worth the price. You'll take it to Almack's, and when you tell Jensen the Trevaine chit is coming, he'll pretend to start whipping the horse and—"

"Hold on, governor. Those swells take their horses seriously. It could get real ugly. Now if Jensen was to beat an orphan . . ."

"The girl likes horses. She'll get hysterical and start an uproar, mark my words. They—that's the Somebodies inside—don't like mingle-mangles, especially if there are dirty, smelly peasants involved."

"What dirty, smelly peasants? I didn't hear you mention any."

"You and Jensen."

"I don't see why Jensen can't do it alone. Claibourne might recognise me."

"You have to identify the girl, you long-legged looby. That's why I sent you to follow her. You'll be in disguise, and you can disappear as soon as there's a crowd. Jensen can just act like the village idiot till it's over."

"He gets the easy part! Uh, gov, I think I'll pass on this one. Clever idea and all that, but Claibourne will be there. He'll kill me if I bother the girl."

"And Jensen will if you don't."

Five hours to prepare were four and a half too many for Percy's precarious hold on sobriety or sanity, especially as he switched from the bottle to his father's pipe as soon as Jensen had carried Fenton upstairs. By the time Jensen was ready with the ancient horse and cart, reality was like last month's weather to Percy, a vague memory. He must not be recognised, he knew, or someone would murder him, but gads, he wouldn't put such foul rags on his body! Not Percival Fenton. No, he had the brilliant notion of donning the costume he'd worn to the last rowdy masquerade at Vauxhall Gardens, half mask and all. Great night, that was, with those French girls. Exiled nobility, they said. Maybe they'd be at Almack's . . .

Jensen's horse made the one Percy bought at the knackers look like a Derby contender. To help it along, the giant-sized servant got out and walked. Then Percy got out. Then Percy led the horse while

Jensen pushed the cart. On King Street, though, one block from Almack's, there was a hill. Not a big hill, mind, just a slight incline. To this horse it might as well have been Mount Olympus. And time was passing. Carriages were starting to turn the corner; fancy coaches with crests on their doors drove past them. Jensen unhitched the cart and put the yoke over his own shoulders, then grunted for Percy to get the nag moving.

Soft words and coaxes got him a few steps. Going to the other end and pushing won him a few more, and a dry throat. He tipped up the flask he'd managed to conceal under his disguise, and remembered that afternoon's spill. He dipped his finger in the mouth of the flask and offered it to the horse. It was sloppy work, but effective, for a while. The horse followed Percy as far as it could, until its back legs gave out and it sat, doglike.

"Aw now, old sod, we've almost got it. A bit more now, you can do it."

But the horse slowly laid its front end down. Percy held up the head, pleading. "Here you go, old chap, you can make it. I have just the thing to set you back up."

That's when the Parkhurst entourage drove up to the red carpets at Almack's doors. Stepping down first, Claibourne looked back. What he saw stunned even him: a huge, ragged man pulling a cart and his cousin Percy, beak nose under a sequined half mask, hairy spindleshanks under a short Roman toga, pouring whiskey down the throat of a half-dead horse.

Claibourne shook his head. The vision was still there. Lord, he'd like a few words with Percy right now, but first he had to see about getting Jacelyn and the aunts, the dowager, and the other antiques into Almack's with the least fuss. He thought of declaiming the classic *"Ave, Caesar, morituri est,* etc., which would be wasted on Percy. Instead he just called out: "Chariots just aren't what they used to be, eh?"

13

Don't expect much, and you won't be disappointed. That's what everyone told Jacey about Almack's, and they were right. The place itself was dingy and dowdy—but oh, the people! Jewels, feathers, finery, she wanted to stare as she'd done at the gallery, but Claibourne tugged her ahead, following her chaperones. What an unlikely trio they made, these three Fates in charge of her introduction to Society.

Mme. Aubonier was in black as usual, tall, dignified, selfcontained. She greeted acquaintances with a nod, like an emir bestowing his favour. She made sure that Jacelyn's first curtsey was to the patroness who had secured her vouchers, Princess Esterhazy.

Aunt Amabel was in lavender chiffon. Her shawl kept slipping as she greeted everyone they passed with an embrace, as if she'd been out of the country for two years.

It was the dowager, though, in her glaring purple and red, short little legs trundling ahead, who kept them moving from introduction to introduction.

"Sooner we get the tomfoolery over, sooner I can find the card room. Chicken stakes only, but it's better than watching these silly geese trip over each other."

"I can see to Jacelyn's introductions, Mother Parkhurst, if you'd rather sit down," Amabel dithered, after Mme. Aubonier left them to sit beside Lady Drummond-Burrell behind the velvet rope marking the still-empty dance area.

"You can't even untangle your draperies, Amabel. The gel needs countenance. Let them all see I approve; that'll hold their clacking tongues. There's Countess Lieven. Not as bad a gabblemonger as Sally Jersey, but bad enough."

Jacelyn had her little how-do-you-do's down pat. "Yes, ma'am, I'm delighted to be here. Thank you for the invitation. The pleasure is all mine," etc. She even had a rote reply to enquiries concerning her London visit, and how much she was enjoying everything, when the matrons were kind enough to ask. She was taken aback, therefore, to meet with a cutting remark à la Priscilla from a total stranger.

The countess was coyly looking around Jacey and asking, "What, no livestock?"

While Jacey was wondering how this woman could be so rude and still be considered a judge of polite behaviour, the dowager was answering. Jerking her head first in Aunt Amabel's direction, then Claibourne's, she said, "The gal's got a peahen and a gamecock, she don't need any stringy old chickens clucking at her.

"Toughest is still to come," the dowager told a wide-smiled Jacelyn, when they paused to let Claibourne fan Aunt Amabel's flushed cheeks. "They call her Silence, 'cause she never is. Damned impertinent, because she can get away with it. I don't know why. Her own history isn't any lily-white. Mind your step, though, child."

Lady Jersey was holding court with some of the older members of the Beau Monde, Alvanley, Petersham, Byng, the Regent's cronies. Most of them raised their monocles to survey Jacelyn like a new species of water bug while Lady Jersey exchanged the usual pleasantries, giving an especially warm welcome to Leigh.

"So nice to see you among us again, Claibourne. I'm glad to see your rakehelling days are over. And here is your little Miss Trevaine," she purred, still addressing Leigh, whose lips were twitching. "I hope she realises what a fortunate girl she is, to have landed such an eligible *parti*. So many girls in this situation find themselves at sea in London. You know, Leigh, all those little country girls with fat dowries who find themselves the target of every flat and fortune hunter in Town."

Jacey looked at Lady Jersey's diamond-studded hand resting familiarly on the earl's arm, and the shy little country girl replied: "Better the devil you know."

Sally Jersey was poised like Julius Caesar about to give the thumbs-down signal. Impudent chit, implying Claibourne was a bounder or a basket scrambler, when she, Sally Jersey, had gone out of her way to congratulate the girl. Poor taste to refer to his financial embarrassment, and poor choice of audience to utter any kind of outré opinion, especially for a girl with a gamey reputation. Esterhazy would hear about this—and all of the ton. But Claibourne was laughing, and old Lady Parkhurst was cackling about the girl's spirit, and the Carlton House set behind her were all smiling and nodding, so obviously the girl was a witty charmer, not a coarse baggage after all. Small, but spunky. Obviously. She, Sally Jersey, decreed it so.

Luckily the music started then, and Leigh led Jacelyn off to the first set. It was the cotillion, with a lot of bowing and curtseying and smiling to complete strangers.

"Unless I miss my guess," Claibourne told her during a quiet interval, "you're about to take London by storm. Look at all the nods you're getting, and all the bucks hanging around your poor Aunt Amabel."

"Silly, that's just Arthur and Carter Sprague. Besides, I noticed how you were welcomed back to the fold with open arms.

"I told you I needed you to give me respectability."

"With *wide* open arms. Soft, clinging, jewel-encrusted arms."

Claibourne laughed out loud, drawing attention to them, and even more when he raised her hand and kissed it, still following the dance's movements.

Tongues ran on wheels. It was true, then, Claibourne was cotched at last. Whatever tales had been circulating about an honour-saving offer could not be disregarded, as well as rumours of a market marriage. It was enough that he was attending Almack's at all, but that he was enjoying it said a great deal about Miss Trevaine. She was certainly worth meeting, the talk went, and her name was added to those mental lists hostesses were forever compiling.

"This is our very first dance, Leigh."

"Why, so it is, my love. And you are as graceful a partner as a man could wish."

"You're much more accomplished."

"Only more practiced. I've been at it a deal longer."

"Leigh, are you . . . that is, did you, ah, find Lady Jersey attractive?"

Claibourne laughed again. "I'm not about to take a page from Prinny's book and admire women old enough to be my mother, if that's what you mean. What has you in a pother now?"

"Arthur said I don't know how to flirt, and she did it so well!"

"Did she? I didn't notice. Come, precious, look up at me with those twinkling eyes, and show your dimples. That's all the flirting you'll ever need."

When the dance ended, he led her to Aunt Amabel, sitting on a little gilded chair behind the velvet rope. Seated next to her was her bosom bow, Lady Ponsonby, so Priscilla was nearby, scowling. The

Ponsonbys had arrived too late for the first set, leaving Priscilla on the sidelines like a wallflower while everyone exclaimed over Miss Trevaine and her earl. Priscilla was waving her fan so vigorously Arthur complained of the draught. After all the insincere greetings, and before the next set was begun, Jacelyn nudged Arthur aside and asked if he was promised for the next dance.

"Only for watching out for Priscilla. I'm to stand by in case no one asks her to dance, you understand."

Jacey didn't. "All night? You have to dance with your sister all night?"

"Of course not. She's very popular, a real Diamond. The company's still a little thin, is all, and her arrival may have gone unnoticed. Quite the thing to do."

"If Priscilla can spare you, do you think you might dance with Miss Endicott, Lady Rhodine, that is? She was very nervous about this evening, and she's very shy, you know. I felt since you're already acquainted . . ."

"Of course, be delighted. Nice girl. I don't know why, but I forgot all about her. Where is she?"

"She just came in, over there by the door, with the stunning redhead. That must be Lady Tina, her stepmother."

"Where? I don't see—Good heavens, is *that* Lady Rhodine?"

Without consulting his mother or Priscilla, he excused himself to go welcome Miss Endicott.

"Doesn't know many people. Quiet girl, don't you know." He only stepped on one dowager's foot in his haste. Jacelyn made sure Claibourne was smiling too.

When the music started for the next selection, a country dance, Mr. Sprague ended his conversation with the earl and headed toward Priscilla. She slowed her fanning and turned her head away. The lady wasn't interested, not in some minor government functionary. He walked right by her and led Jacelyn out! They were headed toward Arthur and Rhodine Endicott's set, and no one had yet asked Priscilla to dance!

None of her other admirers seemed to be around. Damn Arthur. Claibourne was still nearby, though, talking with her mother and Lady Parkhurst. He seemed to be acceptable in polite company, suddenly, and he was certainly handsome, if one didn't mind his nonchalant, almost flippant manner. Those blue eyes and broad shoulders . . . No, it wouldn't hurt Priscilla's consequence in the least to be seen with the worldly earl. They would make quite an attractive pair, in fact, both fairhaired, tall, dignified. Not like the couple he made with that harum-scarum little gypsy. Priscilla paced the fan's rhythm to her eyelash fluttering. The earl didn't seem to notice. Priscilla mentioned, "Oh dear, the music is starting, and my partner hasn't arrived," and the infuriating man asked Lady Parkhurst if she was dancing that evening. After her tittered denials, Claibourne turned to Lady Ponsonby. Priscilla's own mother! One of the spokes of her fan snapped in two.

"How ungallant of your partner, Miss Ponsonby. Might I take his place?" Claibourne finally got around to asking.

"My pleasure," she answered through clenched teeth as he led her past dancing couples to the same set the others had joined. When the movements of the dance brought Arthur as her partner, Priscilla stomped on his foot, hard. He yelped and hopped about, however, instead of taking his punishment like a man, which made her look like a clumsy cow. The dance wasn't over soon enough for Priscilla, who accepted Mr. Sprague's offer to dance even before reaching her mother's seat, lest the shame of being partnerless repeat itself.

Jacelyn was to dance next with Arthur, and Claibourne with Rhodine, so they all stood near Lady Parkhurst, chatting amiably, while Priscilla seethed as she turned down four men she'd rather dance with than that prosy Sprague. At least her dance card was getting full! She absolutely refused to acknowledge that some of her gentlemen had also put their names on Jacelyn's and Rhodine's cards, and two had actually asked Jacey first!

The quadrille was a complicated dance, and both Jacelyn and Arthur had to mind their steps. He did manage to compliment her efforts on Rhodine's behalf, though.

"What, did she say I had anything to do with her new style?"

"She was telling everyone over by Lady Tina how much you'd done to help. Nice girl, appreciates kindness."

"Poo! No, I don't mean Rhodine isn't nice; she's the sweetest thing in nature. I just meant I didn't do anything. My maid and Aunt Simone's did all the work."

"It's more than m'sister would have done, help someone who's much pre—Um, ah . . ."

Jacelyn laughed, and almost missed a turn. "You can say it, Arthur, Rhodine is the image of the English beauty. She just needed a little push, that's all."

"Still, it was a deuced fine thing."

"Why, Arthur, I believe you may even grow to like me one of these years!"

His choking caused a button to pop off his straining waistcoat, causing the gentleman behind him to lose his footing. Skidding, that man grabbed his partner for balance, throwing her off the measure. She stepped back, and right onto the flounce of the lady next on the line, tearing it. It just wasn't Priscilla's night.

Jacelyn next danced the boulanger with Lord Farthingale. She'd hastily introduced Rhodine to Lord Tayson, who was to have partnered Priscilla, and sent them into the dance. Now she was too worried about how quiet Rhodine and the nervous, stammering Lord Tayson would manage a conversation to pay much attention to Farthingale's flattery.

"Come, my lord, there must be a more interesting

topic of conversation than my gown. How did you spend the day, for instance, or have you any fascinating plans, and have you seen any of the new plays? We're to go to Drury Lane next week."

Another contra dance followed, with Lord Tayson with his rose boutonniere. Luckily, the figures kept partners changing, so Jacey didn't have to sustain a long conversation. She did recall the questions she'd put to Farthingale, to stopper his high-flown compliments, and used them to good effect with the young nobleman, until he was finishing whole sentences before moving to the next lady in the figure. She also met three new gentlemen and found they were happy to speak of themselves and their interests, rather than just the usual gossip and polite inconsequentialities.

Jacelyn was becoming so popular with those who had met her, and so attractive to those who'd only seen or heard of her, that the spokes of her fan were nearly filled by the time the next set started. It was a waltz, which she had to sit out until approved for it by one of the patronesses, under some peculiar ruling. No matter, she was glad of the rest, and the cool drink Claibourne had waiting for her.

"Aren't you promised, my lord?"

"Only to you, pet. I'm here to beat off the hordes of admirers, remember?"

She told him, with a giggle, to leave enough of them for her to dance with. "I 'm having a wonderful time! Are you? Are you very bored?"

"Not at all. I danced with Lady Rhodine and

heard you nearly recommended for sainthood; I listened to five dowagers tell your aunt what a delightful girl you appeared; and I had seven chaps tell me what a lucky dog I was while they waited in line to sign your programme. Delightful evening."

"You could go dance with Sally Jersey."

"Minx! Be quiet and drink that insipid stuff, or I'll tell all your admirers how you gallop in the park."

After that, Jacelyn danced straight through to the intermission. She danced with Lord Farthingale again, and all the new young men, and the Spanish count, de Silva, which raised Claibourne's brow, which in turn made it hard for Jacey to keep from laughing during de Silva's long, flowery speeches. She danced with her uncle, passing between the card room and the front vestibule where he could enjoy blowing a cloud. She danced with some of the older set, Miss Montmorency's Lord Milbrooke, for one, who found her refreshing, and whom she found charming and courtly. She did not dance with Anton-Fredricks. She couldn't believe the man had the gall to ask her, and took great pleasure in announcing that her card was filled. Arthur, nearby with Rhodine, crossed his arms over his chest and glowered.

"I see," said Anton-Fredricks, looking from one to the other.

"I thought you would, old boy," said Claibourne.

Arthur and Rhodine strolled off to find what refreshments were available. Ponsonby, like

Claibourne, had danced a few duty sets, and otherwise stood near the chaperones, waiting for the ladies to be returned. He wasn't there for his sister's sake, now, but for Miss Endicott's, whose own chaperone seemed to have disappeared, rather than stay to hear more about her stepdaughter's dewy beauty. Rhodine was dancing nearly every dance too, for the first time in her life, and not just with those who couldn't get near Jacelyn. But Arthur was always waiting there, with a cooling drink, or to wave her fan, or to receive her tremulous smiles.

"He's positively hovering over the girl," Claibourne told Jacelyn. "You were right, she's as helpless as a kitten, and he's a natural guard dog. I congratulate you on your foresight. Now what in hell are you going to do about that puppy Farthingale? He's been drooling over my shoulder all night."

"Now you're encouraging my matchmaking? What an aboutface!"

"I've seen it succeed. While you're at it, what about Sprague? The poor fellow had his dance with the Iceberg and went home."

"I know. Isn't it sad? But don't worry, I'm working on it. I haven't got it quite settled between them, but I think one or the other would be perfect for Sam. You know, Squire's daughter Samantha. She's to come for my ball next month. Can you see Squire with a future duke as son-in-law? And a sports-mad one at that? I don't know if Sam would like being a duchess though. She might prefer Mr.

Sprague's quiet gentility and good sense. Squire would be pleased with a man who earns his way in life too, instead of what he'd call a fribble. I'll have to let Sam decide."

"Kind of you, my dear."

After the intermission, Jacelyn had her second dance with Leigh, and another with Tayson, at ease with her now. All the young men were, in fact. The girl was cheerful and pleasant, without all those airs the Incomparables adopted. Furthermore, she was a beautiful little handful, a regular Pocket Venus. She was soon dubbed an Original, for her style and her outspoken views. Why, she'd argue the merits of crossbreeding as easily as discussing the weather. She was kind, too, didn't make a fellow feel no-account if he forgot the steps, and look what she'd done for the Endicott girl, the one who'd been all over frills and frizz, and no conversation. Miss Trevaine was safe, besides. Some of those other girls, you danced with them twice and their mamas were calling you son. Miss Jacelyn was as good as spoken for, with Claibourne at her side all night, looking as if he were just casually passing time, and giving all her partners a look that would freeze their livers if they had dishonourable thoughts. If they did, they got rid of them fast and simply enjoyed the young woman's unaffected charm. So relaxed were they in her pleasing company that they found themselves excitedly telling her about yesterday's races, and last week's mills, and tomorrow's cockfights in Little Dene.

"We have to stop it, Leigh, can't you see that? It's dreadful, what they do to the poor birds!" They were sitting out another waltz.

"Yes, it is dreadful, Jacelyn, but we cannot stop it. It's the way of the world, and nothing will change that."

"I won't accept that. It's wrong and shouldn't be allowed. We can notify the authorities."

"And what would that do? It might even be legal in that village, for all you know. The authorities don't care, if it keeps the people happy. You've heard of bread and circuses, haven't you? This is the same. The young bloods from London will go bet their blunt, but it'll mostly be country folk, poor farmers and down-at-the-heels workers. It's one of their few pleasures, and no one wants to be the one to take it away. The folks who live there? Think of all the traffic and trade for a little market town. Do you think the locals would be pleased to see their windfall outlawed?"

"But what about the birds, and how immoral it is to wager on another creature's life!"

"I'll tell Lady Ponsonby to pray for their souls. Listen, Jacelyn, whatever notion you're entertaining, get rid of it. This isn't like playing ducks and drakes with Squire. These are rough, violent men. It would be dangerous to interfere with them in any way. Do you understand?"

"I understand you won't help." She was disappointed and disillusioned. As for Leigh, he wanted to shake her.

"Jacey, I am not a Farthingale to parrot every opinion you make, and I won't agree with you when you're wrong. I cannot think your thoughts, nor vice versa. And this time you are wrong. It's sad, sweetheart, I know it is, but you can't save every fallen sparrow, and you cannot change the world singlehandedly."

"Then why did you volunteer to fight Bonaparte, and stay so long? Did you think he wouldn't be defeated, else? Yet you were only one man!"

"I was only one man, but there was a whole army beside me. You are one woman. You cannot take on a whole cockpit!"

It was easy for Jacelyn to discover the location of the cockfight, some few miles outside of London along the Great North Road, and to watch for the crossroads signs at Upper Dene's Landing. The young Corinthians were speaking of nothing else, though once she had the information she needed, Jacelyn refused to discuss it further. One overeager enthusiast kept at it, till she told him to go find a like-thinking friend, put bladed spurs on, flap their arms up and down, and try to cut each other to shreds. It would be better sport! When the man laughed at her "wit" she walked off the dance floor, claiming a ripped flounce.

She didn't even have a flounce, but she went to

the ladies' retiring room anyway, to get away from the chatter and music, and think. She wasn't sure what she could do about the cockfight. That was for later. Right now she had to think about Leigh. They were friends—he'd said it just last night—although she felt so much more. Claibourne was almost a part of her, sharing all those silent jokes at the silliness around them, touching her hand gently when he sensed she needed reassurance. He was there, for her, this whole night that could have seen her disgraced. It was his stature that had lent her the credit to be a success. So why was she so hurt, so angry, that he couldn't support her in this? Maybe because they were so close, to her thinking, and she was beginning to dream of their being one. Which was foolish, she knew. Even if he loved her with his whole heart, they would still be separate people, with separate beliefs and separate feelings. Even if he loved her . . .

The last dance was another waltz. Leigh considerately asked if she would like to go home, rather than sit it out, but Aunt Amabel was still deep in conversation. Mme. Aubonier and the dowager had left ages ago with Lord Parkhurst, so there was no need to consult their wishes. Jacey wanted to talk to Leigh. She glared at de Silva till he veered off, blowing a mock kiss, and then she turned to the earl.

"I owe you an apology, my lord, for not respecting your opinions. I know I must not expect you to agree with all of mine, yet I am sure you will grant me the right to hold them, no matter how cork-brained. As I must yours."

"I don't have cork-brained opinions, poppet, but thank you. I was afraid you were still angry with me. You know, I can't decide if you are more charming at your most sincere or at your silliest. Come." He took her hand.

"But . . . but, Leigh, I can't dance with you! I haven't been given the nod to waltz, and Aunt Amabel said I would be labelled fast if I did it without permission. And we've already danced twice. You know—"

"I thought we agreed on that at least, that all these silly conventions were so much manure to wade through. Do you want to waltz?"

"Oh yes!"

"With me?"

"Of course!"

"Then come."

A corner of heaven must be reserved for young lovers' first waltzes. It was almost like kissing to music, the way Leigh did it, holding her closer than customary. They were breaking so many rules, one more didn't matter. Nothing mattered to her now, except his warm hand around her, the brush of his thigh against hers, those blue, blue eyes staring into hers like eternity.

It wasn't till the dance was over that he told her he'd gotten approval from Sally Jersey. Sally hadn't even asked for a favour back, thank goodness. Some sacrifices he was willing to let Baron make for him, but there were limits to the others. He didn't discuss any of this with Jacelyn, who was still humming the last refrain. Nor did he mention that the third dance was as good as having the banns read. It was time to go home.

14

The window or the servants' door, that was the question. Coming back through the kitchen in britches would be hard to explain, when the staff might be at their own breakfasts. But the dog couldn't climb trees—up or down—so the rear exit it had to be. On second thought, Jacelyn turned back and opened the window for the return trip. She could always scramble up the tree and leave the dog in the courtyard, saying she'd let Pen out early.

Getting into the stable was no problem; the door facing the rear gardens was always unlatched. She didn't dare open the wide stable doors facing the mews, for the noise would surely wake the grooms asleep overhead, so she led the mare back through the courtyard and out by the small delivery gate. She couldn't latch it behind her, of course, but perhaps it would go unnoticed in the morning's bustle. As for getting the mare back, if the stablehands were awake—well, she'd worry about that later. Perhaps she should have taken

Lem, but he would have argued with her till it was too late to go. Besides, as she'd just written in a long letter to her papa, she had to fight her own battles.

Jacelyn had stayed awake for three hours after sharing her success with a rapturous Pinkie, rather than chance staying asleep past daylight. She filled in the time with writing home. She'd previously told her father about the bareback ride and Richmond, so now she related her experiences at Almack's, and the people she'd met, and how nice most of them were, just as he'd said they'd be. Lord Trevaine's last letter, in his fine angular script, had advised her to look for the best in people, and laugh at the worst, if she could. If she was unhappy, he'd written, she should come home immediately. She made sure he wasn't fretting himself that she was miserable, or that she was so enamoured of this new life that she didn't miss him and Treverly. She also explained to him—and herself—some of the lessons she was learning. She'd always been independent; it was easy in the country. Here in London, where she was never alone, other people had a much greater say in her life. The very trip to London itself wasn't her choice. Now there were so many telling her what she must and mustn't do, where she should and shouldn't go, even whom she should and shouldn't talk to. She felt she was losing part of herself, even more by trusting so fully in Claibourne. She must not let herself become a hollow shell filled with social conventions, nor an empty extension of the earl's will. She'd managed by herself at Richmond; she would manage tonight. What she wrote to her father, without mentioning cockfights or solitary 4:00 a.m. rides, was something to the effect that a man—or woman—had to do what a man had to do, and stand on his own two feet to do it.

Or her mare's four feet, as the case may be.

The ride through London was quick. Her route bypassed the less savoury neighbourhoods she had been warned about countless times, thank goodness, and the Great North Road was wide and clear. There were even some travellers about, mostly draymen and farmers going to market. None paid any mind to the boy in the floppy hat, if they noticed him at all by the moon's uncertain light. She reached the crossing at Upper Dene without incident. A few times she thought she'd heard hoofbeats other than her mare's, but the imagination played tricks on dark nights, she knew. Pen never signalled anything untoward so she'd kept riding. Now here she was at the five-fingered crosstie, trying to stand on the mare's saddle to change the direction signs.

Pen was off in the bushes and the mare was fidgety and Jacelyn couldn't quite reach. Every time she got her hands on the Little Dene marker, the horse took a step ahead, or tried to put her head down, or whuffled nervously. Jacelyn then had to sit down and pull the horse back into position, all while she kept looking over her shoulder. It was spooky out here, alone, miles from home, in the dark. She stood in the saddle again, wishing it were Baron's back. His was rock-steady and a lot taller. That sign was high, she was short. "Drat."

"Need some help, sweetheart?" asked a voice from behind the bushes, followed quickly by Jacelyn's shriek, then Pen's barking.

"You . . . you bastard! What do you mean, sneaking up on me, scaring me half to death!" Jacelyn sputtered as the earl slowly, casually, walked over to her and her horse.

"What I'd meant to do, you widgeon, was throw the fear of God into you. What in bloody hell are you doing out here with only your overgrown rug rat for protection, when I specifically told you how dangerous it was?"

Avoiding the question, more than a little nervous at the harsh expression on his usually smiling face, to say nothing of his hand steadily tapping a riding crop against his leg, she countered: "What in . . . bloody hell are *you* doing here?"

"I am following my instincts, which right now tell me to use this"—the whip—"where it will do the most good."

She shivered. Lord, he meant it! This wasn't Squire's burning fury, nor her father's warm, sorrowful regard. This was cold, hard anger. She'd never seen anything like it in the easygoing earl, and she didn't want to see any more of it. She pulled her horse back.

"Stay." She stayed. "Miss Trevaine, did you ever, I repeat, *ever*, stop to consider that you might be in danger, riding around the streets of London by yourself?"

"I did think of it, my lord. No one would bother a poor boy off on an errand."

"Not even a poor boy on a rich man's horse? You foolish little innocent. No one bothered you, my *lady*, because I was a block behind, with a pistol very visible in my waistband. Otherwise you would not have gotten past Portman Square."

"You . . . you followed me from Parkhurst House?"

"To my dismay, I find I am beginning to understand how that hare brain of yours works. Your charming apology didn't quite answer; it never said you'd give up, even if it was a hen-witted idea. Therefore, yes, I followed you, lest someone break your sweet little neck before I got a chance to!"

As he took two steps closer to her, Jacelyn began to speak, quickly: "My lord, I can see where you might be a trifle overset—"

"Hah!"

"—since you are responsible for me, and your aunt is sponsoring me, but you *must* understand that I couldn't *not* do something about the cockfight."

"I must?" He took another step, but the whip tapping was, at least, less frequent.

"Remember what you said about saving every

fallen sparrow? I know I cannot even come close, but what if I could save even *one* rooster? Wouldn't that be worth trying? And I did listen to you. I would have gone to Dene's Landing in the morning and demanded they call off the fight, but for what you said about all the rough folk."

"Thanks for small favours, puss."

Ah, he was back to the pet names. His "Miss Trevaine" was more chilling than the threats. "And I thought of going there tonight and freeing the birds . . . if I could find the place, and if the cocks were there yet, but I decided that would be too dangerous also. See, I'm not entirely fool-hardy."

"Do you know about the simpleton who jumped off the bridge after the ha'penny he dropped? He was clever enough to remove his boots, but he still couldn't swim."

"It's nothing like! If I could just switch the signposts, I'd ride home and no one would be the wiser."

"Certainly not you," he muttered. Louder, he asked, "What, my sweet, did you hope to accomplish? I can see you mean to confound the London bucks, send them off to . . . where? Upper Dene? Bathny Willow?"

"Actually I was hoping they'd get halfway to Scotland before they realized the mix-up. Lord Forster said most of the men would stay up through the night, at their clubs, rather than have a few hours' sleep. I can only think they'll be somewhat worse for it, by seven or eight."

"Which is all the more reason why this was a chaw-bacon scheme!"

"I won't be here then. Besides, most will be driving too fast, racing their curricles as the sporting group seems to do all the time, so they won't be paying careful attention to the markers."

"That's not to the point. You send a few Town bucks to the rightabout, but you haven't ended the cockfight, or even delayed it."

"I know," Jacelyn admitted sadly, "but it was the best I could think of. I reasoned that the young gentlemen from London had the most money, and the most leisure time. If they weren't there to make their enormous wagers, perhaps it wouldn't be so profitable for the local men, who would then go back to their chores. If there wasn't so much betting, maybe, just maybe, one bird wouldn't have to die for their pleasure. Do you understand?"

"Get down . . . For heaven's sake, stop looking like a frightened rabbit. I'm not going to beat you. Yet. You can reach the signs from Baron's saddle." He whistled for the stallion while she dismounted, then lifted her up.

"This is another crime against the Crown, you know," he remarked casually from the ground as she tugged and twisted at the fingerposts. "I'm not sure where it ranks in relation to kidnapping, but you are certainly turning out to be the felonious sort, aren't you? You know, my dear," he added just when she finished, "I think it's time you learned that crime doesn't pay."

Jacelyn thought of adding another misdemeanor: stealing the horse she was on and riding away as fast as she could. Baron would come to Leigh's whistle, though, even if she weren't standing upright. She stayed where she was, but Leigh walked around the horse and, reaching up, grasped her firmly around the knees.

"Yes," he said, "it's long past time you learned that your womanhood won't always protect you from the results of your follies."

He lifted her off the horse, then down the length of his own body to the ground, still in his arms. He brought his mouth down to hers in a fierce kiss, while his arms tightened around her till their bodies touched everywhere. The kiss went on and on, and where his hands or his lips didn't touch she ached for him.

At last he raised his head, but still held her cheek pressed against his chest. "Oh, Lord," she heard him groan, through the smooth fabric of his jacket, and over the blood thundering in her own ears. "What was the deuced lesson?"

"Listen to this, George. Jacelyn writes that they are calling her "Miss Trevaine, the Toast of the Town.' What do you think of that?" Lord Trevaine turned the sheets of his daughter's latest letter while Squire sipped his wine and studied the chessboard.

"To be honest, Elliot, I wouldn't believe a word of it, if m'sister hadn't written the same thing."

"I'm having difficulty crediting it myself! My Jacelyn, in her pigtails and boy's clothes, always in some bumblebath . . . curtseying to the Queen. My sister Amabel says she did it gracefully, too. Jacelyn writes that she had no time for her own spasms over the hooped skirts, she was so afraid Amabel would succumb to the vapours and swoon dead away."

"Damned foolishness, if you ask me," said Squire, capturing Trevaine's bishop.

"I agree, and so does Jacelyn. She says that she enjoyed the literary evening at Miss Kinbeck's much better, but that Amabel fell asleep."

"Shouldn't wonder. I always told you the girl didn't need all that fancy book learning you kept spoon-feeding her. Isn't she going to any balls and such? That's all Clothilda ever writes about. Who danced with Priscilla, who sent flowers. Mrs. Bottwick's interested in that piffle. Says it'll help next year when my Samantha makes her curtsey. Not looking forward to it, all that doing the pretty."

"Indeed, there seems to be a great deal of that. Listen: 'In the week since Almack's I've hardly spent two hours at home, except to change my clothes and sleep. There are so many invitations Mme. Aubonier and Aunt Amabel have long arguments over which should be accepted. Claibourne and I have had to delay our morning rides and

Pen's exercise until after ten, we get home so late. Friday we had tea at Miss Montmorency's, dinner at Lady Hockney's, attended the Royal Theatre (an undistinguished *Richard the Third*) and then went on to two different balls! I need more gowns, Papa, but Mr. Sprague assures me my account is still solvent.' "

"Hell and blast, they never have enough gowns. Be thankful you've only the one daughter, and that one discovered fripperies late in life. For a female, anything over the age of five is late! Lord, what it's cost me in India muslin already, I could have bought the whole deuced East India Company."

"You'll be interested in this, I'm sure: 'I've been helping my friend Rhodine alter her gowns also. You'll remember I wrote about her. She's the over-dressed girl with the sweet nature and the evil fairy-tale stepmother. Except Lady Tina is a real dasher! Anyway, I think dear Rhodine and Arthur will suit perfectly, and they seem to agree! He is very solicitous of her, and she doesn't mind!' Have you heard anything about this from your sister?"

"Yes, and she wasn't best pleased at first, I can tell you. No money there. Endicott's run aground, they say, gambling. The girl wasn't much either, though Clothilda says she's coming along, whatever that means. She wrote Mrs. Bottwick that rumour says Spenborough might come down heavy, if he likes the match. M'sister's reconciled to it, she says, if Arthur's set on having the girl."

"It sounds like it: 'Arthur now rides with us in

the mornings, along with half the Corinthian set, so there's no more riding astride' "—Squire snorted—" 'and he spars with Lord Claibourne at Cribb's or Jackson's, for the exercise. I can only hope this is to impress Rhodine, and is a good sign.' "

"Exercise, eh? That does sound serious. Does she say anything else about the girl? Part of the family, don't you know."

"Let me see . . . no. She did mention in her last letter that Lady Rhodine was coming out in the carriage most afternoons, and she was getting used to Penelope, but still had no liking for horses."

"Pah! Trust that coxcomb of a nephew of mine to find a shrinking violet. But a duke's granddaughter . . . What else does she say?"

"Hm, she writes that her Aunt Amabel took to her bed for three days after the dowager left."

"Parkhurst's mother? That old curmudgeon still around? Cads, she was a tartar when I was a boy on the Town! How did your spitfire deal with her? Like fire and ice, I'll wager."

"Quite the contrary. Lady Parkhurst introduced Jacelyn all around as her granddaughter, or as near as she'd get since that 'twiddlepoop Parkhurst' never provided her with one."

"That sounds like the old bat. You have to give your girl credit. An old besom like that would eat my girls alive. That Frenchie aunt of Claibourne's didn't seem any too accommodating either. How is

234

that working out?"

"Seems ideal. Jacelyn has the fondest regard for her, and even her maid. We didn't see the woman, but Jacey's first letter had her carved in granite. Now they all rub along nicely. Mme. Aubonier has taken Jacelyn to tea with some of the old French aristocrats living in London, and she said I'd be proud of her French now. One old *vicomte* had the girl in alt, last letter. Didn't I read that one to you? It's right here. He was one of the wealthiest men in France; now he's teaching music. Jacelyn was so impressed with his exquisite manners and his courage that she's determined to have her friend Miss Montmorency 'discover' him to her musical friends."

"So your girl seems to have found her feet. I'm glad, Elliot. Nasty business, that was."

"I was worried myself. It seems to be going smoothly and yet . . ."

"And yet there's still no betrothal notice."

"Nor does she mention Claibourne much except by name. 'We go to Covent Garden tonight with Claibourne,' or 'Today Claibourne and I saw the waxworks,' like that, nothing more."

"What do you think it means?"

"You're the one with three daughters, you tell me!"

"It wouldn't matter if I had twenty-three, I'd be danged if I'd understand a one of 'em. And that goes double for *your* daughter. Check."

From rout to ridotto and from balloon ascension to Venetian breakfast, London's newest star was busy every minute, mostly in Claibourne's company, but never solely in Claibourne's company. Mme. Aubonier or Aunt Amabel was always along, or Pinkie during the day, when a young lady was considered less vulnerable. Leigh and Jacey hadn't been alone together since that morning after Almack's, weeks before.

Neither mentioned that kiss, though both carried the memory like a bouquet. And neither mentioned the betrothal Lord Trevaine and Squire Bottwick were so troubled about. Aunt Amabel, Great-aunt Simone, Pinkie, Lem, and Arthur could be added to the concerned list—and all of London to the curious. Claibourne swore he would give Miss Trevaine what was left of her first Season, to be a belle, to enjoy herself, and to reconcile herself to the marriage. He wanted so much more than that, but he would woo her and wait. Even if it killed him. It had to be her choice.

As for Jacelyn, it had to be love. It had to be mutual. The affection was there, she knew, and the attraction. The last was obvious. So many tiny sparks were kindled by even the most casual touch between them, she was surprised no one else noticed. But there was no talk of love. She thought of asking him outright, but even her candid nature quailed at the idea of hearing his affected London drawl say, "What's that to the point, poppet?" or some such. There was no one else to consult, either. She resolved again, as she had almost every day, to accept what she had, his comfortable friendship and his charming company.

He spent so much time with her, doing the pretty as Squire would say, that one day she had to ask, "Leigh, haven't you anything better to do with your time than escort me all over London?"

"You wound me, Miss Trevaine. Are you tired of my company so soon?"

"Silly. I mean, are you bored, or am I keeping you from something important?"

"What could be more important, rosebud? No, you see a man of leisure, your typical London loiterer at your service. Unless you'd rather I filled my afternoons with lewd women, in addition to my late evenings."

"Gammon. Arthur says you go to your clubs with him at night."

"You mean I really am a reformed rake? Arthur would know. Now that he's *cap-à-pie* over Lady Rhodine, he's become even more fusty."

"If possible!"

"If possible. You know, kitten, I have been thinking of a worthwhile occupation for my time, now that I am become so upright. Not that Lady Cowper's amateur theatricals, et cetera, aren't worthwhile or anything, but I've been considering taking my seat in the House of Lords. Your uncle has mentioned it, and Sprague, of course. What would you think of going with me one afternoon next week to see the great statesmen of our time in action, so I might see if it's too dull even to consider."

When they approached Sprague, he was delighted to be of assistance. A friend of his, in fact, was giving a speech next week which Sprague had helped draught, and he would be pleased if Claibourne and Miss Trevaine would be his guests in the visitor's gallery. Lord Medford Broome's speech was in favour of a bill protesting the plight of child labourers in the mills, and it stood almost no chance of passage. Lord Parkhurst hadn't felt he could sponsor such a doomed measure; therefore Sprague had worked with his friend Broome. Sprague mentioned to Jacelyn that he had been thinking of inviting Miss Ponsonby; what did Jacelyn think? She had to tell him, honestly, regretfully, that she didn't think Priscilla would be interested, at all. He nodded in resignation. He didn't think so either, unfortunately.

The gallery was almost empty when the two men, Jacelyn, and her maid attended. So was the floor of the chamber. The few members who'd bothered to appear wore robes and wigs. A few were asleep. Most were chatting among themselves like ladies at tea, or reading the newspapers, or writing notes. No one seemed to be listening as the earnest young man stood to address the assembly. Jacelyn, for one, was not impressed with Parliamentary procedure. She was, however, thoroughly impressed by what Lord Broome was saying, and soon forgot the rest of the audience. Broome spoke of children working ten-hour shifts. Of tiny girls set to bobbins, because their hands were small. Of little boys sent to work underground, because the shafts needn't be so large, then. He spoke of huge, deafening factories, where six-year-olds spent their short lives, without breathing any but poisoned air, without seeing the sun. The money they traded their childhoods for? It wouldn't even buy them a piece of the fine linen they wove, much less decent, nourishing meals.

Pinkie was quietly weeping, thinking of her little brothers, who might have been forced to the mills too, if not for her wages. A muscle in Claibourne's jaw twitched as Broome declared the situation a national disgrace, perpetuated by greed and indifference. Think of your own boys and girls, Broome said, for you are the fathers of all the nation's children.

He bowed his head and took his seat. There were coughs and shuffled papers as the Upper House prepared for the next speaker, and the same undercurrents of muffled conversations. Then there was applause: a steady, determined clapping by a pair of small hands in tan York kid gloves. After a startled moment, Claibourne joined her, then Sprague and a tear-stained Pinkie. Some of the members on Broome's side of the aisle took up the acclaim, and then those who hadn't even heard the speech. The opposition even added to the ovation, and Lord Broome, red-faced, was being patted on the back and having his hand shaken.

Jacelyn turned to Mr. Sprague and congratulated him. "The speech was marvellous. I'm sure the bill will pass, if not today then soon." She impulsively planted a kiss on his cheek.

As they turned to leave, the earl whispered for Jacey's hearing only: "Were you just putting your mark on him for Samantha's sake, or do I have to worry?"

"You have to see about taking your seat here," she told him. "There's so much to be done."

15

Miss Trevaine was enjoying London to its fullest, and London was enjoying her. Her refreshing candour, her innovative styles, her seeming to do what no other woman had ever done—bring Rake Claibourne to heel—all were chewed over with the morning's chocolate. Except in one house on Mount Street, where the new day began past noon, and where anything as sweet as chocolate was as foreign as a Hottentot. Here Jacelyn wasn't considered delightful, effervescent as champagne, or an exquisite wild rose among London's hothouse beauties, as reported in the papers. Here she was that damned interfering nobody, or Claibourne's cream-pot connexion, or his two-bit tumble. Once she was established and accepted, it was worse. Claibourne would never throw her over now.

"You botched it, you bandy-legged boob. You could have shown the girl for an hysterical hoyden. Now we'll have to go the other route, discredit Claibourne. And the demned cub's been acting the saint, from what I hear."

Percy was sprawled on the sofa as usual, dreamily contemplating the wine in his glass. "La Fleur."

"Stop flogging a dead horse, boy!" Fenton didn't even notice when Percy's wince caused the wine to overflow down his shirtfront. "Claibourne hasn't been next or nigh that jade in months."

Percy was busy mopping at himself with his loosened cravat. When he finished, his hands automatically retied the now-splotched neckcloth into its usual crooked, droopy knot.

His father looked on in disgust. "Well," he said, "what are you going to do about it?"

"I'm going to see they meet again, Claibourne and La Fleur."

"You slack-jawed jackanapes, it'll take more than a meeting between the cub and his old doxy to get the Trevaine tart up in the boughs."

"I know that, governor, I ain't as stupid as you think."

"You couldn't be, boy, you couldn't be."

Percy ignored this. He smiled and went on: "They'll meet at the theatre 'n everyone will see."

"So what if they are seen together? You've got to show he's a womanizer, a rakeshame, not that he's polite enough to greet his ex-mistress. Besides, how do you know they're going to meet at the theatre?"

"That fellow Kean's doing Shakespeare Friday. You know, the one the toffs make such a fuss about. *Macbeth? Hamlet?* One of those, no matter. Claibourne will be going, mark my words. That chit's bookish, remember. And Miss La Fleur has box tickets. I made sure of that."

"Well, well. I didn't think you had it in you. You mean you're actually on terms with the woman, to know her engagements? Maybe we'll come about after all, if she cooperates."

"Not exactly. I've been standing her doorman a few rounds now and then, so I know what's what." Percy swallowed what was left in his glass, then undid the neckcloth again to use its ends as a napkin. He belched, then grinned. "She said good day yesterday, though. It's a start."

"Percy, your nursemaids didn't just drop you on your head; they must have played Albert-Had-an-Apple, with you as the ball."

Jacelyn was already disturbed on the afternoon of the theatre party, and it had nothing to do with Percy's machinations, or even Claibourne. Strangely enough, it was concern for Priscilla Ponsonby that was discomfitting Miss Trevaine.

The afternoon's carriage ride had seen Jacelyn and Rhodine riding with Mme. Aubonier and Monsieur Blanc, as the *vicomte* turned music teacher now called himself. Arthur and Claibourne rode alongside for awhile, until the flow of traffic forced them apart. Jacelyn saw Claibourne ride to pay his respects to Lady Tina, Rhodine's stepmother, where that elegant auburn beauty was posed artistically in her pink-satin-lined coach under a stand of trees. Arthur had joined a group around a showy phaeton, where Priscilla was perched on the high seat next to the driver, Lord Anton-Fredricks. Priscilla was tittering shrilly, although whether her nervousness was real or put on for the effect, Jacelyn didn't know. The phaeton was a spindly, fragile thing, no doubt fast, and assuredly dangerous. If Priscilla wanted to risk her neck in such a perilous contraption so the sporting gentlemen would admire her, well, that was Priscilla's choice, wasn't it?

Then Monsieur Blanc held up his looking glass. "That is Lord Malcolm Anton-Fredricks, from Lancashire, *non?*"

"Yes it is," Rhodine answered, "and the beautiful lady with him is Arthur's sister, Miss Priscilla Ponsonby."

"This Miss Ponsonby, she is very wealthy?"

Mme. Aubonier told him in rapid French, to save Rhodine's blushes, that the family was respectable, the girl had a decent portion, but there was more pride than substance.

"If Miss Ponsonby is not very, very wealthy, she has more to worry about than that so precarious equipage," the old gentleman told them.

There was a man in Lancashire, it seemed, Chater by name, was a wealthy mine owner. Monsieur related this, not to carry tales out of school, they must know, but for family. Chater was of the bourgeoisie, better than most. His mines did not collapse as often as others'. Chater wished to better himself, and his family status. To this end he hired a music teacher for his talented daughter, the best instructor he could find, Blanc. The girl had a pleasing touch, but her hands were too small. *Enfin.*

While Monsieur Blanc resided under Chater's roof, the wealthy capitalist contracted a marriage for his daughter with the son of a minor nobleman in the vicinity . . . Lord Malcolm Anton-Fredricks. Blanc had played the organ at the wedding in the local church, at Miss Chater's fond request. In the last letter the new Lady Anton-Fredricks had written, she was practicing her scales diligently, while awaiting the birth of her first child, next spring. Perhaps, she'd added, Monsieur would see her husband in London; Anton-Fredricks was attending Parliament to look after Mr. Chater's interests in labour laws or such.

Rhodine had her hand to her mouth, so it was left to Jacelyn to exclaim, "That swine! That scum! I feel like going right over and telling Priscilla and the others."

"You mustn't, Jacelyn! Oh, please don't! Arthur will have to call him out, you know he will. And Arthur could get hurt, or arrested, or . . . or killed."

"Sh, Rhodine, we won't let Arthur challenge him. But Priscilla has to be warned. She—"

"Pah!" Aunt Simone put in. "That one would

not thank you, *petite*. She likes playing with the fire. *Tiens*, I think a small lesson might do her some good. The Season has only a few weeks left to it, then we all go home, no? And Anton-Fredricks goes to be a papa, and Miss Ponsonby polishes her beauty for the spring Season. Maybe no longer too proud to consider a man of true values, no?"

"Carter Sprague? But the humiliation, *Belletante,* if anyone finds out! I just don't know what's right to do!"

Jacelyn was still undecided by the first curtain that evening at Drury Lane. She wondered if she should discuss it with Leigh during the farce, which no one listened to, or even sat down for. There were so many people coming and going in the box the Parkhursts and the Ponsonbys shared, however, that there was no opportunity for privacy. Farthingale stopped by, acting as if he'd never seen a pink gown before. Jacey's deep rose velvet from Ryefield was regal, perfectly fitted, but utterly unadorned. She wore only her mother's pearls, and a single white rose in the shining coils of her chestnut hair, for contrast. Claibourne wore his relaxed, amused expression, but Jacelyn noticed that he put his arm across the back of her seat while Farthingale rhapsodised about her celestial beauty. "Fustian" was all he said, though, when the viscount left. Lord Tayson silently handed Jacelyn a pink rose, which quite ruined the effect of her gown, but she tucked it into her hair next to the white one, anyway. Tayson blushed, bowed, and left, obviously too overcome by the full box. The *Conde* de Silva visited, weighted with gold braid, diamonds, and compliments so grandiose they could all laugh. Even the young politician, Lord Broome, came to pay his respects, and ended up losing his heart to the lovely young woman who was so enthusiastic over his cause.

Lady Endicott stopped by, to check on her "dearest Rhodine," who was totally ignored as Lady Tina usurped the chair next to Leigh.

"We're old friends, you know," she told Jacelyn, who was staring at that lady's bare arm resting on Claibourne's satin-covered thigh. A lot of the rest of the lady was equally bare. When she left, Jacelyn whispered to the earl, "How come you almost outdid the grandee in your flattery of Lady Tina, and you only told me I looked charming?"

"Because she is nothing without her outward appearance. You would still be your exquisite self no matter what you wore. And stop pouting, or I'll put you to the blush by telling you exactly how I'd like to see you dressed . . . or not."

At least she didn't have to worry about Leigh, not tonight, thank goodness, because through all of this, all the mock courtships and friendly banter, Priscilla was flirting with Anton-Fredricks.

It almost turned Jacelyn's stomach to hear Priscilla's lisp and "La, sirs," and to watch her flutter her fan and her eyelashes at him. The more gentlemen who came to the box to greet Jacelyn, the shriller Priscilla's voice seemed to get; the more heady the compliments to Miss Trevaine, the more coquettish Priscilla's behaviour. Jacelyn could *not* let her make such a cake of herself over such a libertine. As the lights were dimmed before the first act of the major play, Anton-Fredricks was sucking each of Priscilla's fingers in farewell. Ugh. Jacelyn had to warn the other girl. After that, Priscilla could make her own choice.

The play was *Othello,* and the great Edmund Kean was playing the evil Iago. Last month, Jacelyn understood, he'd played the title role. The man was amazing, but she kept seeing Anton-Fredricks as the double-speaking standard-bearer. Watching poor Othello's unravelling, she was glad she wasn't the suspicious type. Jealousy was such a terrible thing.

When the curtain came down the applause rose like a wave, a uniformed footman brought a four-folded note to the box on a silver tray. It was for Claibourne, who unfolded it while the others watched curiously.

"Nothing wrong, I trust," Arthur commented.

"No, not at all," Leigh replied, refolding the note and placing it in his inside coat pocket. "Just an old friend who asks me to visit during the interval. Will you excuse me, my dear?" he asked Jacelyn, and left.

When Arthur and Rhodine also went out, to get

refreshments for the ladies Parkhurst and Ponsonby, Jacelyn was too concerned with her planned conversation with Priscilla to wonder why Leigh hadn't taken her along. If she could only speak to Priscilla before all the chitter-chatter began again and—Speak of the devil.

"Lord Anton-Fredricks, I hate to impose, but could I trouble you to procure me a lemonade? Claibourne was called away, and I have a terrible thirst. You'd like one too, wouldn't you, Priscilla? Oh no, you mustn't go off with Lord Malcolm and leave me alone. Besides, it's been such a long time since we've had a comfortable coze."

Priscilla was glaring. As soon as the gentleman unctuously bowed himself out, she snapped: "What are you trying to do, Miss Hobbledehoy, steal this beau of mine too? You have nearly every man in London at your feet. Isn't that enough?"

"Be still, Priscilla, I have something to tell you. I feel I have to give you warning, as a friend. It's . . . it's about Anton-Fredricks. He's only trifling with you, Priss. His . . . his affections are already committed elsewhere. I felt it best to tell you, rather than—"

"Why, you jealous little cat," Priscilla hissed, her eyes narrowing. "How dare you! You're only telling these nasty lies so I'll stop throwing him lures and you can step in. You spiteful brat, how would you like to hear some home truths, hm? Just look over there at the 'old friend' your precious earl had to visit."

249

She directed Jacelyn's view across the horseshoe-shaped theatre. Jacelyn could recognize Leigh's broad back, narrow waist and tousled blond curls anywhere. The lady alone in the box with him she'd never seen before. Full-figured, raven-haired, red-mouthed, she had a diamond the size of an ostrich egg nesting between her breasts. If the fullness of the woman's bosom was any indication, the blasted thing would hatch soon!

"*Who is she?*" she squawked. "Surely Leigh knows many women."

"He knows them all, Miss Greenhead! This one has always been one of his favourite bits of muslin. La Fleur, she's called. The flower's a bit past bloom, I'd say, but there's no accounting for a man's taste. The *on dit* is that he's always welcome at her house in Islington, no matter that she's another man's mistress. He used to stay there sometimes when he was in London on leave, before he and Arthur took lodgings together. They even say La Fleur purchased his army commission for him." Priscilla gave the dart a moment to sink in, then she rammed it home: "So you don't have to worry about his pride, Jacey, he's used to living off his women's money. Even if they earn it on their backs."

Jacelyn was too stunned to move. She wasn't sure what she was thinking about Leigh and this . . . this Cyprian, for she could now tell that the woman was no lady. The way the two were laughing, and touching, they were far more than

250

friends. Her mind refused to focus, though, only backing to the beginning. "But Priscilla, Anton-Fredricks is—"

"Mine, and you better remember that. Look to your own, Jacelyn Trevaine, before you start making accusations. Here's another 'friendly warning,' all in the family. Watch out for your earl and Lady Tina. Dear little Rhodine's stepmama has been his flirt for the last six months. You knew he was a rake, didn't you? Or didn't anyone tell you what that meant? I'm sure you can figure it out for yourself now." She got up to leave. "One more thing: If you tell your Banbury tales about Malcolm to my mother or Arthur or *anyone,* I'll tell all of London how you spent the night alone in the gardener's cottage with Claibourne. They've overlooked the whispers because of your connexions, but they'll listen if I shout it loudly enough, you can wager on that. See how popular you are then, Miss Trevaine."

Jacey sat, turned to stone. It surely was a good thing she wasn't the jealous type.

There was a bit of confusion in that other box when Leigh walked in and Mr. Farley Unger discreetly left on an errand.

"You mean you didn't send this note, Flo?"

"Lord love a duck, pet," answered La Fleur, Flora Cobb. "My writing's better than that. And I wouldn't put any silly little flower by the name, neither, not to you, Leigh. 'Sides, you should have known I'd never send for you like that, not with your pretty little miss sitting over there, nor Mr. Unger sitting here." She fingered the boulder on her chest. "He's a diamond importer, is Mr. Unger."

"I'm sorry, Flo, truly I am. I did think it must have been urgent for you to ask for me here, so of course I came. I'll explain to Mr. Unger, if you wish, that we seem to be the victims of a hoax."

"No need to worry about Unger. If I can't handle a middle-aged merchant, my name's not La Fleur."

"It's not!"

"So there!"

They both laughed at this foolishness, then Claibourne said, "Since I'm here anyway, Flo, it's good to see you. You're looking as ravishing as ever, but is everything well with you?"

"Nothing's wrong that a little more money and a few less birthdays wouldn't cure."

"Are you in trouble? I don't have much of the ready, but I could—"

"Go on, Leigh. You save your guineas to buy that girl something pretty. If you want me to talk to Mr. Unger for you, just let me know. No? Well, I hear she's a real charmer, and I wish you happy, indeed I do."

"Thank you, Flo. I think I will be. You take care of yourself now, and if you ever do need anything . . ."

"You always were the sweetest, even when you didn't have two coppers to rub together. Oh, Leigh, before you go, you know that cousin of yours?"

"Percy? Don't tell me you know Percy Fenton? I've been looking for him for weeks."

"Have you? If he's the queer nabs I think he is, I know where you can find him."

"Really tall, skeleton-thin, slept-in fancy clothes, a nose like a turkey vulture's, and more money than brains. With Percy, it would only take a shilling. And he's always in his cups."

"That's him, all right. He's been weaving up and down my street for weeks now, days and nights. Sometimes he sits on the bench across the way for hours; sometimes he just passes out in the street. He's been giving my man Remington money, so I make Rem pay for the hackney to get the poor cawker home. He'd catch his death of cold out there, castaway, if the pickpockets or press gangs didn't get him, or the watch. 'Sides, it's off-putting for my guests."

"I'm sure. What does he pay your man *for*, though, Flo? I can't figure what he's about."

"No more can I. At first he wanted to come up, but I'm not currently receiving gentleman callers. Except for a few dear friends, of course. Then he wanted to know if you'd been around. That's why I thought he might be that cousin. Remington knows not to tell any more than he has to, to cover the hackney fare. I pay him plenty enough

253

as it is. This week he told the poor bastard I'd be coming to the theater." She waved a hand around expansively. "Everyone in London is here, so it was no secret. . . . I bet the nodcock's the one what sent the note getting you here. And I just thought he was a harmless mooncalf on the go."

"He is, for the most part. He used to be, anyway. I think he's up to some devilishly queer business now, though. If he shows up again, you might mention that I'm looking for him. That should chase him away. Otherwise you can always send for me if he's a problem."

"If I can't handle a cup-shot cawker, my name's not La Fleur!"

"Flo, it's no wonder I love you. I'll stop by soon to see what Percy's up to."

Claibourne returned to the box just as the curtain was going up for the second act. At the next intermission he noticed that Jacelyn was pale and quiet.

"Do you feel all right, dear heart? Would you like to walk in the corridor where it's cooler? Shall I send for the carriage?"

She waved away his concern. "It's only the play and Mr. Kean. So affecting, don't you know."

The play was finally over. Instead of applauding madly like everyone else, Jacelyn just kept weep-

ing, for poor mad Othello and sweet Desdemona—
and herself. Jealousy was such a terrible thing!

16

"Aunt Amabel, I have to talk to you." It was the next morning. Jacelyn had sent a message down to the stables for Claibourne, saying she was too fatigued to ride. Of course she was tired; she hadn't slept at all last night. Now she was trying to get her aunt to listen to her, never an easy thing before noon. Poor Lady Parkhurst was doing her best to look alert, peering owlishly up from the bedclothes through the frills of her lace cap.

"Yes, dear, what is it? Um, what time is it?"

"That doesn't matter. Aunt, you have to tell me something. Are all men unfaithful to their wives? And if a man is unfaithful *before* she's his wife, does that mean he doesn't care for her at all? Aunt Amabel? Aunt Amabel!"

Jacelyn rushed to the door, calling for Davis, milady's dresser, to come quickly, with the smelling salts. The second footman Eugene, he of the easy morals and roving eye, was carrying the first of the day's floral tributes upstairs, so he ran to help.

Jacelyn slammed her aunt's door in his face. "Not you!"

Next Jacelyn approached Mme. Aubonier, who placed a finger, not a marker, in her book, to show the interruption would be brief. This was between Jacelyn and Leigh, she told the girl.

"You knew he was a man for the ladies; you know he is a man of his word. Take your anguish to him to resolve, *chère,* and stop bothering old ladies. Such romantic hobbles are for the young."

Leigh returned to Portman Square at eleven, with his curricle and a small nosegay of violets. He was not best pleased to see all the other bouquets on the hall table, awaiting dispersal. Nor was he happy to be told by Marcus that miss was not receiving that morning.

"Damn it, man, this is me, not some jumped-up Johnny Raw. Where is she?"

"I'm sorry, milord. That was Miss Trevaine's message."

"Is she in bed? Is she ill?"

"I couldn't say, milord."

"Well, has the doctor been called?"

"Not to my knowledge, milord."

"You're being damned helpful, Marcus."

"Yes, milord."

Claibourne was undecided. His horses couldn't be kept standing, yet if something was wrong, he had to know.

Marcus was undecided. His employers' interests and the generous earl's interests did not coincide, but where were his own best interests? "If I may suggest, milord, perhaps you would step into the yellow parlour. I believe Mme. Aubonier writes letters there. . . ."

Claibourne strode down the hall, calling back over his shoulder, "Have Lem walk the horses, they're fresh." When he came back out to the hallway a few minutes later, his brow was lowered and his mouth was set in a firm line. "Will you please tell Miss Trevaine that I wish to see her, *at once.*"

"Yes, milord."

Marcus turned to Eugene, rigid at attention next to him. Eugene went up the stairs at a suitably dignified pace and scratched on Jacelyn's door. Pinkie answered, correctly, listened to the message, and shut the door behind Pen, who went downstairs to greet the visitor. The dog, at least, was happy to see Claibourne.

Pinkie repeated Claibourne's request to her mistress.

"He does, does he? You can tell my Lord Claibourne that . . ."

Pinkie opened the door, quickly erased the grin from her face, and whispered to Eugene. He went down the stairs and spoke into Marcus's ear.

Marcus gathered all of his butlerish dignity, as much as he could muster, considering his portly figure, less than adequate hair-covering, and reddish nose, from ensuring the quality of Lord Parkhurst's private stock. Shoulders back, looking past the earl's left ear, Marcus announced: "Miss Trevaine, my lord, says your lordship can go hang."

"Does she? Why, that little—" Claibourne headed toward the stairs, Pen happily circling around him. Marcus blanched; Eugene stepped aside, smartly. Then the earl thought better of it, as his hand closed on the dog's collar. "You may tell your mistress that I shall wait in the parlour for ten minutes while she puts on her bonnet. After that, her dog and I are going for a ride. I am not quite sure when we'll return, possibly this evening, possibly tomorrow."

He led the dog to another parlour, where his aunt was not, and proceeded to feed Pen macaroons from the claw-footed end table, so she would stay with him. "London's no good for females," Leigh told the big dog. "Your mistress is putting on airs, and you are getting fat as a flawn."

The ormolu mantel clock with its silly amorettos didn't seem to be working. Claibourne picked it up and gave it a good shake. It was ticking. Ten minutes to the second, he got up and herded Pen out the parlour door. Marcus silently handed over Claibourne's beaver hat and just as silently opened the front door for his lordship, who marched out, to see Miss Trevaine prettily seated on his curricle's bench, staring straight ahead. She, of course, had gone out the back door and walked around the side of the house, rather than give Claibourne the round.

"Witch," was what Leigh said as he climbed up after Pen and took the reins, signalling for Lem to release the pair's heads.

"Kidnapper," was what Jacelyn said, pulling the dog closer to her side, without turning her face a whit.

Jumping up behind, Lem grinned. Nothing more was said until they reached the park and Lem had charge of the horses again. Jacelyn scrambled down from the high seat as best she was able in her gown's narrow skirt, rather than wait for the earl to lift her down. He ran a hand through his already windblown curls. Where to start?

"Jacelyn, listen. I'm sorry if you were disturbed about my visit with Miss La—deuce take it, her name is Flora Cobb. She is one of my oldest friends, just as I said last night. It would have been discourteous not to answer her invitation, even if she didn't—that's beside the point. She has been very kind to me. She even helped me get my army commission."

"So I heard, my lord, and how she helped you."

"That old story, eh? Let me tell you, my girl, sarcasm and snide remarks aren't becoming."

"How about bare bosoms and dampened skirts and arms that wrapped around you like ivy creepers? You seemed to find that becoming! How do you think I felt when my . . . my escort was

260

fondling some . . ."

"Don't say it."

"Woman."

"I told you she was a friend, Jacelyn. I shouldn't have to listen to this."

"What about Lady Tina? Another *friend?* You slobbered over her a good half hour!"

"Lady Endicott too? Good grief, Jacelyn, if I seem familiar with these females, it's just out of habit. I'm used to holding a lovely woman, that's all. It doesn't mean anything. It's only among the debutante set where men and women can't touch except to dance. A man's used to these easy affections."

"You're what? You . . . you lecher!"

This was too much for the earl, who'd been valiantly trying to maintain his composure. He felt badly about Flora, but wouldn't have acted any differently. As for Tina Endicott, he'd thought her obvious lures amusing; Jacelyn obviously hadn't. But to be called a lecher when he'd been living like a monk for two months—and not enjoying the experience—was past his limit.

"Listen, you little shrew, I won't be subject to the Inquisition every time a woman smiles at me, nor vice versa. I told you I would honour you, and that had dashed well better be the end of it! I won't live my life as a Cheltenham tragedy, and I won't answer to you!"

He was really angry now, surprising even himself with his raised voice. Unlike the mercurial Jacelyn, who was always in the boughs over something, then just as quickly all sunshine and smiles, it took a great deal to upset the earl enough to lose his temper. Like that whole table filled with bouquets from Jacelyn's admirers. He wanted to shake her!

"While we're at it, Miss Trevaine, what about your own behaviour? How do you think I feel watching every fribble in Town fawn at your feet?"

"What do you mean?"

"I mean that herd of wet-eared calves you don't wean away. For a girl who didn't know how to flirt just last month, you've done admirably, and I don't like it above half."

"How dare you!" She was rigid, hands clenched at her sides. With the fist, Arthur'd said, not the open palm. Claibourne stomped out of her reach.

"Poor Tayson's bad enough; that Bartholomew Babe won't go beyond the line, though, nor that Broome speechifier. And de Silva knows it's a game, but that Farthingale fop! It's disgusting how you encourage the man-milliner to dangle on your chain when you are just leading him on."

Words dripping ice, Jacelyn said, "Perhaps I'm not."

"What in hell is that supposed to mean?" he shouted. "Perhaps you're not what?"

"Perhaps I'm not leading him on, you bonehead," she yelled back. "You always said I might find a better man than you."

"Well, you haven't, damn you!"

Well, she hadn't. She took a step back and took a look at him. Even with his arms folded across his chest, his jaw outthrust, his hair all mussed, and his blue eyes glaring at her, he was still devastatingly handsome, even if he reminded her of a terrier picking a fight with the kitchen cat. She supposed she must be the angry feline then, hackles up and hissing. What a pair! She had to laugh at them.

It took a moment before the earl could laugh too, but soon they were smiling sheepishly at each other and what gudgeons they'd been. Leigh gathered her in his arms for a quick hug, and kissed the top of her head before he stepped back.

"Come, precious," he told her, tucking her arm in his and starting to amble about the pathways. It wasn't a fashionable hour to be in the park, thank goodness, he thought, though they did receive one or two curious glances. Had they been shouting that loudly? He laughed again at two of London's luminaries putting on a Punch and Judy show for passersby. "We can do better than this, rosebud. Let's start over, shall we?"

He began with Flora. Yes, she was his lover once, his friend still. When he was sent home to convalesce, she was the one who had taken him in. She'd taken him out of the hotel where he'd lain feverish for days, without anyone having sense enough to send for a physician, and no one else in all of London caring enough to investigate. When the man who was then paying Flora's bills objected, she showed him the door. It was her house, after all. She'd worked hard enough for such independence, for just such occasions. She did not have to "entertain" anyone she didn't wish. As for buying his colours, the rumour was totally unfounded. He'd managed the funds by selling off a hunting box he couldn't afford to maintain anyway. Flo's protector at *that* time, however, was an Austrian baron, an officer with the Allied Forces, and a comrade of then General Wellesley. As a favour to Flo, he put in word enough to get the new officer appointed to the general's own staff. "He was a fine gentleman. I named my horse after him, in appreciation.

"As for Tina Endicott," he went on, "the woman is a born flirt. She'll never be any different. If I once accepted what she was offering . . ." He shrugged. "I cannot apologise. I can only repeat that it was before I met you. I shall never disgrace you, and you'll have to trust me for that. I can see where it will take time to convince you, with all the gabblemongers, but we can see our way clear, I know."

It was Jacey's turn. "I really did think Farthingale was just paying me court because I'm the fashion this week. You know how he likes to keep up with the styles. If you think he is really forming a *tendre* for me, though, I'll discourage him from the notion as soon as possible. He's a nice boy; I wouldn't want to see his feelings hurt."

"Boy? The jackanapes is three years older than

you, Miss Maturity. Besides, how are you going to dislodge him without wounding his pride? You make it sound so easy."

"It is, with people who only care about outward appearances, like Farthingale. You'll see."

"Looking forward to it, my dear. There is, ah, one other thing, just to clear the air." He pulled her behind a row of bushes and held her close. "I do love to have a woman in my arms, and that will never change!"

"Just any old woman?" she asked, turning her face up for his kiss.

"Only ones about so high"—kissing the top of her head—"with freckles here . . . and here . . . and here. And lips that taste like . . ."

A short, but not too short, while later the two headed back to the carriage, holding hands.

"You know, puss, how we've had to cancel the trip to Vauxhall Gardens twice because of the rain? What would you think of going tonight? There won't be many more evenings warm enough."

"But we're promised to Lady Manderby's rout tonight."

"There will be five hundred people there, in room enough for fifty. Lady Manderby won't miss us. Wouldn't you rather see Vauxhall's famous Dark Walks, hm, sweetings?"

"Aunt Amabel says I mustn't. Dire things happen to girls who stray down just such primrose paths. What time shall you call?"

The Dark Walks, with their lovers' bowers, the shaved ham and arrack punch, the stupendous fireworks displays, the fairy lights strung from the trees. These were some of the reasons Vauxhall was called London's Pleasure Gardens, and why so many people came. Another reason many of the *belle monde* attended Vauxhall that evening was to escape the crush at Lady Manderby's.

The box Claibourne had rented for their small party was filling up. Lady Parkhurst thought it would be impolite to the Manderbys to renege on her acceptance, so she and her deputised escort, the ever-agreeable Mr. Sprague, waited in the carriage row for half an hour outside the party, inched up the stairwell for another twenty minutes, and shook four hands on the receiving line. When Arthur asked who was on the line besides Lord and Lady Manderby, Aunt Amabel asked back, Who cared? It took another hour to get back down the stairs, have their carriage brought around, and navigate the traffic on Curzon Street. Aunt Amabel was wilted, but had energy enough to describe her travails to all the callers at the box, Jacelyn's usual retinue. An equally exhausted Lady Parkhurst was thankful when Arthur offered her a seat and some punch. Priscilla and her friends would be up shortly, she announced, after they greeted everyone on the esplanade.

It was as good an excuse as any for Claibourne,

eyes twinkling as much as the hanging lanterns, to suggest that he and Jacelyn, Arthur and Rhodine, take a stroll around, before the fireworks. Mme. Aubonier, deep in conversation with Monsieur Blanc, waved them on. Sprague declined playing dogsberry to the two couples, with a laugh, and with Claibourne's permission ordered another supper.

"I didn't think this place would be so large, this close to the city," Jacelyn said, looking around.

"We haven't even seen half," Rhodine told her. "The last time I came we walked the other way, near the boats, where there are all kinds of little tents and booths. You can see a puppet show or have your fortune read or have your eye painted—"

"Ugh! Why would anyone want their eyeball painted?" Arthur exclaimed.

"To give to their lover. I think it's very romantic. Don't you, Jacelyn?"

"I'd rather have my fortune told."

Claibourne laughed. He lowered his voice and solemnly intoned: "Cross my palm, O beauteous maiden, and I will read the leaves. Ah, I see a man . . . tall, dark—oops, fair—and very handsome. He will give you your heart's desire, unless you wish your eyeball painted."

They went merrily on, through the crowds.

"I don't see how these Dark Walks can be very private, with so many people around."

"You should see it on Masquerade Night if you

think this is crowded." A cough and a frown from Claibourne hurried Arthur on: "Of course, Masquerade Night's no place for ladies. Very rough trade here then, you know. Anyone with a shilling can get in, and disguises seem to bring out the worst sorts. You never know if that fellow in the domino is a member of White's or a pickpocket. The, ah, lower orders get rowdy at their revels. No place for a lady. Not at all. Not the thing, you know."

Jacelyn's eyes were shining. "It sounds wonderful! When may we go?"

"Arthur," Leigh informed his friend in disgust, "you are the greatest fool in nature. How could you even think to mention something dangerous, foolhardy, and improper to Miss Trevaine? Haven't you known her long enough?"

"Dashed sorry, Leigh. I forgot."

Jacelyn was pulling on Claibourne's arm. "Oh, don't be so fusty! Say we can go, do! You know the gypsy said you'd give me my heart's desire."

"You cannot believe anything a gypsy tells you! You, madam, with your deuced curiosity, are the perfect illustration of why we got evicted from Eden! Of course I never agreed with that concept. If the Creator was so almighty, He had to be omniscient, so must have known what would happen if He gave Eve the chance. According to Milton, however—"

"I am not going to discuss free will at Vauxhall Gardens! You're just trying to avoid talking about the masquerade. Will you take me, or shall I find someone else to do so?"

"You see that pretty little bench under the tree over there? Why don't we sit and talk about forbidden fruit, hm? Arthur, why don't you and Lady Rhodine find a bench of your own to discuss original sin?"

It didn't take ten minutes. Claibourne promised to get Jacey to the masquerade, if she could slip out of the house, since there was no way either of the aunts would countenance the expedition.

In that same ten minutes Arthur stunned himself by proposing marriage. He was accepted eagerly.

"How wonderful! Let me be the first to congratulate you, old man!"

Jacelyn and Rhodine were already embracing and laughing and weeping. Then Leigh kissed Rhodine's hand, but Jacelyn threw her arms around Arthur in delight. She had to hug Claibourne too, to make things even. "I'm so happy for you both! Can we tell the others? Shall we order champagne to celebrate?"

There were rivers of champagne. Everyone in their box, the surrounding boxes, passing below on the walkway even, was invited to share in the couple's joy. Even Lady Ponsonby unbent enough to permit Rhodine to kiss her cheek.

"You can wipe that cat-in-the-cream look off your face, minx." Leigh smiled softly to Jacelyn. "You didn't do it *all* by yourself, you know."

"Of course not, silly. It's just that they really

love each other, and they'll be so happy. I mean, it's not the marriage of convenience everyone talks about. It's not for money or status or honour, or anything but that they're perfect for each other. *That's* the way it should be." In her excitement, she didn't notice his querying look.

There were at least two people in the box who were not happy to be there, and who didn't care tuppence about the newly affianced pair's happiness. One of these was Malcolm Anton-Fredricks. He didn't like what he read in Claibourne's face, for one thing, and he finally remembered where he'd seen the old man in the back of the box with Claibourne's aunt, for another. There hadn't been a formal introduction, with so many people talking at once, but there was no doubt. Worst luck! He had to get away from here.

The other person who was almost as desperate was Priscilla Ponsonby. She looked around her and saw, not joyous, loving couples, but plainer girls, with less distinguished families and smaller dowries, getting engaged before her, to better catches than she had. That hoyden Jacey, mousy Rhodine, even her friend Marcella Chadwick, who was a simpering ninnyhammer if Priscilla'd ever seen one. They were all nearly settled, whilst she, the Diamond, was still on the shelf. Next Season they'd call her an ape leader . . . if she didn't do something about it tonight. Too bad Farthingale wasn't hanging around Jacelyn as usual; it would have to be Anton-Fredricks. At least he seemed to have a large fortune at his disposal, despite being a mere baronet. Carter Sprague was dismissed instantly. He was a nobody, and too much of a high stickler to fall in with her plans anyway. But what providence! Here was Malcolm asking if Priscilla would like to take a walk, almost as if he could read her mind. Perfect.

"I would be delighted. We can be sure to get good spaces for viewing the fireworks. I *do* enjoy the spectacle so." She addressed the rest of the box: "You'll all be coming along shortly, won't you? It wouldn't do for us to be alone for too long, now would it? Lord Claibourne, do be sure to bring Jacelyn. She won't have seen such a display in Ryefield, or even in her fertile imagination."

"What was that about, my love?" Claibourne asked when Priscilla was gone.

"Nothing much. I tried to warn Priscilla about Anton-Fredricks, that he was,"—she caught Rhodine's unspoken plea—"not worthy of her, but she wouldn't listen."

"You know what they say, Love is blind."

"In this instance it would have to be deaf and dumb as well. I don't think this one is a love match though; I don't think Priscilla is capable of loving anyone but herself. Still, she hadn't ought to be alone in the mawworm's company. Shall we go too? I'm looking forward to the fireworks, no matter what Priscilla said, just like a provincial tourist."

Three or four couples eventually followed Priscilla and Anton-Fredricks down the path toward the cascading fountain, beyond which the fireworks were held. Jacelyn made certain Mr. Sprague came too, simply by tucking her arm in his and pulling. They were going to an entertainment, she teased, not a tryst. They were all laughing and talking loudly enough to be heard over the fountain's noise, when a shrill scream pierced the night.

"By Jove, that sounds like Priss!" shouted Arthur, running down a less well lighted side path. They all hurried after, especially when they could, indeed, recognise Miss Ponsonby's strident: "Unhand me, you brute!"

At the small clearing, Arthur was already Squire-like: redfaced, short of breath, and bellowing. "What in bloody hell is going on here?"

Priscilla was sobbing on the bench, her hands fluttering between the torn lace of her bodice and her disordered curls. Anton-Fredricks, however, was simply dumbfounded. His slicked-back hair was as well oiled as ever, his neckcloth barely crushed.

"What the deuce are you shrieking about, Priscilla? You were enjoying it as much as I was."

Priscilla's sobs grew louder; her shoulders shook. Rhodine ran to put her arms around the other girl, but no one else seemed to know what to do, where to look, though Jacelyn noted that Claibourne appeared more amused than upset as he said, "Your play after all, Arthur."

Arthur was outraged. "The scurvy swine! It's obvious what happened, isn't it? What kind of man would force an innocent girl—"

"I didn't force anything on her, Ponsonby! She led me here and she—"

"That's enough! You cannot get away with this kind of behaviour, not while I've got breath in me to defend my womenfolk! You'll meet me, Anton-hyphen-Fredricks, if you're not too lily-livered to face someone your own size. Leigh, will you second me?"

Rhodine was now sobbing as loudly as Priscilla, on the stone bench. Captain Highet led Miss Chadwick away, commenting, "Disagreeable scene, what? We shouldn't be privy to it at all. Not suitable."

Claibourne put his arm on Arthur's and calmly explained, "It needn't come to pistols for two and breakfast for one, old friend. I think there is a less strenuous method of retrieving Miss Ponsonby's honour than that. You wouldn't want to have to flee the country for killing him, would you? No, I believe Lord Malcolm will be quite content to do the honourable thing. Miss Ponsonby, would a proposal counterbalance the offense?" She sniffed her assent. "You see, Arthur, all right and tight. No need to exert yourself at five in the morning. Anton-Fredricks? You *do* see your way clear?"

His way was clear as mud, but Anton-Fredricks

grunted. He'd be out of London before daybreak one way or another.

Claibourne took the grunt for agreement. "See? No problem. What a night for betrothals. Shall we—yes, my love?"

Jacelyn stopped pulling at his sleeve. "There *is* a problem, Leigh. In Lancashire, with another coming in spring." She glared at the now-furious Lord Malcolm. "Or weren't you going to mention your wife?"

"Wife?" Arthur roared. Priscilla pretended to swoon, right into Carter Sprague's arms.

"Is it true?" Leigh demanded of the greasy baronet and received the smallest of nods. "That does change things a bit. Hold, Arthur. Not with the ladies present. Sprague, would you be so kind as to escort the women back to our box while Lord Ponsonby and I tidy up the grounds here? I'm sure Miss Priscilla would like to go home. . . ." He didn't look back to see that Rhodine and Mr. Sprague supported Priscilla between them, but Jacelyn stayed put. "A moment more, Arthur. You wouldn't want to muss your coat, would you?"

"But, but," Anton-Fredricks spluttered as Claibourne helped Arthur remove his tight jacket and loosen the fitted cuffs of his shirtsleeves. "But what about the duel, pistols, seconds?"

"My, my," Claibourne drawled. "You *do* have a misunderstanding of the social niceties. Duels, old chap, are only for gentlemen."

While the sound of fireworks filled the air, another type of pyrotechnics took place behind the bushes. When Jacelyn couldn't watch any longer, she called out: "Arthur, don't kill him! Think of that poor girl and her baby!" Arthur did, and hit the other man once more for each of them.

Claibourne turned around. "What, you still here, pet? I should have guessed." He faced her in the other direction while Arthur wiped his knuckles. "It's a strange choice, actually, for someone who denounces blood sports."

"I never said vermin shouldn't be eliminated, Leigh. Besides, now you *have* to bring me back for the masquerade. I've missed the fireworks!"

"How is your sister, Arthur?" They were riding in the park late the next morning, and Jacelyn wanted to know how Priscilla was weathering the storm.

"Not as bad as m'mother. She's prostrate, refuses to talk to Priss. She says she'll have to rusticate till next year, at least, before she'll dare show her face in Town. I don't know. Lady Tina's talking of throwing a ball for Rhodine. M'mother would have to come. Maybe not Priss."

"Stuff and nonsense! Another scandal will occur next week, and everyone will forget," Jacey reassured him, which had Claibourne only half jokingly asking what she was planning. "Not funny, my lord. You know, Arthur, if her friends would stand by her . . . Well, I can see that Miss

Chadwick won't be a help, but perhaps one of her other admirers will come forward. For a moment I thought Mr. Sprague might . . ."

He mightn't, it seemed. Priscilla had thrown herself at him till the carriage arrived, according to Aunt Amabel, and he had simply bowed and shut the door on her and her mama, saying he was committed to seeing Lady Parkhurst home. Quite correct, and quite like a man who has finally recognised his idol for what she was: selfish, spoiled, and manipulative. *Vraiment*, Mme. Aubonier had added, Priscilla'd gotten no more than she deserved. Sprague was too nice a young man for her.

". . . But I can see that Priscilla and Carter wouldn't suit anyway. Carter needs a quiet girl who will help him with his career. Priscilla needs a rich, social, shallow—'faith, there's Lord Farthingale! Let's ride over, shall we?"

"Now what was that faradiddle all about, my lady? Since when am I too busy to help you exercise your dog in the park?" Claibourne demanded.

"Since I don't need Farthingale, and Priscilla does!"

"Jacey, men aren't like spigots you can turn on and off, you know. I'm happy to see you hint Farthingale off, and I do think he and Priscilla are well suited. They would spend their days being beautiful together, and save two other unfortunates from being bored to death. I'll even grant you that your motives are admirable, but, my sweet pea-goose, Farthingale is thoroughly smitten with you, and La Ponsonby is currently Priscilla *non grata* in polite circles."

"Minor impediments only. You'll see. No, you won't. You're too busy to ride this afternoon, remember?"

"Of course. Perhaps you ought to remind your fellow conspirator of her role also. For a beast needing so much exercise, Penelope seems quite content to lie by Lem's horse, awaiting our return. That last squirrel almost mistook her for a log and nearly hid a nut under her tail."

"I think she grew bored with the squirrels when she realised she'd never catch one. Leigh, isn't that your friend Miss La Fleur in that barouche over by the fountain?"

He turned in the saddle. "Yes, and her Mr. Unger, the jewel merchant. Very handy occupation, that. Flo thought that he would give me a bargain, but I'd like you to see the Claibourne diamonds first. We could have them reset or—"

"Leigh, will you introduce me?"

"To Mr. Unger? I'm sure Rundell and Briggs is handier for your shopping, pet."

"No, to Miss La Fleur, Miss Cobb. She sounds like such a generous, kind-hearted person, I'd like to know her."

"Of all your strange and varied whimsies, dear

heart, this is one of your most hare-brained. A man don't introduce his fiancée to his mistress!"

"I'm not your fiancée yet, and she's not your mistress, still," she persisted.

"Cut line, baggage. A lady isn't even supposed to talk *about* such women as Flo, much less talk *to* them. As much as I like Flora, there's no denying what she is, and what she is just isn't suitable for you."

"Why? Do you think she'll encourage me to take up the life of sin?"

"Jacey," he finally said in exasperation, "it doesn't matter what I think, or what the social arbiters decree. Flo wouldn't want to meet you. It would only embarrass her and make her feel ashamed of her . . . her profession."

Jacelyn thought about it awhile. "Leigh, does Flora like what she does?"

"Lord, Jay-bird, I don't know! I surely wouldn't ask her!"

"And what about when she's older and not so attractive? What happens to women like her then?"

"With luck, she'll have put some money away. If she's been lucky and her gentlemen have been generous, she can sell off the baubles she's accumulated, like the king's ransom Flo wore the other evening. Why?"

"Just curiosity, I suppose. I never knew any . . . any *demimondaines*. Only Sal, down at the Speckled Pony, but that was different. She was barmaid, so everyone could pretend she didn't do the other."

"In London, gentlewomen pretend that other doesn't even exist."

"Here they come. Can I at least smile?" She did anyway, before he could answer. Leigh raised his whip in greeting, and Flora tilted her head, slightly. Mr. Unger searched his sleeve for specks of lint.

"What a hubble-bubble convention! Leigh, do you think Mr. Unger will marry her? Or maybe one of her other gentlemen will?"

"A man doesn't marry his mistress, primrose. He doesn't need to. Gads, I hope you don't tell anyone about this conversation! You know, the only reason I said I'd take you to the masquerade at Vauxhall was that I feared you'd go by yourself. And the only reason I had this discussion with you was to keep you from accosting some poor girl waiting for business outside the theater or somewhere. I've never been so glad to see Lem. Squire was right: you *do* have an odd kick to your gallop."

Leigh parted from her at the stables, reminding Jacey that he wished to hear all about her dealings with Farthingale, that evening at Wrenthe House. "And if that puppy is still trailing after you, you owe me a kiss!"

"And if he's not?"

"Then I owe you a kiss!"

Consider the man who thinks so much of his appearance that he'd wear the latest fashion, no matter if it were war paint and feathers. In Farthingale's case, he wore his starched shirt collars so high he could blind himself with a quick denial. His waistcoat was nipped in so tightly he couldn't eat in public, and tying his neckcloth in the delicate *trône d'amour* took one valet, seven snow-white linens, and forty minutes. All this was for a walk in the park with Jacelyn and her dog.

Farthingale cared inordinately for what he looked like, but more for what he looked like to others. Perhaps it was because the viscount had such a high position to live up to, or that his mother was so disapproving, or just that the other boys hadn't let him play knights and dragons. Jacelyn didn't know what made a man—or a woman—wear such a social façade with so much pride, but she knew how to handle him gracefully, without injuring that same *amour propre*. With a dog, of course.

That same dog who is such a friendly topic of conversation among strangers, its antics and ancestry, is not quite as comfortable up close. A person-to-canine meeting, among strangers, is a hound of another colour. The lovable star of all the anecdotes is liable to embarrass its companion worse than a split seam to sternward. The darling pet will happily relieve itself as near to the stranger's boot as possible, in full view of passersby, of course, and then indulge in a loud, vulgar display of personal hygiene. If two of the little dears get together, their introductory rituals could send a gently reared female into palpitations. As for four-footed romance . . .

That's why no one ever brought any but the tiniest lapdogs to the park, and rarely put them down.

That's why Jacelyn fed Pen a large meal at noontime, and a whole bowl of broth, and did not have Lem walk her near the house as usual, before getting into Farthingale's carriage. And that's why she insisted they get out to walk right at the entrance to the park, where all the fashionables were gathered to see and be seen.

Jacey had to hold her parasol; could Lord Farthingale please hold the leash?

Pen was your typical dog, only more so, since she was larger. Farthingale was used to hunting-hounds in the woods, not this. He was mortified. People were turning their backs, snickering, lifting their noses and their skirts to step around them, and Miss Trevaine was twirling her parasol! He prayed the ground would open up and swallow him—or the unconventional girl and her impossible pet! No such luck, as Jacelyn just kept chattering, walking onward slowly, behind two ladies whose skirts the dog was sniffing! Death couldn't undo this blow to his self-esteem. The shame was bound to haunt him throughout eternity.

Jacelyn finally took pity on him when she saw the tears start to form in his eyes. "Shall we go, my lord? I think Pen has had enough exercise now, don't you? You have such a way with dogs, we have to do this again soon. Perhaps tomorrow. No? I'll see you this evening at Lady Wrenthe's, shan't I? You have other plans? That's too bad."

As Jacelyn told Claibourne later, making herself and Pen into Scylla and Charybdis was the easy part. Getting Priscilla to look like safe harbour was a little more difficult.

"Did you hear about Arthur and Lady Rhodine? Lady Tina is throwing them a ball on Friday. It will be one of the premiere entertainments of the Season, I'm sure. Everyone will be there."

Farthingale was having a little smoother sailing, now that they were in the carriage and out of the park. His colour changed from green back to its usual baby pink. The chance to gossip enheartened him further, especially the word "everyone."

"I wonder if Miss Ponsonby will attend? Shocking thing, that, everyone's talking of it."

"Poo. Anton-Fredricks was a cad, that's all. We were all right there; no harm was done, except to him, of course. Priscilla will naturally attend her own brother's betrothal ball, and I'm sure she'll be all the rage. She was so brave, fighting off that madman and calling out for help. I'm sure everyone will want to hear her story. I'll wager there won't be any getting near her. And dear Priscilla will be looking as beautiful as ever, despite such a harrowing experience. I don't know how she does it, never a hair out of place, never a spot on her glove. What do you think?"

"Mother thinks Priscilla's no better than she should be, but the way you tell it . . ."

"You couldn't think *Priscilla* was at fault, could you? Why, everyone knows Miss Ponsonby is the most *proper* girl who ever lived. My own aunt is forever holding her up as an example to me. I may have acted a trifle impulsively at times, which everyone has so kindly overlooked, but Priscilla? Never!"

"Deuced fine looking woman."

"A real Diamond." Jacelyn sighed. "I'll never be like her. At least you won't have to worry about not having a dance with me at the Endicotts'; my card is never as full as Priscilla's."

"I might just pop over there this afternoon and ask her to save me a couple. Quite the thing to do, you know. Show the dear girl all men aren't bounders."

"How kind of you, Lord Farthingale. You won't come in for tea, then? Oh, and I so wanted to show you how Pen drinks from the saucer."

"So now you and Arthur have to see that Priscilla comes to the ball and acts noble," Jacey told Leigh.

"She's way ahead of you, sweetheart. Arthur says that after Farthingale's visit Priscilla actually started to believe she was a heroine. By the night of the ball she'll have vanquished Anton-Fredricks herself, in single-handed defense of British morality. If no one else dances with her besides Farthingale, Arthur and I will, and I suppose we could ask Sprague, now that his eyes are open. That will be enough, with her pride. I salute you again, ma'am, for successfully completing another difficult mission in enemy territory. I only wish we'd had you in Spain for the Peninsular Campaign! Shall we proceed to the balcony where I might give you the decoration for valour?"

17

Sniff . . . sniff? "What's that smell, boy? What are you doing over there?" Fenton put down his newspaper.

"Roses, gov. I'm writing a note to go with them."

Fenton rolled his Bath chair down the long room to where Percy sat at the desk. On the desk, the floor, his lap, were piles of little calling cards. Some had ink splotches, some had spatters. Others had messages: *fondly, Claibourne,* or *with affection, Leigh. Yours truly, Merrill,* etc. Close by was a large parcel, two dozen red roses tied in tissue with a silver ribbon. The roses were already browning at the edges from being out of water so long.

Fenton looked at the roses, flipped over a few of the cards. "Your mind doesn't work fast, Percy, when it works at all. I assume you're still trying to get Claibourne and his straw damsel together; I just can't understand why. He saw her at the theater, in front of the girl and the whole ton. So what? The *Gazette*'s still full of their doings, Claibourne and the chit, together."

"He called at her house."

· "Did you see him there?"

"No, thanks be. Miss La Fleur had her man tell me Leigh was there looking for me."

"You brandy-based bubblehead, that means he suspects you're involved with the theater contretemps, not that he's interested in the woman! Besides, even if he does call there, he'll be discreet. It won't have any damned effect on the Trevaine twit. The only way your cork-brained scheme could work is if the doxy is on our side. That's like hoping the Tower of London falls on Claibourne's head. Have you even talked to her yet?"

"She likes me. She wouldn't have her man warn me, else. You're right though, Da, I should be trying to win her affections to m'self, not my cousin Leigh."

"Percy, your attics are to let! You could rent your brainbox to a couple of starlings—and still have room for a squirrel!"

Percy wasn't listening. He was torturing a new set of cards. *Fondly, Fenton? With affection, an Admirer? Hopefully, Percy?*

Fenton read two of the blotched efforts, shook his head. "At least I won't be going to hell. I've already done my penance. . . . I have a new idea, boy, lucky one of us does. Percy, put down that damn pen and listen to me!"

Percy blotted the nib on the penwipe, then naturally tucked the blackened cloth into his waistcoat pocket, like a handkerchief. "Listening, governor."

"Aargh." Fenton backed away. "There's a ball tonight, according to the *Gazette,* and Claibourne's sure to be there. It's for his friend Ponsonby and Endicott's daughter. The girl is friends with Claibourne's chit, so it's the perfect time."

"Perfect time for what? You know La Fleur won't be at any fancy nob's ball."

"Use what little wit you have, Percy. It's the perfect time to show the gel Claibourne's character, make him out a libertine and worse, a debaucher of women."

"Is a debaucher anything like an accoucheur?"

"You skitter-witted slowtop, it's a man who would seduce a virgin, get her with child, then just walk away."

"Oh, a bounder. Whyn't you just say so? It won't fadge, though. Claibourne ain't one. Everyone knows he don't go near the innocents, except for Miss Trevaine, of course."

"Exactly, but she *doesn't* know it. She'll believe the worst, if she sees proof right outside Endicott's door."

"Huh?"

"You stage a show for her, Percy, before the party, one to give her a disgust of Claibourne for once and all. They'll all see it. He'll be cut dead, tossed out of his clubs, finished in polite circles, just like they did to me."

"Uh, gov, what kind of show is that? That horse bit outside Almack's wasn't any great success, you know."

"Did you think I wouldn't know, you gnag-nosed nodcock? This plan is so simple even you can do it. All you need to do is find a woman who's breeding. A young, pretty one. You point Claibourne out to her, and you pay her to stand outside Endicott's yelling the brat is his. That should settle his account, by Jupiter!"

"But, gov, where am I going to find a pregnant woman? You know I ain't in the petticoat line."

"You ain't in the petticoat line, you ain't in the banking line. You ain't in the shipping line, and you damn well weren't in line when they were handing out brains!" He wheeled his chair to the doorway, calling for his man Jensen. He shouted back toward Percy: "You'd better do it, boy, if you want to stay in line for my fortune."

Percy sat thinking for a minute. You could tell: his mouth was open. Then he took the pen, dipped it in the ink, and painstakingly inscribed a fresh card: *Please let me love you. Percy.*

"You want a pretty young woman who's breedin', for one night? I don't know, Mister Percy." Cook was eyeing him as if he was some kind of pervert. She was backing toward the meat cleaver. "There's my sister's girl Fanny, but I can't say as how she'd oblige. Her man's a mail driver, so they don't need the ready. I'll ask for you, if you just get along now, so I can do up these nice trotters your father likes."

But it had to be tonight, and Percy had to have a pregnant woman, guaranteed. The only women besides Cook he ever dealt with made sure they never found themselves in an interesting condition, so that option was out. Down by the East End, Seven Dials, or the Docks, though, there were always half-naked urchins begging in the streets. That seemed as likely a place as any to search.

Percy was lucky. It only took three dingy taverns, and a few rounds of cheap gin in each, to find a pregnant woman. But she wasn't very pretty, with her scarred face and stringy hair, and she wasn't even very far gone. He gave her the time, address, instructions, and half the fee, in case he couldn't find a more suitable increasing actress. He secured the deal with another drink, and a bottle to carry with him. What do you know? His luck was getting better. There were two big-bellied women at the next grogshop, sitting sideways at the table. One of them was almost pretty, too. Sure, she'd claim King George was the babe's dad, for a half crown and a few drinks. Only thing was, she was very close to her time and didn't like being out alone, so far from home. Could her friend come too?

If one unwed mother was a disgrace, two really ought to put Claibourne in the basket, so they drank to their success.

The barkeep couldn't watch those half crowns being tucked into bodices without wanting a share for himself. "What about m'wife upstairs?" he volunteered. "We got a tyke and a infant at suck. Your swell can't have all his buns in t'oven at oncet, can he?" Furthermore, the barkeep had a cart; he could see all the "delicate" lasses got to the right place on time. That had to be worth an extra crown or two, but the next round was on the house.

A cat can look at a king. But why would one want to, Jacelyn wondered, seeing the larger than usual crowds on the sidewalk in front of Endicott House. Whenever there was to be a huge ball, hordes of the uninvited gathered to watch the nobility. They oohed and ogled, and in general acted as vocal theater critics for the aristocratic play. Jacelyn would never get used to it, nor the way the invited guests had to queue up on the red carpet outside the house, waiting to have some stiff butler intone their names and titles.

Tonight was no different, except there were more women than men and—gracious, nearly every one of them was breeding or had a babe in arms. Aunt Amabel was asking if the lower orders held conventions for that sort of thing, while Lord Parkhurst facetiously wondered aloud if the Regent was expected. All these women were here, he surmised, to hold the infants up and the babe-filled bellies out, for the future king's blessing—so he wouldn't beggar the country before they were weaned.

The women weren't holding those children for Prinny, however, they were just waiting for Claibourne to step out of the coach.

"There he is! There's the man what ruined me!"

"Here, Claibourne, see what your wicked ways have brought!"

"Hey, yer lordship, how'm I to feed the brat you left me?"

"He done me wrong—twice!"

The situation was absurd, of course: every *enceinte* woman from the East End accusing Leigh Claibourne of siring her child. Soon the ladies on line were atwitter, and the men were laughing outright. The crowd on the pavement was delighted, calling uproariously vulgar comments and ribald suggestions. Lord Parkhurst and Mme. Aubonier had to lead Amabel back to the carriage so she could faint without dirtying her gown, leaving Leigh and Jacelyn on center stage, without a script.

After the first moment's shock, Leigh began to chuckle, and then trade jokes with the bystanders, most of which Jacelyn could not understand, luckily. "Come ladies," he was saying good-naturedly, while she was wishing someone would shake her and tell her to wake up, it's only a nightmare. "I have only been home from Belgium for five months. Wellington himself couldn't have done the job from there."

"Them British musketeers have good aim, Major."

"Not that good, friend, so I'm thankful to all you lads at home for standing in for us so nobly."

They were finally at the door. Before entering the house, Leigh told the women to meet him around back in ten minutes, he'd buy the babies their first pairs of shoes.

"What are you doing, Leigh? You're going to go talk to those women—and leave me here all alone to face *this?*"

This was everyone in the room laughing and pointing and holding fans over their mouths. Even Arthur, on the receiving line, had heard about it.

"Great show, Leigh. Here we were all wondering how Priscilla would be received, and you go set them all on their ears. No one will have a spare tongue-wag for her. Thanks."

"You'll find this hard to believe, Arthur, but I really wouldn't have subjected myself and my friends to such a spectacle, not even for Priscilla. Lady Endicott, may I please trouble you for the use of a back room to interview some of the mamas-to-be? I've got to find out who has the quirky sense of humour. Would you also look after Miss Trevaine? Her aunt didn't appreciate the jest much either."

292

"Leigh, you can't!"

"I'm sorry, pet, you have to stay here and look amused."

Amused? She hadn't been so amused since she'd caught her hand in the barn door. Now she felt like Farthingale must have with the dog—only worse. Farthingale merely looked less elegant than he wished; Jacelyn looked like a red-faced fool. She didn't want to become an outraged fishwife, and she didn't want to marry a man who could even be suspected of such behaviour. She didn't believe any of it, needless to say, but if not these women, then others. And he'd said he'd never disgrace her. Hah! What did he think tonight's display was? A schoolroom tea party?

A farce, that's what Leigh thought, in the small pantry behind Tina Endicott's kitchen. He was surrounded there by seven, no eight, women who looked like a pod of beached whales. It was a comedy and they were all laughing at the hoax. The real disgrace was the women's condition. He left them a moment so he could bribe, threaten, and otherwise coerce the horrified cook into serving them cake and ale. He swore to make it right with Lady Endicott's household account, for the wheels of cheese and fresh apples and oranges he brought back to the pantry.

His lordship was a real fine gent, the ladies decided. Kindhearted, generous, polite even to the likes of them—and so devilishly handsome with his easy pearly smile, they wouldn't mind if the babes wore his butter stamp after all. Asides, he'd laughed right along with them, not run off like that queer nabs who'd hired them. The women were happy ·to oblige Claibourne with anything he wanted to know, even if they were disloyal to their employer. He wasn't there with the other half of their pay; Claibourne was.

Fifteen minutes later, the earl sent his latest conquests home in the barkeep's wagon, having emptied his pockets and the cook's larder. He now owed his life's savings to Endicott's servants, if his life was worth saving, after Jacelyn got through with it, for here was Lady Tina herself. She had come to thank Claibourne for enlivening Rhodine's dull little gathering, and to lead him back to the party. Tina's gratitude was almost as deep as her neckline, but not quite, and she guided him to the ballroom with all the sinuous grace of a tigress stalking her prey. Since he'd been using her house as a home for unwed mothers, common courtesy required him to ask her to dance. Bad luck made the orchestra choose a waltz.

Jacelyn was dancing with the Spanish count, barely listening to his ornate compliments, when Claibourne danced by with their hostess nearly wallpapered to his shirtfront. If Jacelyn's looks were daggers, both of them would be skewered like ducks on a spit.

Her next dance was promised to Lord Tayson, but Claibourne persuaded the young lordling that Miss Trevaine needed to catch her breath and would be sitting out—with him.

Jacey ignored the earl as he took a seat next to her. She couldn't ignore the smell of cheap perfume, or the lip rouge on his neckcloth. She glared at him. "I see you were as friendly to your back-room brood mares as you were to Lady Endicott."

Laughing, he wiped at his cheek where she was staring, and said, "Don't be shrewish, darling, and don't worry. If you're breeding, I'll marry you."

The wound wasn't like a clean cut that bled, hurt, then healed. This was more like the pain of a deep splinter, which festered and throbbed.

All those women, all those Lady Tinas. The world was full of them, Jacelyn knew, and the only thing presently keeping Leigh away from them—if he was, indeed, keeping his distance—was herself, her reputation, her money. It wasn't enough.

If he loved her, she could laugh at the silly prank last night, and she could shrug off Lady Tina's clinging with simple pride in his attractiveness. If he loved her, she could even disregard all the thinly veiled hints about what an ideal match theirs would be, for both of them.

She knew, had always known, how much he needed her money, and she really didn't care. She would be glad her fortune could ease his way, if that wasn't the only reason for this continued parody of a near betrothal. Everyone, even Leigh, she thought, assumed they would make it official soon, at her ball, perhaps, or over Christmas. It wouldn't happen, not if it killed her, for he didn't love her. They—her father, Squire, Aunt Amabel, Leigh himself—could no longer argue that her good repute and social well-being depended on Leigh's name. Just look at Priscilla; it only took a bit of courage and a fresh scandal. As for Jacey's future happiness . . . that did depend on Leigh. She didn't quite see how she would live without him, but she'd have to, rather than slowly being nibbled to death anyway, by all the doubts and uncertainties. Just a few more weeks, and she and Pen could go home, alone.

Claibourne was relieved to see that Jacelyn wasn't angry when he met her at the stable for their ride. He'd been prepared for fireworks, vowing to hold his own temper in check this time, for last night *had* been an awful experience for the young girl. It hadn't been any picnic for him, either, so he was pleased there wouldn't be any brangling now. If Jacelyn seemed quieter than usual, it matched the overcast, dank morning. The dog wasn't interested in chasing sticks, and even Baron took exception to the bare branches clicking in the raw wind. Claibourne's mood was all of a piece.

His lordship had a lot on his mind, not least of

which was figuring out what in Hades Percy was trying to do with these skipbrained schemes to humiliate his cousin. To find out would mean finding Percy, most likely at Flora's place in Islington. Claibourne's presence there was sure to get back to Jacelyn, and cause her still more upset. Unless he was to tell her beforehand. Deuces, just when he was glad there were no storm clouds. He decided to take the cowardly path, mentioning Flora only as he left Jacelyn at Parkhurst House later, so they could keep on with the quiet, reflective ride now.

Percy could wait. Claibourne's finances couldn't. Mr. Pettigrew hadn't had any good news lately, and he couldn't take any more money out of the estate. Applying to Trevaine was out of the question, as was visiting the cent-per-centers. Leigh had no intention of paying twice for what he used once. There were no calls for Baron's services, and the cards just weren't falling right. Leigh was too astute to wager where the chances of winning were so poor, and no one would bet against him in other contests, like culping wafers or three-round sparring matches, where the odds were so heavily in his favour.

It was dashed expensive, this London living, if you added the price of courtship to clothes, lodging, and horses, besides incidentals like last night's unexpected debts. With all the gratuities he was handing out, he felt like Golden Ball on Boxing Day.

He was thinking of selling the curricle and pair, but he'd only have to rent job horses and rigs to take Jacelyn driving. He could ask Arthur for a loan until the dibs were in tune, but with his own marriage to plan, Arthur mightn't have as much of the ready, and Claibourne hated to ask his friends, anyway; he'd had more than enough teasing about his coming change of fortune. There might be a position for him at the War Office, but not necessarily in London. Then again, he might take himself and his pistols somewhere away from Town, to Bath or Brighton, perhaps, where his skill wasn't as well known. He only had to hold out a few weeks more, until the end of the Season, when he could ask Jacelyn to marry him. It would be the shortest engagement in history if he had anything to say. If she said no . . . It didn't bear thinking of, and the money had nothing to do with it at all. He could live on very little at the Abbey, and without Jacey's laughing eyes, that's all it would be, barely existing.

"Will you come in for breakfast?"

"Thank you, pet, no. I have some errands to run. One of them is tracking down my cousin Percy. Ah, he may be at Flora's house, so I'll have to stop there this afternoon."

"Will you take me with you, Leigh?"

"Don't be a widgeon. Flo isn't suitable company for you, but she's a Sunday-school teacher compared to Percy."

"That's all right, I forgot I'm promised to Rhodine after luncheon anyway. We're to select a pattern for her wedding dress."

Jacelyn half-expected him to question plans for her *own* bridal gown, and it was almost on the tip of his tongue to do so, but he'd vowed not to pressure her, and he wouldn't. Instead he asked: "Incidentally, Jacey, are we promised anywhere for the next few days?"

"I don't think there is anything very grand until the ball at Lady Hockney's country home next week, except you did promise to take me to the Vauxhall masquerade Saturday. Why?"

"I didn't forget the promise, dear heart, I already hired the closed carriage. I just might have to be out of town before then."

She looked at him like he'd crawled out of the kitchen tiles. "Tell me again. You are going to visit your mistress, and be out of town for two days?"

He blinked, then grinned. "Ah. She's not my mistress, remember? And one trip has nothing to do with the other, you adorable peagoose." He quickly kissed the tip of her nose, then said he would see her at tea.

Trust him, he said. Don't listen to the gabblemongers, he said. He'd be there for tea, he said. That was easy for him. He wasn't at the dressmaker's where even the fitters giggled about how Claibourne was raising his own army. He wasn't at the silk warehouse where Lady Tina teased about his lordship's taste in women: warm and willing. And he wasn't on time for tea. Of course not, he was visiting his mistress! Fortunately for the Sèvres tea service, there were other callers in and out all afternoon.

Leigh's luck was still gone begging. Percy hadn't shown at Flora's, it being earlier than his usual time, but Unger had. Rather than cause Flora any embarrassment, Claibourne had left by the kitchen door. Gads, creeping out of a noted courtesan's door like some guilty, henpecked husband! Then Arthur had reminded him that no one but crones, consumptives, and caper merchants were in the resort areas at this time of year, so that notion was discarded. He hadn't wanted to be out of town anyway, not without seeing Percy.

All in all, his lordship was in a foul mood. Seeing Jacelyn entertaining some mushroom in yellow pantaloons did not improve his temper.

"Lord Claibourne, how nice of you to join us." Jacelyn managed to get anger, resentment, and nagging at his tardiness into the one sarcastic statement. She hadn't gotten up from the Queen Anne desk where, Claibourne could see, she was writing a cheque. The cit had stood, though, so she introduced him.

"Lord Claibourne, I would like you to meet Mr. Godfrey Durbin. Mr. Durbin is the founder of a new group, the Benevolent Protectors of Innocent Creatures. Its goal is to provide food and shelter for all the homeless dogs and cats of London. Remember last month when Aunt's people were having all those difficulties with strays? I'm to be a charter member. Oh, Mr. Durbin, this is Leigh Merrill, Earl of Claibourne."

Durbin didn't know whether to bow or put out his hand. Neither would have mattered, as his lordship pointed to the door.

"Get out, you charlatan," he ordered, "and don't ever let me see your ugly phiz in the neighbourhood." Then Claibourne took the cheque from Jacey's fingers and ripped it in two. "Still too green by half, my girl," he drawled.

Jacelyn jumped up in furious indignation, hands on hips, and shouted the first hateful thing that came to mind: "How dare you! I'm not your girl and it's not your money yet!"

All the colour left Leigh's face, then returned in a quick bloom of red. He turned on his heel and left.

Percival Fenton was not your average fool, nor even your average drunk. He had to be the unluckiest inebriate idiot on earth. He was so stupid, he thought he was lucky to have missed his cousin Leigh earlier. He was so drunk, he didn't even duck. Of all the times and places to be where he was, Percy'd picked the worst.

Claibourne had been wanting to talk to Percy for weeks, ever since the Roman scene outside Almack's. That is, he felt he should, whether he wanted to see the muckworm or not, to find out what all the tomfoolery was about and put a stop to it. With one thing and another, he'd never run him to ground, until today. Leigh wasn't a vicious, violent maniac, either, until today. Today, however, he didn't want to talk, he wanted to murder anyone in his way—who just happened to be Percival Fenton.

Maybe being hit on the side of the head knocked some sense into the clunch, because he did the only intelligent thing possible: he stayed where he was, flat on the ground.

"Get up and fight, you bastard!"

"Oh, do you think so, too? M'father swears I'm none of his but I—"

"I don't give a damn about your ancestry. I only wish you were no relative of mine." Leigh had him up, willy-nilly, by the neckcloth, and was roaring at him. "What I want to know is what the bloody hell is going on?"

Percy dangled there, thinking, then he said, "I could be wrong about this, mind, but I think you're going to beat me to a pulp. Knew it would happen, told the governor so."

Claibourne shook him like a sandy rug. "Why, Percy? No, blast you, not why am I going to pop your cork. Why have you been bothering me and my friends?"

"It's the governor. He don't like you. I never had anything against you m'self."

"Thanks," Leigh said dryly. "Why did you do all those crazy things then?"

"He said he'd have his man Jensen kill me, else."

"Well, I'll kill you now if you don't tell me the rest. I don't like your father any more than he likes me, but I don't go near him. What does he want?"

"It's your marriage. He don't want you leg-shackled and starting your nursery. He says I'm to be your heir."

"*You!*" Claibourne shook Percy so hard his previously loosened teeth rattled. "You cannot be my heir," Leigh raged, "because you're not going to outlive me." And he hit him again. Picked him up and shook him again.

"Uh, Leigh?"

Claibourne paused, right arm way back.

"I never hurt that horse, that time. The one I left at Parkhurst's stables. Found him that way at the knackers. I wouldn't have done that to a horse, honest."

So Leigh didn't kill him.

Even if he didn't love her, even if he only wanted her for her money, even if there really had been a Benevolent Protectors Society, which Mr. Sprague confirmed there wasn't, she should not

303

have said it. Even if he was high-handed, arrogant, and smelled of patchouli when her own scent was lavender, she should have bitten off her tongue before uttering those words. But she hadn't, and he was gone, most likely back to La Fleur's house, where he'd be welcomed with kind words and satin sheets. Fallen women always had satin sheets in the novels she read, and they never yelled like fishwives. He would stay there and help La Fleur count her diamonds, and never, ever know how sorry Jacelyn was.

In a pig's eye, he would.

She put on her dark blue merino dress with the long sleeves, grabbed a shawl, told Marcus she was going to the stable, turned the corner, and kept going. The hackney driver took her to Islington, but baulked when she ordered him to find Miss La Fleur's direction.

"I knows where the Flower lives, I does, 'n I knows it's no place for the likes a'you, miss."

"Don't be impertinent, sir. We are having a meeting of the Benevolent Protectors of Innocent Creatures Society, and Miss La Fleur and I are charter members. She is a great champion of the downtrodden."

"That right? 'N here I allays thought she were a rich man's whore. Beggin' your pardon, miss."

He set her down at a pleasant little whitewashed house with a brick wall, and hedges all around. She paid the fare, the jarvey took off, and she wondered what on earth she was going to do now.

What if Claibourne wasn't here? Worse, now that she considered it further, what if he *was* here?

She was standing in the roadway, debating with herself, when she heard terrible noises coming from the hedges. She ran to the moan's direction, and found what had to be Percival Fenton, from Claibourne's description of him: an elongated scarecrow, losing its stuffing. He was also losing a lot of blood from above his right eye, which was quickly swelling shut. His jaw was already empurpled, and he held one of his teeth in his hand. Jacelyn hurried to his side and started to mop at the blood with her handkerchief.

"Percy? Percy, it's Jacelyn Trevaine. Can you understand me?"

He looked up and nodded. Then at the same time, they both asked, "Is Leigh still here?"

"Gads, I hope not," swore Percy, and Jacelyn *amen*ed it, then asked, "Was it Leigh who did this to you, because of the pregnant women?"

"Yes'm, but I didn't hurt the horse."

"I should hope not. If you touched Baron he would kill you for sure."

"He's an earl, not a baron. You should know that, if you're going to marry him. M'cousin's a downy one. He won't like a widgeon-wife."

Jacelyn had Percy's neckcloth off and was making a pad for the cut, while trying to make sense of his conversation. He must be concussed, she decided, leaning over to press the bandage in place. His breath nearly made her eyes water.

"You're foxed!"

"Yes'm, usually am."

"You mean you're never sober?"

"Not if I can help it."

"Oh dear. I think you'd better get inside. Can you stand?"

He couldn't, so she wadded up her woolen shawl and put it under his head. "Wait here," she told him unnecessarily, and went to pull the door knocker. Miss La Fleur herself answered the door, in a pink satin negligee—in the daytime! Jacey didn't have time to consider the implications as she tried to explain who she was, why she'd come, and what Percy was doing groaning in the grass.

"That bag of bones? I had my man warn him to stay away, but he wouldn't listen. It's Remington's day off, or I'd have him put your friend in a hackney, like usual."

"But he's hurt badly, and Leigh said how kind you are. Couldn't he come in? We could clean him up and—"

"What's this *we?* Leigh would kill all of us if he found you here! I'm sorry, miss, about Percy, but I've got a, ah, gentleman caller due soon, and it would be awkward-like having the cawker bleeding in the parlour."

"It can't be any worse than having your guest trip over him in the walkway. He really needs someone to take care of him. Will you at least come look at him?"

The next time Percy opened his eyes, two thinly

covered breasts dangled right above him. He thought Claibourne must have killed him after all. His horizon filled with satin tits, he must have gone to heaven. Wouldn't the governor be surprised! It was better than heaven, by Jupiter; it was La Fleur herself, come to wipe his brow!

"I love you."

"I know you do, you poor sod. Here, let's have a look at you."

"He loves you?" Jacey asked, incredulous. "Then you *have* to take him in."

"He says he loves me, he writes me notes and sends flowers. I never met him before today, though. He sure don't look like much."

"Leigh did this to him!"

"He's got no chin," Flo pointed out, as if Percy were an inanimate statue—sculpted by a Bedlamite. "Leigh didn't have anything to do with that."

"True, his chin is a bit weak, but his nose is strong enough to compensate."

"It's a shame Leigh didn't break it for him, could only be an improvement. He sure is skinny, too."

"He only needs fattening up, some healthy food, regular meals, you know. If it's a matter of money . . ." Jacelyn was fumbling to untie her reticule.

"It would be another mouth to feed, now that you mention it."

Percy, who'd been lying on the grass worshipping, now put his hand to his waistcoat and pulled out a bulging wallet. "I've got plenty of blunt," he said, handing it to Flora, his one good eye never leaving her face.

Flora glanced through the wallet quickly. "He's getting prettier by the minute."

"You know, Miss La Fleur, Leigh says he is very wealthy, and he really seems quite fond of you. His name isn't such that he has to worry over what connexions he makes, if you understand me. Who knows where it might lead?"

It led right upstairs to the bedroom, Jacelyn under one shoulder, Flora under the other, Percy grinning like a roast pig with an apple in its mouth.

"I'll let him set a bit, I suppose, if only to keep an eye on him for Leigh's sake."

"I'm sure he won't trouble Leigh anymore, will you, Percy?" Jacey asked, giving his arm a jerk.

"Oh no, ma'am, Miss La Fleur. I wouldn't do anything you didn't like, ever."

"Pitiful. Sweet, but pitiful. All right, you stay. And it's Flora, to my friends. Flora Cobb."

They had him on the bed now, his boots off. "Flora . . . Flora Fenton," he whispered before he passed out.

"He'll keep till Remington gets back to help. You better leave, miss, before Mr. Unger gets here. This is going to be hard enough to explain as is."

When they reached downstairs again, Flora couldn't resist asking, "What were you doing here anyway, miss, if you don't mind my prying? I mean, it's not every day grand young ladies drop in to tea, if you ken my drift."

"Well, I did want to meet you, but Leigh said I mustn't—"

"So you did anyway."

"I wouldn't have, but he said he was coming here, after Percy, and . . . and I wanted to apologise to him for something terrible I said."

"Here? You were going to apologise to him here, in my house? I don't know who is more addlepated, you or the tosspot upstairs! I can see where you'll lead Leigh a merry chase. Good. He needs that."

"You're not mad, then? And you'll tell him I'm sorry, if you see him?"

"I won't be seeing him, dearie, if that's what's on your mind, and no, I'm not mad. If that rummy sobers up decent, you may have done me a good turn. Now I'll do you one and get you a hackney. And, miss, take my advice, don't ever mention to Claibourne that you were here, or you'll be sorrier still."

"Thank you, Flora, and thank you for being kind to Leigh when he was ill, and for taking in Percy. It's been a pleasure meeting you."

"And you, miss. You're a real lady, and I don't mean titles and such. Leigh'll be proud. There's no question either; he'll make you real happy."

* * *

"*Ar . . . Ar . . . Ar-choo. Choo. Archoo.*"

"Typical, you twit. Other men come home from two days of raking with the pox. You come home with a head cold!"

"Not a cold, Da, it's snuff." Percy was practicing opening the small enamelled box with one hand. So far there was a damp layer of brown powder all over him.

"*Snuff!* You're shoving tobacco up your nose so you can sneeze? Only a simple-minded sop would get pleasure from that!"

"Gave it up, gov. No more Blue Ruin."

"Gave up gin, did you? That only leaves brandy, wine, port—"

"All of it. Am doing snuff instead. It's more manly. *Ar-choo.*"

Fenton rolled his wheelchair away, out of range, and dabbed at his sleeve in repugnance. "Manly? Boy, you're as manly as the sultan's soprano. Just look at you!"

It took a strong stomach to do so: one totally shut blackened eye that shaded off to bilious yellow; a huge purple bruise on the jaw; swollen, split lip; missing tooth—and lace ruffles.

"That bastard Claibourne did this to you?"

"Told you he would. He didn't like your idea about the pregnant women."

"My idea? *My idea?* You paper-skulled popinjay, I told you to get a female who was increasing. *One.* What do you bring? Ten! If you can count to twenty-one with your pants on I'll be amazed!

Besides, I'm surprised Claibourne didn't kill you, hanging around his mistress like that."

"You were right: she ain't his mistress anymore." He grinned proudly. "She's mine. I'll be staying there. Just came 'round to tell you."

"Gads, that woman will do *any*thing for money."

"Not so. She likes me."

Fenton shook his head. "You poor deluded dunderhead. Will she help us queer Claibourne's marriage plans?"

"No, she likes him too. She doesn't want me messing with him neither."

Fenton slammed his fist into the armrest. "And you call yourself manly! Look what he's done to you! Look what those bastards have done to me! You'd let him get away with it all; you'd throw rice at his demn wedding!"

"Doubt I'd be invited, gov. Leigh ain't too keen on our branch of the—"

"Shut up! *I* won't sit still and watch it happen, boy, I won't. If I can't get rid of the wedding, I'll get rid of Claibourne. It's what I should have done from the first. Yes, once and for all."

"Uh, I'll just be toddling off now, before you get another of your ideas."

Fenton sneered. "Did you think I'd send you against Claibourne? As well send an ant to itch an elephant's arse."

"Well, I don't want anything to do with it. Don't want the title, don't want any draughty old castle in Durham."

311

"Percy, somewhere, somewhere on this earth, I say, there's got to be a greater fool than you. But when that man dies . . ."

18

Two days had gone by with no word from Leigh. Two very long days. Jacey wondered what the rest of her life would be like, if he never came back. Her restless sleep left her more exhausted, and she couldn't eat, not with the lump of granite in her throat. The dog might have cheered her, but Pen had grown fat and lazy in her London life, and was content just to lie by the fire. Shopping held no attraction either, not if he wasn't around to dress for.

It was Saturday, the night of the Vauxhall masquerade, and she didn't know what to do. She'd begged off accompanying her aunt to Lady Richardson's rout, and she'd told her watchdogs Pinkie and Lem that she wouldn't need either of them that evening. She was going to read a book and retire early, she'd claimed. The book never got opened.

What should she do? They had talked about meeting at the corner by the stables, but no time was given. She couldn't very well go stand on the street corner in her evening gown and wait to see if he remembered. On the other hand, if he did come and she wasn't there, he'd think she was still angry.

The best solution she could devise was her usual one for these situations: the boy's clothes. She could get out by the tree and over the garden wall, and no one would think anything odd about a lad out at night. She'd be safer from recognition at Vauxhall too, in Lem's castoffs.

"The only problem," she told the dog sprawled at the hearth, "is that I want him to see me looking pretty." The dog thumped her tail twice and went back to sleep. "You're no help," Jacey complained from the bottom of the clothespress, where she'd stowed the outfit.

She was stuffing her hair up under the floppy hat when someone scratched at her door. Good grief, what if it was her aunt home early, or Aunt Simone? She mustn't be seen in britches! She went to the door, but didn't open it. "Yes, what is it?"

"It's Eugene, ma'am. A parcel just came for you."

"Would you put it down by the door, please. I am not, ah, presentable. Thank you."

She cracked the door an inch and peered out. It would be just like that libertine to lurk in the hall to catch a glimpse of her *en déshabille*. Why Aunt Amabel kept such a creature was a mystery. She scooped up the paper-wrapped bundle and scurried back inside her room.

It was a scarlet domino, a long, hooded cape that would conceal nearly every inch of her! He didn't forget! The note read *Ten o'clock*. It was already nine-thirty, drat the man, and she would *not* go in britches! Off they came and back to the closet. Out came one of her new gowns, a low-cut pink crêpe. She chose it because of its fuller skirts, besides its daring neckline, in case the side door was locked later and she had to climb up the tree to get back inside. She was pleased at how the gown swirled around her feet and clung to her hips when she moved, but she couldn't do up three of the tiny buttons at the top of the back! There was no time to change, and she still had to do something with her hair. She brushed it so fiercely it crackled, then hurriedly plaited it into one long braid she could pin into a circlet atop her head. She tied a matching pink bow around the knot, laced pink sandals on her feet, and donned a dark wool pelisse to cover the gown's gaping back—and therefore sagging front. She refolded the domino and held it against her body, under the pelisse.

"Come on, Pen. I know you'd rather spend the night here, but I need you as an excuse to leave the house. Don't worry, old girl, I won't be out all night."

Marcus and Eugene were both at the front door. To avoid having the footman delegated to accompany her, Jacelyn headed for the library, whose glass door opened to the courtyard.

"I'm just taking Pen out to the stable, Marcus. You can lock up the library when you wish. I'll come back through the kitchen to get some warm milk, and I'll most likely use the back stairwell. Good night."

"Good night, Miss Jacelyn. I hope you're feeling more the thing by morning."

"Thank you, Marcus. I know I shall. I'm feeling much better already."

Leigh's reasons for staying away were twofold. First, they both needed time to calm down after those angry words. He shouldn't have been so high-handed with her, and she shouldn't have said what she did. Second, his face didn't bear looking at. Not as gruesome as Percy's, Leigh's black eye gave him a raffish look, but it still declared he'd been in a fight. Leigh had chosen not to make explanations to the ton or to Jacey. In the closed carriage, with a black domino pulled low over his brow, the bruise was hardly noticeable. He wouldn't have to lie that his ragtag cousin had landed a lucky punch, nor tell the truth, that he'd been in a prizefight for the money.

When he was finished with Percy, two days ago, he still wasn't quit of his anger, so he visited Jackson's Boxing Parlour. Everyone there was talking of a promising young pugilist they'd seen working out that day. Even Jackson was impressed. Lord Alvanley was so confident, he wrote an open wager in the betting book, offering five-to-one odds to anyone challenging Treadway for a three-round match, Jackson to judge. Claibourne took the bet.

"Arthur, can you lend me a hundred pounds?"

"Are you sure, Leigh? You're good, but, fiend take it, man, Treadway's twenty-two. He's got ten years on you!"

"Ten years of practice, Arthur. The money?"

"Of course. No need to borrow it, in fact, it's yours. Remember that night at the Cocoa Tree, after the Victory Celebrations? I borrowed five hundred from you. Forgot all about it till now."

"Lord, I don't even remember going to the Cocoa Tree that night! Arthur, you're a prince. A little late, now that I've entered my name in the book, but a prince nonetheless. Give me two and hold the rest for me, will you?"

The fight had taken place Friday morning. The first and the second rounds were Claibourne's. His skill and finesse left the younger man dazed, punching air, and losing his footing. In the third round Treadway found his tempo and landed a few solid, punishing blows, but it was too late, as long as the earl could stand. A fourth round would have finished Claibourne, but the match was his. Now he had a black eye, a bandage holding his ribs together, and enough money to last a good long while, if he didn't make any more foolish desperation bets. He wouldn't. He'd much rather spend the blunt on Jacelyn, making sure she enjoyed herself.

Like tonight, at Vauxhall, if she came. She shouldn't be there at all, certainly not alone with him, so Leigh had made plans for her safety, and more, which was why he was so late. He just couldn't move as fast as usual. Those ten years felt like twenty, today.

The hackney driver slid the call box open. " 'Ow much longer we goin' to wait, then, gov?"

"A few minutes more. She has to come."

"Its your silver, mister. 'Avey-cavey business though." He slid the little door shut with a snap.

Then she was there. He helped her into the seat opposite him and tapped on the coach roof with his cane for the driver to start.

Jacelyn was staring at him, her face filled with joy. "You came."

"I promised, sweetheart."

"I'm so sorry about that other day, Leigh. I didn't mean what I said. I don't care about—"

"Shh. I'm sorry too, kitten. I missed you."

"Oh, Leigh." She threw herself across the carriage into his arms. He almost fainted from the pain. A good soldier never complains though, so he just held her close while he caught his breath. In a minute she sat back, withdrew the domino, shaking it out onto the other seat. She started to undo the bow holding her pelisse closed, and made a silvery little laughing noise. "I had to let Pinkie have the evening off, Leigh, and I couldn't do up all the buttons. Would you . . . ?"

"I recall volunteering to be your dresser once, didn't I? Come here, my wanton, so I can reach."

She took off the pelisse and made an effort to hold up her bodice while turning around, but even in the dim light from the lanterns on the coach doors, Leigh could see the creamy glow of her skin above the fabric. He had to catch his breath again. His ribs be damned. With her back to him, he folded her in his arms, his cheek against the softness of her neck. Then his lips moved to caress her shoulders, her ear, and his hands moved slowly over the material of her gown. Instead of doing up the top three buttons, he undid three more, until he could cup her breast in his hand and slowly stroke the nipple. Jacelyn moaned softly, calling his name. She turned to face him, and then she was lying in his arms, the gown at her waist, and he was kissing her heart while she grasped his neck and combed her fingers through his curls.

"Oh, Leigh," she whispered again, until his mouth was on hers and there was no more bumpy carriage or flickering street lights, only his kiss and his hands, waking her like Sleeping Beauty to his passion.

His hand was caressing her thigh, through the silky crêpe, and down her leg, drawing the skirt and petticoat up till he was touching bare skin and their breaths were more like gasps.

Snick. The sliding door opened. "By Jupiter, I knowed it! We're at Vauxhall, governor. D'you want me to pull up or should I just drive 'round a few times?"

Vauxhall was vastly different on Masquerade Night, from when the ton attended. There were more soldiers, and more girls in low white blouses with rouged cheeks. There were Pierrots and Elizabeths and Henrys. Cats and devils and nuns and nymphs. And a lot of hooded capes and half masks, like theirs. Not just the outfits differed; the outlook was more relaxed, noisier, jollier. These people didn't have every night of the week to eat, drink, and be merry. They had to do it all at once. At first Jacelyn was enjoying herself. The people seemed so happy, dancing with enthusiasm never seen at Almack's, cheering and singing, laughing out loud. Then, as she and Leigh meandered along the paths, she realized that most of the crowd was on the go. They all, men and women alike, had bottles and flasks and full glasses waving in their hands. Those who looked so companionable were often holding each other upright, and beneath the laughter and the music she could hear angry shouts, an occasional scream.

"I can see that you and Arthur were right, Leigh. This is no place for a lady." She moved closer to his side.

"Have you seen enough then? Shall we go?"

"After the fireworks, all right? I'd really like to see them."

"Of course, my sweet."

But not tonight. Just past the cascading fountain, near a huge oak tree, a roughly dressed man staggered out of an unlighted alley. He bumped into Jacey, and his hands were groping at her body. She pushed him away and turned to Leigh, but he was grappling with another man! The first, a thickset man with long, bristly sidewhiskers, saw her attention turned and grabbed for her reticule. Jacelyn pulled back, shouting, "Thief! Thief!" to which no one paid the least heed. The strings broke in her hand, and the man was headed down the alley. "Leigh! He's getting away."

Claibourne had dispatched his assailant while Jacey was diverted, and now raced after the thief. "Stop, you!" he shouted, and caught the man by the shoulder. He swung him around and connected his fist with the man's chin, it appeared to Jacey, from where she stood next to the tree. The man went down, and Claibourne retrieved her reticule. He hurried back to her, while the thief scuttled under the hedges.

"Oh, Leigh, how terrible! Are you all right? How can things like this happen?"

"It's all over, my dear, nothing to concern yourself about."

"How can you say that? You might have been killed! And if you weren't so quick and strong and brave, I might have . . . have been . . ."

"There, there," he told her, gathering her against his chest, patting her back, and smiling. His plan

321

was a success! His man Haggerty and Haggerty's friend Jack had played their parts just as they'd rehearsed. In one easy lesson he'd taught his madcap love never to come here on a lark, to listen when he warned her of danger, and that he'd lay his life on the line for her. Impressing her with his prowess was a bonus. He hadn't intended to dally in the Dark Walks, but she was clinging so trustingly, tightly—blast Treadway's right cross—and temptingly.

Someone pushed him from behind. "Haggerty, what the hell are you—" It wasn't Haggerty. Possibly it wasn't even a man. It had a little head with piggy eyes all red and squinty, and a huge body with oxlike muscles bulging under its clothes. In a hand the size of a coal scuttle, the creature held a knife. Oh Lord. "Haggerty!"

Leigh got in a quick jab. The attacker hardly felt it, but at least it showed Leigh he wasn't fast with the blade. He didn't have to be. Leigh couldn't disarm him, not without the cane he'd dropped for the first act. He surely couldn't overpower the beast, even if his ribs weren't broken, and he couldn't run—not leaving Jacelyn there.

"Jacey," he shouted, circling, crouching, never taking his eyes off the giant. "My cane!"

His cane? Jacelyn found it, but how to get it to him? Then those other men came running out of the bushes toward Leigh, the ones who'd assaulted them first. Attack the earl three-to-one, would they? That bear-man had a dagger too, so it was even more unfair! Jacelyn stepped into the fray, beating Haggerty and Jack with the cane before they could get to Leigh.

"Hold, miss, we're on your side," Haggerty yelled, shielding his head. "His lordship needs his cane!"

The other man, Jack, was indeed pounding on the giant's back. Not Leigh's, and not to any effect, but he was definitely coming to Claibourne's aid. She let the man Haggerty take the cane from her and toss it to the earl, still keeping his distance from that deadly blade. Now Leigh could act: feint, parry, thrust, counter. *Whack* with the cane and the dagger was in the leaves under the tree. The cane snapping was the last Jacey could see clearly, as the four men made one blurry pile of moving arms and legs.

Jack went down first, flying over the bushes to land with a thud. Haggerty was straddling the giant's back, whomping on his head like a berserk piggyback rider, while Claibourne was bruising his knuckles on the behemoth's midsection. Leigh didn't want to get in close, knowing that one jab to the ribs by the tree-trunk arm, and he'd be out for the count. Then Polyphemus growled and whirled, flinging Haggerty off his shoulders like a sack of cornmeal. Haggerty stayed down.

By now Jacelyn had found the dagger, again with no way to get it to Leigh, so she kicked it farther into the leaves. She also found a big branch fallen from the oak. She managed to give the man-mountain a good wallop on his arm, getting his attention, which finally allowed Leigh to connect with a scientific right that would have floored Mendosa. The colossus shook his head. He looked at Jacey with her stick, Claibourne with his right, and Haggerty on his feet again and coming, and shook his head once more. He gave Claibourne a shove, not even a punch, but a push in the chest that flattened Leigh, and then he took off into the alleys.

"Should I follow him, Major?"

"Not without reinforcements, Haggerty, like the entire Fifth Cavalry. Are you hurt? What about Jack?" The earl managed to drag himself to the tree where he could sit, propped up by the trunk and Jacey's arms. "You were valiant, my lady," he told her, gasping.

Jacey looked around: the dagger, the broken cane, the two thugs standing by on guard. "Leigh, I don't understand what's going on."

"Not surprising, dear heart. I haven't the foggiest idea myself."

"Can we please go home?"

"You didn't get to see the fireworks."

"They'll have to hold them in Portman Square. I'm never, ever coming back to Vauxhall!"

"Incompetents! I'm surrounded by idiotic, imbecilic incompetents!" Fenton raged. "Jensen, you mammoth mole-mind, you've been hanging around that fool Percy too long."

He scrawled a message on a piece of paper and shoved it into Jensen's hand. "Here, take this to the Red Lion in Cheapside. Ask for Newgate. That's what I should have done months ago, hire a professional. . . ."

"If this is another of your freakish schemes, Leigh Merrill, I am not amused!"

"Shut up, you peagoose, and get down! Those were real shots!"

He had a pistol in hand and was looking for something to aim at. There was no need to tell Lady Parkhurst to duck; she'd collapsed unconscious to the carriage floor at the first cry of "Stand and deliver." Luckily *Tante* Simone had decided she needn't come.

They were about a half hour outside of London, halfway to Hockney Hall, the duchess's country residence. Not the Farthingale family seat, it was just a huge pile where the duchess liked to entertain. They were already late when the message came from Lord Parkhurst, telling them to go ahead, he and Sprague might be hours more at their meeting. Because of the delay, there were few other carriages on the road this dark, moon-clouded night.

The carriage came to a lurching halt. Jacey could hear shouting, from Lem up on the box with the coachman, then another shot! The door was wrenched open, and a voice growled, "Out, all of ya, or yer coachie gets killed. Girl first."

Leigh nodded and Jacelyn got out, stepping over her aunt's limp body. A gun was pointed at her by a mounted man in a brown frieze coat, cagily positioned behind the door, out of Leigh's line of fire. The highwayman leaned down, grabbed her arm, and pulled her next to him. When Leigh came out, he had no chance to act. The one bandit held a gun to Jacelyn; the second, shorter, man was covering the servants on the box, having taken their weapons. The Parkhurst outrider was on the ground, but alive, moaning. His horse was halfway back to London.

"A'right, yer lordship, drop the popper, or I glom the skirt."

Leigh tossed the pistol and raised his hands. "There's no need for anyone to get hurt. You're welcome to whatever we have."

"Oh yeah? What if we wants the mort?"

Leigh charged him, Jacey screamed, the horse reared, a shot was fired and went wide. Leigh was grappling with the frieze-coated rider, trying to unseat him, when the other highwayman rode over and smashed the earl on the head with his pistol. Claibourne went down, hard, and didn't move.

"Leigh!" Jacelyn was on her knees beside him.

"Whyn't ya shoot him?" Frieze-coat demanded.

"The skirt was in the way. 'Sides, I got a better idea. 'Is Royal Navy'll pay pretty good for a able-bodied seaman, willin' or no. We kill him, we get

326

paid oncet. We dope him 'n ship him off, we gets it twice, and the old coot's none the wiser. Here, gimme a hand gettin' him up."

Frieze-coat dismounted, and together the bandits dragged Leigh across Shorty's horse's withers, face down, despite Jacey's screams, kicks, and flails.

"Should we see if the flash mort's got any baubles?"

"Nah, we got what we come for. Let's ride 'fore someone comes. You there"—to the coachman—"you keep your dubber's mum till we're out a'sight or yer fine gent gets it. Understand?" The two men took off, Leigh's head and feet bumping against the horse's sides. There was nothing for Jacelyn and the others to do but watch the bandits ride away through the dense forest along the side of the road.

"Oh, God, we've got to save him! Lem, cut the horses loose! Zack, go see to the outrider. Oh, Leigh!"

"We can't follow them through *that,* miss," Lem told her, "not in the dark, on carriage horses. And they took all of our weapons with them."

"I know, I know! Zack, how is he?"

"Bleedin', but it's just his shoulder, miss. His pistol's still here."

"Good. Listen, here's what we'll do: Lem, you take one horse and ride ahead to Lady Hockney's and tell them what happened. Get a search party, men, lanterns, guns. Zack, you'll stay here with the coach and the pistol. You guard the postillion and my aunt, but don't try to wake her. She's better off in her faint! A coach should come along soon, I hope. I'll take the other horse and ride back to Town for help."

"But, miss, we can't even begin to track them until daybreak."

"*We* can't, but Pen can! Are you done with the knife?"

Lem was through cutting the traces of the lead coach horses. He finished and handed over the knife. Jacelyn gathered the hem of her gown in one hand and slashed it up the middle with the other. She repeated this with the back, then snatched his lordship's greatcoat off the coach seat and drew it around her. Lem led one of the horses to her, gave her a leg, and she was up, and away. "Hurry!" she yelled back.

"Get up, you lazy good-for-nothing mutt! Get up, Pen!" Jacey was pulling on her britches. The house was in an uproar around her. *Belle-tante* was for once *not* placid. She was wringing her hands and sending Marcus off to the Watch, to Bow Street, to the Magistrate, and the War Office!

"There's no time, Aunt! I've got to go now! Marcus, get a message to Lord Parkhurst. Tell him to get people to watch the ports and the press gangs. Tell him Henesley will follow me with the dog cart, but I can go faster on my gelding, and get through the woods, too. A pistol! Marcus, find my uncle's pistols—and load them!"

"Run, Pen, run. We're almost there, you can keep up!" The coach was up ahead; she could see its lanterns. She spurred the gelding on. "Zack, have they come?"

"No, miss. A carriage came by and took up milady and the outrider, on to Hockney with them. Help should be getting back here soon."

"I cannot wait! Henesley's behind me with fresh horses, but Pen will do better while the scent is fresh. I wish she weren't so out of shape! Here, girl, smell this. It's Leigh's greatcoat, Pen. Leigh. Here, his cane is still in the carriage. Leigh, Pen, find Leigh!"

The big dog was panting, her sides heaving, but she gamely followed Jacelyn's horse to the woods where Jacey thought the men had entered the forest. Yes, the branches were broken. "Here, Pen, please!"

The dog put her nose down and wuffled. She wagged her tail and whined—and she set off! "Good girl! Not so fast, it's dark. We have to watch out for low branches, Pen. We're coming. Good girl!"

Jacey lost her hat to the next trailing vine, and a twig scratched her face and caught in her hair, undoing all of Pinkie's efforts to send her to Hockney House an elegant lady. After five more minutes of this mad rush, all the pins were out,

329

and Jacey had to keep brushing the hair away from her eyes just so she could see. Pen was slowing down, thank goodness. Unless, it suddenly, horribly, occurred to Jacey, the dog was tracking a rabbit all along!

No, there was a glow up ahead.

"Pen," she whispered, "to me, girl. Let's scout around first." Jacelyn dismounted and tied the horse to a bush. She could hear the dog's almost wheezing breaths, and patted her on the head. "You did fine, Pen. Shh, just a little closer." Her intentions, as she crept closer to the light from a small cottage's window, were to get a good look at the place, see where the horses were, count if there were more than the two highwaymen's mounts, etc. Then—and she wasn't decided yet—she could either try to find her way to the carriage and lead the rescuers back, if she didn't get lost and if the bandits didn't ride on, or she could stay where she was, waiting. The men had to move Leigh, if they were going to take him to a ship or something, and when they came outside for the horses, she could shoot. The shortcomings of this plan were that her aim wasn't terrific at this range, and she wasn't entirely sure she could pull the trigger on a real person. Both of her choices had a common drawback: the men could decide to kill Leigh at any time.

Jacey stopped while she was still in the trees' cover, about twenty yards from the house. She couldn't see any horses or hear any voices. There might be two men or twenty; she had no way of knowing. Five yards more and she let go of Pen's collar to take out the pistols. One was in her waistband, uncomfortably; the other was in the pocket of Claibourne's caped greatcoat, still buttoned around her. The pistols were not the light duelling weapons her father owned, but were heavy, double-barrelled guns. At least she had two shots to each, which ought to be enough for Frieze-coat and Shorty. She *had* to know if there were others. Maybe she could follow the forest line around back, where the horses must be. She moved slowly, stealthily, trying not to step on fallen branches—then Pen barked. The dog headed right for the front door, following orders to find Leigh.

Immediate tactical revision: attack!

Jacelyn started howling like a banshee, zigzagging, calling out to Arthur and Lem and Zack. Pen kept barking. Jacey fired a shot and called, "Over here, men. The dogs have them." Another shot. "Surround them, boys!" *Boom.* "Let's go in!" She was at the door with one shot left, and her army of rescuers was one loud, tired dog. Oh dear!

The kidnappers didn't know that, however. Frieze-coat and Shorty dived out the back door for their horses as Jacey crashed through the front and fired at a retreating figure. "Yeow!" came back to her, and she was satisfied. So much for scruples.

331

Pen was racing around the room, licking Leigh's face, coming back to Jacelyn, panting and whining. "Down, Pen, let me see."

Leigh was on a faded sofa, his head hanging over the back. "Leigh! Leigh, darling, wake up! Oh, Leigh, please!"

Her voice roused him. With an effort, he opened his eyes and smiled that sweet, lopsided grin. "Changed your hair style, did you, pet?"

"Leigh, you have to get up! We have to reload the guns in case they come back. Can you walk? Oh, Lord, don't go back to sleep! I know your head hurts, but help will come soon. Here!" She spotted a bottle of wine and a glass on the mantle and brought the glass to him. "Just the thing."

"No, Jacey, not that." He weakly brushed the glass away.

"Yes, Leigh, it'll set you right back up. Please, we have to leave. Oh God, what now?" Pen was howling. Was she hurt? Had one of the pistol balls ricocheted and hit her? Jacelyn hurriedly pushed Leigh's limp head back against the sofa and tipped the contents of the glass into his mouth.

"Thanks, sweetheart, I needed that," he told her, slurring the words. She was already on the floor near the fire, though, where Pen was whimpering and writhing. Leigh managed to pull himself up to see. "Pup . . . puppies."

"Puppies! *Now?* Pen, how could you? And I made you run so hard, poor baby. Leigh, what do we do?"

"Do? You keep her in . . . inside during her season. Now . . . nothing to do but wait. The guns . . . I'll reload. Not much . . . not much time left for me."

"What do you mean? You're not going anywhere!"

"To sleep, Jay-bird. . . . You just poured half a bottle of lau . . . laudanum down my throat, remember?"

A few hours later Jacey was holding a pistol in one hand and a tiny brown and white puppy in the other. "You lightskirt, Pen. This could only be Jasper's get. Won't Squire be pleased?" There were six others nesting in the only quilt the place had, next to an exhausted Pen. The earl was draped across the sofa as comfortably as Jacey had been able to manoeuvre him, his greatcoat covering him. Jacelyn put more wood on the fire, and tried to stay awake.

The highwaymen hadn't come back; help mightn't locate them until morning. She couldn't go in search of the rescue party, not with the earl unable to defend himself or Pen. Even if she could lift or drag Claibourne to her gelding, Pen and her babies couldn't travel, so there was nothing for it but to wait. The cottage was dusty and smelled of mildew, and had no foodstuffs whatsoever. She was tired, hungry, dishevelled—but her

333

two best friends were safe!

Leigh woke up at first light, cramped and headachey and with a throat so dry he could barely swallow. Jacelyn was curled up in a chair, fast asleep, a pistol in her lap. He got up slowly and tucked the gun in his waistband. He sniffed the bottle on the mantel, then drank some of the wine. Poor quality, but not drugged, at least.

"Good morning, mama," he whispered to the dog. "I forgot all about you and your pups. Can I see them?" Pen wagged her tail, so he picked up a soft little wriggler making piggy noises. "Foxhound, eh? Well, they always say that where there's a will, there's a way. Good girl."

He made up the fire again, then lifted Jacelyn in his arms and carried her to the sofa. She stirred and mumbled "Leigh?"

"No, its Simple Simon. Go back to sleep." He cradled her in his lap, wrapping them both in his coat, and went back to sleep himself.

That was the way the rescuers, all twenty-odd of them, found them two hours later. Some of the saviours were liveried servants with ancient muskets. Some who had been searching the woods all night were still in their evening clothes. There were two soldiers and a few yeoman farmers, draughted, presumably, because they knew the countryside. There were Lem and Arthur and Farthingale and de Silva, all the other young men Jacelyn usually danced with. They were standing around in varying degrees and combinations of astonishment, aggravation, and embarrassment at the cozy little scene. Jacelyn, in britches, hair tumbled down her back, was wiping her eyes in confusion while Leigh stood and drawled, "Congratulate me, gentlemen. Not only am I still alive, but I am already a proud papa." He held a puppy in each hand. "Oh, yes, Miss Trevaine and I will be announcing our betrothal next week at her aunt's ball."

19

"Damn your luck, you blue-blooded bastard."

20

"Jacelyn had dinner with the Regent last week," Lord Trevaine told his friend, over the chessboard.

"Did she, b'gad. What did she think of our Prince Florizel?" Squire asked, making his move.

"Not much. More to the point is what he thought of her. She took him to task for the opulence of Carlton House, when so many of the people are hungry, to say nothing of the condition of the animals in the Royal Menagerie."

"She didn't! On second thought, I'm sure she did just that. Lord, I'd like to have seen Prinny's face! What did he say?"

"According to Jacelyn's letter, he is going to visit the Menagerie with her, to see for himself."

"Claibourne better keep an eagle eye out. Our Prinny's been known for his appreciation of the, ah, finer things in life."

"Jacelyn didn't mention Claibourne. She wrote about seeing *Othello* and a new opera, and a picnic. Not a word about Claibourne. I received a letter from my sister today also. Hers was dated Saturday, three days after Jacelyn's."

"Can't trust the mails these days. What did Lady Parkhurst say?"

"She recrossed her lines so often I had trouble deciphering. As far as I can tell, she's in a swivet. Her servants said Jacelyn and Claibourne had some kind of row, and he hadn't been seen nor heard from since."

"I knew it was too good to last. That gal's too hot at hand. You should have—"

"Wait. I got another letter this afternoon, an express from Claibourne. That's why I asked you over. Where is it? Here, listen: 'Informing you I shall announce the betrothal at Lady Parkhurst's ball Saturday. Yours, Claibourne.' That's all. What do you think?"

"I think Miss Jacey's up to her usual bobbery! That girl's never done what anyone expected."

"I don't want to see her make a mistake and have to live with it for the rest of her life."

"Course not, but who's to say what's the right thing? Look at my nevvy, Arthur. Getting betrothed before talking to Spenborough. What if the Duke don't take to Arthur, and he cuts the girl out of his will? Arthur says he'll have her either way. These young people go around making life hard on themselves."

"Still, I wish I could go to London. This curst cough of mine, though . . ."

"We'll be going down, come Friday, the wife and

338

I and Samantha, for the party. There was no peace in the house till I agreed. I'll take a look-see for you, find what the rumgumtion is this time. You don't want to move there, man, leaves your queen open."

"Oh, sorry. My mind's just not on the game. Friday will be too late, George. By the time you get to London, you won't be able to stop the announcement."

"Stop it? It'll be the best thing for the gal! What she needs is someone to shake some sense into her!"

"The doctor says I mustn't travel, at least not until it is warm again."

"Quite right, you might take a chill. You know, Elliot, the fox season's nearly over. . . ."

"Is it? You know I don't pay attention to those things."

"The ground gets too hard. Dogs can't pick up the scent. The hunt wasn't so fine this year anyway."

"That's strange. I would have thought with Jacelyn gone . . ."

"I know. I thought so too, but, oddly enough, it wasn't the same. I'd ride out *knowing* nothing untoward would occur. Oh, Vicar might take a toss, or a horse might refuse at the wall at Kraft's farm, but it was dull! I even pulled the dogs back, when I could, letting Reynard go, by damn."

"Jacelyn would be happy to hear that."

"She would, wouldn't she? It's been quiet with-

339

out her. Too quiet. Maybe I'll toddle off to Town early. Give m'womenfolk a treat, extra shopping and all that. It'll cost me, but dang, it's been dull here."

A treat? When their gowns weren't ready, the house wasn't in order, Lady Ponsonby couldn't be warned to expect her relatives three days early? Samantha was *aux anges,* but Squire's wife was not pleased, until Bottwick told her about Trevaine's three letters. They managed to reach London on Thursday, only one day early.

They were to call at Parkhurst House at eleven Friday morning, having heard conflicting reports from the Ponsonbys about kidnappings and such. Priscilla was in her usual high dudgeon, having decided that Farthingale would finally have come up to scratch at his mother's ball last Saturday, if not for Jacelyn's latest hobble.

Another imbroglio, eh? Squire thought along the way. Well, look how neatly he'd tied up the last. There was plenty of time to set Miss Trevaine right and reassure her father. See? There was Claibourne, standing right beside the girl to greet them. This should be easy as pie.

Five minutes later Squire was lost, heart, mind, and body. He forgot all about Jacelyn and her questionable engagement, all about his ailing friend's concerns, all about his waiting wife and daughter. No amount of pleading could pry him out of the kitchen, where Pen and her brood were star attractions.

"Settle your own hash," he told Jacelyn when she brought him tea at the servant's table. "You never listened to me anyhow. What do you think? The one with the white spot on his tail or this fellow here?"

It was up to Mrs. Bottwick and Samantha to make sense of Jacelyn's explanations.

"So you're going through with the betrothal because of the night at the cottage?"

"Yes, I see where we must, but Leigh says we still needn't marry."

"Don't you want to marry him, Jacey? He's *so* attractive," Samantha enthused.

"I know, you peagoose. I'm not blind, you know. And I do want to marry him, more than anything. But it wouldn't be right."

"But if you love him, dear, the other reasons, the cottage and all, are nothing to the point."

"I know that too, Mrs. Bottwick, but it's so confused. He never said he *wants* to marry me, only that we should be engaged. Now he doesn't even want me near him. He says we cannot ride in the park or go for carriage drives or anything, until he decides it's safe."

"Safe?"

"He thinks someone is trying to harm him, and the fool tells me not to worry! As though his

341

telling me not to worry takes away the danger! How can I not worry when men attack him in the park with daggers and kidnap him on the King's highway? What kind of unthinking, uncaring, unloving man would tell me not to worry?"

"None, dearest. I think you'd better have him anyway, when all this is over."

"I think I intended to from the first. I just wanted to make the gudgeon love me!"

It was her ball and it was beautiful. Her friends were all enjoying themselves, even the guests Squire dragged one by one into the kitchen, giving the chef palpitations. Arthur and Leigh had managed to pry Squire away to White's for the afternoon, leaving Chef to his creative concentration. The resultant dinner had been a masterpiece.

Aunt Amabel was so relieved that her mother-in-law had decided not to attend that she relaxed and enjoyed the meal too, especially since Jacey had done all the work of organising the ball.

Jacey was proud of all her efforts, not just the superb dinner she and Chef had consulted over for days. The seating chart had taken almost as long, with equally satisfying results. Monsieur Blanc had been deep in conversation, between Aunt Simone and the musical Miss Montmorency; Squire was pleased to find Arthur's intended a gentle, quiet sort of girl who let a man eat in peace; Samantha had charmed both Mr. Sprague, who found her an intelligent listener, and Lord Tayson, who found her full of bubbly chatter, so he didn't have to strain to make conversation. Jacey couldn't imagine Squire complacent about the dandified Lord Tayson as son-in-law, but he was a likeable enough sort, and well connected. Carter Sprague was still Jacey's first choice for Samantha. They made a handsome couple, she noted, as they passed by together on the way to the ballroom.

Jacelyn was standing in the hallway, greeting the rest of the evening's guests with her aunt and uncle—and Claibourne. This made it official, then, even before the announcement Uncle would make at the first dance. Leigh looked so handsome she wanted to sit down and stare at him! What she didn't want was him kissing the hands of all those women whose mouths said congratulations, but whose eyes said they were still available, what was a little engagement, between sophisticated friends? She caught his eye and he winked at her. That was all right, then.

The last guests having arrived, Aunt Amabel led the way to the ballroom, which was decorated with the usual swagged greenery and pots of flowers. When Jacey decided to wear the cream gown from Ryefield, with its bodice embroidered with butterflies, she also thought of adding silk butterflies to the decor, as a novelty. Now the multicoloured creatures seemed to hover over the flowers, on gold threads, and flit among the greens. With all their airy shimmer they seemed to epitomise the evening for Jacey: bright, insubstantial beings dancing their courtship rituals till the end of their short seasons. Don't let her love be as ephemeral, she prayed, as hard to hold and to keep. She squeezed Leigh's hand, and he brought hers to his lips, just as Lord Parkhurst made the announcement. Everyone applauded. She and Leigh walked to the centre of the room to begin the first waltz while they all watched.

Butterflies on the walls, butterflies on her gown, and butterflies in her stomach. Tonight she was going to ask Leigh, once and for all, if he could love her, if not now, then some day. Otherwise . . .

"Smile, dear heart, these are all your friends."

"I know, Leigh, it's just that—"

"Shh, pet, we'll talk later, when there aren't two hundred people watching. Just think, now that we are officially engaged, we'll be permitted ten minutes or so alone. Perhaps we could disappear after supper without causing an uproar. I still haven't presented the Claibourne diamond to you."

"I don't know where we could find any privacy! There are card tables in the east parlour, Monsieur will be playing pianoforte in the west, with Lord Milbrooke, if I'm not mistaken, and Squire Bottwick has decided Pen would do better in the library."

"I'll wager the petty despot in the kitchen tossed him out. Don't I see lanterns in the courtyard?"

"Yes, but it's cool out there."

He swung her in a twirling flourish to end the

dance. "Don't worry," he whispered in her ear, "I'll keep you warm."

After the waltz came the congratulations and well-wishes, Aunt Amabel's tears, and *Tante* Simone's contented *bien*, before she left for the music room. Arthur and Rhodine teased about who would be wed first, and Samantha just hugged her. Even Priscilla was magnanimous, now that Jacelyn was no longer a threat.

Squire's words, though, affected Jacelyn the most. He led her aside, on a stroll to the library, in fact, and took a small suede pouch from his pocket.

"Your father asked me to give you this tonight, but it, ah, slipped my mind until now. It was your mother's. He sent a message too, said to tell you he hopes you'll be as happy as he and your mother were, but that your joy should last forever."

There were tears in Jacey's eyes as she opened the drawstring. Inside was a simple gold heart on a chain. The inscription read *With all my heart, for all time*.

Jacelyn undid the topaz necklace she was wearing and slipped it into her uncle's desk drawer. She asked Squire to clasp the locket for her, which he did with trembling hands.

"We haven't always seen eye to eye, Jacey, and you're not what I'd want my girls to be, but damn, I'm as proud of you as if you were my own, as proud as your father would be, if he saw you here. I had my doubts, I'll admit it now, that you could play the lady or fix Claibourne's interests. You proved me wrong, lass, and I'm glad. He's a fine man, Claibourne is, and . . . and if he doesn't make you happy, you tell him he's got me to answer to."

Squire patted her back awkwardly while she wept on his shoulder.

"There, girl, you don't want to go all splotchy for your own ball," he said, sniffling himself. "Come see, I think the lads have grown an inch since noontime."

By supper, Jacey's hand ached from being shaken, her face hurt from smiling. It was a relief to sit down to lobster patties and champagne, even more of a pleasure to leave all the music and laughter behind as she followed Leigh into the library. Squire was helping Farthingale choose a pup while Priscilla tapped her foot in impatient aggravation. Farthingale should be out under the stars proposing to her, not picking names for dogs! Leigh and Jacey smiled at each other as they walked out the open library doors to the courtyard.

Leigh took off his jacket and draped it over her shoulders.

"Now you'll be cold," she protested.

"So come warm me." So she did, walking into his embrace as naturally as breathing.

346

"But, Leigh, we have to talk," she told him a few minutes later.

"Indeed, it's not proper to kiss a woman without putting a ring on her finger." He fumbled in the inside chest pockets, next to *her* chest, longer than strictly necessary, but Jacey wasn't complaining. He finally retrieved a tiny box. They walked until they were directly beneath one of the lanterns, before he opened the lid.

"Oh Leigh, it's beautiful. It really is. I was afraid it would look like one of Flora's investments, from what you said."

"Will you wear it for me, then? Not just for tonight, or for appearance's sake?"

"You mean forever? And really get married?"

"Don't sound so surprised, dewdrop. That's what an engagement ring is for, isn't it?"

"Of course it is, but we have to talk more about this."

"Talk, precious, I'm listening." But he wasn't, really. He was leading her away from the lantern's light and nuzzling at her neck.

"This is serious, Leigh. I have to know if you—"

"*Boom!* Something flared between them, and it wasn't any spark of desire. It hit the wall and sprayed concrete shards. Leigh yelled "Down!" and pushed her flat to the ground, covering her body with his. There was another explosion, then pandemonium. Priscilla shrieked, and Farthingale shouted for help. People were running outside with

347

candles, others were panicking in the ballroom. Pen was barking. The grooms were pouring out of the stable, shouting, "We're under attack! They're trying to assassinate the Prince!"

Arthur came running, yelling, "Leigh? Are you all right? Is Jacey with you? Was it another attempt on your life?"

And Squire roared, "Are the pups safe?"

The earl was helping Jacelyn to her feet. Her face was smudged and her skirt was torn, and she was trembling.

"Don't you *dare* tell me not to worry, Leigh Merrill!" She stood there, shaking her fist at him.

"Damn, woman, at least get inside where it's safe to do your fussing!"

"Don't you talk to me that way! I told you to go to the magistrate's. I said hire a Bow Street Runner, and you said you'd handle it! *This* is how you handled it?" She swept her arm out, now they were back inside. The guests were frantically taking their leave; even the orchestra was packing. Whistles were blowing up and down the street as the Watch was called. Aunt Amabel was being carried upstairs, and Aunt Simone had streams of tears down her wrinkled cheeks. The chef was running after the departees, crying in French about his dessert *extraordinaire*. Arthur was trying to direct the carriages, getting in Marcus's way, and Lord Parkhurst and Mr. Sprague were in conversation with two men in uniform, discussing round-the-clock guards.

Squire stopped by Jacelyn and Leigh on his way out, herding his wife and a white-faced Samantha. "I knew it," he said. "I knew you wouldn't get through a whole night as a lady without at least one ruckus, riot, or rowdydow."

21

"What do you mean, you know Percy's not involved with the attacks?"

It was late afternoon of the next day, Sunday, and the first Jacelyn had seen of Claibourne since the shooting incident. He'd been holding his own investigation, while she'd been to church, then tea at the Ponsonbys' with Mrs. Bottwick and Samantha. She'd also made a few other calls. Leigh now adjusted the tassel on his Hessians. "I, ah, was not aware you knew my cousin."

Oops. "I happened to make his acquaintance one day. So when all of this happened"—she waved her hand—"I thought he might have knowledge of the matter. He didn't. You know, he's not half as awful as you said; he's just a trifle peculiar."

"If Percy's just a trifle peculiar, Prinny's just a trifle overweight. Jacelyn, pet, I am not sure I wish to know, but it does occur to me that Percy's been deuced few places recently. You mightn't have spoken to him—by chance, of course—at Flora Cobb's?"

"Now that you mention it, wasn't that a strange coincidence? There I was, visiting my old nurse in Islington and who should live next door—"

"Jacelyn!"

"It doesn't matter! Flora's very nice, and her looking out for Percy is precisely what he needs. He wasn't the least on the go, I don't think."

"It's hard to tell with Percy, isn't it?"

"Leigh, be kind. They're both concerned over you, and want to help. So do I!"

"No. I told you I don't want you anywhere near me, except here, of course, in my arms."

She pulled away. "What, for an hour? Then you are going back on the street by yourself? That's the most chuckle-headed notion of all."

"I explained, puss, I'm not alone. Arthur will meet me here, and my man Haggerty is right outside. He'll walk ahead of us, scouting. His friend Jack from Vauxhall will trail after, to see if anyone follows."

"But that still leaves you exposed to whatever madman is hiding in an alley or doorway. Why can't you just have Fenton arrested?"

"Because there is no proof that he's done anything. You cannot charge a man with hating you. This is the only way, baiting the hired killer into a trap, then snabbling him. He'll name his employer, rather than hang, and there, it's all over. Otherwise we'll never be safe."

"I don't like it." She stamped her foot.

"I'm not thrilled myself, dear heart, but it's the only way. Let me tell you something else that wouldn't thrill me: finding your perfect little nose in the business. You didn't listen to me about Percy, and you didn't listen to me about Flo. You *shall* listen to me now. If I find you out there in your britches, or tagging along with your uncle's pistols, or putting yourself in any kind of danger, you'll wish that bullet last night hadn't missed. Understand?"

"Yes, Leigh, but how am I to know you are all right? You cannot expect me to sit with my knitting while you're providing target practice for a paid assassin!"

"Can you knit?" He kissed her and stepped back quickly, before he was tempted to stay. "Don't worry, I'll send messages."

The messages came regularly, a boy with a rose at six, a book of poetry at seven. Leigh, looking like he was actually enjoying himself, and Arthur, just looking weary, arrived in person at nine, to share tea and reassure the family. They were going back to Half Moon Street, in case anyone was waiting for Leigh at his lodgings, and then onto the clubs. Squire was going along with them, and Lord Parkhurst and Mr. Sprague thought they too might pop into White's, Watier's, or Crockford's. Claibourne smiled but told them he was trying to look vulnerable, which was hard to do amid a phalanx of armed defenders.

"I'll wait up till I know you are home safe," Jacelyn warned as she walked him to the door. Marcus pretended he was another piece of furniture as they shared a hurried embrace.

"It won't be much past one or two. We cannot stay inside; that would be a waste of time. I think the attack, if there's to be one today at all, will be waiting outside Half Moon Street when we get home. I'll send a messenger over, when we're all tucked in bed. Just think," he teased, "if we were married you could be waiting there for me, in something soft and lacy. I'd come home at eleven."

"If we were married, my lord, you wouldn't be going out without me!"

."Oh-ho, is that the way it's to be, under the cat's paw? We'll have to see about that."

"We haven't even seen if there's to be a wedding!"

"We never did finish that conversation, did we?" Arthur coughed, over by the door. "Right. It will all be academic anyway, if there's no bridegroom. Rest easy, rosebud, everything will work for the best."

The message didn't come at eleven, or twelve, or one. Jacelyn was in bed, reading, when it finally came at two. *Home safe,* it read. *Sweet dreams, sweetheart.* She tucked the note in the book and blew out the candle. Now she could unclench her muscles and relax. If that message hadn't come soon she was all prepared to climb down the tree and go to the earl's lodgings herself, no matter what he'd threatened.

The tree. Were there trees at Half Moon Street? Leigh and Arthur rented the second floor. What was to stop someone from climbing up and shooting Claibourne through the window while he slept? He thought he'd be safe in his bed, and most likely had no guards outside the house. Someone could even break in and strangle him, without waking Arthur. Or they could put poison mushrooms in the pantry. Anything could happen!

This time she took Lem. She knew he was awake; he'd brought the message up from the stable. She needed him to help watch the back entrance while she took the front. Besides, if his lordship found her, he'd be less likely to beat her in front of witnesses. Leigh's warnings didn't give her pause, beyond that. If she was willing to risk her life for his, it was her own decision to make, not Leigh's. Of course, he still didn't know how little her life meant to her, without him. . . .

Jacey and Lem separated at the house, each taking one of the pistols and tiptoeing to a sheltered hiding place, to watch. There *was* a tree, and no one keeping lookout. Good thing she came! She pulled herself into the shrubs to the right of the doorway and crouched down, trying to make herself comfortable, but not enough to fall asleep. The Watch went by, then nothing. No bird sounds, no carriage wheels, nothing. And then a sneeze.

The noise came from the opposite row of hedges. A cat? No cat sneezed so loudly. It had to be the attacker, or a guard Leigh had set out after all. There was only one way to find out. Jacey stood, pointed her pistol, and called, "Halt. Who goes there?"

Instead of calling back that he was a lookout, the lurker panicked and bolted for the street, so Jacey shot him. She heard the man cry out—then yell for Flo! Oh God, she'd shot Percy!

Jacey ran over. "Percy, it's me, Jacelyn! Did I hurt you? What were you doing here? I thought you were the gunman!"

Percy was holding his arm. Jacelyn undid her loose neckcloth to wrap around it. "I knew they'd hang me if anything happened to Claibourne," he said, "so I came to protect him." Jacey threw her arms around him.

Claibourne, meanwhile, came flying down the stairs while lights went on all over. He was barefooted and bare-chested, but had a pistol in his hand. He saw Jacelyn struggling with a man, so he hit the assailant over the head with the gun barrel. The man folded like a house of cards. Jacey screamed.

"Whatsit? Whatsit?" Arthur was yelling, in his long white nightshirt and tasselled bedcap. He was waving a sabre around.

"It's Percy! He came to save Claibourne, and I shot him, then Leigh bashed in his head. Poor Percy!"

"Haggerty," Claibourne shouted. "Come help get this cawker inside, and send someone for the surgeon. I suppose I'd better send for Flora too."

"Lem can go. Where is he? He should be right here, with all the yelling and shooting. Lem?"

Then they all heard what they'd missed over the other confusion, the sounds of a scuffle at the rear of the house.

They all ran back, Arthur flapping like a ghost, Leigh, Haggerty, Jack, and Jacelyn with her one remaining shot—leaving poor Percy flat on the sidewalk.

Lem was struggling with a man who was a lot larger than himself, but the second man, Shorty, had already emptied two cans of alcohol and was setting the house on fire!

Haggerty tackled the torchbearer, and the earl came to Lem's aid, shouting, "Don't kill him, Haggerty. Someone run for the fire brigade!" He pounded his fist into Frieze-coat's face, then again for good measure. He pushed the now-limp figure toward Arthur. "Find some rope and keep them safe. I'm going to make sure Mrs. Dawe from upstairs is out. She's hard of hearing." He went into the house, through the flames.

Jacey was in the way of Lem and Jack with the well buckets, so she raced around to the front of the house to make sure Percy didn't get stepped on by all the people running around. An old woman with a shawl over her nightgown grabbed her arm. "My kitty's in there, lad. My poor, poor kitty."

"Where?" Jacey asked, but the woman just kept crying about her poor kitty.

Leigh wouldn't even know to look for a cat! The front of the house wasn't touched by flames so, without hesitating, Jacelyn tore up the stairs, and up to the third floor. It was smokey here. She couldn't see well, and was coughing, but she got down on her hands and knees to look under the sofa. No cat. She scrambled along till she found the bedroom—and Leigh's boots.

"What the hell?" He tugged her upright. "By all that's holy, girl, don't you have any sense?"

"Mrs. Dawe's cat!" she gasped, from the smoke and her arm being yanked nearly from its socket.

"Damn!" He let go of her and looked around. "We'll never find a blasted cat!"

"Stop yelling and help me. He's under your side of the bed." Jacey couldn't quite reach. Claibourne got down on the floor and grabbed the animal—and got bitten for thanks.

"Is Mrs. Dawe outside?" he asked, shoving the cat at Jacey who at least had on a jacket. There were claw marks across Leigh's bare chest. "Then you and the deuced cat get the hell out of here. I'll see about the fire downstairs." He gave her a not so gentle swat. "And listen to me for once!"

Jacelyn waited till the fire was out, and Flora'd come in a hackney to take Percy home, and Leigh was talking to the magistrates. When it appeared that the earl, dressed now, might have time to remember her presence, she called to Lem.

"We're not needed any longer, Lem. We better go home."

"That is the only clever thing you've done all night," Leigh called out, his arms crossed over his open jacket. "I'll be finished with these men in five minutes. If I see hide or hair of you when I'm done . . ."

"Good night, my lord!"

"You mean you're just going to let him go free?" Jacelyn wanted to know the next morning, walking in the courtyard.

"What would you have me do? Plant him a facer or have him sent to Botany Bay? He's a sick old man in a wheelchair."

"But all those terrible things he did! It doesn't seem right he shouldn't be punished."

"Whatever happened to that sweet little girl who wanted to save every fallen sparrow? You've shot at least two men this week, that I know of."

"At least I didn't brain my own cousin twice."

"Only because you don't have a cousin. Fenton will be punished enough, knowing he failed. He's lost Percy, besides, for what that's worth. Percy and Flo are emigrating to the colonies."

"I know. Percy wants to go into government."

"Good grief! And how do you know that, miss?"

"Flora sent 'round a note, telling me that Percy was doing fine, and wasn't mad at us for what

358

happened to him."

Claibourne started to exclaim, "Mad at *us?*" but Jacey hurriedly put in: "Percy is better off abroad, but I still think Fenton is getting off too easily. What about Mrs. Dawe's cat? Fenton didn't care how many people he hurt, besides you."

"Thank you, my dear," Claibourne said dryly, "for considering my life as valuable as the cat's. The actual criminals, the ones Fenton was paying, will go to prison. They have confessed, and named Fenton, so he is just as guilty. The magistrates and I have offered to keep him on parole, since he never leaves his house anyway. He knows, however, that if there is the slightest hint of trouble, his gargantuan Jensen goes to gaol too. He'd be lost without the man. Beyond that, if anything whatsoever *ever* happens to you, or me, or our families, Fenton hangs, wheelchair or no. He's sworn *pax*, and I am tempted to believe him."

He led Jacey to a stone bench. "Enough of Fenton and Percy and the magistrates. It's time for another reckoning, Miss Trevaine. What the devil were you doing there last night?"

"Saving your life. Again."

"Oh." Claibourne abruptly sat down next to her. "Did I thank you?"

"No, you didn't. You threatened and yelled and sent me home like a schoolboy caught putting worms in teacher's desk."

"You know, I hadn't quite seen it from that perspective. From where I was standing, it looked a great deal as if you were endangering your life and your reputation, despite my orders to the contrary. You don't make a good soldier, pet."

Jacey giggled. "Too bad, now you can't have me court-martialled."

Claibourne was serious. "Indeed. So what am I supposed to do with you?"

Jacelyn took a deep breath and spouted: "You could tell me you love me, for a start." There, she'd said it!

Claibourne raised an eyebrow. "I could? I've been thinking about this a lot, Jacelyn"—and about time, she thought, but didn't say it—"and I think perhaps you were right all along, we don't really need to marry."

"*What?*"

"I know it's an about-face, but it's for the best. You should have someone younger, not an old officer like me who'll be forever telling you what to do, and getting angry when you do the opposite. You should have lots of Seasons, beaux, and balls. You deserve someone who doesn't drag around a parcel of dirty-dish relations like the clanking chains on a castle haunt. And you need someone you can trust, not someone with such a spotted past that you'll always wonder."

"What do you need, my lord?" Jacey asked quietly.

"I need to return to Durham. I should have been there ages ago, to see to the land myself. And I need to know I can support my wife, without living off her income. The money would always come between us, Jacelyn."

"No, Leigh—"

"Shh, let me finish. You say it doesn't matter, but it does. You wouldn't respect me, and I would resent being in your debt."

Jacey's eyes were wet. Leigh couldn't see because his back was turned. "It's because of my distempered freaks and silly scrapes," she decided.

"Never, Jacey," he said, turning and taking her limp hands in his. "All of that is just part of your bright honesty, your goodheartedness. You mustn't ever change. You're like a rose. The thorns are there, certainly, but oh, how sweet the blossom." His voice was breaking. He stood and walked away.

"I . . . I'll be leaving after dinner, I think. It will be easier all around. I've spoken with my aunt. She'll stay on in London with her French friends for a while.

"You should send a retraction to the newspapers when you return to Treverly. By spring everyone will have forgotten all about the engagement. Will you make my farewells to Lady Parkhurst?"

Jacey couldn't talk, for the lump in her throat. She just nodded, eyes down. He came closer and kissed the top of her head. "I only want what's best for you, Jacelyn. I'm not it."

And he walked away.

Jacey cried for an hour, out in the courtyard, then she got mad. The concrete benches fought back so she went inside and attacked a row of china shepherdesses on Aunt's mantel. Then she found Pen and cried some more, hugging each of the pups in turn.

There wasn't a soul, from the scullery maid to the Squire, playing three-handed whist with Lord Parkhurst and Mr. Sprague in the parlour, who didn't know that Lord Claibourne was gone, and Miss wasn't half pleased. Aunt Amabel locked herself in her bedroom. Lord Parkhurst and Mr. Sprague shrugged helplessly. Squire waited until he could hear Jacelyn's footsteps trail up the stairs before he went into the library to help Pen wipe her sodden puppies.

Jacelyn was spread-eagled on her bed, damp, drained, devastated.

Tante Simone passed Pinkie, weeping on a chair in the hall outside, and scratched on Jacey's door. "*Petite,* may I enter?"

"*Entrez-vous, madame.*"

The old woman, dressed in black as always, sat at the foot of Jacelyn's bed. "He is gone?"

"Yes."

"And he told you why?"

"He gave me a barrelful of reasons. The sense of it would fit in a thimble. He doesn't love me."

"*Non, cherie,* he loves you a great deal."

"Aunt Simone, he wouldn't leave if he loved me."

"He leaves *because* he loves you."

"I don't understand."

"How could you? He is only a foolish man, trying to be noble. Logic and reason have nothing to do with a man's pride, child."

"Then you think he really does love me?"

"I know it. He told me."

One half hour later Jacey was in the library, wearing Lem's britches and jacket, her uncle's pistol in the waistband, unloaded, her streaming hair held back with a ribbon. She'd never replaced the hat, and she didn't care. Lord Parkhurst had turned craven and disappeared to his club. "Private affair, I'm sure," Sprague had mumbled, bowing himself out. Squire appeared not to notice her odd ensemble as he continued his hand of solitaire.

"I'm not going to let him just ride off without a by-your-leave! It's my life he's ruining too, for the most hare-brained reasons I've ever heard. Arthur could reason better than that. Pen could reason better than that!"

Squire turned over a red three. He needed a black three or a red four. "Damn."

"And I am going to ride through the streets of London just like this so he sees I don't care what anybody else thinks of me. It makes no difference if I'm ruined, if he won't come back with me."

The red four. "Ah!"

"Did you hear me? I'm going after him."

"What's that you say, m'dear? I wasn't attending."

"I said I'm going after him!" she shouted.

"Of course you are. I'd be shocked if you weren't."

"You would? But . . . but . . . ?"

"You're still Jacelyn Trevaine, ain't you? Never did the conventional thing in your life, nor let anyone hold the bridle for you. I don't figure you to start now."

"Then you approve?"

"You never paid that any mind before, either. There's just one thing you should know, missy. If you go off like that, you better be prepared to marry him. I sent your uncle out for a special license and a vicar. There's been enough of this harum-scarum engagement. You understand?"

"Stand and deliver," came the command from the bandit up ahead.

"What the blazes?" Haggerty was on the box; his lordship was inside, sleeping after being up all night. Baron trotted along behind.

Haggerty peered and pondered. This was the strangest holdup he'd ever seen. Broad daylight, the gun wasn't even drawn, and the highwayman's face mask was a paisley scarf. He grinned and pulled up.

Jacey rode over and dismounted, taking the pistol out of her waistband. She entered the coach and aimed it directly at the earl, who had woken at the carriage's change of tempo.

Claibourne was not amused. "You little fool! I suppose you rode through Town like that, too, after all we've done to protect your deuced reputation. We settled it all this afternoon, Jacelyn. Your dramatics won't change anything, so what the hell is this about? And if that damned pistol is loaded, I'll put you over my knee right now. If it isn't, and you rode out here alone and unprotected, I'll use the carriage whip!"

Jacey ignored the last, saying, "This, my lord, is a kidnapping. We settled nothing this afternoon, and now we are reopening negotiations. I am holding you for ransom."

Claibourne laughed bitterly. "Wasn't this where I came in? Jacey, that's the whole point. I haven't enough money to buy farm seed, much less my freedom. You've made a bad bargain, my dear. There *is* no ransom money."

"Then I'll just have to keep you."

He took her firmly by the shoulders. "Listen, dearest, I'll try to explain again."

"No, Leigh, I only want you to answer one question. Do you love me?"

"More than I've ever loved anything in this world. That's why—"

"Shush. Here, take this." She put the gun in his hand, pointed it at herself, and whispered, "Help!

Help! I am being held prisoner!" She took a cheque out of her pocket and handed it to him, as he sat there, grinning foolishly.

"It's blank," he said, putting the gun down and drawing her onto his lap.

"Of course it is," she told him. "You've just captured me, my lord, for all time, and you can demand everything I own." As she turned her face up for his kiss, she added, "You already own my heart."

For all time.

A Loyal Companion

To Yang-Sho Sundial Jim,
who is my sunshine

Chapter One

Squire Elvin Randolph was a proud man. He was proud of his vast, well-tended Berkshire acres, and proud of the wealth they brought him, so he and his wanted for nothing. He was proud of the ancient name he bore, and of the sons who would bear it after, and the daughters who graced his fireside. If Squire Randolph had any misgivings, it was that his beloved wife had passed on to an even better life, if such were possible. His chest still swelled, albeit over a comfortable paunch, when he recalled the day Allison Harkness, daughter to the Duke of Atterbury, had chosen him, a simple farmer, to receive her hand and heart. She had never regretted her decision, despite that widow in the village, no, not even when he turned down Atterbury's offer of a title. "A title does not make a better man," she'd said, to his everlasting gratification. He missed his dearest Allison still, despite that widow in the village, but he took comfort knowing she would have shared his pride in the fruits of their union.

The boys were George and Hugh, an heir and a spare as the saying went, solid lads with good bottom. They'd be educated as gentlemen farmers the same as their father: as much book learning as they'd sit still for, with the mud of Randolph's Deer Park Manor only temporarily scrubbed off their hands and faces. There was enough property for Hugh, the second son, to claim a tidy parcel, or enough income to purchase his colors if the little hellion didn't outgrow his love of knights and dragons, pirates and Indians.

The girls would be well provided for, too, their mother's portion making them heiresses in their own rights. Catherine, Squire's firstborn child, had also inherited her mother's delicate beauty. She was soft-spoken and well mannered, even as a tiny moppet in sparkling, starched pinafore and smooth blond braids. A lady to her fine-boned fingers, she was destined to grace London ballrooms, to shine as an ornament of society, to make a noble marriage. Her grandmother, the dowager Duchess of Atterbury, was already planning her come-out, with the squire's blessings. Frankly, Catherine's perfection terrified Randolph. What if he got her dirty, or uttered a profanity in her hearing, or touched her soft skin too hard with his rough hands? Better the dowager saw to such a paragon. He'd look after the boys, and Sonia. . . .

If the dark-haired, sturdy boys were as alike as two cherries on the same vine, the squire's daughters were as similar as apples and oranges. Catherine was refined elegance, with the cool essence of silvery moonlight. Sonia was exuberant sunshine, all bouncy golden curls and bluebell eyes and a dimpled smile that could melt the frostiest heart, which the squire's certainly was not. The baby of the family, younger than Catherine by ten years and soon left motherless besides, Sonia was pampered and spoiled and adored by the whole household.

"You'll ruin that child," the dowager duchess warned. "Letting her run wild after the boys like that, taking her up on your horse with you every time she holds her arms out, instead of sending her back to the nursery where she belongs. Mark my words, Elvin, that gel will be a rare handful. No man will take a hoyden to wife."

"But she's just an infant, Lady Almeria," Squire replied, brushing cookie crumbs from his now-rumpled cravat. "Time enough to worry about a husband later."

The dowager only sniffed. "She doesn't even know the meaning of the word 'no.' "

"Of course she does." Randolph tossed the babe up in the air and asked: "Precious Sunny, do you want a fussy old rich man with a title to take you away and keep you in some cold, dark castle?"

"No," she shouted between squeals. "No, Papa, no!"

Squire called her Sunny, not Sonny with an *o*. He denied his mother-in-law's claims that he was trying to make another son out of the girl. He was content with his boys, and absolutely delighted with this pink and white bundle that was soft but not fragile like porcelain, sweet but not cloying like wedding cake. Besides, no little boy would be so generous with sticky hugs and sloppy kisses. He called his youngest child Sunny simply because she lit up his life. When she looked up at him with adoration, he saw her mother, Allison, and he was proud all over again.

Unfortunately, when Sonia looked up at him like that, Squire Randolph could deny her nothing. Even more unfortunately, perhaps, Sonia also inherited, beyond Allison Harkness's beauty, fortune, and loving nature, her mother's knack of knowing her own mind. Allison had always known what she wanted, and had accepted nothing less. Didn't she marry plain Elvin Randolph, Esq., despite an uproar that shook stately Atterbury House in Grosvenor Square to its very foundations? So, too, did Miss Sonia Randolph make her wishes known. Poor

Elvin had more than one opportunity to think back on the dowager's dire warnings. Especially when it came to his hounds.

Now, as proud as he might be, Squire Randolph did not take credit for his lands. They were passed down to him, as he'd hand them on to George. That they were fertile was a gift from on high, to be nurtured and tended as best he could. Even his children, as much as he loved them, were more products of Allison's goodness than his own, he felt. But his hounds? Ah, now, there was something a man could brag about to his cronies. He could invite those toffs down from London and show off his darlings till the titles turned green with envy. Hadn't he bred the dogs himself, for generation after generation, to get just the right conformation, just the perfect pitch, color, and temperament? Hadn't he trained them all himself, right from the weaning box, till he had the best fox-hunting pack in the county, maybe the country? By Jupiter, he had!

Sheltonford was not Quorn territory, and the squire was too conscientious to let anyone destroy his tenants' fields or disturb their herds, fox or no, but an invite to ride with the Deer Park pack was seldom refused. When there was no company or no fox, Randolph had one of his kennelmen drag a hide for him, just so the hounds stayed keen, just so he could have the joy of riding behind, a fine piece of horseflesh between his legs, the wind in his face, and the sound of a dog on the scent like music in his ears. Aw-roo! Aw-roo!

Squire could pick out the individual hounds' voices the same as he could identify his children's. Better, for there was Belle, first to find the scent, loudest to bay, sweetest in timbre. Belle was the best dog Squire ever owned. Gold and white, with velvet ears and doe eyes, her tail arched just so, she stood foursquare and jaunty, always eager. Her heart was in the hunt, and Elvin Randolph's heart rode with her.

* * *

Bud Kemp was also a proud man. He ran over three hundred head of fat and fluffy black-faced sheep on hundreds of acres of land he leased from Squire Randolph, just like his father before him, and he'd never missed a rent day. He had three strapping boys to help him at lambing, shearing, and market days, with another gone for a soldier. The youngest was studying with the vicar to see if he'd suit the priesthood. His wife still looked good to him, especially in the dark, and they had enough money set by in case times got hard. Bud Kemp could rest easy nights, knowing he'd done right by his family, his landlord, his church, and his country. He could also sleep soundly knowing his woolly assets were safe out in the valleys with his dogs, the smartest, loyalest, most competent sheepdogs in the shire. Hadn't Bud bred them himself for generations, right since crossing his older border collie bitch with Shep Hayduck's Belgian herder? Damn right, he had. And kept breeding the good 'uns back to the lines to weed out the bullies, the daydreamers, and the weak of body or soul.

Those sheep were the stupidest creatures on four legs. They'd get lost in the front yard if not for the dogs. They'd panic at the slide of a pebble on a slope, graze clean off a cliff, or baa in the face of a long-knifed poacher, if not for the dogs. Bud Kemp's sheepdogs kept him snoring, and the dog that brought a smile to his weathered face, even in his dreams, was Jack.

Jack was a handsome black dog, well-furred to keep him warm out in the hills on cold, wet nights. He had a white blaze and a white bib, and half-cocked ears that were always vigilant for warning sounds. He carried his feathered tail low, in the habitual low profile that let him swivel quickly or bunch his muscles for a quick burst of speed. Jack was so smart, Bud boasted, he could drive those sheep through the eye of a needle. And he never harmed a one of the plaguey beasts, nor ever let anyone or anything else hurt one either. Jack was so smart, Bud swore down at the local, he could sense danger when it was two valleys away.

The only thing Jack never did understand was market day. He and the boys and the other dogs brought the sheep to whatever place Bud told them and then . . . nothing. No sheep, no job, just a saucer of ale on the floor of the tavern.

Now, Squire Randolph wasn't too stuck up on his own worth to bypass the local alehouse on his way home through Sheltonford village, nor to share a mug with his tenant, nor to admire Bud Kemp's fine working dog. The two men had a lot in common, but this was not France. Neither man, in fact, would think of getting their dogs together any more than they'd encourage the sheepherder's sons to go courting the landowner's daughters. There was just no way in King George's England for Squire's Belle and Kemp's Jack to know each other, in the biblical sense, that is . . . except for Miss Sonia.

"But, Papa, they were only playing!"

Squire's bellow of rage could be heard two counties away. "Hell and damnation, Sunny, didn't I tell you I wanted Belle in the house tonight? I should have listened to your grandmother and beaten you years ago. It's not too late. I'll ship you off to boarding school, see if I don't!"

"But, but, Papa," she said, sniffing, "you just said Belle was to keep me company tonight because you had to go visit Mrs., um, someone on business." At his narrow-eyed look, Sonia hurried on, her bottom lip trembling. "And, and Belle missed her friends in the kennel so much, she was crying by the door."

"You are never, ever permitted to open the front door by yourself at night!"

Sonia shrank back from his roar, her blue eyes awash in tears. "I didn't, Papa, truly. Jack came around by the library door, you know, the one Taylor leaves open for you when you're coming home late from—from wherever you go. Isn't Jack clever, Papa?"

Squire Randolph sank down in an old leather chair in what used to be his orderly library, in what used to be his well-ordered life. He shook his head in resignation and motioned to Sonia, who promptly launched herself into his lap. "Ooph, poppet, you're getting too big for your poor old da. And you are surely too old to be in such scrapes. Why, you are all of ten now—"

"Nearly eleven."

"And country-bred. You know what happens when a, uh, ram and a ewe get together."

"Yes, Papa, but you didn't tell me that Belle was feeling motherly like you say about the ewes and the mares and the sows and the hens and—"

"All right, Sunny, I should have—"

"And I didn't know Jack was feeling frisky like you say when the stallion—"

"Enough! Here, blow your nose."

She took the handkerchief he held out to her, snuffled into it a few times, then squirmed around to look up at him, blue eyes shining despite the tear streaks, dimpled grin showing a missing tooth. "Papa, can I keep one?"

Squire Randolph was still saying "No" some two months later. "You know you cannot have one, poppet. They just wouldn't make good house dogs. They'd be too big, too wild. I'll buy you a puppy, love, see if I don't. What would you think of a little pug you can carry around? You know, with those cute little squashed-in faces? Or a Pekingese you can comb and brush and put ribbons in its hair. You'd like that, wouldn't you, Sunny?"

Sunny stamped her foot. She wouldn't like a lap dog at all. She was too old for dolls.

"No matter, the pups'll likely be sickly anyway."

And she was too old not to know what happened

to unwanted puppies and kittens. Someone would tell her the babies were sickly, and the next day they'd disappear. Not this time, she vowed.

The men in the stables were like jackstraws under the weight of Miss Sonia's desperate coaxings: they crumpled immediately. So she managed to be on the scene for the grand event and could see for herself that all three of the pups were strong and shiny, suckling avidly. Her eyes big with wonder, Sonia turned to share this marvel of new life with her father, and intercepted his signal to the head kennelman, Tom. Squire jerked his head once to the side, and Tom nodded.

Sonia ran to her father and clutched his hand. "No, Papa! No!" she cried in a pathetic little voice.

Randolph stroked her gold braids, tumbled, as usual, out of their ribbons. "I'm sorry, Sunny, but the bast—babies are neither fish nor fowl. You know they're no good for anything."

"No, I don't know that, Papa, and you don't either! You can't yet. Why, that would be like deciding someone was guilty before you heard the evidence. And you wouldn't do that, Papa, I know. Everyone says you are the fairest man in the shire. They made you magistrate, didn't they? You didn't even send Eddie Spears away when everyone knew he was poaching. No evidence. That's what you said, Papa. So you have to give Belle's puppies a chance, too."

The pups were weaned young, though not for lack of attention, despite Squire's best efforts. He wanted to avoid future disappointments and heart-wrenching scenes. But no governess or nanny or nursemaid had yet kept Miss Sonia from where she wanted to be, so she knew Tom's report before he gave it to her father.

"Very well, Sunny, we'll keep the blondish pup for now. Tom says she follows a scent right smartly for such a young bitch, and sticks to it. She won't look so out of place with the pack, either. But she's not a pet, mind, and if she doesn't work out, she's gone. Now, let that be the end of it and these other two wretched whelps. I don't want to see them around here anymore."

Sonia patted his knee. "Of course not, Papa. Mr. Kemp will make sheepdogs out of them."

"I'll keep the spotted bitch, sir, Miss Sonia. Seems to take to the sheep. Quiet-like an' gentle with 'em." Kemp not-so-gently nudged the last pup, the only male, away from chewing on his heavy boot. "Not like this fool. Barked in their faces, he did, then ran the silly beasts in circles till we could catch 'em, and him no bigger'n a minute. I got no time for a dog what only wants to play."

The mostly black dog had noticed Squire's riding crop, tap-tapping against Randolph's thigh, and was lunging at it, trailing mud and straw and other stable debris down the well-clad leg. Squire kicked him away. Ferocious infant growls turned to a soft whimper as the squire nodded sagely. "My man Tom had no better luck with him. He wouldn't stay on a scent, just hared off in twenty directions at once. Wouldn't bring a stick back, so he'd never make a retriever, and he sure as Hades isn't quiet enough to go on point." Squire turned to his daughter to make his final, sad ruling in the case.

And there she was, his baby, his heart's ease, sitting cross-legged on the stable floor amid the muck, with a miserable mutt on its back in her muddied lap, teething on one of her blasted braids!

"I'm sorry, poppet, but there you are. No one wants this one."

She looked up at him, his angel, with that smile so like her mother's, and his eyes almost watered. Then she declared, in a tone of voice also reminiscent of Allison Harkness Randolph: "I do." She set the dog on his white feet and ruffled his shaggy black coat, pulled straw out of the arched and

9

plumed tail with its white tip. She bent over and kissed the puppy right between his clownish gold eyebrows.

"But, Sunny," her poor father tried one last time, the same as he'd tried to convince Allison her sons did *not* need to be sent to boarding school, or that fox hunting *was* pious enough for a Sunday. "But, Sunny, he's not good for anything!"

"He's good enough for me."

And that is how I, Fitz the dog, by Jack out of Belle, came to share my life with Miss Sonia Randolph.

Chapter Two

 $\mathcal{T}$ hey named me Fitz, which in ancient times was used to denote a blot on the family escutcheon, the old bar sinister, a product of an unsanctioned joining. A bastard. Human persons seemed to care a lot about cat dirt like that. I didn't. After all, wasn't everyone always praising both my parents? What more could a body ask? My sire was the finest sheepdog between here and Canis Major. He could think like a sheep, they said. Then again, a *rock* could think like a sheep. Jack could think *for* a sheep, for a whole flock of sheep and for the shepherds, too. And my dam never lost a fox. A few horses, their riders, the master of the hunt, but never the fox. No, I had nothing to be ashamed of in my forebears. In fact, I wanted to be just like them.

But sheep? Moving them from place to place to place, when all they talked about was grass and grass and grass, just to let the harebrained shepherd lose them for you? That made no sense to me, no more than fox hunting did. You kill the foxes and what do you get? More rats. And everyone knows what you get then, and it's not just the bubonic plague.

Still, I yearned to fulfill the promise of my breeding, to go beyond mere existence toward excellence. I looked around and there she was, Miss Sonia Randolph. I knew right away—they say it's like that with true vocations—that I had found my calling. I was going to be a companion! Not just any companion; I was going to be the best companion since Hector was a pup.

Please note that I consider myself a companion, not a pet to be pampered and sheltered, smothered and caged for another's pleasure. I accept my soft bed, my regular meals, but I work for them, training Miss Sonia.

There were no more tantrums. Miss Sonia soon learned that *I* would be banished to the stables for her misbehavior. There were no more missed sessions in the schoolroom either, and no more unfinished lessons. If Miss Merkle was pleased in the mornings, Miss Sonia quickly deduced, then Papa was pleased at luncheon, and we were free to do as we pleased for the afternoon.

No one ever needed to worry about us when we were out and about. Where I was, she was. Where she was, I was. No one had to feel guilty that there were no other children for Miss Sonia to play with, or had to take a groom away from his chores just to shadow her about. No one had to worry about the eggs disappearing from the henhouse or the vegetable garden being torn up, either. I was a responsible dog now; people trusted me. They knew that, like my mother, I would never get us lost and, like my father, I would defend Miss Sonia to the death.

We went everywhere. We knew every bird nest, every new foal, every gingerbread baker and sausage maker for as far as we could go and still get home in time for supper. We *never* missed supper.

It was a time to learn, a time to talk. We had discussions with birds, beasts, bugs, even bats. Socrates' cave had nothing on theirs!

As time went on, we were more on our own. Miss Catherine completed her schooling and her Season with honors: a ring from Lord Martin Backhurst, marquess, from Bath. Master George left university to study the bachelor life in London; Master Hugh became Lieutenant Hugh Randolph, posted to Portsmouth. And we expanded our horizons. The pianoforte, watercolors, the reins of a pony cart, the reins of the household, it was all the same. We knew which groom to chivy, what new tweeny needed a kitten in her bed so she wouldn't be homesick, where the sun cast the prettiest shadows, and when Papa liked to hear "Cherry Ripe." We kept growing, learning. I even stopped teasing Deer Park's tame deer. They were too easy.

Squire Randolph was happy. He threw into the trash Lady Atterbury's letters demanding that he send Sonia away to school before the provincial hoyden was permanently freckled. The neighbors were happy that there was a real lady at Deer Park, and Miss Sonia was happy. Why not? Everyone loved her.

I loved her, but I was not happy. I was five years old.

Five is not old for a dog; sixteen is not old for a human person like Miss Sonia. But I worried. We were no longer ignorant children. I, at least, had learned from everyone around me—sparrows and sows, milkmaids and meadow mice—that there is a higher purpose beyond mere survival, beyond even personal success. We each have another calling, a universal—

dare I say divine?—raison d'être. Succession. We must carry on.

Sirius knows I was doing my share, and so were those maids out behind the barn, but Miss Sonia was sixteen, and playing chess with her father.

But enough of teleology. I once knew a badger who fancied himself a philosopher. Fellow could bore the fleas off a ferret. I decided to take matters into my own paws. As soon as the family returned from London, I was going to start holding up carriages.

The heir was getting married. George Randolph was taking in holy matrimony the hand of Miss Jennifer Corwith, and he was doing it with all pomp and glory at St. George's, Hanover Square, in full view of half the ton. According to Squire Randolph, smug in the first pew, the boy hadn't done half-bad for himself. Miss Corwith was a handsome enough female with a more-than-handsome dowry. She came from a good family—her mother's people were distantly related to royalty, but not so uppity that they could look down on George's ancestors. Squire scowled at Lady Almeria Atterbury seated next to him, looking more like a jewelry shop mannequin than a dowager duchess. Uppity didn't half describe his mother-in-law. He turned back to the ceremony. The bishop was still spouting incomprehensible eloquence.

The Corwiths were doing themselves up proud. Of course, this affair wasn't nearly as grand as the bash Squire threw for his Catherine's wedding. Then again, Catherine married the Marquess of Backhurst. The Sheltonford chapel in Berkshire had been laughingly dismissed, and a simple ceremony at Atterbury House was out of the question. Balls, breakfasts, bride clothes, Lady Almeria spared no expense. Why should she, when Elvin Randolph was paying? Roses were not good enough;

she wanted orchids. A handful of attendants was paltry; every classmate of Catherine's at Miss Meadow's Select Academy became a bridesmaid, it seemed, with every gown, slipper, and hairpiece added to Squire's account. And the reception after, well, the food could have fed every dirt-poor tenant in Berkshire for a year, if the wealthy members of society hadn't devoured it all in a matter of hours. He frowned again, this time encompassing the whole congregation of overfed, overdressed jackaninnies. Then his brow cleared.

It had all been worth it, to show the ton that Backhurst wasn't marrying down, by Jupiter, and to show Lady Almeria Atterbury that Elvin Randolph was no countrified coin clutcher. Mostly, though, it had been worth all the blunt, and the time and botheration, just to see his girls walk down that long aisle.

He didn't actually see Sonia, naturally, for as flower girl, she went before him and Catherine. And his Sunny didn't quite manage to walk down that white-carpeted path; she skipped. Flowers twisted into her hair, a gap-toothed grin for the bishop, the minx turned and winked at her brothers. Lady Atterbury clutched her vinaigrette the whole time.

Then came Squire's turn, with Catherine. He would never forget the joy on her face nor the hushed awe in the vast cathedral as he led to the altar the most beautiful bride in decades. Not since her mother, they whispered, and tears came to his eyes even now, at quite a different wedding, just remembering. He took out his handkerchief and blew his nose.

The dowager poked a bony finger in his ribs. "It's they who ought to be crying, you twit," she hissed, nodding across the aisle to the bride's family, "not you."

His collar was starched too high for him to look. He nodded, barely.

"My goddaughter heard that silly Corwith chit

didn't want anyone to compare her wedding with Catherine's—gel can't hold a candle to our Lady Backhurst—so she just picked two attendants. No chance of being cast in the shadow on her day in the sun that way, especially with Catherine stuck in Bath in her condition."

"You know what Backhurst said," the squire whispered back. "Maybe this time, if she stays quiet . . ."

Lady Atterbury twitched her scrawny body a hairbreadth away on the cushioned seat. "My granddaughter, sir, is not a barnyard creature whose breeding is subject to one of your interminable speculations."

Squire mopped his forehead with the linen he still clenched. "Sorry," he muttered.

The dowager nodded and edged closer so she could continue her conversation. There was nothing Lady Atterbury liked better than a good gossip, unless it was baiting her son-in-law, especially in church, where he couldn't raise his voice or flee to the stables.

"Vain as a peahen, that Corwith girl," the old lady confided. "So she chose her spinster stepsister from Corwith's first marriage as maid of honor. Leah's a plain, shy old ape-leader who never took. And for bridesmaid, Jennifer picked George's harum-scarum little shire-bred sister. Heh heh."

Squire shifted his eyes to see if anyone had heard the old harridan's cackling, then he checked to make sure Sunny hadn't brought a mouse into the church or had her petticoat dragging. No, she was standing there next to Hugh as pretty as when they'd left Atterbury House, for a miracle. Her golden curls were as bright as the braid on her brother's dress uniform. Those same curls, or most of them, anyway, were held up for the first time with a wreath of blue silk flowers. She wore her grandmother's pearls, her mother's smile, her sister's elegant charm—finally, thank heaven!—and that glow that was only Sunny's.

Minds might be wandering as the bishop droned on, but from what the squire could see, most eyes were on the altar where the bridal couple knelt, their attendants to either side. Unfortunately, no one was looking at the bride.

Lady Atterbury did not want Sonia at the wedding breakfast. "Chick ain't full-fledged yet," she said, excusing her granddaughter's early withdrawal. "We'll fire her off next year." Actually, the dowager wanted Sonia out of the way before the untutored chit did something outrageous to give the Quality a disgust of her, before the wedding toasts got too ribald, or before the bride murdered her. She made sure Sonia was escorted home as soon as politely possible.

The squire was not so lucky.

"That one is going to make a stir," the dowager announced to him after she'd dragged Randolph away from a gathering of cronies and a discussion of the latest improvements in crop rotations and opera dancers. "What are you going to do about it, Elvin?"

First he was going to rub his knuckles where she kept tapping them with her fan, then he was going to make sure he wasn't back in short pants. "Do about, uh, what, Lady Almeria?"

"About finding her a husband, you looby! That one could land a duke, if there was a decent one among the bunch, but she's as sure as salvation going to attract trouble like a magnet. And what are you going to do about it, Elvin? Are you going to find an eligible parti and arrange a good marriage before she lands in the basket? Or are you going to do what you've always done, and give the chit her head?"

"It's a good, level head, ma'am, not stuffed with gewgaws and gossip. Sunny's not more hair than wit like most females her age. She's a wise little puss."

"That's not enough, Elvin. You wouldn't send her to me, you wouldn't hire the females I recommended to school her properly, you wouldn't even send her to Miss Meadow's Select Academy that turned Catherine out so nicely. Sonia don't know how to go on. She could embarrass us all." Before her victim could work himself up to produce the ladylike governess Miss Merkle as a good loud parry, or deliver a thrust about London manners and mores, right there at his son's wedding reception, the dowager delivered the coup de grace. "Worse, planted like a cabbage out in Berkshire, she'll make a mésalliance."

She didn't say it. She didn't say, "like Allison." But he heard it, and his ruddy tan grew ruddier. "If Sunny wants to marry a farmer," he said through gritted teeth, "she has my blessing. She's got too much in her brainbox to fall for a here-and-thereian."

"She's got you wrapped around her finger, you mean, as always. The chit's got more energy and enthusiasm than a colt, and about that much sense of what she owes her name. What if she throws her bonnet over the windmill for some linendraper's assistant? What will you do then?"

He'd bellow the rafters down, that's what, the same as the Duke of Atterbury had done. And he'd swallow his own tongue before he admitted it to this diamond-decked she-devil. "Sunny's young yet; no need to worry about her marrying for ages."

"No? Well, you think about it, you twiddlepoop; you're not getting any younger!"

Squire Randolph did think about getting older, and Sonia getting older, and even that old-maid daughter in the Corwith household getting older. The only ones getting younger were the successive widows he kept in the cottage in the village. He thought about it on the carriage ride home, and looked around when they arrived in Sheltonford.

He looked at the local boys with new eyes and saw gangly gossoons and unlettered lumpkins. Then he compared his Berkshire friends' sons with his son's London friends he'd met at the wedding, and started sending out invitations. Surely among George's Corinthian set there'd be a young buck who could appeal to Sonia, appease Lady Atterbury, and not displease himself too much. Surely, when pigs flew.

"Never seen so many cow-handed fiddlers," he muttered into his newspaper at breakfast, after seeing off the latest of his invitees. This one limped so badly, he wouldn't even stay for the hunt, which was the ostensible reason for the blasted visit.

"What's that, Papa? Did Lord Northcote get off all right?"

"Just fine, poppet." Fine, except for a smashed curricle and worse-damaged ego. The poor fellow'd had to be carried up the drive, chicken feathers blowing out of his hair. Sunny's damn fool dog was barking to raise the dead, so Squire couldn't even get the viscount inside and cleaned up before she saw him. A viscount, deuce take it. He shook his newspaper. "What in the blazes were chickens doing on the roadway? That's what I'd like to know."

Sunny narrowed her eyes and looked sharply at the dog at her feet. She shook her head. No, it couldn't be. "Good dog, Fitz."

"That mutt's not begging at the table again, is he?"

"Of course not, Papa."

"Of course not, why should he beg? You feed him everything in sight anyway. And you cannot deny he caused Sir Findley to part company with his horse last week."

"Fitz was chasing a rabbit, Papa."

"Findley swore there was no rabbit, just a berserking wild beast."

Fitz had his head in Miss Sonia's lap, softly brushing his tail along the floor. She stroked back his shaggy eyebrows. "Of course he did. The silly man couldn't very well admit he'd chosen to ride more horse than he could control. I think the problem is that while George's friends are sporting-mad, they are all city drivers. They're not used to our country roads. What was that other gentleman's name? The one who put his phaeton in the ditch just because a few sheep were blocking the road?"

"L'duc de Bourville," her father said with a groan.

Sonia came around the table to place a kiss on his cheek. "Are you very sorry you'll have no company on the hunt tomorrow?"

Sorry? He wouldn't be sorry if he never had to see any of the quick-tempered, bad-mouthed young bloods again, especially the one whose whining he had to listen to for a whole week before the sawbones declared him fit to travel. He wouldn't let a single one of the chubs call on his daughter. B'gad, he wouldn't let a man jack of them drive her the half mile to church! Perhaps he should tell Hugh to bring some of his officer friends home for his next leave. No, he couldn't bear the idea of his little girl off somewhere following the drum. Or of telling Lady Atterbury.

"Sonia." Squire only called her Sonia when he was troubled. She sat on the arm of his chair to listen carefully. "Sonia, your grandmother thinks it's time we started thinking about a Season for you. Perhaps you should spend some time with her in London, quiet-like until your come-out, you know, but meeting some of her friends', er, daughters, so you'll have acquaintances of your own when the time comes."

"You mean meet all those exquisite coxcombs, don't you? I know what Grandmama wants, and that's a fancy title, no matter that the sprig of nobility has less upstairs than an oak tree in winter."

Squire Randolph laughed and pinched her cheek. "What do you know of dandies and such, huh, puss?"

"I know Backhurst. Why, he buys more clothes in a year than most men buy in a lifetime. He's always complaining about his health, and he can't even give Catherine a ba—"

"Sonia!"

"Well, I never did see why she married him."

"Then you don't want to go stay with Lady Atterbury?"

"Heavens, no, Papa. You won't make me go, will you?" Sonia giggled. "Grandmama terrifies me."

"Me, too, poppet," he confessed. "Me, too. No, I won't force you to go. What would I do here without my sunshine?"

She slid into his lap and threw her arms around him for a hug the way she always did. "And I won't leave till Grandmama finds me a man just like you!"

Right, when hell freezes over.

Chapter Three

$\mathcal{I}$s there such a thing as hell? What about heaven? Are there sausages there? For that matter, is there a God? Many gods? There used to be pantheons of them, Osiris and Thor, Baal and Vishnu. Gods are immortal, so where did they go?

I wait outside the doors of the Sheltonford chapel every Sunday listening to the psalms and the hymns and the sermons, but I still do not understand this one omniscient, omnipotent being theory. I mean, look around. We've got rabies and hunger and fleas. Shouldn't someone get rid of the cat dirt if they've got the shovel?

Human persons have a great deal of imagination. That's a fact. Think of all their inventions, all their books, a heaven with no dogs allowed. Think about that cockamamie idea they cherish: that some divinity created us ... to serve them. What a quirky sense of humor this creator must have had, making an entire horse just so some scribbler could glue his book together, teaching suchamany worms how to spin just so ladies didn't have to wear fig leaves. Hogwash! And what possible use could they have for gnats? Only mankind could subscribe to such a notion.

Yes, they are helpless, so we help them when we can, but that's as far as it goes. We kick dirt on this theory of dominion. Animalkind embraces the mysteries and worships only one religion: survival. My survival, my children's survival, my children's children's ...

So I ate a cat.

The honeymoon was over, the nuptial visits to aunts in Scotland and cousins in Ireland were complete. In other words, the bride was in a family way. George was ecstatic; he could be home for grouse season. Jennifer was less thrilled. She'd looked forward to at least another Season in town, this time with the freedoms of a married lady. At last she'd flirt with rakes, gamble at polite hells, wear bright colors. Now she was condemned to making eyes at the footmen and playing whist with her father-in-law. As for clothes, she might as well start ordering tents!

She swept into Deer Park prepared to hate it, and she was disappointed again. The mellowed brick manor house was handsome and set among lovely grounds and well-kept gardens. The furnishings were tasteful and the staff was polite. Even her new sister-in-law was properly deferential, personally escorting her upstairs to Jennifer's spacious and freshly decorated rooms. Jennifer's only recourse was to pick on the dog.

"I'm sorry, Sonia, but I cannot abide dogs in the house."

"Oh, dear, I'm afraid you'll have to get used to them. Father often brings his hounds in, you know." From the look on Jennifer's face, she obviously had not known. Sonia smiled and went on:

"Please feel free to call me Sunny as George and Father do. And I'm to call you . . . ?"

"Jennifer. This will never do. No, Sonia, I have to insist this . . . creature stays in the kitchens. I'll speak to Father Randolph about the hounds. I'm sure he'll understand. Why, Muffy wouldn't be safe." She shuddered dramatically and clasped her white fur muff more closely to her chest.

Muffy was a white long-haired cat with gold eyes and pushed-in face. She was as fat as she was lazy, content to be hauled around on Jennifer's hand warmer like a dowager on a sedan chair. Jennifer thought the cat and muff, especially when she wore her ermine-trimmed pelisse, gave her a cachet. Her signature, she called it, like Poodle Byng.

"Like Poodle Byng?" Sonia choked, trying to stifle her giggles. Right now poor endangered Muffy was doing a fair imitation of a cushion atop a burgundy velvet-covered slipper chair.

"Oh, I forgot you couldn't be au courant with what's à la mode in Town," Jennifer sniped, recognizing the younger girl's levity, "in notables or fashions."

Sonia fidgeted with the ribbons of her new dimity round gown, which her grandmother had sent down from London and she'd saved for this special day. She didn't reply.

"Nonetheless, I shan't have my dear Muffy distressed by any rowdy dogs."

Muffy had finished her pillow act and was now portraying a Staffordshire porcelain fireplace dog, batting Fitz aside to get the warmest spot on the hearth.

"Fitz is the gentlest creature on earth," Sonia said, scratching behind the dog's ears in consolation. "He would never hurt anything."

"But he sheds! I don't want any awful black dog hairs on my light-colored muslins."

Sonia just looked over to the burgundy velvet chair where white hairs clung like threads on a cutting table. "That's why Fitz is not permitted on the furniture. Nor are the hounds, of course. And we'll just have to make sure Muffy is in another room when Father brings them in. Is there anything else we can do to make you more welcome?"

Jennifer gave up, for now. "How do you stand it in the country, Sonia? What is there to do with all this time?"

Sonia didn't know how to answer, since studying with Miss Merkle, running the house, looking after the tenants, helping at the Sunday school, and keeping Papa company seemed to leave no free time at all. She was hoping George's wife would take over some of the responsibilities, but didn't want to discuss housekeeping on Jennifer's first day. She tried to remember what Catherine liked to do. "We have a lovely pianoforte, and a good library, and the church is always needing new altar cloths." No response. "We go riding, of course, and walking, and visiting with the neighbors. They are so anxious to meet you, I'm sure the vicar's wife and the Minch sisters will be over for tea Sunday."

"The . . . vicar's wife and the Minch sisters?" Jennifer threw herself on the bed. Sonia sank down on the rug between the cat and the dog, stroking both. She missed Jennifer's look of disgust.

"Oh yes, they run the lending library. And the postal office." Jennifer moaned, and Sonia hurried on: "We have card parties and dinners, and informal dances sometimes when there is company for the hunt. And there are assemblies over in Seldenridge, the nearest town of any size"—Jennifer brightened—"once a month."

"Oh." Jennifer stared up at the swagged canopy over her bed. "At least you have linendrapers and dressmakers, don't you?"

Sonia busied herself retying Muffy's bow, barely whispering: "Just the Minch sisters."

Jennifer shrieked.

"But they get all the latest fashion journals from

London, or Papa could have them sent with his newspapers, and . . . and there are lots of shops in Seldenridge. You could ride there anytime you want. George said you were a bruising rider. That's what first attracted him to you, he told us at the wedding."

Jennifer sniffled. "The physician said I mustn't ride anymore!"

"Then you can take the pony cart. Or maybe George will buy you a curricle of your own. Father says I am too young."

"I don't know how to drive a cart," the bride wailed. "I never needed to know, in the city."

Jennifer was sobbing now, and Sonia was patting her hand, pouring tea, ringing the bellpull. Fitz pushed the door open and left. "Oh dear. Don't cry, Jennifer. Please. I know, I'll teach you to drive. Then you won't need to call out half the stable staff every time you want to buy a new ribbon or go visiting. It'll be our surprise for George. What do you think of that?"

Sonia was thinking that George was in for more than one surprise. She was also wondering where she was going to find time to teach her bubble-headed new sister-in-law how to handle the ribbons. Anyone who would name a cat Muffy . . .

Jennifer sat up and clapped her hands. "How absolutely perfect! You shall teach me how to drive, and I shall teach you how to dress like a lady!"

Oh dear.

The new Mrs. Randolph—Mrs. George below-stairs and in the village—grew about as content as she grew competent at the reins. Coco, the old mare who was used to finding her own way home from the village while Miss Sonia drove with her nose in a book, seemed to have forgotten which foot went where. She did manage to find every rut and bump on the road to the village, however. When Jennifer finally reached Sheltonford, she was usually too queasy to step down outside the tiny emporium.

"Too high in the instep," Miss Petronella Minch declared.

"We won't call again," her sister, Miss Marietta Minch, added.

"But Miss Sonia serves such a lovely tea."

At first Sonia tried to keep Jennifer busy with driving lessons, renovations to the nursery, introductions to the local society. She even agreed to be poked and prodded and pinned into a new wardrobe of sheer muslins and soft silks, just so Jennifer could have the pleasure of talking fashions and fabrics for endless hours. Sonia still preferred her kerseymeres and calicos for the long walks and comfortable times she managed to fit in. She thanked her lucky stars that Jennifer slept late in the mornings and rested after lunch, so Sonia could get her own chores done. George's wife refused to look at the menus or go over the household accounts with Sonia, saying: "Oh no, you're still the daughter of the house and still your father's hostess."

As Jennifer's shape got more unwieldy, though, her temper grew more uncertain. She took her pettishness out on George when he was available, so he made himself less available, checking out new breeds of sheep in Weymouth or Wales or the West Indies, for all Sonia knew! With George off on his trips, Sonia was left to bear the brunt of Jennifer's spite, until Squire Randolph had the downy notion of inviting Jennifer's stepsister to Berkshire.

"You remember, that quiet gel from the wedding, Leah."

"Papa, you are brilliant! She seemed so pleasant and mild-mannered. Perhaps she won't mind Jennifer's megrims."

"I don't think she was very happy in London; might be glad for the change."

"It might be that she wasn't happy with Jennifer, but I'll write this very morning. Oh, I hope she comes, don't you, Father?"

Miss Leah Corwith came, and with her soft-spoken ways, charmed everyone, even Jennifer for a while, for Leah was able to relate all the news from London. She kept up a large correspondence, so was au fait with the latest on-dits. Miss Corwith pleaded to assist Sonia with the household, for she was used to keeping busy, she said, and felt like a hanger-on otherwise. She was a skillful whist player and an enthusiastic if not expert rider. She even liked dogs. Sonia and the squire and George and the staff thought Leah was wonderful; Jennifer thought she was useful.

Now that Leah was here to take over the drudgery of a chatelaine, Jennifer didn't have to be so tolerant of Sonia. She saw no reason why the heir's wife shouldn't sit at the head of the table or take precedence going into dinners with company. The villagers should not call during Jennifer's established nap time, nor ask for Miss Randolph. The servants should take their orders from the future mistress of Deer Park Manor, not from some half-grown hoyden whose hair was always falling down and whose gloves were always soiled, when she remembered to wear them at all. Mrs. George gave up trying to make a lady out of that sad romp. She even stopped advising Sonia about her clothes, after all the gentlemen noticed and admired the forward chit—and made Jennifer feel more like a bloated cow than ever.

Jennifer knew better than to complain to George or Father Randolph about Sonia—she saw the way they fawned on the girl—but she did not hesitate to complain about that dog.

The dog was spoiled, the dog was ungoverned. He was no proper pet for a lady of fashion, and he was certainly not a proper chaperon. Sonia had no business running around the countryside like a veritable draggle-tail gypsy with nothing but a mongrel for escort. She and that flea-hound were going to land them all in the scandal-broth. Besides, the dog was always underfoot. Jennifer could trip and lose the child. Fitz had to go.

George went to his father, and the squire went to Sonia, after a quick helping of Dutch courage from the brandy decanter.

"Give me a pregnant bitch or a mare in foal, poppet, I know what to do. But women get queer as Dick's hatband. It's more'n a man knows what to do."

Sonia had her arms folded over her chest and her chin thrust out.

"It's only till after the baby comes, Sunny."

"If Fitz goes, Muffy goes." She turned on her heel and left.

Squire had another glass of brandy. This was going to be one very long pregnancy.

Miss Sonia tried, she really did. She stayed in her room, she stayed in the kitchen, she even stayed in the schoolroom. Fitz stayed with her, of course. She stayed out of the house till her nose turned blue and icicles hung off Fitz's fur; then she stayed in the warm stables, drying and brushing the dog till there wasn't a loose hair to fall out of that animal for a week. Jennifer took to putting her hands over her protuberant belly every time she saw Fitz, protecting the unborn babe.

Matters came to a head the day Jennifer refused to go to church in the family carriage if the dog came along, even if Fitz rode with the coachman as he'd done since her arrival.

"It is not seemly," she said, waving her fur muff around. "I refuse to be a laughingstock in the village where I expect to live the rest of my life." And she sat right down on the hall bench, put her muff on the floor beside her, and started untying her bonnet.

The servants disappeared. George was scarlet-faced with embarrassment, and Miss Corwith was suddenly memorizing her hymnal. The older Randolph looked beseechingly at his daughter. Sonia looked back at her father, and for the first time saw not a hero, not a god, just an ordinary, peace-loving, incompetent male. She looked outside; it was raining too hard to take the pony cart. She looked at the clock; they were already too late for her and Fitz to walk. She looked at Fitz; yes, he'd race them to town no matter what, meet them on the church steps, and likely shake raindrops all over Jennifer's ermine-edged pelisse. "Very well," she said, gesturing for them all to precede her out the door, and quickly. "Fitz stays home. This time." She never looked at Jennifer at all.

Squire invited the Pinkneys to take luncheon with the family after church. The Pinkneys were prosy old windbags, but a man couldn't be selective when he was looking for a smoke screen. Before they were all out of their carriages and inside the door, General Pinkney was bending George's ear with the same old tales of the Mahratta Wars. Mrs. Pinkney was giving Sonia and Miss Corwith her interpretation of the vicar's sermon. The host followed last, escorting his daughter-in-law at her slower pace. It wasn't until they were all gathered in the hall to hand over their wraps that Fitz came slinking down the stairs.

The big black dog didn't bound down the hall to welcome Sonia the way he usually did if she left him home. Furthermore, he wasn't quite as black and shiny as when they'd left. Instead he seemed to have played in the snow, only there was no snow on the ground. He didn't bark his usual welcome, either. He couldn't, his mouth was full. A piece of something white and furry dangled from between his long, white fangs. A piece of—

"Muffy!" Jennifer screamed. And screamed and screamed for two hours solid until the doctor could be found, out by Peg Wilson's. Not even dangling Muffy in her face, *felis intactus*, could halt the hysterics. George scrambled around finding bits and pieces of ermine skin and satin lining to prove the hand muff's demise. Miss Corwith burnt feathers. The squire suffered a very boring luncheon with the Pinkneys . . . and Miss Sonia wrote a letter to her sister in Bath, accepting Catherine's long-standing invitation.

A few days later Sonia burst headlong into her father's study the way she used to when there was a new litter of pigs, or the first dewdrop was out.

"Papa, is it true? Did you really tell George to hire some workmen to fix up the Dower House? Oh, Father, that's the best idea you've ever had! Now things can get back to normal."

"Whoa, poppet. Don't go crammin' your fences. Things are never going to be the way they used to be. We're all older now, Sonia. We have to think about the future."

"Yes, Papa." She knew to be quiet and listen when the squire was in such a serious mood. She took the seat across from him, her hands carefully folded in her lap.

"A man gets lonely when his wife is gone, his children are grown." He held up his hand when she started to speak. "No, hear me out. If not today, someday you'll want a husband, babies, a home of your own, and this isn't it. And that's the way it should be, like chicks leaving the nest. George and Jennifer will do better on their own, too. She'll settle down as soon as the baby comes, you'll see. Then I'll have no one."

"You'll always have those widows in the village."

The squire dropped the pen he'd been holding. "Tarnation, you shouldn't know anything about any— And you sure as hell shouldn't mention 'em! Didn't anybody teach you anything?" He looked away from the knowing smile she flashed him. "That's neither here nor there. What I wanted to say was, I'm thinking of stepping into parson's mousetrap myself. With Miss Corwith. Leah."

"That's just wonderful, Papa," she said, beaming. "I am so happy for you, truly. She's a lovely girl—uh, woman—and I think she will make you an excellent wife. And we already get along, so you'd never have to—"

"I know you like Leah, and she likes you. I wouldn't have her else, and she says she won't have me unless you give your blessings. You do, don't you, Sunny?"

Sonia giggled. "I thought the young man was supposed to ask the father's blessing. Of course I wish you every happiness!"

"Good, good. We're going to have a quiet wedding right here as soon as the banns are read. I mean, no reason to wait, at our ages. Might even start a new family. Leah's not much older than Catherine, after all. But the fact is, Sunny, you'd always be mistress here. And Leah's so gentle and kind, she wouldn't even mind. But it's not fair to her."

"I see, I think. I was planning on visiting Catherine anyway, so I'll just stay in Bath until Jennifer's baby is born and you and Leah are all settled in." She forced a laugh. "Perhaps I'll even nab some rich old duke there taking the waters, and make Grandmama happy."

Squire didn't join her laughter. "Thing is, Sunny, I wrote your sister a few weeks ago. Got a letter back today. She's finally increasing again and says she's too sick to take you around or anything, and can't jeopardize the baby, after so many disappointments. And, well, you never did get on with Backhurst. Catherine's just not up to that kind of brangling."

"I never did see why she married that milksop," Sonia muttered, studying the design on the Aubusson carpet—and her options. She swallowed, took a deep breath. "Grandmama?"

Her father nodded sadly. "Lady Atterbury."

Among wolves, only the dominant female gets to mate.

Chapter Four

Of all the courtship rituals I have studied, the London Season sounds the most bizarre. My information comes from Muffy, the greatest feline impersonator of my experience. I have seen that cat portray a snowdrift, a dish towel, and a tea cozy. Such virtuosity!

According to Muffy, whose observations I cannot discount since she was witness to two Corwith sisters' come-outs before Jennifer's, human persons' mating behavior seems contrary to nature.

For one thing, the proper breeding age is arbitrarily set—by a committee, mind you—regardless of individual maturation. Then all of those selected (debutantes) to meet the most eligible males (catches) are herded together (the Marriage Mart) and dressed alike. In white, no less. The brightest colors, the most sparkly jewels, the finest plumage, are reserved for those who already have a mate! If a female loses her mate, she is forced to wear darkest black, even if she wishes to encourage another male.

In many species, the males fight for the females. Muffy says the London gentlemen often participate in fisticuffs, swordwork and marksmanship contests, even hold races. But the young women are not permitted to view these activities, or the unclad males, so how can they select the mate who is strongest, fittest, fastest, best able to protect them and their children? The debutantes are not permitted to be alone with the men, no, not even to dance more than twice in an evening with the same partner. How can they make a proper choice? No wonder they have so many ugly babies.

Muffy calls me naive. They choose for two things, she says, purity and property. The sexes are kept so firmly apart because chastity in females is valued above beauty or intelligence. There are chaperons and open doors and enough rules to choke a Chihuahua. This I can understand. A male wants to know that his own progeny will inherit his property, not some other stud's in the stable. The females accept this because property means possessions and power in London, and security for their families. A man does not have to be as brave as a bull, as strong as a stag, as fast as a falcon, as smart as a dog, to win the maiden of his choice. He has to be rich. The wealthier the female, the wealthier the male has to be to prove he can provide for her.

In her descriptions of the marriage contracts, Muffy has never mentioned anything about affection, devotion, or respect, which is not surprising for a cat. I question the absence of love in these negotiations, however, since mankind has made so much of that emotion over their centuries. Muffy just laughs. I shall wait until visiting Almack's to see for myself.

While I am looking forward to the Metropolis and exploring its possibilities, Miss Sonia does not share my enthusiasm. Her steps lag, her words come slower, her mouth droops. She grieves at the loss of her home, and I am sorry. I drop my bowl into her half-filled trunk to say, "Don't be afraid, I am coming with you." She smiles, but I can see she is sad. She's torn, having to leave her beloved father to make him happy, feeling guilt that his joy causes her pain. She does not understand: he is not her mate, she is not his dog. I lick her nose.

"Well, let me take a look at you, girl." The old lady raised her lorgnette and motioned for Sonia to turn around, like a horse on the auction block. "Now let me see a curtsy," she barked.

Sonia dipped into a bow suitable for royalty, and only ruined the graceful effect by making the obeisance to the dog at her side instead of toward her grandmother. Fitz lowered his head, as he'd been taught. Lady Atterbury made a sound almost like a chuckle. "You'll do. The hair is atrocious, of course, that sunburned skin is an abomination, and whoever had the dressing of you should take up upholstering. What do you think, Bigelow?"

Lady Atterbury's abigail, as venerable in her starched black uniform and lace apron as her employer was in taffeta and turban, made her own inspection. Sonia held her breath. "Monsieur Gautier. Lemon juice mixed with strawberries. Celeste's. Breathing lessons."

"See to it," the dowager said, as if making a silk purse out of a sow's ear overnight were as easy as matching ribbons. Lady Atterbury nodded to Bigelow, dismissing the poor woman to her Herculean task, then raised the looking glass again.

"And I suppose this is the animal that stirred the bumble-bath in the first place."

With a slight hand gesture Sonia had Fitz approach her grandmother's chair, sit, and offer his paw for shaking. Her Grace twitched her skirts aside. "A gentleman always waits for a lady to offer her hand first, Sonia. Remember that."

"Yes, Grandmama," Sonia said, ordering Fitz back to her side. "But he truly is a well-behaved dog. He won't cause anyone any trouble at all."

"Well, it's all the rage for ladies to carry their pets around with them. Margaret Todd even brought her parrot to tea at Devonshire House, I understand. All the unmarried women had to flee the room when it started to talk. I have a feeling you'll be an Original on your own, dog or no, but we'll see. Once the Season gets rolling, you'll send him back to Berkshire fast enough, I'm sure. He'll be company for you till the ball, anyway."

"The ball, Grandmama?"

"Of course; didn't think I'd fire you off without the proper *affaire*, did you? Invitation list is in the study; you can start on them tomorrow, after your fittings. Marston, he's the butler, don't you know, can help with the details, orchestra, refreshments, that type of thing."

"I . . . I'm to plan my own ball?"

"You don't expect me to do all that work at my age, do you? I'm too weak for that fardling nonsense. Don't get your garters in a welter; Marston knows how I like things. The ball will be in a month. Plenty of time. Bigelow should have you in shape by then. I've arranged with the war minister's wife to have your scapegrace brother here on leave to stand up with you. That clunch Elvin writes that he will still be on his wedding trip, and George cannot leave the milk-and-water miss he married. We cannot wait."

Sonia ignored the insult to her father; he'd warned her she'd better get used to them. "I'd be more than happy to delay the ball, Your Grace. Couldn't we just hold a quiet dinner, a small party?" she asked hopefully.

"Hmph. I know what's due the Harkness name, no matter if some don't. Wouldn't want those old gabble-grinders thinking I'm a lickpenny, would you?" She didn't wait for an answer. "Elvin's paying anyway. That's not to the point, girl. You are not Out till you've been presented to the queen and to the ton. And until you are Out, you can't *go* out. No balls, no picnics, no theater. I don't even want anybody seeing you looking like something that's been dragged through a bush backwards. Perhaps next week we might entertain some of my particular friends for tea."

"That sounds . . . lovely. May I at least go sight-seeing?"

"I am too old and frail to go gawking like a tourist at the Tower and Astley's Circus, and it ain't fitting for you to go with no one but servants. You'll make friends at your ball, gentlemen who will be in alt to escort you to such pawky places. In a group, of course. My goddaughter Rosellen has agreed to take you around with her after your presentation, so I won't have to drain my strength with those routs and venetian breakfasts. Lady Conare, Rosellen is now. She's good ton even if Conare's only a baronet. Carlton House set, don't you know, and only one away from the earldom now."

Sonia did not care about routs or the Regent's friends; she couldn't bear the idea of three weeks in the house with this crusty old tartar. Grandmama was about as frail as medieval armor. "Fitz will need exercise, Your Grace."

"You may take him to the park. The one in the square, of course, not Hyde Park, where you'd be ogled by every half-pay officer and libertine on the strut. Nothing will ruin a gel's chances faster. You'll take servants with you, naturally. We'll hire a groom and a maid for you. No reason to disturb my regular staff."

"But, Grandmama, I'll be safe with Fitz, and I am used to doing for myself."

Lady Atterbury rapped Sonia's knuckles with her lorgnette. "And I am used to being obeyed, young lady. You kick up a dust and I'll send you off to that academy in Bath so fast, you'll be there before Miss Meadow gets the note saying you're coming. You will go to the park and no further, you will wear a bonnet at all times so you lose that gypsy complexion, and you will always be accompanied by servants. Is that understood?"

Sonia bowed her head. "Yes, Your Grace." She thought of one appeal Lady Atterbury might heed. "But the expense . . ."

"Elvin can afford it. Better he spend his blunt on you than squander it on that young filly."

Sonia had already heard the dowager's opinions on her father's remarriage. All of Grosvenor Square must have heard. Before she was dismissed into Bigelow's charge, Sonia was treated to another lecture about what was due the family name, the Harkness name, that is. Grandmama felt the Randolphs could go to hell in a hand basket, and the sooner her granddaughter shed that label, the better. Here she shook her finger under Sonia's nose, saying: "And I won't have you throwing yourself away on any soldiers, scholars, or starving second sons."

Gamblers and gazetted fortune hunters were also forbidden, as were rakes, widowers, and Americans. Nabobs might be tolerated if they were Oxford-educated, and émigré French aristocrats, if their property had not been confiscated. Lady Atterbury did not bother to mention the rising London merchant class nor, in a rare moment of noblesse oblige, the gentry. Welcome, of course, were wealthy peers, preferably above the title of baronet. Impoverished noblemen were only slightly less acceptable, since the duchess was not unreasonable and there were more of the latter than the former. Sonia was well dowered enough, if the title was noble enough. After all, that's the way things were done in the *belle monde*.

"But don't think I mean to push you into a marriage you cannot like, Sonia. Those gothic forced marriages just create the foundation for scandal. No, I'll make you the same offer I made Catherine. If you cannot find a suitable gentleman to wed, you may stay on here as my companion."

"Well, now I know why Catherine married Backhurst." Sonia had conferred with Marston and confirmed appointments with Bigelow. She had taken tea with Lady Atterbury after the dowager's nap—no second servings, fidgeting, or feeding the dog. She had enjoyed a fifteen-minute airing in the park with Fitz—no running, shouting, or talking to strangers—and was finally sitting alone in her bedroom with something on her face that smelled like what the pigs got, if there was nothing better for them. She couldn't even hug her own dog, because he was too clever to get near her. She could talk to him, though, the way she always did.

"Do you know what I think, Fitz? I think I hate it here. All this effort and extravagance for a ball I didn't want in the first place. And for what?"

Fitz thumped his tail.

"To show off an expensive piece of goods to discerning buyers! That's all this is, you know. Grandmama means me to land a title to make up for Mama's 'lapse.' She thinks my portion is bait enough for a viscount at least, especially when dangled alongside the Harkness connection." She sighed. "She's most likely right."

Sonia scrubbed the mess off her face as though she could wash away the disquieting thoughts. When she was finished she sat on the floor with her arms around Fitz and watched the fire burn down in the grate.

"Well, I don't care. I'm not going to let her sell me off to the highest bidder, and I'm not going to stay here as her lackey either! I'll marry the first nice man I meet, see if I don't. I don't want any stiff-rumped nobleman looking down his nose at me and Papa, always expecting me to act the lady. And I don't care if he's poor. In fact, I might like him better if he needs my money, for then he might be more manageable about the settlements."

A few minutes went by while she thought, then: "He has to be pleasant, of course, and he absolutely must prefer the country. On the other hand, perhaps I could use my money to purchase a country estate—nothing too grand, naturally—and he could use the rest to stay in the City. That might be even better. We could work it out later." She yawned. "He should have a nice smile . . . and smell good."

So I dragged in the butcher's delivery boy.

Chapter Five

*W*hat is beauty? What is the mystery of one creature's attraction to another?

Someone likened truth to beauty, but you cannot taste truth, or touch it, or feel it. It won't get your heart thumping, your pulses racing. It won't lick your ear. Besides, what a frog might find fascinating won't hold true for the titmouse. Then again, human persons find beauty in daubs of paint, chunks of marble, and Italian sopranos. Who can understand taste?

Take ticks, please. No one likes the bloodthirsty little buggers, no one finds them the least attractive—except other ticks. I truly believe this is where love enters the equations. The ugliest equine in horsedom could be grazing in the field, all swaybacked and moth-eaten, but let that mare come into season, and the stallion is in love. Old Gigi is the most beautiful creature he's ever seen. The sap rises, his heart sings. If he cannot be with her, he'll die. That's love. That's the fire that lets creatures as silly as sheep perpetuate their species, and the flame that helps a lady starling select one gentleman out of a flock of a hundred identical males. It's magic.

If marriage has nothing to do with love, as Muffy so firmly believes, there is no reason for cosmetics or corsets, padded shoulders or hairpieces. Solicitors could handle the transactions. We could be home in the country. Instead we spend boring hours planning for balls—dancing parties, not the fun chase-me kind—and improving Miss Sonia's appearance. We are *not* laying a trap, as Miss Sonia so inelegantly puts it; we are kindling a blaze.

Obviously Ned the butcher's boy did not generate any warmth. No magic. I myself thought he smelled delightful; it seems Miss Sonia prefers a gentleman to smell of Hungary water or snuff. I admit I have made mistakes before, but he seemed to fit her specifications so well. I guess I was barking up the wrong tree.

Lady Almeria revived after the Watch left. The already too-long-suffering Marston took charge, clearing the front steps of curious bystanders and the entryway of slack-jawed servants. Next the butler paid off the butcher and saw that the delivery boy was reimbursed for a new pair of breeches, plus a handsome tip for the trouble. The unfortunate animal was remanded to house arrest in Miss Randolph's room, and young miss, still giggling, set off for her appointment with the dressmaker. Properly escorted, of course. Then, his duties discharged with what dignity befitted a ducal residence, Marston withdrew to the butler's pantry, firmly locking himself in with a bottle of the late duke's vintage port, not to reappear until dinner.

This was not what he was used to, no, not even when Lady Allison, Master Thorndike, and Viscount Harkness, the heir, were young. Lady Atterbury and the late duke—and Marston—agreed that children were best raised in the country, by someone else. That was how the new little duke was being reared, in the country with his mother and an entire army of nursery staff to see that he did not burn down Atterbury Hall. He would seldom be in London to cut up Marston's peace until he reached his majority. Viscount Harkness did not live long enough to succeed to the title, predeceasing his father due to overindulging in brandy and underestimating a jump. He never got to see the son everyone said was in his image, and Marston was almost hoping he himself wouldn't be around to see the lad either.

In all of Marston's days at Atterbury House, there had only been one ignoble episode, that concerning Miss Allison and her would-be betrothed. The event was of such monumentally vulgar proportions, it was still spoken of at the nearest pub. Now Miss Allison's daughter was here for just one day, and Marston could never show his face at the Red Stag again.

Oblivious to Marston's distress, Miss Sonia was shopping. For once, she was enjoying the experience. Madame Celeste did not make her feel like a cabbagehead, instead encouraging her—and her father's remorse-driven generosity—to create a style of her own.

"I can see that Mademoiselle is not in the usual mode," Madame understated when her newest customer blew into the shop. Miss Randolph, with tousled tresses and laughing blue eyes, had instantly pleaded that, if she absolutely had to wear white for her come-out, Madame would please find a way to make it different from every other white debutante gown.

Sonia had never had so much choice before, and the new styles were looser and more comfortable. Sunny thought she'd feel more herself in them. Madame unerringly brought what was suitable for her coloring and situation, and wooden-faced Bigelow was an unobtrusive guide. "The blue to match the eyes. No frills; we have nothing to hide. Colors are unexceptionable for daytime."

Sonia held up a fashion plate of a gown cut daringly low, winking at the assistant who was standing by to record the order. Madame Celeste clucked her tongue and threw her hands in the air, but Bigelow did not fail Sonia. "Haymarket ware." Sonia and the girl laughed, until Madame frowned at them.

After Sonia was measured, two ready-made gowns were presented for consideration. "An improvement," Bigelow decreed, so Miss Randolph was helped into the peach muslin in order to complete her shopping with less embarrassment to her grandmother's abigail. Best of all, Aimee, the shopgirl, was found to be of a size and shape with Miss Randolph, and was willing to stand in for all but the final fittings. Sonia handed the girl a handsome douceur. "Just please do not use it on so many strawberry tarts that I'll have to undergo those hours of pinpricks," she said, laughing.

"*Mais non*, mademoiselle, I save for my *dot*. Better a girl make a good marriage than make a good meal, *n'est-ce pas?*"

Further stops saw the crested coach fill up with bonnets and boots, fans and feathers, parasols and petticoats, stockings and . . . gloves. Sonia still had energy left to visit Gunther's to see about ices for the ball, and a florist to order the flowers. Bigelow was limp on the facing seat for the ride back to Atterbury House. "Youth" was all she said.

Monsieur Gautier called that afternoon. The coiffeur studied Miss Randolph from every angle. He lifted a curl, he let a wave drift through his fingers. He chewed his mustache. Then he began to cut. He cut and he cut, muttering all the while. Sunny was beginning to wonder how many sheep Bud Kemp could have shorn in this time when the slender Frenchman stood back, kissed his fingertips, and proclaimed, "A la cherubim." He had to pause to wipe his eyes. "I am a genius."

Sonia shook her head and felt three pounds lighter. She laughed in delight. Then she finally turned to look in the mirror. "Oh, sir, you are." What had been unruly wisps and wayward locks was now a golden halo of naturally and Gautier-tumbled curls, curls that couldn't fall down or fly away. They framed her face, revealing the high cheekbones and ready dimples. Her blue eyes sparkled even brighter. Not quite an angel, not quite an imp, and very, very appealing.

"What do you think, Fitz?" Hearing his name, the dog ran over and barked, bestowing the cut hair more liberally around himself and the room. "And, Bigelow, do you like it? Do you think Grandmama will? What about the gentlemen?"

"Yes. Yes. Heaven help them."

The next major project, in addition to writing out two hundred invitations, hiring an orchestra, and planning a menu, was finding servants. One of the underfootmen was promoted—or not, depending on who you asked, Marston or Bigelow—to be Miss Sonia's personal man. Redheaded Ian was big, strong, and liked dogs.

An abigail had to be hired from an agency. Bigelow thought they should request an experienced older woman to pilot Miss through the shoals of society. Marston wanted to hire a warden from Newgate. Sonia selected her own maid partly because Maisie Holbrook had freckles and partly because she looked as if she needed the job. Holbrook's last mistress had suddenly eloped—"with no connivance from me, on my honor, ma'am"—and Miss Martingale's parents had turned the abigail off without a reference. The position was secured when the neatly dressed young woman, not very much older than

Sonia, said, "That's a fine-looking dog, ma'am. Can I walk him for you sometimes?"

At first Maisie and Ian were inclined to be over-protective, especially after receiving their instructions from the dowager duchess, through Marston and Bigelow. Ian was terrified of all three of them, and Maisie knew another social misstep would end her own career. Ian insisted on holding Fitz's lead in the park, lest Miss Randolph be tugged or tripped. Maisie wanted to fuss for hours over Miss Randolph's hair and clothes.

Sonia swayed the pair to her way of doing things with two simple sentences: "Lady Atterbury does not pay your wages. I do." After all, she was Allison Harkness's daughter. So she got to Astley's Amphitheater and the Menagerie and London Bridge and the cathedrals with no one the wiser, and struck up friendships with flower girls and pie-men and the Watch and a kindly old gentleman who fed the squirrels in the park. He didn't even mind that Fitz chased the squirrels away, as long as he didn't catch any.

Lady Atterbury was pleased with her grand-daughter's progress. Bigelow judged her passable, and Marston was relieved there were no further Incidents. With more than a fortnight still to go before the ball, they deemed her ready to get her feet wet with minor socializing, to test the waters, so to speak, at small, private gatherings of the dowager's set. Sonia nearly drowned from boredom.

Lady Atterbury's crowd was not comprised of the great hostesses of the day, the Almack's patronesses and such. Her coterie contained instead those powerful figures' mothers and aunts and *belles mères*. The old beldams were therefore an even greater force to be reckoned with. They got together of an afternoon for silver loo, charitable committee meetings, musicales, poetry readings, and scientific dissertations. They also served up the latest gossip along with their tea and culture.

Sonia was not expected to participate in the conversations, thank goodness. In fact, she was often waved away to a secluded corner after her appearance and demeanor were scrutinized, lest her innocent ears be sullied. Many of the ladies refused to carry their ear trumpets, however, so the conversations were perforce loud enough not only to reach Sonia, but to rise above Herr Mitteldorf's performance on the harpsichord. Few of the grandes dames could rise without a footman's help after the performance, in fact, and fewer could see Herr Mitteldorf at all without their spectacles or looking glasses. Sonia thought she must be the only one there with all of her teeth, until she noticed another young woman across the way, concentrating not on the music or the chitchat, but on the book in her lap.

The young woman read her way through a lecture on the electrical properties of wool carpets, and through a dramatic presentation of an endlessly epic poem by a lisping young man with flowing locks.

Sonia made sure she sat near the young lady at the next gathering, a report from the directors of St. Bartleby's Institute for the Destitute, to which no one listened. The girl, for she could not be much older than Sonia, did not raise her eyes from her book, but she did reach into her reticule and pull out a matching purple-covered volume. "Here," she said, "you'll need this."

"This" was a purple-prosed gothic from the Minerva Press, and the young woman was Blanche Carstairs.

"Lady Blanche if you care for those things," Sonia's new friend and literary advisor introduced herself at the intermission. "I'm a countess in my own right, but don't let that bother you. I don't. It's one of those ancient land-grant titles that can pass through the female line. That's my aunt over there, the one in puce who is snoring."

Blanche—they were quickly on a first-name basis—was a drab, graceless type of girl, with little conversation and less fashion sense, but she knew everything. She flipped the pages of her book. "They think I'm not listening, so they say anything. Like how you're expected to make a grand alliance, despite coming from the gentry, if you don't make a mull of things."

Sonia gasped in indignation, but Blanche held her hand up. "It don't fadge. They"—she nodded toward the clusters of crones—"say I won't take, especially being fired off the same time as you, but Auntie says the lands and title will turn the trick. Of course, my dowry isn't as large as yours."

"Do you mean they all know the size of my dowry?"

"Goosecap, they all know the size of your shoes!" Blanche went back to her book. Sunny shrugged, then opened hers.

Some new, younger faces were added the afternoon Grandmama held open house. The old ladies trotted forth spotty-faced, stammering grandsons just down from university, bored middle-aged bachelor sons, and the occasional rakish man-about-town nephew who owed his living to the ancient relative.

"The hounds are on the scent," Blanche commented, making Sonia smile. They'd reluctantly put their books away for the afternoon. Sonia liked reading about the dashing heroes and put-upon heroines far more than she did pouring tea and listening to empty chitchat and insincere flattery.

Sonia finally got to meet Grandmama's goddaughter Rosellen Conover, Lady Conare, a brittle young matron who covered her slightly faded beauty in flamboyant dress. Rosellen was supposed to chaperone Sonia for the season. The older woman's eyes narrowed to slits when she saw Miss Randolph's fresh young beauty.

"Why, Lady Almeria, whatever can you be thinking?" Lady Conare chided. "Surely the chit's too young to be presented. She looks a veritable schoolgirl. Or a little milkmaid."

Lady Atterbury just cackled and waggled her sticklike finger under the woman's nose. "Told you she was a Diamond, didn't I?"

Lady Atterbury's assessment was quickly and eloquently seconded by Lady Rosellen's escort and brother, Lord Ansel, Baron Berke. The baron was a fairly attractive man of about thirty, trim if not muscular, and exquisitely tailored. There was just a touch of dandyism in his patterned waistcoat, crossed fobs, and heavy scent. Nor could Sonia appreciate the way he looked at her through his quizzing glass. Still, he was friendly and polite, and his compliments went far to restoring Sonia's confidence after his sister's cutting remarks. She was further impressed with Baron Berke when she saw him cross to where Blanche sat alone and unpopular—until she spoke to her friend later as they exchanged books.

"Berke? He's one of the season's catches, you know. They say his pockets are to let, so he's bound to settle on some heiress or other this year."

"Are you sure? He certainly didn't look like he was all to pieces."

"Don't be a goose. The worst wastrel in town can dress elegantly; he just don't pay his tailor. Berke's not that bad off. Yet."

"Well, he seemed pleasant enough."

"Of course he did; he'd never land an heiress else, title or no! Did he tell you that you were a breath of springtime, a bud of perfection just waiting to open? Did he kiss your hand and say he was honored to be among the first to touch the bloom?"

Sonia giggled. "You, too? Oh dear, and I thought he was the nicest of the gentlemen here today."

"You mean he was the only one with any conversation at all, even if it was Spanish coin. They"—Blanche nodded toward where her aunt and Lady Atterbury had their heads together—"say he was dangling after a rich Cit's daughter, but he'd sooner take you with your looks and money, or me for the title and lands. Do you think you'd have him?"

Sonia laughed, saying, "After you convinced me not to believe a word he says?" She tapped the book in her hand. "I'd rather have Count Rudolpho than a husband I couldn't trust!"

So, like Diogenes, I set out to find an honest man.

Chapter Six

$\mathscr{I}$was taught that honesty means I am not to sleep on the furniture, even if no one is home. Honesty means not taking food from the kitchen when Cook isn't looking, unless it falls on the floor. I am a good dog.

Human persons are different. They make laws about honesty and then they break them. Sometimes this is a crime, sometimes not. Poaching happens to be a crime, but it is also dishonest—and confuses the game animals. Squire Randolph was very strict with poachers, yet he had no scruples about telling lies: "Here now, Bossy, we're just going to borrow your pretty little calf." To excuse these moral lapses, humans call them social lies, white lies, flummery. For Spot's sake, even poor color-blind Bossy can recognize a faradiddle when she hears one.

They do it all the time, calling such falsehoods polite fibs: "Delighted to see you. So glad you could call. You are looking lovely. I adored your gift. Please come back soon." Miss Merkle explained that gentlemen and ladies bend the truth a shade here and there so no one's feelings will be hurt. When the knacker comes and they tell the decrepit old plow horse, "Here, boy, we're just going to take a little walk," you know something more than feelings are going to be hurt!

No wonder animals have learned to distrust men. Still, I say don't listen to the words, listen to the heart. An animal can tell the truth. Just like I listened to what Lord Ansel Berke didn't say.

I was waiting in the hall when company came, quiet so Marston would not notice. Having studied under Muffy, I was pretending to be a scatter rug. Not my finest role, but I was not dragged back to the kitchens. Miss Sonia spotted me right away—she always does—when she walked some of the departing guests to the door. As soon as Marston turned his back to fetch Baron Berke's gloves, hat, and walking stick, she introduced us. We shook hands. He patted my head and said, "What a fine dog, Miss Randolph. Smart and handsome." Then he wiped his hands on a cloth.

He did not commit a crime, like stealing eggs from a chicken coop, or a sin, like stealing the chickens. But he does not have a true heart. A dog always knows.

Miss Sonia deserved better, so I had to expand our horizons. Somewhere in this great city of London . . .

I had never been on foot beyond the park before. Always we went sightseeing in the carriage, and I waited on the box with the driver outside the Tower or Westminster, marveling at mankind's achievements and wondering why they bothered. I could only sniff at the passing strangers from my high perch; now I would be down among them. I was looking forward to exploring on my own while Miss Sonia had her final fittings. Tippy the turnspit dog says there are rats as big as cats!

I saw one myself, a surly fellow with a half-chewed ear. He wouldn't give me the time of day, much less any hints as to where I should begin my search. Muffy was right, city folk aren't as friendly, for even the horses didn't stop when I asked directions. The heavy workers were short-tempered beasts in a great rush to get nowhere that I could tell. The fancier cattle were all twitchy nerves and bunched muscle, ready to explode. I stopped asking. I kept going, following my nose as it were, and oh, the smells! And the sights and the noise and the traffic. Even the air had myriad tastes. And men, hustling, bustling, busy. A few glanced my way, one tried to kick me, another held out a cup—and it was empty! Mostly they were in a hurry. I may have been a tad optimistic about my search.

I always knew where I was, of course. Hadn't I been carefully marking my way? Much too soon, though, I had spent every penny, out of sheer excitement, I suppose, so I decided to return home. But there were buildings in the way and high fences, and alleys no dog should walk down by himself. The smoke was so thick, I could not even sniff my own scent in the air, and a pair of livery horses pulling a hackney poked fun when I asked my way back to Grosvenor Square.

" 'Ere now, who's 'e think 'e is, some poodle wot gets 'is blinkin' toenails painted?"

"Oi say 'e ain't no gennlemun's dog, 'e's one of those baa-baa baby-sitters. Ya wants th' sheep pens out Marlybone way, ya 'airy botfly."

I wished them high hills and heavy loads, then I showed them my heels.
Did Diogenes ever get lost?

"Damn and blast! First those fools at the surgeon general's and now this!" The curricle was stuck in traffic, between a mail coach with a bunch of unruly schoolboys on top and a barouche whose high-pitched occupant was obviously no better pleased than the officer at the curricle's ribbons. Most likely some high-priced cyprian en route to her lover, he deduced from the garish red and gold trim on the outside of the expensive turnout, and the unlady-like expressions coming from within. The officer cursed again, that he'd have time to listen to the high flyer's entire repertoire before this mess was cleared.

Gads, how he hated the city! He hated everything about it, including those clunches at the War Office who wouldn't send him back to Portugal without the medicos' approval. They, and that popinjay from the Cabinet, wanted him to sell out now that he'd come into the title. As if England needed another blasted nobleman more than the general needed him at the front. As if he ever asked to be earl in the first place. He cursed his brother Milo for up and dying. Well, he'd told them he wasn't selling out yet, and he wasn't using that damned title while he was in uniform. Major Darius Conover, Lord Warebourne whether he acknowledged it or not, was barely holding his high-bred cattle in check, and his temper not at all.

His batman, Sergeant Robb, got down to soothe the impatient bays, and to put a distance between him and the major's ill humor. The major liked to throw things when he was in a taking, and Lord knew, there wasn't much in a curricle to toss.

Church bells chimed the hour, and Major Conover whacked his driving whip onto the floorboards.

"Dash it, I told my nieces I'd drive them in the park this afternoon. Now they'll hate me even worse!"

Thinking he might do better to soothe his employer after all, Robb said, "Here now, Major, them tykes don't hate you, they hardly know you. They're just upset, both parents poppin' off like that, and then bein' shipped to relatives what didn't want 'em, and now landin' back here with you. It's no wonder the little ones are confused."

"Confused? That's gammon. The baby Bettina cries if I get near her, Genessa in the middle tries to kick me—my bad leg to boot—and the eldest, Benice, is so stiff and polite, I'm afraid she'll shatter into a million pieces one day." He beat his cane against the curricle's rail. "My blackguard of a cousin Preston and his bitch of a wife set them against me. Confused? I'm the one who should be confused. I've never been around children in my life!"

"You're doin' fine, Major. It just takes time."

"I don't have time, Robby. I want to go back and see Boney put down at last. And it's not as if I'm doing the girls any good here. I even thought of marrying to get them a mother, so I could go back and get myself killed. But no respectable female would have me, with my name as black as mud."

"Not with the army, sir. Why, you're one of the heroes of the Peninsula, Major. I 'spect that's because you'd go back to all that mud and heat and poor grub, if you had your druthers, rather than stay here and be a nob." The sergeant's dour expression conveyed his own opinion. Lord knew he'd follow the major to hell and back, but Robb figured they'd already been to hell. "I don't see what's so bad about two country properties," he said with the familiarity of shared battlefields, "a huntin' box, the London town house, and a healthy income. Why, you could take a seat in Parliament if you wanted, sir, and get the army boys better rations.

56

So what if some Tulip cut us in the park? At least we don't have to go forage for food."

The major didn't throw his cane. He didn't want to scare the horses. "Stubble it, Robb. Go see what the devil is holding us up."

While his man was gone, Major Conover tried to shut out the bawdy ditties from the mail coach and the less frequent screeches from the barouche. What was so wrong with being an earl? How about dragging up all the old scandal, or not being admitted to his brother's clubs, or his nieces thinking he was so terrible, he ate children for breakfast? How about not being trained to administer those vast holdings? How about worrying about the succession? He'd do anything in his power, including giving up his commission and his career, just to keep Warebourne and the girls' inheritances safe away from Preston. Tarnation, he'd even marry the lightskirt in the barouche.

He threw his gloves as far as he could. An urchin scooped them up and ran away. Good, let someone benefit from this hellish day.

When the sergeant returned, he related a minglemangle of stunning dimensions, even by London standards. A racing phaeton, it seemed, had been tearing down the crowded road at a high rate of speed. The driver, a young cawker who was more than a little on the go, started to take the corner where an organ-grinder and his monkey were working. A dog came out of nowhere and ran between the horses' legs, barking. The spirited horses took exception, but the choice spirit at the reins lost control, so his carriage veered, into the path of an oncoming barrel wagon. The drayman pulled his brake and managed to avoid the curricle, but the barrels started rolling out the back of the wagon. Some split open on hitting the cobblestones, but others rolled merrily along. One hit a vegetable stall on the sidewalk, another exploded a newspaper delivery cart. One barrel headed for the chaise behind, which overturned, dumping out an irate cast from the Italian Opera House. The phaeton and its castaway driver, meanwhile, had continued on out of control, scattering pedestrians and other vehicles until coming to rest, sideways, alongside a poultry cart, with foreseeable results. Beggars and street urchins and nearby residents were all in the road, grabbing up the fallen bounty while shopkeepers and lorry drivers got into fistfights. The local fire brigade was called out to catch the chickens, and the Italian Opera Company decided to conduct an alfresco rehearsal. And the monkey . . .

"Oh, and the barrels were full of pickled herring. But most of the action was over when I got there," the batman concluded with regret. "They should have it cleaned up in a shake, leastways enough for us to get through. I 'spect they'll be fightin' over who pays for what for the next two years."

They eventually made their way through the scene of the devastation, holding their noses and turning down offers for fresh-killed chickens and kippers wrapped in newspapers. They had to travel slowly around the debris of wagons and carriages, slowly enough for the major to spot the black dog lying in the gutter. He pulled the curricle to the side, receiving one last vulgar imprecation from the passenger in the barouche, which now had to negotiate around them.

"What are you doin', Major? We're late as is."

"Here, take the ribbons. I'm going to see if the dog is alive."

"I 'spect they would have killed it," Robb said, indicating the knot of angry men still arguing with the Watch. "If the horses and barrels and wagon wheels didn't." He took the reins and shook his head as the officer got painfully down from the curricle and limped to the animal sprawled on its side in the filth. Conover pulled a sticky newspaper away from the dog's face and felt its chest for a

58

heartbeat, then ran his hands over the animal's legs. He lifted its eyelids and looked in its mouth.

"Is it dead then?" Robb called.

"No, just in shock. And it's a male. He's got a broken leg, but nothing else I can find. Hand me down the carriage blanket."

"B'gorm, Major, you can't mean to take on some broke-up mutt. It's nothin' but a stray. There's a million of 'em in London."

"Stow it, Robb. Look, he's got a collar, and he's got too much meat on his ribs to be a street dog. Someone took good care of the poor chap once. Now it's our turn."

"But, Major, sir, you wasn't thinkin' of takin' the poor sod home with us, was you? For all you know, it could be mean, or have rabies. Leastways fleas."

Conover was already wrapping the dog in the throw, taking care not to jar the broken leg. "I would have died alone out in that field if those peasants hadn't taken me in. He deserves the same chance. Besides, the children might like him. We always had pets when we were growing up. At least maybe they'll understand why I didn't keep our appointment."

Robb could only shake his head while the major carefully lifted his burden to the carriage seat, then slowly climbed up. "You drive, I'll hold the dog steady," Conover said.

The batman made one more plea for sanity. "But what if he up and sticks his spoon in the wall then? How are those little tykes goin' to feel if somethin' else dies on 'em?"

The major held the dog firmly, stroking his head. With the same tone of voice the officer used to command his men to hold the ranks, to take that hill, he ordered: "He will not die."

"She's the prettiest dog I ever saw. Let's call her Beauty."

"No, I want to call her Bess, after the queen."

59

From the baby: "Me. Me."

"Beauty."

"I say Bess. Maybe Queenie."

"Mimi! Mimi! Mimi!"

"Ah, sweethearts, those are all good names, but the dog is a, uh, gentleman dog."

Six-year-old Genessa gave him a dirty look. "You're just saying that because you don't like girls."

"I like girls, Gen, truly I do. But the dog is a boy." The major was mopping his brow. Robb was smirking, leaning against the table in the kitchen, where the dog lay on blankets in front of the fire, his leg splinted and wrapped.

"How do you know?" Genessa challenged.

Conover mopped harder. "I just do," he said, in a voice loud enough to make Bettina, the two-year-old, start crying.

Ten-year-old Benice solemnly declared, "If Uncle Darius says he's a boy, Gen, then he must be." But she didn't sound convinced.

Genessa moved to kick her sister, but the major got in the way. "Ouch. Boy dogs are ... bigger, sweethearts, and have broader chests and—"

Genessa had already rolled the unconscious dog over. Conover hastily threw another blanket over him.

Robb cleared his throat. "Whyn't you just call him Trouble, sir?"

What they say about the evils of the big city are true. I've been dognapped.

Chapter Seven

*W*hite slavers! Press gangs! Procurers for houses of ill repute and perversion! (Miss Sonia and Blanche Carstairs had been reading their lurid novels aloud to each other.) Anatomy professors! Oriental chefs! (I had nightmares of my own.)

Instead, a man in uniform, an officer by the markings, was cleaning my coat with a dampened cloth, and telling me what a brave fellow I was. I did not feel brave; I felt like a fool. Only a nodcock would ask directions from a dancing monkey wearing a skirt.

I smelled. My head hurt and I was sleepy, and my right hind leg was broken. I was never so glad I wasn't a horse. The soldier had strong, gentle hands and a nice voice; he brought me some warm broth with bits of meat in it. If he wanted me to be brave, I would be brave.

The next time I woke up, my new friend—Major Conover, I heard him called—carried me to a walled-in garden behind the house. He helped me stand, then turned his back. An officer, and a gentleman. I noticed on the way back that he limped, too, and wondered if the same barrel had rolled over him. Later I learned he was shot in an act of heroism.

He was certainly a coward when it came to the little girls. They say, never show your fear to a wild animal. Well, children are worse. The major was afraid of hurting them, afraid of frightening them, afraid of talking to them. And oh, how they knew it! So the fool never got to know them, never got to cuddle them, never got to love them. So how could they love him back? They were turning mean, moody, or timid, as will any creature lacking affection and security. I started straightening them out while my leg healed, before I could go home.

If there was anything I knew, it was little girls. Soon I had them laughing and playing without arguing. Of course, I was wearing bonnets and taking tea with a bunch of glass-eyed dolls and giving Baby rides on my back. Worse, I had to pretend I couldn't find three giggly little girls smelling of milk and porridge when I was It, but no one from the old neighborhood would ever know, and it was all for a good cause. At night after Baby was asleep, I had two little bodies pressed against me while the major read nursery tales. So what if they were stories I'd heard suchamany times? Gen and Benice wouldn't sit in his lap yet, but they didn't mind that we crept closer to his chair every evening. Two more Little Penny Partridges and we'd be at his knees.

Major Conover was a harder bone to chew. He was too restless to stay in the house, but came home in a blacker mood if some old acquaintance snubbed him. When the children were abed he'd help me down the stairs and we'd go to the library, where there were so many books, Miss Sonia and I could have spent every rainy day from now till kingdog come. He never read out loud. The major mostly stared at the fire and poured wine from the decanter.

Sometimes when we went out to the back garden he'd throw rocks and sticks as far toward the rear wall as he could. Now, there's a cruel man, I thought at first, until I realized he didn't intend a three-legged dog to go fetch. He was just angry. I felt bad that I couldn't stay to set him to rights, but I had a job of my own to do. Miss Sonia must be worried.

I whimpered, yes I did, wanting to go home. The major asked if my leg hurt and poured me a saucer of brandy. I could stay a day or two more, I decided, recovering my strength before I had to face that London maelstrom. Meanwhile I'd see what I could do to get Major Conover's ducks in a row. Those slovenly maids, the cook who stole, the nursemaid who spent more time with the footmen than with the children, the castaway butler, they would all feel my wrath. That was the least I could do.

Miss Sonia could do more. I made the obvious connection, then rejected the thought. One and one did not always equal two; sometimes they just stayed that way, one and one. The major did not fill the bill. He was a soldier and a sir, not a my lord, so Grandmama would be unhappy. He wasn't well to pass, judging from the run-down house and his ill-fitting uniform, so Squire might object. He gambled in low kens, Blue Ruin on his breath, saying, "Blister it, what else is there to do?" He used bad language, was cow-handed with children, and smelled bad from the cigarillos he smoked. He was so used to giving orders that he'd never make a manageable, complacent sort of husband, and he'd never be a good dancer, with that limp. Miss Sonia loved to dance. He wasn't even handsome enough, with lines on his face and a scar on his cheek, and he never talked about going to the country at all, only Portugal. Besides, I didn't even know if he was honest. He hadn't given me back yet, had he? And he never smiled.

"Blackie must be ready for more exercise, girls, the way he's bothering the servants. What do you say we take him across the street to the square for a run?" Major Conover was almost trampled in answer, as his nieces ran to find mittens and have their bonnets tied. He wished some of the eagerness were for his company, not the dog's, but he was a little heartened when Benice paused, halfway out the door, and called back, "Hurry, Uncle Darius."

He followed down the steep front steps of Ware House as quickly as he could on a leg that refused to heal, his cane in one hand, the lead Robb had fashioned for the dog obviously de trop in his other. "Do not cross the—" he started to command from the marble landing, scowling that the nursemaid was nowhere in sight. Then he noted how Blackie put his body in front of the girls at the edge of the walkway, keeping them back until there was a break in the traffic. The dog was a better nanny than any he could have hired. He stopped trying to catch up.

He followed happy squeals and excited barking to the park entry, where Blackie was whining at a pieman outside the gates. Lud, the major thought, the mutt eats everything in sight. Why does he have to act like we've been starving him? The vendor was handing out meat pasties to the girls and Blackie when Conover got there, just in time to pay, he thought, reaching for his purse.

"Oh no, sir, it's that happy I am to see Fitz again." The man did accept a coin for the pie Major

Conover munched on as he followed his noisy pack. Fitz?

Hampered by his still-splinted leg, Blackie was galumphing through the gates of the square. The children skipped behind him, playing this new kind of tag. Then Blackie started dancing clumsy circles around a flower girl on one of the paths. "Aw, Fitz, y' near t' broke our 'earts, y' did, disappearin' like that," she said, tying a bunch of violets to the dog's collar. " 'Urry on 'ome now, Fitz. Poor missy's been lookin' 'igh 'n' low."

Uncertain now, the two older girls ran after the limping dog, leaving the baby in their wake.

Darius looked around for the blasted nursemaid, who was paying them no mind at all, chatting up the pieman outside the gates. He awkwardly lifted Bettina, hoping the child wouldn't start screaming. "Come on, Tina, let's go find Blackie. Or Fitz."

"Me. Me. Mimi!"

"I don't think so, sweetheart."

Blackie-Fitz made one last stop at the opposite end of the small park. He halted in front of a silver-haired figure on a bench, barked once, and wagged his tail. He waited for the old man to put down a sack of nuts, accepted a scratch behind the ears, then took off again. When Darius and Bettina reached the bench, the elderly gentleman got slowly to his feet.

"Found our Fitz, did you, Major? Good job, soldier." And he snapped a still smart salute.

The major transferred his cane and the leash to the hand holding the baby, to return the courtesy.

This time, when the big dog reached the edge of the park, he turned on Benice and Genessa, barking in their faces, showing his teeth. They were not to cross the road behind him. He dashed between a hackney and a brougham.

Benice silently put her hand into her uncle's as they waited for a break in the traffic. Gen held the trailing end of the leash. No one said anything, listening to the dog's near frantic yelps as he made his clumsy way up a wide colonnade of steps outside a mansion even bigger than Ware House.

Sonia was trailing down the stairs to join her grandmother's company for tea. She didn't want to. She had no interest in the old ladies' gossip or the younger gentlemen's flattery. She only wanted to put on her old cape and sturdy half boots and continue searching for her dog. Maybe there was a paper she hadn't sent an advertisement, or a street urchin she hadn't told about the reward. Someone had to find Fitz. They just had to.

But she'd promised her grandmother to make an effort, with the ball just a few days away now. Maisie had taken a few hasty tucks in her gown, and Bigelow had come in to use the hare's foot to bring some color to Miss Randolph's wan cheeks. She was presentable, even if she didn't shine. Sonia didn't care.

She heard the barking, but she heard Fitz barking in her dreams these days. Or someone was bringing her another emaciated, scrofulous stray for the reward. She gave them each a coin for their trouble, hoping they would feed the animal, at least, before sending it back on the unfriendly streets. She hoped someone was feeding Fitz.

The barking was getting nearer. Sonia wouldn't get her hopes up; she'd been disappointed so many times. No, she'd just open the door an inch and peek out. Marston would look down his nose at her, but the butler must be in the parlor serving tea, for only Ian stood in the hallway. Just an inch, Sonia told herself, just to be sure.

By the time the major's small, grim-faced party climbed the covered stairs to the open door, Fitz was engulfed in sprigged muslin, a cap of golden ringlets mixed with his black fur. The dog was yowling, trying to bury himself in her lap, licking her hands, her face, wriggling with joy.

"I, ah, guess there's no question he's your dog then," the major said quietly from the doorway.

The girl raised her head from the dog's back. Darius saw her reddened nose, tears streaming down her cheeks, and the most radiant smile he'd ever expected to see this side of heaven. "We'll leave you to your reunion then," he choked out, when he could breathe again. He could feel Benice's hand trembling in his—or was it his trembling in hers?

"Oh, please don't go so fast!" The girl, no, young lady was struggling to rise, encumbered as she was by ecstatic dog. The major was too burdened himself to help her, and the chuckleheaded footman was blubbering into a square of linen in the corner. At last she was on her feet, and Darius could see that her form was as lovely as her face.

"I'm sorry for enacting you such a scene, ah, Major," she said, recognizing the insignia. "We've never been apart, you see." One hand still on the dog, she fumbled for the tiniest scrap of lace to blot her eyes, eyes he could see were the color of a summer sky. Darius wondered if he was looking at this vision any less worshipfully than the dog. He tried to pay attention to her words.

"How can I ever thank you, Major? You must have taken such good care of my Fitz, for look how shiny he is. And his leg is wrapped better than a surgeon could do. Please, please do come in, sir, you and the children, and let me offer you . . ." Sonia was going to offer the reward, noting how the officer's uniform hung on his frame as though made for someone else. His face was too thin, with haggard lines, and he was leaning heavily on his cane. But the silent little girls were in crisp white pinafores, all expensive lace and fancywork smocking.

". . . Some chocolate, at least, and Cook's macaroons, so you can tell me how you found my Fitz."

Reality intruded when the major heard voices

from a room down the hall. This sweet angel didn't know who he was. She'd never invite him in, else. "No, thank you, my lady, we mustn't impose."

"Then please, may I have your direction, that I can call on your wife to show my appreciation?"

The major looked blank for an instant, then: "Oh no, these aren't my children. They are my brother's. That is, they were. Now they are my wards." Blast it, he was as tongue-tied as a raw recruit.

"Then their mother," she persisted, fully intending to bring a gift and some toys for the children.

"She's gone, too, regretfully, and I don't have a wife, ma'am, bachelor quarters, you see, so it wouldn't be at all the thing for you to call. And not necessary, I assure you."

Truly the man was exasperating! "But there must be some way I can thank you."

"Just seeing your joy was reward enough." He smiled, and Sonia realized he was not as old as she'd first supposed, not even thirty, in fact, young to have attained such a high rank. And he was quite attractive, in a rugged way, with the same dark hair and eyes as the little girls.

"Now come, children, make your curtsies," he continued.

Benice made a wobbly bow, her lower lip quivering. When she realized they were leaving, without the dog, Bettina in the major's arms started clutching his uniform collar so tightly that Conover's face turned red. She started screaming, "Blackie! Mimi!" at the top of her lungs. And Genessa jerked at his cane so the major's bad leg nearly went out from under him.

"I won't!" she shouted. "He's our dog, Uncle Darius, you said! She lost him and we found him. Make her give him back, Uncle Darius, now."

Some of the guests in the drawing room decided to make their departures, timely enough to satisfy their curiosity as to the commotion in the hall.

"Look, Lord Berke," Sonia addressed the baron,

"Fitz has come home! These kind young ladies and their wonderful uncle just brought him." She laughed. "And I was so excited to see Fitz, I never even got their names, to make introductions."

"Just as well, Miss Randolph." Lord Berke had drawn himself up to his full height, not quite that of the officer. He raised his quizzing glass and surveyed the untidy, fractious group. One side of his lip lifted in a sneer. "He's no one anyone with taste wants to acknowledge."

Sonia gasped. She had never seen such rudeness from the baron.

"It's true, my dear, everyone knows his reputation. I am just surprised swine like that has the nerve to cross your doorway."

The major grabbed the back of Gen's dress before she could go kick Ansel Berke. What could Darius say in front of a young lady, especially one whose eyes, so recently shining with innocent tears, were now filled with shock and horror? What could he say with Baby's hands closing his windpipe? He made his bow, such as it was, to Lady Atterbury where she stood in the hall, her lips gathered in a tight O of disapproval. Then he bowed again to the young woman. "Your servant, Miss Randolph." He hauled Gen and Baby awkwardly down the stairs, Benice carrying his cane and sobbing behind them.

They didn't move fast enough to miss hearing Lady Atterbury's instructions to her butler before the door was closed: "Marston, we are not at home to Major Conover. Or Lord Warebourne. Whatever the scoundrel chooses to call himself."

A dog with a bad reputation is given a wide berth. Or shot.

Chapter Eight

$\int$ ome things are better left unknown. Like the meaning behind the expression "It's a dog-eat-dog world." We know such things exist, but we do not have to speak of them, no more than we would explain the origin of "hangdog look," at least not in polite company. Shame, either personal or collective, does not need to be aired in public. For once, I agreed with Lady Atterbury when she commanded Miss Sonia to have nothing more to do with Major Conover–Lord Warebourne, and then refused to say why. "The details are too sordid for your ears," she said.

Human youngsters are forever asking why. Why can't they fly like birds, why can't they breathe underwater like fish? How in a badger's backside can anyone answer that? Why must they stay away from silver-tongued strangers with shady backgrounds?

The answer is usually "Because I say so."

This answer seldom satisfies anyone.

Every fox cub ever born has been told not to

look under a hedgehog's skirts, and every fox cub ever born has had a swollen snoutful of prickles. Forbid a lass to step out with a rake and a rogue, she'll elope. It's been that way since men started falling off the edges of the earth, looking for the unknown. Danger, forbidden fruit. Think of Eve. Everyone blames the snake—they aren't my favorites either, right down there with tapeworms—but Eve was just young. Curious and contrary and a bad dresser.

Anyway, Miss Sonia always did have a soft spot for the underdog.

"Suffice it to say, Sonia, I would not be doing right by you or the Harkness name if I permitted you near a blackguard like Darius Conover. Or Warebourne, though he shames the title."

"But, Grandmama, I am sure I have read his name in the dispatches. He is one of our own brave soldiers. Surely he deserves better than this Turkish treatment. And he took care of Fitz and brought him home. I am in his debt, Your Grace, and cannot dismiss him so cavalierly."

"Write him a letter," the dowager snapped, rapping Sonia's fingers with a teaspoon. "Then have nothing more to do with the knave, do you hear me, missy? That is all I am going to say on the subject. Drink your tea."

So Sonia asked Blanche.

"The new Lord Warebourne?" Blanche asked, her eyes wide. They were pretty hazel eyes, when she took them out of a book. The two girls were best of friends now, and Blanche had lost most of the gruff cover to her shyness. They were on their way back from Hatchard's when Sonia startled her companion with the question. "However did you get to meet him? He's not accepted anywhere."

"I know he's scorned by society; what I want to

know is why. As for meeting him, he brought Fitz home. He seemed sad and tired and overburdened with cares. I'd like to help him."

Blanche shook her head. "But, Sonia, he's not a pigeon with a broken wing or a kitchen maid needing your encouragement to see the tooth drawer. I don't think there's anything you can do, except make mice-feet of your own reputation."

Sonia's chin rose. "If you don't tell me, I'll ask the servants."

Blanche shrugged. "The original scandal happened years ago, at least five or six. Everything would have blown over by now, except that the girl he ruined was well placed, and he came back from the wars." Blanche could feel Sonia's impatience, so she got more specific. "The girl was Ansel Berke's sister Hermione. Lady Rosellen's sister, too, of course, although I think she was not long married to Conare at the time. Anyway, Hermione was found to be breeding, and she claimed Darius Conover was the father. Darius denied responsibility and refused to marry the chit."

"Perhaps he wasn't the father?"

"Who's to say? But the whole coil could have been kept quiet if he had married the girl anyway. Or if Berke had just sent her off to Ireland to have the babe. Instead Berke challenged Conover to a duel, so naturally Hermione's name became a byword. Again, things might have been settled if Darius took the usual path, but he didn't. He would not accept Berke's challenge, saying the chit wasn't worth dying for, or fleeing the country for if he killed Berke, or losing his commission over. Conover had just signed up, I think, and Sir Arthur was very strict about his officers not dueling."

"That sounds very intelligent. Dueling is barbaric."

"Yes, but Berke didn't see it that way. He'd thought to force Darius to marry Hermione one way or t'other. So he called Conover a coward, and still

Darius would not fight. Ansel Berke convinced everyone that Conover acted without honor. You have to know the store men set on honor, so Darius was cut. At first his brother Milo kept the worst of it away. He was the Earl of Warebourne, after all, but then his wife was breeding and he stayed in the country. And then Hermione killed herself."

"Oh my. The poor young woman."

"And Conover's hopes of being received in London were destroyed with her. They say he threw himself into the Peninsular Campaign to try to regain his honor, volunteering for hazardous assignments, making daredevil rescues."

"Surely that must have proved he was no coward, at least."

"I daresay it did. That would have turned the tide, too, especially after Milo Warebourne and his wife, Suzannah, were both lost in a carriage accident without leaving an heir. An eligible, wealthy earl can be excused many a youthful indiscretion."

"Except?"

"Except Berke would not let the matter rest. Nor would his other sister, Rosellen, whose husband, Preston Conover, Lord Conare, is incidentally next in line to the earldom. I think Lord Conare would not be upset if Warebourne is convinced to return to the perils of war. Conare has Prinny's ear, and Rosellen the Almack's hostesses', so your major's case is next to hopeless. Forget him."

"But what about the children? I should think Lady Rosellen would want Lord Warebourne received if only for their sakes. What will happen to them if they can never take their places in society?"

"What has that to do with Rosellen? Haven't you seen she cares for nobody but herself?"

Sonia nodded, dreading the time she would be consigned to the arctic lady's chaperonage.

"There's another thing," Blanche recalled, "and it's about the children. When Darius came home on injury leave, he stopped at Conare's place in Sussex to visit with his nieces. Neither Preston nor Rosellen were there, naturally, since they are always in London or Bath or at some house party. Darius scooped the little girls right out from under their care, saying they weren't taking proper charge of the children."

"Good for him!" Sonia exclaimed. "And much better for the children. Just think, leaving those dear little girls for the servants to raise!"

Blanche frowned. That's how *she* was raised. "Anyway, Lady Conare took it as an insult. I heard her saying so to your grandmother. They are thinking of petitioning the Crown to have themselves named as guardian instead of Warebourne, on grounds that he is not morally fit."

"That's outrageous. Why, anyone could see he loves those children." Actually, Sonia had seen right away that he knew as much about little girls as she knew about steam engines, but she, at least, was willing to give him credit for trying. "And as you say, Rosellen cannot claim affection for the children."

"No, but the Warebournes left a vast, unentailed inheritance to their children. Whoever gets them as wards gets to control that money for a long time. So you see, there is every reason to keep Darius Conover discredited."

"I see that the so-called polite world is an evil place of manipulation, greed, and ambition. Why, one man's life is being ruined for a crime he might never have committed, and three little girls will be ostracized for no wrongdoing of their own at all!" Sonia stamped her foot. "Well, I don't care. They were good to Fitz, and now I have to repay the kindness. That's how *I* was raised. I shall stand their friend."

Blanche almost dropped her books. "Don't be a ninnyhammer, Sonia. You'll be ruined. And you can't have thought; you're so good, you think there's good in everyone. What if he really is a cad?"

"What if he isn't? You cannot expect me to take the word of Rosellen. I'll have to know Lord Warebourne better to decide for myself. I certainly owe him that much."

Blanche sighed with relief. "That's fine then. He'll never be invited to ton affairs, so you'll never see him again. And not even you would think of calling on him at home. Would you, Sonia?"

"Of course not, goose." But there was nothing to stop her from walking her dog in the park.

Fancy that, Sonia thought after one simple inquiry, Ware House was just across the square from Lady Atterbury's. She might have seen the Warebourne children in the park any number of times, if she'd been looking. Now that she was, she decided to leave nothing to chance. She sent her footman, Ian, over to find out when the girls were usually taken for a walk. She met them and their nursemaid at the gate closest to Ware House.

The nursemaid had no fault to find with Sonia's taking the children off. The brats finally stopped whining and moping when they saw the dog; Miss Randolph was obviously a lady; and that handsome red-haired footman had a fine line of Irish blarney that fair turned a girl's head. Besides, her employer would never know. The major had not come out of his library since bringing the children home yesterday without the dog. A fine job that'd been, too, trying to stop all the crying and screaming so she could get some rest before her evening engagement with the head groom. Some fine lady wanted to play with Meg Bint's charges, she had Meg's blessings.

At first the girls were uncertain of Sonia, considering the scene at her house yesterday. Fitz's exuberant greeting quickly had them laughing and babbling like old friends, especially when Sonia fetched some gingerbread from the tapestry bag at her feet and suggested they sit on the bench awhile to catch their breaths.

"There," Sonia told them, "now we can be comfortable. I was so sorry that I didn't get to thank you properly for taking care of Fitz yesterday. I didn't even catch your names. I am Miss Sonia Randolph, and this, of course, is Fitz."

Ever conscious of the proprieties, Benice stood and made a curtsy, her dignity somewhat marred by the crumbs that fell off her lap. Sonia took no notice. "We are pleased to make your acquaintance, Miss Randolph," Benice solemnly recited as if from memory. "And we are the Conover sisters of Ware House. I am the oldest, so I am Miss Conover, but you may call me Benice."

"Very prettily done," Sonia congratulated, causing the pale child to blush with pleasure.

"My middle sister is Genessa, but we call her Gen. Gen, make your curtsy!" The minx in the middle crammed the last of the gingerbread in her mouth and bobbled up and down, grinning. Sonia grinned back and handed over a napkin.

"And that's Baby. She doesn't curtsy yet. She doesn't talk much, either. She used to talk more, before . . ." The child's voice faded and her smile disappeared altogether. "Her name is Bettina. Uncle Darius says she's too old to be called Baby, so he calls her Tina. That's what our father called her." Benice's lip trembled.

"I'm sure you must miss your father ever so much. I miss mine, and he's only in Berkshire. He always called me Sunny. Do you think you might do that, so I don't feel so lonely?"

Three heads nodded somberly, then Gen asked, "What about your mother? Ours is gone to heaven with Papa."

"Mine is there, too. Maybe they'll meet and be friends, just like us. What do you think? Meantime," she said, changing the subject, "I brought you some gifts, just to say thank you from Fitz. I didn't quite know what you would like, so I hope I chose correctly." She reached into the carpetbag. "This is for you, Benice," she said, pulling out a tiny gold locket on a chain. "See, it opens. I put a snip of Fitz's hair inside—from his tail, where he won't miss it—so you won't forget him. Of course, if you have a beau, you might put his miniature there," she teased. Genessa hooted, but Benice was smiling through her blushes, and asked if Sonia would please put it on for her. "I'll wear it always, Miss Sunny. It's beautiful."

"And, Gen, this is for you." It was a bilbo-catch toy, a wooden ball meant to be caught in the wooden cup tied to it with string. "Topping!" Gen shouted, running off to try it.

The littlest Conover was jumping up and down on the bench, yelling, "Me. Me."

Sonia laughed. "I wouldn't forget you, Tiny! Here." She pulled out a little stuffed pillow in the shape of a dog, with buttons sewn on for eyes and nose, and a ribbon around its neck for a collar. "Mimi!" the baby cooed, hugging the pillow to her.

Then Sonia had Fitz do some of his tricks, to show what a smart dog he really was, even if he did get lost and run over. Fitz sat and lay down and rolled over, he shook hands and barked and fetched. He went right at a hand signal, left at another, and concluded with his bow, head lowered between his legs. The children, and a few passersby, applauded happily.

"Can we play hide and seek?" Gen asked. "Blackie was the best finder."

So the little girls ran squealing behind trees and under benches, and Fitz and Sonia made believe they couldn't find them. Then they played blindman's buff, with one of the napkins as blindfold, and, finally, a lively game of tag before it was time to go.

"Do you think you might come tomorrow?" Sonia

77

asked, and three dark heads nodded vigorously. "At the same time?" More nodding. "Maybe your uncle will join us." Three little girls shook their heads no.

"He says he doesn't want to go anywhere, only back to the army," Genessa confided.

"And he stays in the library, throwing books," Benice fretted.

"Oh dear. Perhaps he would come if you tell him that I need to consult with him about Fitz's leg. What do you think?"

They all grinned. They thought it just might work.

Tag, hide-and-go-seek . . . cat and mouse?

Chapter Nine

Sometimes I envy Tippy the turnspit. Granted, her life is narrow, lived entirely between the kitchen and Cook's bedchamber, but she is too small to face the world on her own anyway. Her responsibilities are no bigger than her short little legs. Her kind has it easy now that there are enclosed stoves, so she has two jobs. By day she has a few hours on a wheel. The scenery is boring, but she says she uses the time to compose verse. By night she is a foot warmer. How hard could that be? She has none of these anguished decisions I now face. No one's future hangs on her actions. Nowhere does she feel the Great Dane's torment, unless it's to baste or not to baste.

I am torn. I have been wrong in the past about Major Conover. He does have a title, he is well to pass, and he did not accept a reward for bringing me home when we both know I found my own way. But he is still an outcast and he still smokes. Furthermore, he throws books. A desecration!

Worse, there is an alarm going off in my head. It's clanging Cinderella, Cinderella, Cinderella. Aristocratic humans have wet nurses, so ladies don't even have to see their babies, much less care for them. Stepmothers have no bonds whatsoever, neither blood nor milk; they don't have to love their adopted children at all.

I do not think Miss Sonia could ever be an evil stepmother, but how much love is there to go around? I know I grew fond of my "Blackie's" family, but I only truly love Miss Sonia. Of course, I am a good dog; I do not expect such devotion from mere humans.

Miss Sonia was growing fond of the Warebourne girls. Wouldn't she feel guilty about loving her own children better? Worse, what if there was not enough love to share so many ways? Benice, Gen, and Tina needed so much, perhaps Miss Sonia wouldn't care about having her own babies? I could have been flattened by a barrel for nothing!

No, I dare not take a chance. 'Twas better to nip this relationship in the bud now, than have to nip a butt later. I will play with the children when we meet in the park. I will play with them so hard and so rough, we'll never be allowed near them again. They'll all thank me someday.

Sonia took an inordinate amount of time selecting an outfit to wear to go for a romp in the square with her dog and some children. Goodness, she chided herself, she wasn't trying to fix Lord Warebourne's interest or anything, she just wanted to be friends with the man. Besides, he mightn't even come. She finally selected a rose-colored walking dress with its fuller skirt and higher neck than many of her new clothes. She pinned a bunch of silk violets under the brim of her chip-straw bonnet, and tied its pink ribbons along her cheek. She took her maid along with her as well as Ian, the footman, so she broke no minor rules, on her way to break major ones. She also brought a ball, so Fitz and the girls could play on their own. She sat on a bench near the Ware House side of the little park, Fitz at her feet, and waited.

He came, following slowly behind the excited children, who immediately ran laughing and tumbling after Fitz and the ball. Darius bowed stiffly, then took a seat on Sonia's bench, as far from Miss Randolph as possible without toppling off. He did not look in her direction. To a casual observer, they would appear chance-met strangers enjoying the day. Ian stepped behind a tree with the nursemaid, Meg, but Maisie Holbrook very properly kept vigil from the next bench over, keeping Miss Randolph quite in view if not exactly in hearing, while she mended a bit of lace in her lap.

Sonia studied the major while he observed the noisy game of catch. He seemed even more careworn today than she remembered, older, harder. He sat rigidly erect, military fashion, only his injured leg angled for comfort. Sonia could feel his disapproval and wondered if she had made a mistake, asking him to come where he had no wish to be. She never meant to add to the officer's discomfort.

She was about to call to Fitz, to leave Major Conover to his solitude, when he frowned, then spoke, still without looking at her. "The dog does not seem to be in a decline, Miss Randolph. He hardly favors the leg at all."

Sonia looked to where Fitz was barking and jumping, chasing the ball. "No, sir, and I am sorry the children told you such a bouncer. I did want to thank you properly for saving him, however, and to apologize for that scene at Atterbury House."

"No need, I am sure." He cleared his throat. "Miss Randolph, I appreciate your attention to the children. They are in alt over their new friends. I don't know which impressed them more, your kind-

ness or Fitz's repertoire of tricks. Now they won't
be so miserable until I can find them a puppy of
their own. Or a kitten. There is some disagreement
among the ranks, so the decision is still pending. I
do thank you, ma'am, but this"—holding his hands
out to encompass the park, the bench, his own presence—"was not well done of you. You must be aware
by now that I am not fit to be in your company. I
heard your own grandmother make that plain."

Sonia raised her chin. "I make my own friends."

"You are very young and foolish, then."

"I am eighteen, and old enough to know when
someone has done me a great service. Fitz means
the world to me, you see."

"He is a lucky dog to win such affection." He
stood to leave. "Still, I cannot let you—"

"Please, don't go yet," she pleaded. "At least tell
me how you found Fitz. The children's tale was all
full of brave derring-do, mixed in with monkeys and
schoolboys and opera singers. That sounds like
quite a bumblebroth, even for Fitz."

Darius could not resist the appeal in her voice.
He made the mistake of turning to her. Deuce take
it, he knew he shouldn't look at those blue eyes, or
catch a hint of those adorable dimples. Or note how
the pink ribbons of her bonnet brought up the tinge
in her velvet cheeks. And those silly violets nestled
in gold curls. Gads, he loved violets. He was lost.
He'd tell her about the dog's addlepated exploits,
then he'd leave. For good.

The telling of the story, the vegetables, the herring, the scattered newspapers, softened the major's features and even brought a twinkle to his
brown eyes. Sonia was pleased to see the years and
worries slip away. She was also happy to have her
own instincts confirmed: He was a good man. Sonia
couldn't begin to imagine Lord Berke or any of his
friends stopping for a half-dead dog, much less soiling his hands to help the filthy animal.

"I truly am in your debt," she said.

"No, I think I am in yours." Darius smiled and gestured to where Fitz and his nieces were frolicking. The ball long lost, the dog and the girls seemed to be taking turns rolling in a mud puddle. Then they went wading in the decorative fountain, splashing water on an irate matron with a beady-eyed mink tippet draped about her neck. Next Fitz took Baby on a ride through the public flower beds, scattering blossoms for the older girls to make into neck chains and hair wreaths. "I have never seen them so happy."

"And I have never seen Fitz behave so badly. Goodness, he knows he's not supposed to go near the fountains or the gardens. I'm sorry about the little girls' clothes, Major. I don't know what's got into Fitz these days. Perhaps it's spring fever. I'll just whistle him back before someone calls the Watch." Fitz was now digging a hole in the soft dirt with his powerful front legs, spraying debris on the girls and a clerk who hurried past, cursing. Benice found a stick and came to help dig. Gen and Tina just used their hands.

"No, leave them. I've never seen the girls act so . . . childishly. Especially Benice. They don't laugh enough." Just then Fitz turned and nosed Baby right into the hole. Darius laughed out loud at the stunned expression on the little girl's face.

"Nor do you, I think," Sonia murmured. She hadn't meant him to hear, and blushed when he turned back to her.

"Miss Randolph, you are very kind. Your compassion does you credit, but you mustn't let your tender heart lead you astray. For your own sake, I must go. I can see you have a strong will under that sweetness, but you must not exercise it on my behalf. I am not a charity case." He spoke gently, to discourage her, not to insult the enchanting young miss. "Truly I do not need your sympathy."

Sonia stared at the reticule in her lap. "I had hoped to enlist yours." She untied the strings and withdrew a white envelope and handed it to him. "Tomorrow night is my come-out ball. I wish you would come."

Darius looked at the envelope and read his name neatly inscribed, Major Darius Conover, Lord Warebourne. He laughed harshly. "Haven't you heard anything I said, Miss Randolph? Not even the title will keep me from being tossed on my ear."

"Not at my ball, my lord, not if I invite you myself. I am acquainted with so few people, you see, I should like to have someone familiar there. Everyone else will be Grandmother's friends."

"Deuce take it, my girl, you'll know fewer and fewer if I sit in your pocket. You'll be cut by them all."

Her lips formed a determined line. "I am not asking you to sit in my pocket, my lord, just to stand my friend. One dance is all I wish."

He gave that same humorless laugh. "I cannot even dance, Miss Randolph, with this blasted leg. A fine figure of fun that would make of us, were I to try and fall on my face in front of you and half the ton."

"I am not permitted the waltz yet, so I shall not be dancing every dance, even if I am asked."

"Even if you are asked? Are you fishing for compliments, Miss Randolph? You are beautiful, charming, and well dowered. There will be bucks and beaux lined up along the sidewalks of Grosvenor Square just waiting to ask you!"

Sonia's face was as pink as the ribbons on her bonnet. "I never meant to be so forward, my lord, truly I did not. I just do not know many of those . . . bucks and beaux, and thought I might be more comfortable sitting out a waltz with someone I know. I'm sorry. It was very improper of me to ask."

"Miss Randolph, your being here in the park with me is improper, and you dashed well know it. Your handing me an invitation your guardian didn't issue is deucedly irregular. Asking a gentleman, and

I use the term loosely, for a dance would set you beyond the pale. I am beginning to think there is the heart of a hoyden under that demure exterior," he said sternly, until he caught the beginnings of her dimples. "Are you really comfortable sitting with me?"

She nodded.

"Every other respectable female goes off in a swoon if I half nod in her direction. Why aren't you afraid?"

She countered his question with one of her own: "Do I have any reason to be afraid?"

"Beyond fearing to be tarred with the same brush? No, Miss Randolph, you never need to be afraid of me. Never."

"There. I knew Fitz wouldn't befriend a bounder." She called for the dog and turned to leave, kissing the muddy children and giving Darius one last brilliant smile. "Will you at least please consider the invitation?"

He nodded. That was all he could do, considering Miss Randolph's smile turned his brain to mush.

Darius did contemplate the invitation as he carried two exhausted, grimy children home. Blister it, where was that wretched nursemaid anyway? Benice could hardly drag his cane, while he suffered along with both Gen and Tina in his arms. Gen was smiling at him, which was worth a walk to the Isle of Wight. He knew he had Miss Randolph to thank for that, and again considered the engraved card. He thought about the ball, picturing Miss Randolph twirling in some lucky devil's arms, laughing up into some fortunate chap's eyes. Then he thought what a wretched mull he'd made of his life. Heaven seemed to be waiting just out of reach behind a locked door, and everyone but Darius Conover had the key.

* * *

Sonia and Fitz, his tongue hanging out of his mouth, made two stops on her way out of the park. First she checked with the flower girl to make sure lots of violets were on order for the ball. Most of the flowers and greenery for the formal arrangements were coming from Lady Atterbury's favorite florist, but Sonia saw no reason her friends shouldn't profit from the party, too. The pieman was already providing a quantity of gooseberry tarts to augment the Atterbury kitchens.

Sonia's last stop was by the bench of the silver-haired man feeding the squirrels, where she sat down before the elderly gentleman could struggle to his feet. Fitz sank to the ground next to them. A squirrel ran right over the snoring dog, and he didn't move. Sonia took another card out of her reticule and handed it to the old man.

"I already got one, missy," he rasped.

"I know, and I already got your refusal. I am hoping you'll reconsider and accept this one." She proceeded to tell him why. He shook his head no. She teased and cajoled until he nodded yes, then she kissed his cheek and went home humming a waltz.

So much for the best-laid plans of mice and mongrels.

Chapter Ten

*T*onight I stand guard like Cerberus, watchdog of the underworld. I wish I had three heads like mighty Cerberus, to keep better vigil at the ball. Marston, the butler, defends the front entry against indignity, calling off the guests' names and honorifics with resonant cadences. I have been assigned the rear garden. I was told, "Fitz, you stay outside tonight." That is a lot of responsibility. I patrol the yard to make sure no intruders come over the walls. I watch the lantern-lighted paths to guarantee no young couples go beyond the line. I pace the balcony outside the ballroom to keep rakes from taking advantage of the darkness and a miss needing fresh air. Mostly I try to keep sight of Miss Sonia as she dances and strolls about, meeting this handsome youth, smiling at that likely lad, granting a quadrille to a paragon in puce satin.

I wish Muffy were here. She could imitate a wig and sit atop one of the footmen's heads and guard the refreshments. Tippy assures me there are always leftovers, but this is my first London ball. I admit I am nervous.

I am not apprehensive that Miss Sonia will not "take." She has been considered an Incomparable since the receiving line. From the drawing room window I hear Miss Sonia discussed in glowing terms, thank St. Francis. She is described as no niminy-piminy girl, but not too coming either. She has fresh charm, not airs and affectations. She is just right, and her dowry is nothing to sneeze at either. We are a success. I am worried, however, that *she* will be taken with the wrong man. Lady Atterbury says that the crème de la crème of society is here tonight. What if its dregs arrive, too?

I wonder if he will come, this lord who would be a soldier. If he likes Miss Sonia, he will come, because he wants to be with her and because she asked. If he likes her, though, he won't come, lest he hurt her chances and disturb Lady Atterbury. More complications. Sometimes I think my life would be easier if they were like trout, the females laying their eggs in one place and the males coming there to leave a token of their affection before going about their own business.

Major Conover or not, tonight is a turning point. I can feel it in my belly. Maybe that's the wine I tasted with Ian earlier, just to make sure it hadn't turned. But Miss Sonia's beau ideal might be here tonight. He might be kissing her fingertips this very minute, while I make fog-breath on the glass doors. Rats!

Still, I am curious about this diversion they call a ball, a toy, a plaything. I am trying to understand what they find so entertaining about cramming four hundred people in space for three, standing on line for hours to shake someone's hand, having their feet trod upon, their names vilified behind their backs, and

88

their heads muddled with champagne. They gamble beyond their means, and they dance like performing bears.

At first the men are in groups on one side of the room, and the women on the other. Then some of the braver lads ask the most well-favored lasses for the set. Lady Atterbury and her friends go around forcing other gentlemen to take the floor, but some of them escape to the card room or the balcony to blow a cloud—incidentally obscuring my view. Some of the girls are therefore left without partners, so they take up positions around the perimeter and pretend they are just another flower arrangement.

When the music begins, the dancers all follow the same patterns and movements. Everyone to the right, everyone to the left, as if they are being herded by a Chopin-loving collie. The waltz is different, but of course, the young ladies, the ones in whose honor the ball is thrown, cannot take part. They sit and watch their older sisters and widowed aunts snabble the most dashing bachelors while they are left with sputtering striplings.

I am intrigued to see the elite at play. Are they having fun yet?

Lady Atterbury was pleased. Not even Sally Jersey or those other rattlepates from Almack's could find fault tonight. Every surface of Atterbury House gleamed, the staff was superbly and unobtrusively efficient, the refreshments extravagant. The dowager had expected no less.

At first she was annoyed with the floral arrangements, banks of daisies and ferns in the ballroom, baskets of violets on each table in the supper room. Common, the dowager decided, wrinkling her patrician nose. And just like her goosecap of a granddaughter, flaunting her humble country origins.

Lady Almeria sent upstairs for another diamond brooch to join the three she already wore, next to the ruby and diamond parure, the blinding tiara, and the eight rings. Heaven forfend anyone mistake the household of Her Grace, the Duchess of Atterbury, for a woodland meadow. Then various matrons came to compliment the dowager on how cleverly the decorations reflected her granddaughter's fresh charm. Just the right touch, Princess Lieven enthused, for a miss not yet jaded by the Season. A joy to see a gel bright as a daisy, Emily Cowper congratulated, so sweetly friendly and lively, not like one of London's delicate hothouse blooms. Lady Atterbury commended herself on her excellent taste and grasp of the social niceties. She also graciously accepted credit for her granddaughter's appearance. Yes, the chit did the Harkness name proud tonight.

Madame Celeste had done the impossible: created a white gown that wasn't white. The slip of a satin undress was white, but the skirt, which began right under a minuscule bodice, was covered with three layers of tissue-thin net in three shades of blue. The gauzy mesh floated at Miss Randolph's feet, changing colors to reflect the dancing lights in her blue eyes. The white bodice was embroidered all over with forget-me-nots, the center of each flower a pearl. Sonia wore Lady Atterbury's gift of pearls and, in her fair curls, a sapphire butterfly sent by her father for the occasion. George had sent the matching earbobs, and her younger brother, Hugh, arriving barely in time for the dinner before the ball, brought her a gold filigree fan.

"Bang up to the nines, Sunny," he told her approvingly as he led her out for the first dance. "Never thought you'd hold a candle to Catherine, but demmed if I didn't have my blunt on the wrong filly. Your dance card is already filled, and you have the blades lined up two-deep to fetch you a lemonade. By George if you ain't a success. Little Sunny with her dirty face and skinned knees and mare's-nest hairdos. Who'd have thought it?"

Sonia chuckled. "Thank you, I think. I just wish Papa was here to see it."

Hugh looked quickly to make sure she wasn't getting weepy on him. No, Sunny was a Trojan. "He'd just grumble about the expense and disappear into the card room anyway. Then he'd brag to everyone for days how you looked fine as five-pence."

"In case I didn't mention it earlier, you are looking very fine yourself, Lieutenant, in your handsome new dress uniform. In fact, I can see the hopeful mamas ringing Grandmother now, waiting for their chances."

Hugh missed his step and nearly trod on Sonia's toes. "Sorry, but hang it, Sunny, I ain't going to dance with every fubsy-faced chit in the place. Just because Pa got himself leg-shackled and George is under the cat's-paw don't mean I have to do the pretty all night. I'm no hand at this blasted dancing anyway. Now, put me on the parade grounds . . ."

"Just one dance, Hugh, with one particular friend of mine, Lady Blanche Carstairs. She hasn't many partners yet, and I do not want her to be unhappy at my ball. Besides, you'll like her. She's a good listener."

Sonia was pleased, later, to see Hugh return from the card room to escort Blanche down to supper. She herself went down with Ansel Berke, as earlier arranged. She laughed, she flirted, she was having a wonderful time at her own ball. Sonia made friends with the other debutantes, happily distributing her leftover suitors among them for the remaining dances. She met so many charming gentlemen, she couldn't keep their names straight, although Lord Wolversham impressed her with his knowledge of farms and crops and sheep. She sat out one of the waltzes with the good-looking marquess, listening raptly, sending more than one gentleman hurrying to change his bets at White's.

Not till long after the supper dance did Miss Randolph betray the least nervousness, and then only by frequent glances toward the ballroom door. No one else noticed her distraction, she hoped, as she fluttered her fan and discussed the weather and the king's health with her latest partner.

He wasn't going. He was in his dress uniform, hastily tailored to compensate for the weight loss from his injury, but he wasn't going. The formal sword lay polished in his hand, ready to be strapped to his hips, but Major Conover was not going to buckle it on. He'd sooner walk through the French lines than walk across Grosvenor Square to Atterbury House. A carriage would save his leg, but get him there sooner. No, he put the sword down. Again. His batman, Robb, was like to skewer him with it if he didn't decide soon. "Deuce take it!" Darius stormed. Robb hurried to remove the sword from the major's reach. Then they heard the pounding at the door.

"Who the devil could that be? Dash it, no one calls for weeks, then someone comes banging in the middle of the night when I am trying to dress. We've been so long without guests in this wretched place, the blasted servants have forgotten whose job it is to open the door. Go get rid of whoever it is, Robby, while I try to make my mind up."

Robb was happy to get out of the way of his employer's impatience. Damned if the major didn't need a good fight to settle him down, he thought. Prebattle jitters, that's what ailed the man. Robb nodded sagely on his way to get the front door. He returned a few minutes later, pale and shaken.

"Well, what was it, Sergeant, a lost traveler or some accident in the square? I hope you got rid of the nuisance, whatever it was. I'm in no mood to—"

"Admiral Cathcart, sir" was all poor Robb could utter.

"What's that, Robb?" The major was recombing his newly trimmed hair, for the fourth time. He was wondering if the gray showed less, now that his hair was in the shorter style currently in favor. "I thought you said Admiral Cathcart. Old fellow must be dead these ten years or so."

"Downstairs, sir. He's downstairs!"

"Admiral Cathcart, who fought with Nelson? Who won so many commendations, they had to make up new ones? Good grief, what's he doing alive? No, I mean what's he doing here?"

"I left him having sherry in the drawing room, Major, but I don't think you should keep him waiting, sir."

"By Jove, I should think not." He snatched up the dress sword and buckled it on as he raced down the stairs. "Admiral Cathcart, in my drawing room."

The elderly man in the drawing room was blinding in his gold braid. He had enough ribbons on his chest to open a shop. Major Conover knew he had never met the silver-haired admiral before, but he had saluted him once. He gazed admiringly at one of the nation's greatest heroes, an old man who fed squirrels in the park.

"Sir, this is a great honor, but . . ."

"Come to request your escort, young man. Told a lady I'd honor her ball. Don't get out much, though, don't want to make my big appearance lookin' like a dodderin' old fool, leanin' on some pesky civilian footman. Spoil the effect, don't you know. The lady suggested you. Fellow officer and all, even if you're not a navy man."

"So you want me . . . ?" He looked at the cane in his hand, then laughed. "I am not so steady on my pins, Admiral Cathcart. I think the lady was just using every weapon in the arsenal."

"Aye, bringin' out the heavy artillery. Good tactician, that girl, don't take no for an answer. She seems to want you at her ball. I aim to get you there, short of callin' out the militia. Can't tell you how the chit brightens my day. Least I can do, then."

"But, Admiral, sir, you can't know—"

"I still have my oars in the water, lad. I know it's no easy thing she's askin', but just one dance. You've faced worse."

"Have I, sir?" Put like that, no self-respecting soldier could refuse. The credit of the regiment, the regard of this venerable old seadog, his own honor, were at stake. "You don't leave me much choice."

"Never meant to, soldier. Never asked more of a man than I thought he could give, either. Don't disappoint me. And don't disappoint that little girl's trust either, or I'll have you blown clear out of the waters."

Marston, the butler, did not know whether to filch another bottle of His Grace's port, or just start packing. The ball had been declared a sad crush, which is to say a great success, and then disaster struck. An appearance by the reclusive Admiral Cathcart would be the coup of the season. An appearance by the reprehensible Major Conover would be the end of Marston's career. But the fellow had an invite, in miss's own hand, and the admiral was leaning on the major's shoulder, waiting to be announced. Marston took a deep breath. In loud, ringing tones, he called out the admiral's name and honorifics. Everyone gasped and turned toward the door. In not so loud, barely tinkling tones, Marston announced Major Darius Conover, the Earl of Warebourne. Everyone gasped again. Not another word was said. The orchestra was not even playing, between sets as it was. The crowd on the dance floor parted as the two militarily erect men, neither bowed by age or adversity, made their slow, careful way across the room to where Lady Atterbury held court on a sofa, Miss Randolph by her side.

The general bowed to Lady Atterbury, then turned and made her a formal introduction to "one of our fine, brave lads."

Lady Atterbury could only smile and nod. Sonia made her curtsy, then relinquished her seat next to the dowager to Admiral Cathcart, with a wink. Two chairs appeared alongside, and Sonia gestured to one. "Will you join me for the waltz, sir?" At the major's nod, she gestured to her footman, who signaled the orchestra. A waltz was instantly begun, to the consternation of those who had reserved a *contredanse*. When Sonia's court had departed to find their own partners, Darius finally took his seat beside her.

"Do you always get your way, minx?" he asked, motioning toward the admiral.

She flashed her dimples. "Was it so terrible?"

"Like walking the world's longest gangplank," he said with a laugh, then fell silent, looking at her.

Color rose in Sonia's cheeks, and in the expanse of white skin left exposed by the narrow bodice. "Major, you are staring," she whispered from behind her fan.

"I am trying to memorize your dress and such so I can describe you to the brats tomorrow. I think I'll just tell them to imagine a fairy princess floating on sunbeams over sky blue lakes."

"How lovely! I didn't know you military men had such poetical turns, Major."

He looked at her and smiled. "Neither did I."

Sonia was relieved to see him smile. He wasn't mad, he wasn't miserable. He was, in fact, so handsome when he smiled, she half hoped none of the other girls saw it. But that was part of her plan, so she made every effort to keep him smiling, telling about Fitz's exploits, asking about his nieces, describing her hey-go-mad brother's latest effort at

gaining preferment. He told about his own childhood pets and some of his milder army pranks. She
thought she'd gladly trade all the night's compliments for one of his laughs.

Soon the dance was ended and Miss Randolph's
next partner hesitantly approached to claim her.
The major rose and bowed over Sonia's hand, then
brought her hand to his lips. He did not say anything, but he squeezed her fingers, and held them
a fraction longer than strictly proper.

**I believe that is called putting the cat among
the pigeons.**

Chapter Eleven

They say elephants have long memories. Mankind better hope the immense creatures don't also hold grudges. Imagine such large, long-lived beasts being persecuted for keyboards, dice, fans, and hairpins. That should be enough to make anyone cross as crabs. Crabs as big as cottages. I hope to have a coze with the elephants at the Tower Menagerie someday.

Human memories, by contrast, are as fickle as fleas, like tonight at the ball, when the doyennes seated inside recall that they always considered Darius Conover more dashing than his brother Milo, even if he was a bit of a rake. A bit of a rake? Half an hour ago he was a debaucher of women! The gentlemen in the book room are re-telling war stories, with the major featured as the bravest man in the British army, when yesterday he was too cowardly to accept a duel. And the young females who last week shivered in fright if he passed them on the street, tonight shiver in delight if his eye catches theirs.

Are their loyalties as inconsistent as their

memories? If Baron Berke and his sister Rosellen do not forget about their dead, dishonored sister, will their friends and the rest of the ton forget the major's role? Their loyalties seem to be king, God, and country, with expediency a close fourth. And the king is all about in his head.

Consider Lord Felton making a liaison with Sir Norbert's wife on the balcony right now, while Sir Norbert is enjoying the favors of Mrs. Quentin-Jones in the curtained alcove next to the library. Perhaps they temporarily forgot their marriage vows. Or perhaps they change their loyalties as often as their outfits.

Sirius, I am not expecting human persons to be as faithful as dogs. That would be like barking at the moon. Just ask Odysseus. His wife may have stayed true all those years, unpicking her weaving and all, but she didn't even recognize the poor sod when he finally got home. Nor did his son, his friends, his servants—only noble Argos, his old dog. That's loyalty. That's a good dog, Fido.

I do not think Miss Sonia will be inconsistent once she gives her affection. She loves me forever, of course, but she has never forgotten her old friends either, or given up on an idea she believes in. Perhaps I am premature; the Dog Star knows I've been wrong before. Possibly Miss Sonia is just repaying a debt, and maybe she will consider her job done, now that she has brought the major back into the fold. His staying there will be up to him and the rest of the sheep, ah, society. I cannot tell from here, blast it! I cannot even tell if there are any lobster patties left.

Admiral Cathcart and the major stayed through one more dance, the admiral remaining seated on the couch next to Lady Atterbury. Major Conover might have left, but the admiral signaled for the officer to take a position beside him, guarding the flank. Leaning slightly on the sofa back, Darius did not intrude on the conversations, but anyone wishing to shake hands with the admiral perforce had to shake Conover's hand. And Lady Atterbury had to make the introductions. She looked as if she had an oyster stuck in her throat, and someone had just reminded her it was alive.

Many of the company wished to greet one of the great heroes of Trafalgar, to proffer an invitation or mention a promising nephew in the navy. With a nod or a gesture Darius made sure the old gentleman had wine to drink and space to breathe and pauses between introductions. He was the one to note when the admiral's voice faltered, and laughingly suggested they retire to fight another day. Even Lady Atterbury had to commend his solicitous regard for the admiral, although it rubbed against the grain. She went so far as to offer her hand when he made his adieus.

Others noted Warebourne's kindness, his quiet dignity, and chiseled features—they also recalled his title and fortune—and began to reconsider their long-held positions. No one could doubt his bravery, not with a chestful of medals and the admiral's patent endorsement. Nor could they question his conduct. For tonight, at least, he had been all that was proper, charming the little Harkness heiress without enticing her to the balcony, the alcoves, or the primrose path. No one was ready to rush home to send him a bid for a card party or to request his presence at their daughter's come-out, but they were thinking it mightn't be such a bad idea to acknowledge a young, handsome, wealthy earl. As for the rest, the jury was still out. The haut monde would wait to see Lord Conare and Baron Berke's reaction to Warebourne's reentry into society before issuing a verdict or an invite.

* * *

Lord Conare and Baron Berke were presently in the rear garden. Their reactions, if anyone could have seen them, were at best anger and disgust. At worst, vicious fury and violent loathing. They both took care that the polite world never saw such raging emotions. That wasn't good ton.

Preston Conover, Lord Conare, was as tall as his cousin Darius, with the same dark hair and brown eyes. Unlike the soldier's well-muscled body, however, Conare's frame was thin to the point of emaciation. His indoor pallor and fashionable but somber clothes, all black and white without a hint of color, made him appear even more cadaverous. His hair was never out of place, he never exerted himself. He'd perfected the art of ennui to where he could take snuff, utter a set-down, and yawn at the same time. Since he could both drink and gamble to excess without apparent effect, he was a welcome member of Prinny's coterie.

Preston's austerity was the perfect foil for his wife, Rosellen's, lush beauty. Her auburn tresses, emerald eyes, bountiful curves, flamboyant dress style, and flirtatious manner captured the attention, but Preston did the behind-the-scenes social maneuvering. They made an interesting couple, invited everywhere. That's why he married her, that and her Berke and Atterbury connections. Which he was regretting more heartily every day.

Ansel Berke was not a large man, but he was as fit as most idle members of the aristocracy, working out occasionally at Gentleman Jackson's or Cribb's Parlor, riding in Hyde Park at the fashionable hour. What exercise and nature had not provided, Berke augmented with padded shoulders and nipped-in waists, which seemed to require more gaudily embroidered waistcoats and more extravagantly tied neckcloths. He wasn't quite a dandy, he told himself; he did not wear yellow Cossack trousers or soup-plate-size buttons. He might have—high-heeled slippers particularly tempted him—but he had a position to uphold.

He was a baron. He was also nearly run off his feet. Where his brother-in-law Preston was always cool and seemingly unaffected, Ansel was something of a hothead. He usually managed to keep his emotions as hidden as his financial state, for the sake of his social standing, but tonight his temper was unchecked. No one could hear him out in the garden behind Atterbury House, so far from the ballroom, and no one could see him in the faint light of the Chinese lanterns strung along the garden paths. No one, that is, except his brother-in-law Preston, who already despised Berke. The sentiment was returned.

"I thought you said the bastard would return to the wars and get himself killed if I brought up the old scandal," Berke raged. "Did you think I wanted my family name dragged through the mud again, you prig?"

Preston flicked a speck of lint off his sleeve. "In case you have forgotten, brother, Conover is my name also. Furthermore, I did marry your sister, you know. Despite the unpleasantness, I made sure all doors would stay closed to him. His pride could not let him remain in England."

"In case you haven't looked, he's inside now, cozying up to Lady Atterbury."

"Then you haven't done your job, old chap. Remember your vows of vengeance?"

"No amount of scandalmongering is going to bring Hermione back."

"No, but it might save the little heiress for you. Did you see the look on her face when he kissed her hand?"

Berke did. That's why he had to leave the ballroom before his anger erupted like a raging volcano. Sonia had never smiled at *him* that way. "Leave Miss Randolph out of this, you muckworm. I noticed the way *you* looked at her, *brother*. She might have been dessert, the way you drooled."

Preston smoothed his cuffs. "I am never so gauche

as to drool, although la Randolph is a tempting morsel. Never fear," he added when Berke started making growling noises in his throat, "I shan't hunt your covers, at least not until the vixen is caught. After the chit is married, of course . . ."

Berke would worry about that when the time came. "Well, that's not getting rid of Warebourne. Besides, there's no guarantee he'll be killed even if he does go back to the front. The devil's been lucky all these years."

Preston sighed. "I know, I know. Gunshots, innumerable saber wounds, to say nothing of infection and the various plagues that carry off most of the wounded. He's survived them all. Wearisome, isn't it? No, you'll just have to call him out."

"What?" Berke shouted. Then, quickly looking around and speaking more softly, he asked, "What do you mean, I'll have to call him out?"

"Simple, dear boy. You'll merely demand he meet you on the field of honor. You never had satisfaction, remember? You cannot swallow that and still call yourself a man."

"No more than one who lets another do his dirty work for him," Berke sneered.

"You're not suggesting I challenge Cousin Darius myself, are you? Think, Ansel, as hard as the effort might be. My motives just might be a tad suspect. You, however, have righteous indignation on your side, your family's honor to be redeemed. Popular sentiment shall be in your favor; you'll have everyone's sympathy."

"He refused before. Who's to say he'll take up the gauntlet this time?"

"By all accounts he's no coward." Preston shrugged. "If he does forfeit, he'll lose whatever acceptance this night's work has gained him. Not even that doddery old relict Cathcart will take his arm. No visits to Atterbury House, no playing the hero for the Randolph chit. Mark my words, he'll

102

rejoin his regiment, and I'll start praying for Bonaparte's success again."

Berke kicked a stone out of his way. "And what if he does accept the challenge? Fellow must have learned to shoot straight in all these years."

"What, dear Ansel, balking at the gate?" He looked over to the other man, where a paper lantern cast a reddish glow on the baron's already empurpled cheeks.

"I ain't no craven," Berke stormed. "I'd call you out in a minute if I thought you'd accept, you blasted mortician."

"Sorry, too, too fatiguing."

Ansel muttered something under his breath. Then, "But what if I kill him? Having Warebourne out of the way is all fine and good for you, but my chances with the Randolph girl ain't improved if I have to flee the country."

"Do I have to do all the thinking? You are a crack shot, Ansel. You don't aim to kill, for Satan's sake. You've seen the condition he's in. One more wound, another loss of blood, that should take the trick. Perhaps we might even help him along some, but not with your bullet, my dear baron. I'll guarantee Prinny won't kick up a dust. After all, if I as nearest relative don't complain, how can the Crown?"

"I still don't see why I have to be the one to force the duel," Berke complained. "I ain't the one who'll inherit the title and the fortune."

"And I'm not the one who needs to marry an heiress. Of course, there is still the Carstairs female."

Berke grimaced, but said nothing. Conare went on: "Of course, her title is older than yours. I shouldn't think a gentleman could sleep well, knowing his wife outranks him. Then again, waking to face Lady Blanche at the breakfast table . . ."

"She's not as bad as all that, especially since Miss Randolph's taken her in hand some."

"Then why haven't you offered? Why not go inside and sweep her off to the balcony, get down on your knee, and ask for her hand and fortune this very night? There's no competition, no chance she'll say no, not if she ever expects to wed, that is."

"Rosellen wants me to have the Randolph girl," Berke mumbled.

"What's that? Oh yes, dear loving Rosellen, who's agreed to bear-lead an Incomparable, just so you two will be thrown together. Imagine her chagrin if all those thousands of Atterbury pounds go to Hermione's seducer. I'm afraid she might even stop helping you with those pressing debts of yours."

"Are you holding the money over me, you bastard? It won't wash. There's always a rich Cit looking for a title. And don't keep harping on Hermione, either. You don't care about her, you never did, so don't pretend you give a rap because she was Rosellen's sister, too. You have everything to gain here, Preston, and you don't even need the blunt. You'll get control of the three Warebourne brats' fortunes at the least, and all of Warebourne at the most."

"Yes, dear boy, but what both of us, you and I, will get the most satisfaction from is ridding the world of Darius Conover."

As the two men started back toward the balcony from the garden's farthest wall, neither saw the black dog dash ahead of them between a topiary unicorn and an ornamental fountain. Neither noticed when the dog's route intersected the graveled walkway they were taking back to the ballroom, nor were they the least aware that the animal paused a moment where the hanging lanterns cast the least light.

I hope you get a lot of satisfaction from ridding your satin dancing pumps of that, you maggots.

Chapter Twelve

And they say we fight like cats and dogs. I'd rather have an honest swipe at my nose than a knife in my back.

The ball wasn't over till nearly dawn, and yes, there were leftovers. Tippy had saved me a nice bone, so I agreed to peruse her poems the next morning while I gnawed. At first I was reluctant, and not just because I had weightier matters to consider, like the conversation in the garden. Commenting on a friend's work can be embarrassing. It can even cost the friendship. I did not want to hurt the little bitch's feelings or discourage art in any form, but, quite frankly, I was expecting mere doggerel.

I was happily surprised. Tippy's verses were on eternal themes, the turning cycles of the seasons, the orbits of the planets, the ultimate circle of life and death, dust to dust, ashes to ashes. Why should I have expected less from one who goes round and round half the day in a wheel? Tippy says her mentor, a mouse who used to live behind the wainscoting in the library, had advised her to write what she knew.

I suppose that is what I am doing, writing what I know, trying to write *everything* I know, in case I never get the chance again. This could not be how true novelists go about the thing, for I cannot believe Maria Edgeworth and the other ladies who write for the Minerva Press have ever been locked in dungeons, tossed from cliffs, set adrift, or sold into harems. They could hardly have time to write. No, they must have imagination, at which human persons excel.

When he couldn't reach the grapes, Reynard decided the grapes were sour; he didn't imagine sprouting wings and flying after them. Now, think of the poor dog of Icarus. The hound puts in a hard day guarding the house, warning of strangers, making sure his master is not disturbed. He looks up—and gets melted wax in his face. There is no way in hell that dog thought he had to protect Icarus from the Sun. He had no imagination; Icarus did. I admire creativity. Some have it, some don't.

Consider the flowers that are arriving all morning. The custom here in London is for gentlemen to send a token of appreciation to the ladies who honored them with a dance, especially the young lady in whose honor the ball was held. The gifts are supposed to be trifles, not personal items such as clothing, nor expensive offerings like jewelry. As a result, the footmen have been carrying in floral tributes since before breakfast. Think about it. Not five hours before, those same gentlemen saw Atterbury House filled with daisies and violets and formal arrangements. We need more flowers like an affenpinscher needs more fleas. No imagination at all.

Baron Berke's bouquet was the biggest. I suppose he sent his florist imaginary shillings.

Lord Wolversham had his groom deliver a

treatise on sheep dips, with his compliments. This may have been too imaginative a gift. Miss Sonia went into whoops over her chocolate.

Sir Montescue Pimford, one of the new young men from last night, sent a lovely poem. Unfortunately it was one of Byron's, according to Tippy.

Major Conover's offering was everything a gift should be for such an occasion: appealing without being extravagant, original instead of outré, sensitive. Brilliant, in fact. He sent a picture of me.

As I said, some have it, some don't.

"Whatever that man sent, Sonia, you'll have to return it." Lady Atterbury was clutching her vinaigrette. "I shall not scold anymore over the damage done last night, but I shall not countenance a further disregard for proper behavior."

Sonia held the wrapped package on her lap. "Fustian, Grandmama. If people were going to snub us because we—" she caught her grandmother's glare "—very well, I invited Major Conover, they would not have sent flowers. Furthermore, I shouldn't want to know anyone so stiff-rumped and prosy."

"Sonia Randolph, your language! I told Elvin he was raising you up to be a shameless baggage. He never listened. Now look, low company, cant language. You'll soon be a byword on the Town. I am too old for such a hubble-bubble." She took a restorative sip of sherry, for her nerves' sake only, of course. "Elvin has a lot to answer for, and I've a mind to send for the nodcock, wedding journey or no. At his age, it might kill him anyway. I could be doing the cod's-head a favor."

"Humbug, Your Grace, you know Father would tell me to trust my own judgment. And keep my own accounts. Besides, you loved every minute of the admiral's visit. Why, I wouldn't be surprised if he became your cicisbeo. See, you are blushing! And Sally Jersey almost tripped over Mrs. Drummond-

Burrell to meet him and invite him to her rout, so we are not sent to Coventry yet."

"Yet. And that's Admiral Cathcart, not some black sheep soldier. Conover ain't been accepted yet, missy, and might never be. That remains to be seen, and till it is, he ain't to be seen in my drawing room!"

Sonia raised her chin and looked her grandmother straight in the eye. "Then I shall meet him in the park if he asks."

Lady Atterbury clutched her heart. "Catherine was such a nice, biddable girl."

"I am not my sister." She returned to the tissue-covered parcel in her lap.

"Whatever it is, I'm sure it's unsuitable." The dowager's nostrils flared in disapproval. "What could a reprobate like that know about genteel manners? If that's jewelry, miss, he is as much a loose screw as they say. I won't stand for any havey-cavey business. Do you hear me, Sonia? No Harkness has fallen from grace yet, and I don't intend you to be the first. There will be no expensive gifts and no clandestine meetings!"

"Yes, Grandmother, I shall invite him for tea, then." She was too busy unwrapping the package to pay attention to her grandmother's moans. Under the tissue were three separate rolled papers, each tied with a ribbon.

"By Jupiter, if he's sending you the deeds to a love nest, I'll have his liver and lights!"

Sonia chuckled. "Why do you insist he has designs on my virtue? They are most likely just poems like Sir Montescue's." She sounded disappointed. Then she untied the ribbons and just said, "Oh."

"Well? What does the rake say that's got you so moonstruck?"

"He doesn't say anything. In fact, the gifts are not from him. They are from his nieces. Look."

The first scrolled page was a black smudge, as if someone had rubbed ashes into the paper. The second was a definite drawing, a black many-legged figure on a green foreground, with a tree or perhaps a building in the back. Large, messy letters across the top identified the picture: "Fitz, by Genessa Conover." The third page, though, needed no label. Benice had painstakingly colored Fitz, gold eyebrows, white bib, splinted leg, and all. He was sitting in a field of flowers, or perhaps on a Turkey carpet, and he was smiling.

Sonia searched in her pocket for a handkerchief to wipe her eyes. "This is the nicest present I've ever had."

Lady Atterbury, her own eyes suspiciously damp, just said, "Humph."

Lady Rosellen paid a morning call. Stunning in cherry-striped lutestring, she was everything gracious about the ball to Lady Atterbury. She ignored Sonia entirely, as if she were a schoolgirl permitted to take tea with her elders, or some type of upper servant.

"The darling flowers were just the right touch, Your Grace. So sweetly innocent, no one could blame Sonia for her faux pas. I mean, entertaining a man the *belle monde* turns its back on. Too, too farouche. I can only hope the Almack's hostesses are as forgiving of the child, Lady Almeria. I was so looking forward to introducing her in King Street. Now, of course, I doubt she'll get the vouchers."

"They arrived this morning, Lady Conare," Sonia was delighted to announce. "Lady Jersey's own footman delivered them first thing. She even wrote that I might attend in her party if Lady Atterbury is not up to the outing, so if you'd rather not escort such a green girl, I understand perfectly."

Lady Rosellen's eyes narrowed. She wondered how much the chit actually did understand. Did she know, for instance, how much Rosellen needed Lady Almeria's continued approval for the times her own behavior sailed a little close to the wind, or how much Rosellen's brother needed the little bird-wit's blunt? "Nonsense, my dear, of course I'll be your duenna for the evening." She gave her tinkling laughter. "Though I am scarcely old enough for the role."

Both Sonia and Lady Atterbury nodded politely, but without the reassurances Rosellen expected. She pursed her painted lips. "Perhaps I am older and wiser enough, my dear, that you'll heed my warning. Young girls cannot be too careful of their reputations, and the man is dangerous."

The man didn't look dangerous, Sonia thought, sitting as he was among Lady Atterbury and her cronies, trying to balance a delicate china teacup on his knee and fend off the circling sharks at the same time. He looked more like a minnow than a barracuda, and there was nothing Sonia could do but smile from across the room. She and Blanche had been assigned the tea cart and the pianoforte, respectively, half to keep them safe from his rakish clutches, half not to spoil the old ladies' fun.

Lady Atterbury had complained that life was wearying enough keeping fortune hunters away from her granddaughter; now she had to worry about libertines. "Lud," she said, "Catherine never even *met* one, much less brought one home to tea!" She was determined to send this thatch-gallows to the right-about. At least he'd be sure someone was looking out for Sonia's interests.

Blanche was pounding away at the instrument, looking more than passable in a new pink frock that didn't make her skin look so sallow. Sonia, in buttercup yellow, took every opportunity to refill cups, pass macaroons, and in general stand ready to toss a lifeline. So far the major was holding his head above water. He even managed to wink up at her once, when she brushed past him with a plate of almond cakes.

Darius hurriedly gathered his wits from where they'd gone begging after a sunbeam. "What's that, Lady Atterbury? I'm sorry, you were saying . . . ?"

"I was asking why you don't use the title, boy. It's a fine old name, almost as old as Atterbury. You ain't ashamed of it, are you?"

"Ashamed? Of course not. I'm just not used to it. My brother was Warebourne for the last ten years. I still look around for Milo when I hear some-one call Warebourne."

"Then you're not rejecting the title because you'll bring shame to it?"

If a gentleman asked another man such a ques-tion, he'd have to name his seconds. Darius took a deep breath and contemplated the tiny teacup in his hand. He carefully placed it on the table in front of him, out of temptation's way. "I am proud of my family name," he said, "but I did nothing to earn it except get born into it. This"— he touched his scarlet regimental sleeve —"I earned. Until I sell out, if I sell out, I am a soldier, and damned— pardon, ladies—dashed proud of it."

Lady Atterbury cleared her throat. Before she could get in her next question, one of the other la-dies asked, "Then you don't mean to abdicate? Talk is going around that you might."

"I don't know where such talk arose, except in drawing rooms such as this." He smiled to take the sting from his words, then rose to take his leave. "I never wanted to be earl, and certainly never counted on it, by Jupiter, but Preston Conover shall not stand in my father's shoes, or my brother's, while I hold breath in my body. Is that what you wanted to know, ladies?" He bowed to each in turn. "If there are no further questions, I shall wish you a good day, and thank you for an . . . entertaining tea."

The dowagers sat shamefaced, knowing even they had gone too far, and indeed, the boy handled him-self well under fire. Sonia took their momentary loss of speech as an opportunity to say, "I'll just walk the major out, Your Grace."

As they walked down the hall toward where Marston stood with the major's hat and gloves, Fitz bounded up to them. His greeting of the major was enthusiastic to the point of endangering Darius's balance.

"I always seem to be apologizing for your treatment at Atterbury House," Sonia told him.

He scratched behind the dog's ears. "Think nothing of it, Miss Randolph. Fitz and I do fine."

She laughed. "I didn't mean Fitz, sir. I meant Grandmama!"

He gave her a crooked smile. "I was captured by the enemy once. Your grandmother and her friends were only slightly less humane than my French interrogators. In truth I was glad to see she keeps such a careful watch over you, the way you take up with strangers."

Sonia turned away, petting the dog. "You make me sound a veritable peagoose."

"No, no. I didn't mean that, Miss Randolph, just that you are so trusting, so good. Not everyone is worthy of your regard." He laughed, more at himself than anything. "Having said that, will you do me the honor of driving out with me this afternoon?"

"Oh, I'm sorry, Major, but I am already promised."

"I see." And he did. She had played Lady Bountiful, done her good deed for the day. Now they were even in her eyes, he supposed, and he could only thank her for her efforts on his behalf and be on his way. He accepted his hat from the butler. "I'll be off then."

Sonia could feel his hurt, despite the forced smile and the polite words. She stopped him with a touch on his arm. "Major, I really am promised for today. I would be more than pleased to have your company in the park tomorrow, though. Perhaps the children . . ."

Drat the children, he was thinking, his spirits soaring once more as he read the message in her blue, blue eyes. Then he came back to earth and remembered who, and what, he was. Yes, the children and the dog, the nanny, two footmen and a maid, anything to protect her reputation. From him. It wouldn't always be so, he promised himself, while Sonia was having to hold her hand back from smoothing the lines on his forehead.

Marston coughed and pointedly opened the door. The two sprang apart and were completing their plans for the morrow just as a carriage pulled up. When the tiger went to the horses' heads, Ansel Berke got down and strutted up the stairs when he saw Miss Randolph framed in the open doorway. He blew out his chest the better to show off his new waistcoat, green hummingbirds embroidered on crimson marcella. Then he stopped at the threshold as Darius Conover came into view. Red anger burnt up the baron's neck to his face, clashing horribly with his outfit.

Ignoring the major as if he did not exist, the baron stiffly asked if Miss Randolph was ready for their drive.

"I'll just go get my bonnet, my lord. Excuse me, Major."

Somehow, as Sonia turned to go up one side of the double arched stairwells, and Darius made to step around the other man, the baron's foot got in the way of the major's cane. Darius saved himself from falling by painfully clutching the hall table, overturning a salver of cards and invitations.

"Clumsy oaf," Berke jeered.

The officer's jaws were clenched, his hands made into fists. "Don't play your games with me, Berke. I don't like you, and you don't like me. Leave it at that."

"Or else what? Or else you'll run to Admiral Cathcart to wipe your nose? No, I won't leave it, or leave you to ruin another innocent girl. You have no business around Miss Randolph," he ranted.

In a quiet, deadly voice, Major Conover replied, "As Miss Randolph is fond of saying, she picks her own friends." The look on his face expressed what Darius thought of some of her selections.

Marston, the butler, was holding out the major's cane. He stood between the two men, pleading, "Gentlemen, gentlemen, remember where you are."

Berke took the officer's cane and broke it across his knee.

Marston bowed, turned, and with stately measure marched into the butler's pantry beside the front door. Sonia could hear the lock turn as she started down the steps.

"We'll settle this another time, I think," Darius said, nodding to Sonia.

"We'll settle it now! Name your seconds, you dastard!" Berke threw the pieces of cane across the hall.

"I don't need seconds to fight you, you little fop." Darius waved his fist under Berke's nose. "You name the time and place and I'll make you sorry you ever started this."

"You can't even fight like a gentleman!"

Darius grabbed the smaller man around the neck and practically lifted him off his feet. "Why should I? I don't see any gentlemen around." He drew one fist back.

Sonia screamed. The dog barked. The old ladies and Blanche came running.

I waited for the crash of antlers; the stags were in rut.

Chapter Thirteen

$\mathcal{N}$ow that was more like it! Man to man, *mano a mano*, tooth and nail. We were going to get this thing settled once and for all, the survival of the fittest, may the best man win, and all that. Of course, I knew who the best man was, bad leg notwithstanding. I'd been lifted by the major when my leg was broken, lifted as easily as I can pick up a big stick. I'd felt Ansel Berke's languid pats, and smelled the sawdust padding in his calves, even through all the scent he drenched himself in. The baron worked out occasionally to stay fit; the officer stayed fit to stay alive.

This is how it should be, combat between two males, just raw power, no weapons. The strongest wins, the loser slinks away.

Weapons in the hands of man are great equalizers: weaklings can challenge the brawniest bruiser. They are also great distancers: a man who cringes at the sight of his own blood when shaving hesitates not at all to put a bullet in someone else. Weapons make killing easy. Why, someday even females might learn how simple it is to pull a trigger!

If man had never invented swords and pistols, there would never be war, which has to be the oddest manner ever devised for thinning the population. I've heard of famine, disease, and increases of preying creatures, to weed out the old, the ill, the young, and the weak. I've never, ever heard of another system for culling out the strongest, healthiest males in their primes. Furthermore, if there were no killing weapons, human people would still be huddled by their fires, waiting for the saber-tooth tigers and cave bears to finish them off!

Ah, civilization, which makes fistfighting ungentlemanly, and killing one another the proper way to settle differences. Now I was seeing primitive man with no social veneer, lips drawn back, muscles flexed. Let the games begin.

Sonia was screaming, "Don't you dare, either one of you!" She was pulling the flowers out of the big vase in the hallway, getting ready to pour its water over the two men as if they were cats on the garden wall. The elderly ladies had run out of the drawing room and were huddled together across the hall.

"My stars!" one cried.

"My salts!" another called.

"My spectacles!" the third complained. "I can't see a bloody thing!"

Lady Atterbury picked up half of the broken cane and shook it at the two men, one of whose feet were still not touching the ground. "This is conduct unbecoming a gentleman, sirrahs! Indulging in rowdyism, and in a lady's hallway!" She didn't say which was worse. "You should be ashamed of yourselves. Now, put him down!" she demanded of the major, who did, letting go of Berke so suddenly, the baron fell to the ground, skidding on the strewn invitations. He didn't stay down, though, just kept coming at Darius on his knees. Lady Atterbury started swinging the half cane at Berke's back, and Sonia tossed her vase of water, but Fitz got in the way, ruining her aim. More water landed on the dowager than on the cursing baron. Sonia shrugged and brought the vase down on Berke's head.

Berke was out cold in a pile of porcelain, Lady Atterbury was sputtering, the dog was scampering around in the spilled flowers. The dowagers were gathered together like Macbeth's witches, cataloging every detail for future reference. Blanche was standing with her mouth open, exclaiming how no novel had ever had this much excitement—and Darius was laughing!

"Why, you—" Sonia flew at him.

Then Hugh came in.

His uniform not quite buttoned up, his hair every which way, Lieutenant Randolph rushed into the hall without a second's thought to the open door or the missing butler. He had eyes for no one but his sister, whom he immediately scooped up into his arms and spun around. "It's a boy," he shouted as loudly as he could. "A boy, Sunny! Do you know what that means?" He didn't give her time to answer, just kept spinning. "It means I can put in for transfer to the front! Papa has to let me go now that George has an heir!"

Sonia beat at his chest until he put her down. "What are you talking about, you rattlepate?" she demanded.

"George! I intercepted the messenger from Deer Park on his way to you. Didn't you hear me? Old George has a son! A month early, too, the sly devil!"

"Were you both born in a barn?" Lady Atterbury shrieked.

Hugh made a hurried bow. "Uh, good afternoon, Grandmother, Your Grace. Sorry, didn't see you in my excitement. Uh, don't suppose I should have said that, about George, I mean. My apologies, ma'am, but congratulations, Your Grace, great-great-grandson and all that." Then he tried to make a hurried departure before Lady Almeria told him what she thought of the grandchildren she already had, something she was wont to do at every occasion. "I'll just be toddling off now, visit the War Office, don't you know."

Before Hugh could make good his escape, Sonia grabbed his sleeve. "Don't you dare leave yet, Hugh! How is Jennifer?"

Hugh stared nervously at his grandmother, who'd always made him tongue-tied. "The, uh, messenger just said everyone's fine."

"What's the baby's name, you looby? Has Papa been sent for?"

"Deuce, Sunny, it's a boy. I didn't stay to hear any more." He looked over her shoulder and caught sight of three other grandes dames down the hall. He made strangling noises in his throat. Then he noticed the girl near them and brightened. "Hallo, Blanche, ladies. Uh, Lady Blanche. Meant to call on you, thank you for the dance and all, you know. Forgot, what with the news. I'm finally getting to go to fight Boney; what do you think of that? Uh, pretty dress. Call tomorrow, what?" His social obligations fulfilled to his satisfaction, Hugh turned to go, and finally began to notice a few oddities in the ancestral hall. Like a peer of the realm groaning on the floor amid potsherds and posies and the post. Hugh's eyes popped open wide. "What have you done now, Sunny? I told the governor you needed a keeper."

"Me? Why does everyone blame me?" Sonia yelled. Then she moderated her tones to a ladylike level. "I believe the two gentlemen had a difference of opinion." She waved toward the shadows where the major was leaning against the wall, having laughed himself silly all over again at the Randolph siblings' wrangling. "I daresay Major Conover can explain the details," Sonia said coldly, although the dimples were starting to show as she realized how they must all look.

Darius bowed in the recumbent nobleman's direction. "The baron took exception to my cane."

"Your cane!" Lady Atterbury snorted. "I never heard the like in all my—"

She got no further, because Hugh was striding up to Darius. "It *is* Major Conover!" He hurriedly rebuttoned his uniform coat and smoothed back his hair, then snapped a salute. "Sir, it is an honor."

"At ease, Lieutenant." Conover saluted, then leaned back against the wall. His leg was paining him like the devil after the contretemps with Berke, who was sitting up now, with the aid of a footman. The servants had finally come forward after Sonia's repeated pull on the cord. They'd been waiting for instructions from Marston; they'd have a long wait. Bigelow took charge in her usual efficient fashion: "Mop. Broom. Sticking plaster. Dry clothes. Gaol."

Hugh, meanwhile, was so in alt at meeting one of the heroes of the Peninsula that he was pacing back and forth in the hall, trampling rosebuds into the carpet. "I heard he was at the affair last night, Sunny. Couldn't believe my ears. Here I was, at the same dull ball with Major Conover! And you never let on he was coming."

Sonia was used to Hugh's passions. "If you'd been doing your duty in the ballroom, you wouldn't have missed him. And my ball was not dull."

"That's what I heard, today! Dash it, Sunny, you could have sent word to the card room!"

"But, Hugh, how was I to know you cared to meet the major?"

"How? I'm in uniform, ain't I? Everyone in the army wants to meet the major. The fellows at the barracks will be knocked cock-a-hoop that I got to see him, right here at m'grandmother's." He looked around as if wondering what in the world a top-of-the-trees officer was, in fact, doing at stodgy Atterbury House. That farrago about a cane, the prone

119

peer, all went by the board as a new thought struck Hugh. Generally he had room for only one at a time. "Deuce take it if you couldn't put in a word with old Hokey for me, Major. They say if he don't listen to you, he don't listen to anyone."

Berke was on his feet now, looking around groggily. Sonia quickly turned to her brother. "Major Conover was on his way out, Hugh. Perhaps you can convince him what a fine fellow you are if you lend him your arm down the stairs. His cane seems a bit the worse for wear."

Like an eager puppy, Hugh offered his arm, his escort, his eternal devotion. Did the major want him to call a hackney, or should they borrow the prime rig out front, since Berke didn't look to be going anywhere soon? Maybe the major would like to come meet some of the fellows at the barracks, share a toast to Hugh's new nephew and new freedom. Was he free for dinner? Hugh knew a bang-up tavern.

Sonia looked at the awakening baron and the shambles of her grandmother's hall. Then she gazed beseechingly at the major. One look from those blue eyes and Darius allowed as how he'd like nothing better than to spend an hour or two in young Randolph's company.

"I will not have my family's dirty linen washed in public!" Lady Atterbury raged.

Sonia looked up from where she was holding a damp cloth to the back of Lord Berke's head, in the small withdrawing room. His eyes were closed, and she worried that he might be concussed. They were waiting for the doctor. The least Sonia could do, she felt, was make him comfortable, which included hushing her grandmother's angry tirade. "I am sure your friends won't say anything about George and the baby."

"George? What need have my friends got to say anything about George? Do you think the ton can't count for themselves? Half of them were at the wedding, you nimwit. What's that to the point? Half the infants born these days come early. At least George can be fairly certain he's the brat's father, which is more than I can say for a lot of treacle moon babies. No, I am talking about that disgraceful scene in my hallway, miss, the likes of which Atterbury House has never seen, I can assure you. When that gets out we'll all be laughingstocks or worse."

The baron groaned. "No one will hear a thing of it," Sonia reassured both the dowager and Lord Berke. "The servants have all been with you for years and won't be disloyal now. They know better than to gossip about the family."

"You mean they know they won't keep their jobs if they go prattling in the pubs." Lady Almeria sipped some of the sherry Sonia poured out for her.

"And I cannot believe your dearest friends would betray you by bandying the tale about."

"Oh, they'd talk, all right, if I didn't know worse dirt about their own families. Why, I could just tell Sally Jersey about Empora's daughter and the second footman. And the third footman. That would put paid to her visits to Town. I never did mention exactly why Philomena's son got sent down from Oxford, either, but she knows I could. As for Sydelle, humph! The ton always did wonder about why her last son didn't take after either side of the family."

"Grandmother!" Sonia jerked her head toward Lord Berke.

"Oh, that's all old news, and he'll be the last one to talk. Not after making such a cake out of himself." The baron held the cloth over his face and whimpered.

"Blanche will never tell either, Grandmama, she swore."

"She better not, if she knows what's good for her. After all, she just might have to take this chaw-bacon if you don't." Lady Atterbury ignored the baron's muffled protests. "No, it's that ninnyhammer of a grandson I'm worried about. His tongue runs on wheels. Loosen it a bit with Blue Ruin or whatever poison the young cockle-heads imbibe these days, and he's liable to sing his song in every officers' club and army barracks. Especially since he's gone moonstruck with hero worship."

"You don't think the, ah, major will spread the tale on his own?" Sonia asked.

Lady Atterbury hesitated a moment, then uttered a decided "No. Don't get me wrong, I don't hold the boy blameless. Too hot at hand by half. But I saw him. He left here with dignity, at least. Somehow I don't think he'll lower himself." That was as close as Lady Atterbury was going to get to approval of the disgraced earl.

Sonia nodded. She trusted him implicitly. "See, Grandmother, you have nothing to worry about then. Major Conover will keep a lid on Hugh. I'm sure he took his measure right off, and must be used to young subalterns who hang on his every word. No one will ever hear there was a fistfight in the foyer."

"You haven't thought, girl. What are we going to tell the sawbones who comes? And what about Berke's tiger, who must have seen the whole thing? To say nothing of every passerby and delivery person in Grosvenor Square. The blessed door was wide open! I'll strangle that Marston, if I ever find him."

The baron took to moaning again, so the dowager turned on him. "Stop your caterwauling, Berke. You have no one to blame but yourself. I heard enough to know who was at fault. You could have let him walk by."

Berke took the towel from his face. "You're forgetting m'sister Hermione, your own goddaughter's sister. I can't let him get away with that."

"Forget Hermione! She was no better than she should be. Why keep blaming some cad for not doing the right thing, when you should have blamed Hermione for doing the wrong thing in the first place! Besides, he said he didn't ruin her then. There is nothing to be gained now."

"Except keeping him away from other innocent young girls."

"You sapskull! He was a pariah and would have stayed that way if you hadn't stirred things up, made him look persecuted. Now he's an object of sympathy, dunderhead, and you did it yourself. If he gets taken up by the ton despite all your scandalmongering, you'll look even more the fool. You, sir, would have done better to let sleeping dogs lie."

Dogs don't lie.

Chapter Fourteen

$\mathcal{W}$hat's in a name? Oh, I know that cat dirt about a rose by any other name, but that was Romeo and Juliet, and look what happened to them. Tippy says to remember Othello, and "He who steals my purse steals trash, something, something, but he who filches from me my good name, something, something, makes me poor indeed."

Names, good or otherwise, have little to do with truth. Ask Othello. Better yet, ask poor Desdemona. Reputations can be made, or unmade, by malicious claptrap or even circumstantial evidence. For instance, a fox with feathers in his fur is considered just as guilty as a fox with a fowl flapping in his fangs. Maybe the first fox happened upon an old pillow. And maybe the major didn't ruin Berke's sister. Try to prove either one. So how do you restore a ruined reputation?

Major Conover seems to be Miss Sonia's choice of mate, and he is equally taken with her. Even a cow could tell. Why, all they have to do is brush against each other getting into a carriage or something, and their scents are almost embarrassing. The carriage horses perk up their ears, the birds start chirping louder. Smelling of April and May, indeed. That's not what we call it.

Of course, the humans can't sniff the *eau d'amour*. (I once knew a poodle named Mon Cher. He could make sarcoptic mange sound elegant.) Men are nose-dumb. They can't tell when a fire is starting, strangers are coming, or a baby needs changing. They can't even smell rain when it's minutes away. They need us.

Anyway, since the major is so obviously Miss Sonia's pick—and I must say, having now observed the other gentlemen in the park, he is the likeliest candidate—I see no reason to delay. I have reconciled myself to the children, especially once I realized the major will want a male heir. And his smoking could be worse. He could chew the stuff like Jem in the stables, then spit it out to get on someone's feet. Lady Atterbury is not quite so antagonistic to the match, although she still suspects it to be no more than mere friendship, which will wane as Miss Sonia meets others. The only impediment I can see, beyond the major's and Miss Sonia's bound-to-be-temporary ignorance of the state of their affections, of course, is his reputation.

Social standing is very important here in London. The rats who live in the stables won't associate with the rats who live behind the dustbins. I met two of the latter, Lex and Drip, who advised me the major's case was hopeless.

"You've got *habeas corpus*," Lex pointed out. "That's the party of the first part, the dead girl, Hermione. Then your party of the second part says *nolo contendere*. He does not refute the accusation in the *modus vivendi* or ac-

125

cepted manner, but goes *ex patria*. The prosecution rests. The verdict is guilty."

I say, *"Amor vincit omnia,"* to which Lex replies, *"De minimis non curat lex*, the law takes no account of trifles."

Lex forages behind a solicitor's office at night.

Drip, so called because of his nose, sniffled and said, " 'E ain't never goin' t'be accepted into 'er world"— snuffle —"never dance at Almack's. Iffen 'e's any kind a gent at all, 'e'll never ask 'er to share 'is hu"— snort —"miliation. 'At's like askin' a moll rat to jump on th' trap wi' you."

Despite their discouragement, I am determined to see the major take his proper place in society, Miss Sonia by his side. She is doing all she can, going to the park with him and the children so people can see he is not an ogre. She sings his praises every chance. Even Lady Atterbury has had him back to tea, with no untoward events. Master Hugh tells everyone what a capital fellow he is, and extols his friend's acts of valor over every mug of ale. And Lady Blanche, making a foursome with the Randolphs and Conover, whispers to the other debutantes that Darius is the most romantically tragic figure she's ever known. Like a hero in one of her novels, she sighs.

It is not enough, so I have to take action. After all, what could prove a man more worthy than the affection of a dog? I positively fawn over him in the park. I dog his footsteps. I pay him the supreme compliment of trusting him with my mistress. Everyone has to see and take note: I am by his side, therefore, he is a wonderful fellow. Dogs do not lie.

"Oh dear. I am so sorry, Major, I don't know what's gotten into Fitz these days. He never used to be so . . . so coming. I'm sure the footprints will wipe off your uniform."

Sonia was even more embarrassed later that day when her dog seemed to miss the bush he was aiming at and dampened Baron Berke's shiny Hessians instead. She'd apologized profusely to the baron for braining him with the vase: "An accident, I assure you. I merely meant to toss the water to get your attention." And she tolerated the milksop's company on occasion to keep peace with her grandmother.

Berke graciously forgave her the headache and still squired her about whenever she permitted. He needed a wealthy wife more than ever. The duns were on his tail, and even his sister wasn't handing over the ready, most likely on Conare's orders. Damn Preston's black soul. Mostly, Berke just wanted Sonia Randolph because he'd be damned if he'd lose her to any loose-screw craven. Once she was his, he'd tame her madcap ways, beat them out of her if necessary, or send her off to some country place out of his way. The first thing he'd do was get rid of that unmanageable hairy beast she took everywhere with her.

"Think nothing of it, my dear," he forgave again, as a toadeater must. "Dogs will be dogs."

Sonia was careful to keep the two men apart, mainly because another confrontation could deal the major's reclamation a setback. His reacceptance into the upper ten thousand was coming along by inches instead of miles, but it was coming. If strollers did not stop to chat when Miss Randolph and the major walked along the Serpentine while the children fed the ducks, at least they nodded and smiled at the pretty picture the little girls and the black dog made. If people passed them when Sonia and Darius, Blanche and Hugh, walked along Bond Street, no one crossed to the other side or looked through him. When Darius attended the theater with Hugh and called in Lady Atterbury's box at intermission, only Rosellen Conare turned her back.

He was even receiving invitations, and not just from the military or old friends of his father's. Most of the new requests for his company came from gentlemen for an evening of whist or a day at the races, but they were tentative offers of friendship all the same. If the hosts were men with no young daughters to worry about, well, he wasn't interested in a bunch of whey-faced debs anyway. He accepted some of the invitations, preferring the company of his nieces and even the rattlepate Hugh and his young friends—when he couldn't have Sonia's company—to the heavy gambling and heavier drinking common among the leisure lords. For a man used to risking his life in battle, there was no thrill in the turn of a card.

Darius was careful not to attend any dinners or sporting events where his cousin Preston or Ansel Berke was likely to appear, not from fear of an encounter, but from fear of distressing Sonia. Part of the major's dawning acknowledgment was due to his title, part to his uniform. A good part of his acceptance, he knew, was due to Miss Randolph. Sonia was the pet of the ton within a fortnight of her come-out. She delighted the old ladies, thrilled the old men, captivated the young gentlemen, and made friends with their sisters. She listened, she laughed, she enjoyed everyone's company, even the worst bores and the most muse-struck mooncalfs. She still made time for three orphaned children. Half a dozen hostesses vied for her presence every evening; seven sprigs fought for her every dance. The least they could do was be civil to the soldier she insisted was a friend. They weren't ready to introduce Conover to their sisters or daughters, but a smile, a nod, a half bow or curtsy, couldn't harm anybody. Perhaps when he used the title . . .

No, Darius wouldn't disappoint his "friend" by creating any more scenes. And he wouldn't push

Sonia for more than friendship until he could meet her as an equal, someone she needn't be ashamed of being seen with, or who was invited to the balls and routs she attended. Even though her companionship was more than he ever dreamed of having, he knew—and he thought she knew—how much more than friendship he wanted from her. How could she not, when his heart beat like a drumroll in her presence?

The major's heart may have tattooed *Charge*, but his head was sounding *Retreat*. Don't rush her, he kept telling himself, don't try to monopolize her and ruin her chances of finding a more eligible parti. Don't let her be cursed for your past. So he waited and was polite when people offered him the crumbs of hospitality, for suddenly, being recognized as a member of society mattered to him. He rested, he gained back the lost weight, and he didn't harass the surgeons about declaring his left leg fit for duty. The waiting was the hardest part.

"Why does it take these stupid people so long?" Sonia fretted to Blanche one morning as they tried on bonnets at a fashionable millinery establishment. She made a face in the mirror at a cottage bonnet with artificial cherries on the brim. "Can't they see what an honorable man he is?"

"Can't *see* such a thing, Sunny," Blanche answered, not even needing to ask who the *he* was. "Handsome and broad-shouldered, assuredly, but honorable?"

"Well, he is! And kind and smart and interesting and fun. Have you ever seen him really smile, Blanche? It's like . . . like . . ." She dropped the lavender cloche.

"Like Count Minestrono's in *Araminta and the Arab Sheik*," Blanche breathed. " 'When the brooding ends and the soul's inner beauty is revealed.' "

Sonia frowned. "I don't think so."

Blanche wasn't sure if Sunny referred to the

ruched satin bonnet or the quote. "Well, they can't decide, not when his own cousin looks down on him. Conare and Rosellen have a lot of influence."

"I've seen how Rosellen looks at him, like a hungry spider looks at a fly. Then she turns away."

"Society will accept him in time, no doubt. Maybe not the highest sticklers, but opinions are swaying in his favor. If he used the title, they'd sway faster."

"He is honoring his calling and his comrades, and I respect him for that."

"So much that you'd follow the drum?" Blanche asked. "Your grandmother would have spasms for sure."

Sonia looked uncertainly at her reflection in the mirror, a hussar-style hat in her hand. "I always thought of a house in the country, with children and dogs. What about you? Should you like to travel with the army?"

"Above all things! Why, it would be like *Melissandra on the March*. Only more dusty and dirty, I expect. But think of the excitement!"

Sonia did not want to think of Major Conover or Hugh going off to war and danger. The thought wasn't exciting at all; it was frightening and upsetting. "I think Grandmama may be right. You do read too many lurid novels. Here, try this bonnet. The wide brim should set off your high cheekbones."

Blanche rushed to the mirror to see if she really did have high cheekbones. To cheer her friend, she said, "Don't worry, in a month or so everyone will have forgotten any unpleasantness in the past and he'll be invited everywhere."

"But I want to dance with him now! He is not limping half so badly. What if he goes back to Spain in a month? Besides, I am tired of going to all these silly balls and dancing with every other man in London, from empty-headed boys to empty-pocketed rakes."

"Give it time. The doors are starting to open."

Before Sonia had one measly waltz with Darius, the doors slammed shut in his face. A few even closed to Miss Randolph.

"Well, missy, you've done it now. You may as well go on back to the country and raise roses and other people's children. You'll never make a match in London, that's for certain. And I don't need any harum-scarum companion either."

"But why, Grandmama?"

"Why? Why are you the most willful chit I've ever known? Because that slowtop Elvin Randolph had the raising of you, and he never raised anything in his life right but sheep. I need my hartshorn."

"No, Your Grace, why did Lady Blanche's aunt suddenly decide I was not a good influence on Blanche?"

"It has nothing to do with influence. Philomena knew you did the girl good, got her out of those wretched novels and into prettier styles. It has everything to do with your pet. No, not that caper-witted dog, that rogue of an unacknowledged earl you've been trying to foist on the polite world. He was a wolf in wolf's clothes, and you tried to convince 'em he was a lamb. Well, you didn't pull the wool over their eyes for long, missy, and now they're mad. The tame beast's turned, and they're turning on you for bringing him into their parlors. You'll be lucky if they don't rescind your vouchers to Almack's."

"What could he have done that was so awful? I refuse to believe he compromised another girl, because he's never been anything but a perfect gentleman with me. Did he and Baron Berke have another go-round? Just what are they blaming him for this time?"

I've met a few fish in my day, but never a card-shark.

Chapter Fifteen

$\mathcal{A}$ cheat. Ivory tuner. Captain Sharp. I got that straight from one of the old carriage horses who used to take the last earl to White's. Among the privileged class, cheating at cards was a worse crime than beating one's wife. Then again, among the lower orders, stealing a loaf of bread was a worse crime than beating one's wife. There was not even a law making the latter illegal.

A male dog will half die before turning on a bitch, no matter the provocation, yet men, who spout of honor, think nothing of harming persons smaller and weaker. This is all of a piece, I suppose, with their considering women chattel. Women are not allowed to vote, hold property, take part in government, or manage their own estates, because they are not deemed competent. Yet, and here is the part that truly muddles my mind, men let women raise their children!

Anyway, from what I could hear from gossip on the street, the pigeons who roost at Boodles' at night, Major Conover has been accused of cheating at cards by—who else?—Ansel Berke. Lord Conare was in the game, held in a private room of Scully's, a gambling hell in Half-Moon Street. Conare, predictably, seconded the charge of double dealing. Two other noblemen held hands in the fateful game, but they were so castaway, they could only recall seeing Conover enter the room. They were assured by both Conare and Berke that Conover had, indeed, won their blunt. They were suitably outraged to be shown the extra ace, found on the next deal, after Conover was gone.

The major had gone to Scully's with Captain McKinnon of the Home Guard, the pigeons understood, but they separated after half an hour or so. McKinnon lost sight of Conover in the smoke and crowded rooms, he later said. The major took a few turns at hazard, played a couple of rounds of vingt-et-un, and held the faro bank for a short while. Then he wandered into some of the back parlors, according to Scully himself, looking for more interesting play. After that he went home to bed—and awoke to find himself branded a cheat.

I smelled Preston Conover's hand in the plot: another vicious whispering campaign, with Berke doing the dirty work, more charges that couldn't be disproved, Major Conover an outcast again. I could howl at the injustice of it. All my hard work! By St. Bernard's beard, if I had that mangy Conare here, I'd tear him limb from limb, I'd shred him from guts to gizzard, I'd . . . be chained in the backyard.

If a man fuzzes the cards, loads the dice, or deals from the bottom, he mightn't pay his debts either. No one will play with him. They won't even talk to him. Men don't seem to mind losing fortunes honestly; they only care when they think they've been diddled.

Strange, no other creature but man gambles. Tippy says betting can be a disease, just like distemper and rabies. Sometimes men who cannot afford to lose gamble just as hard as those who can. They only need a stake and a little luck. Or just a marked deck.

"You can't send a letter, Sunny, it ain't proper." Hugh was having breakfast at Atterbury House at his sister's insistence, and not enjoying his gammon and eggs at all. A man didn't like a bear garden jaw with his kippers. At least Lady Atterbury never left her chambers till noon.

"I didn't send a letter, Hugh," Sonia insisted. "I sent Fitz." She was too distracted to sit still, which wasn't doing much for Hugh's digestion either.

"And?"

"And nothing! A footman brought Fitz home. He said there was no message, nothing. The young misses have already been sent to visit their mother's people in Lyme. That's all the footman knows, or would say." She banged her cup down on the table. "I've got to see him, Hugh!"

Hugh spread jam on a piece of toast and pondered the matter. "Can't see how you can if he don't want you to. He's got the right of it, too. Got to keep your name out of the bibble-babble. Best you stay out of the coil."

Sonia snatched the toast out of her brother's hand. "Hugh, you don't mean to say you think he's guilty?" she demanded before taking a bite of the bread.

"I never said I do, just that you should keep clear while he's under such a cloud."

"Then you do believe Darius would never, ever do something dishonorable?"

"Darius, eh? I thought the wind sat in that quarter. Too bad, sis, you'll have to set your cap at some other poor sod. The governor will never hear of you marrying a dirty dish." He held a hand up in defense. "Not that I think he ain't honorable. Play cards with him m'self any time, if my pockets weren't always to let." He made sure she was eating while he buttered another slice. "And look who's laying evidence against him. Everyone knows Conare wants the title and Berke wants you."

"Me?" she squeaked, spitting out crumbs. "You mean this is all my fault?"

"Don't be a ninny. The feud with Berke goes back years before you put your hair up and your skirts down. Be hard to prove they set the whole thing up, though, with the only witnesses admitting they were drunk as wheelbarrows. It'd be Berke's word against Conover's, if Berke said it outright. Instead it's all lies and rumors."

"Then what's to be done?" Sonia wanted to know.

Hugh swallowed a large bite. "I told him to ship out. Nobody'd think the worst of him, least of all the fellows who've fought by his side for years. He said he's thinking on it."

She pounded her fist on the table. "It would be just like him to think he could simply go off without saying good-bye. Well, he can't."

Hugh munched some more. "Yes, he can. Better that way. Can't say I want m'sister in such a hugger-mugger mess."

"Hugh." He knew that tone from old. He left his toast and bolted for the door. "Hugh Randolph, you get that muttonhead of a major in Grosvenor Square Park at two o'clock this afternoon or else."

"Or else what?" he asked from the door, sure he didn't want to know, wishing his orders had come through yesterday.

"Or else I'll go to Ware House myself, or I'll inform Grandmama he compromised me, or I'll just tell Blanche Carstairs you wet your bed till you were twelve."

Sonia sat on the same bench where she'd first spoken to Darius just a few weeks ago. It seemed

135

like forever, he was so much in her thoughts. Now he could be leaving England, and she might never see him again. She wouldn't think of that. Instead she'd let her anger cover the pain, anger that he'd go away without a farewell, without leaving her one last memory to cherish. She sat rigid on her bench, her hands folded in her lap, a statue in a blue velvet pelisse. Even Fitz couldn't tease her into playing.

Maisie sat on the neighboring bench with her knitting, and Ian was getting up a flirtation with two nannies pushing prams. A nearby clock struck the hour. He was late. He wasn't coming.

Then he was there, looking more handsome than she'd ever seen him, now that his face was fuller and not so wearied. He bowed to her, but didn't take her hand or sit next to her. He didn't speak, either.

She cleared her throat. "You came."

"Hugh seemed to think it was worth my life, and his, had I not."

"But you did not want to." It was a statement, not a question. If he heard the hurt in her voice, he did not, could not, respond. He stared toward the trees, not looking at her.

"No, it is not wise. And there is nothing to say."

Nothing to say? Sonia bit her lip. "I, ah, wanted to know about the children. Will they be happy in Lyme?"

"Happier than here, I hope. Suzannah's parents are well on in years, but they love the girls. They used to visit, before . . . Her old nurse is still there, anxious to help coddle them, I am sure, so they'll do. They wanted to say good-bye, you know, but it was very early in the morning."

"I see," she said, but her coldness told him that she didn't see at all, didn't understand that he couldn't have borne another emotional scene. 'Twas hard enough parting with the three moppets he'd come to love as his own, without watching them cling one last time to her. Not when he had hoped for so much more.

"They swore they would write. And they were excited about visiting their grandparents and the seashore. I promised they could each have a pet of their choice when they got there. Benice can pick between a puppy and a kitten, and Gen already decided she wants a pony. Tina seems content with her stuffed Mimi. Not quite fair to the grandparents, I'll admit, but now they have something to think about on the journey."

"That was clever of you." She pleated the velvet of her pelisse. "They are wonderful children. I'll miss them."

"I, ah, had my solicitor draw up new papers, naming their grandfather as guardian if . . . just if. Milo wanted them to be raised at Ware, but this is better, I think. I know I have no right to ask you to look after them or anything—you'll have children of your own before long—but could you write to them? About Fitz or whatever, just at first, so they don't feel abandoned?"

She waved that aside. Naturally she would write the children, and visit them, too, but what about her? Didn't he care that she'd feel lost, abandoned? "Shall you write?" she asked, knowing how improper, how forward, was her question.

Darius chose to misinterpret. "The children? Of course, if I can."

Sonia thought that if she had a gun, she'd shoot him right then and save the French the trouble. "When do you sail?"

"Sail?" Now he turned to look at her, but Sonia had her head down so the brim of her bonnet hid her face. "I thought you knew, I am not rejoining the regiment just yet."

She looked up at that, blue eyes filled with hope. "But Hugh said . . ."

He turned away quickly. "I thought about it, but I cannot." He started to pace along the path in front of her, jabbing his cane into the loose dirt. "I made a mistake years ago." He paused at her sharp intake of breath. "No, not with the girl. I had nothing to do with Hermione but a few dances here and there. The mistake was in not meeting Berke. Milo thought it best, since her family already suffered so much grief, and I was off to the war anyway. He said he'd rather chance losing me to a better cause than a sordid affair."

"He loved you," she said softly.

"I shouldn't have listened. The hatred festered in Berke, and backing down did me no good. I let him win without firing a shot. Berke and the other highborn asses who rule this town control my life. I cannot go where I choose, I cannot make friends where I wish. I cannot speak my mind. Or my heart."

That traitorous organ made him turn back to Sonia, to see if she understood what he could not put into words, what his circumstances and his principles would not permit him to say.

Sonia nodded. At least his suffering matched her own. She hadn't been mistaken, then. The last threads of her anger melted away.

He went on: "I am sorry for so many things. I regret my troubles have rubbed off on you, but I am not sorry to have had your ... friendship. Never that."

"You intend to duel him, don't you?"

"It's the only way. The first time they called me lily-livered for not meeting him. I didn't care. I knew I was no coward, and Milo knew, and the men who served with me and under me knew. They were all who mattered. I did not have to prove anything to these useless, empty-lived parasites. Now I do, so I can reclaim my birthright, my freedom. I need to live my life the way *I* want."

"What if you kill him?" She couldn't bear to think of the other.

One side of his mouth lifted in a grim half smile. "Thank you for the confidence. I'll have to leave the country, of course. The family has property in the Colonies if the general won't take me back. But I'll try not to have it come to that if I can."

"Please," she told him, bringing the rest of the smile to his face. Then she asked "When?"

"You don't need to know that. You know too much already. Lud, a proper gentleman never discusses such things with a lady."

"When?" she asked again, quietly.

"Hugh was right, you are a determined little minx. No matter, for I do not know the time or place yet, and would never reveal them if I did. You might get some odd notion in that thick, pretty head of yours to interfere or notify the magistrates. No, don't look so innocent. I can almost hear the wheels spinning in your brainbox. I haven't confronted Berke yet, although I doubt he'll be hard to find. He's waiting for my challenge so he can have the choice of weapons. He knows I'd pick swords, for I am much the better fencer, even with a bad leg. With swords there is less chance of an unintentional mortal wound, too. That's not what he wants, so he'll make himself available. This afternoon in the park, tonight at some gaming hell or other."

"And there is no other way?" Sonia held her hand out, and he took it in his.

"Believe me, this is not the way I would have chosen. Berke thrust it upon me, and now it is the only solution."

She nodded. "I do understand."

He squeezed her hand in his larger one and tried to make light of the matter. "What, no arguments? No stiff lip and crossed arms? No stamping feet as Miss Randolph demands her own way?"

She shook her head.

"What? Not even one plea or threat to make me change my mind?" he teased. "Don't you care?"

The tears shining in her eyes told him how much

she cared, but her words only said: "How can I come between a man and his honor?"

Easily. You hit him behind the knees.

Chapter Sixteen

$\mathcal{N}$ow he couldn't stand on his honor, or on his leg.

I looked up at the trees, searching for the squirrel I was supposed to be chasing. What do you know, the little nutter got away! As I rushed past, though, I heard an audible snap as the major's bad leg gave way beneath him. Once the chaos died down, the sawbones eventually found a bit of shrapnel in the leg when he went to set it. He said that's why the thing never healed in the first place. Now the major will not even have a limp, once the bone mends. Oh, what a good dog I am!

So was I wrong, or does the end justify the means? Darius seems to feel that a life without honor is not worth living. I, however, need him alive for what I consider the greater goal. I never argue with another's beliefs. He had his, I had mine. Mine won.

Still, this honor thing bothers me like a flea bite I can't quite reach. Tippy says to remember the "But Brutus is an honorable man" bit. Sure, with his knife in his best friend's back.

Keeping the promises that suit one, repaying gaming debts and not merchants' bills, this is not honor. Honor is when no creature molests another at the water hole.

Tippy says that what goes around comes around, yet I am satisfied with the results of my actions. There will be no challenge while the major is flat on his back. There will be no duel while he cannot leave his house.

Happily, and the more so for being unforeseen, he also gave up his cigarillos. The stench in his bedroom was too great even for the major, when he couldn't step outside or stand by the window to make the noxious smoke dissipate. Unfortunately, he took up drinking. What goes around comes around?

Master Hugh moved into Ware House to help the major and his batman, Robb. Then some of Hugh's friends came to call, to help bear the major company. Without the children, the place soon resembled a barracks, with hard drinking and gambling. The other officers made a point of playing cards with Major Conover, standing by one of their own, as it were, and drinking toasts to his health.

I took to visiting Ware House evenings when Miss Sonia was out on her social rounds. This was better than sitting up on the carriage box with the driver, who tipped his jug a few times himself. At least at Ware House there was food. The major held no grudges, so most nights I was also offered a sip of something, which I refused after watching his friends muddle their minds, curdle their stomachs till they cast up accounts, turn mean, sleepy, sad, or just plain silly. The next day they drank the hair of the dog! The hair of the dog! That's disgusting!

They say Dionysius gave wine to men as a

blessing. Some favor he did them! The god taught Icarius how to ferment his grapes, the story goes, and the villagers killed the first vintner in a drunken rage, thinking he'd poisoned them! They hid his body under a tree, and Icarius's family would be looking for him still if his dog hadn't stayed howling at the grave. Good dog, Moera. They named a star after her, too.

Robb makes sure the worst drunks get sent home, and the belligerent ones are not invited back. The batman and Hugh—on Miss Sonia's orders—and I, for obvious reasons, keep watch over the major like three hens with one chick. We don't let the visitors tire him, we won't let him use the crutches until the physician gives approval. He is healing; he hasn't got Berke's bullet in him; he is not on some boat for America. I am delighted. I just hope Major Conover isn't drinking to drown his sorrows.

Sonia was still a Toast. Everyone knew a duel had been avoided by her dog's clumsiness, which they thought hilarious. Anytime a nobleman falls on his arse, especially one who disdains the title, society is amused. They all wanted to hear Miss Randolph's account. As soon as Hugh revealed that the major had indeed intended to call Ansel Berke out, that a challenge would be forthcoming directly he was fit, the ton gave Darius back some respect. They might laugh at him, but they did not despise him so much. Curiously, the charge of cowardice had been more a black mark against him than the trumped-up accusations of cheating. Hugh was relieved, and so was Admiral Cathcart, who made the trip from three doors away to visit the fallen officer. And laugh.

Lady Atterbury swore she never wanted to see the mongrel again, that he'd brought nothing but trouble. Elvin Randolph should be horsewhipped, she decreed, for foisting a hobbledehoy female and her harum-scarum hound on unsuspecting gentle-people. Then she commandeered all of Blanche's novels, shut herself in her bedchamber, and didn't come out for days.

She gave copious orders through Bigelow that under no circumstances was Sonia to visit the household across the square, no, not even if her own brother was there. Sonia was not permitted to stay home, either. Nor, under the direst of threats, was she to create any more scandals. Bigelow's translation: "Bachelor fare. Ape-leader. Great-Aunt Sophrina in Yorkshire." Sonia didn't even know she had a Great-Aunt Sophrina in Yorkshire.

Lady Atterbury, or Bigelow, also had a few choice words for the disappearing butler: "Guard the front door, or leave by the back door." Every time Miss Randolph or her dog went by, Marston wished he were tied to the hall table, like Jason to the mast, to resist the temptation to flee. But he stayed and held the door, accepted calling cards and nosegays, and sighed with relief when Miss went out of an evening. He nearly wept with thanksgiving when she came home without incident.

So Sonia resumed the social whirl. If she was considered too ramshackle by the highest sticklers, keeping low company and getting into scrapes, she behaved prettily enough for the rest of the Quality. If she had to go out, she decided, she would show the shallow elite what a Randolph was made of, not hide her head nor wear the willow. She wore her prettiest gowns, gathering compliments and admirers like fallen leaves. She laughed with them over Warebourne's predicament, when she was not staunchly defending him. Mr. Brummell was heard to chuckle at Fitz's antics, and Sir Montescue Pimford wrote a poem to Miss Randolph's loyalty to her friends.

Hugh raved to the major about Sunny's success, and the other officers reported that Miss Randolph danced like a dream and smiled like an angel. Darius had another drink.

Unfortunately, Sonia's foray into society threw her into close association with Lady Rosellen Conare and her brother, Ansel Berke. Sonia could not renege on previous commitments without seeming horribly rude, so she learned to tolerate the baron's company. Perhaps she could make him see what a goosish thing this was, his pursuit of vengeance. She even felt sorry for him. Pursuing heiresses was degrading enough.

"I'm glad to see you laughing at the bounder," Berke gloated. "For a moment there I was worried. I know how you females admire a uniform. And your tender sensibilities must have been aroused by the unfortunate orphans. Very proper sentiments, my dear. No one can fault you for having a gentle heart. Now, of course, you've discovered for yourself what a paltry fellow he is. I'm glad. Now I can reveal that as soon as this unpleasantness is over, I plan to ask you a particular question," he said with a simpering smile, while his teeth gnashed at the delay. His creditors were lining up at his door. He needed some crumb to toss them. "Dare I hope what your answer will be?"

He could hope all he wanted. She didn't feel that sorry for him.

Darius thought he'd be ready for Bedlam if he didn't get out of the house soon. For sure they'd have no china left, the way he bounced it off the walls. And if he had to listen to more praise for Miss Randolph from men who could call on her, go riding with her, dance with her, hold her, blast them, he would soon be calling out half the British nobility and all of the Home Guard!

So he exercised his leg while his watchdogs were still abed, and the confounded real dog was scrounging breakfast at his own house across the square. He couldn't chance Fitz getting under his feet and toppling him again. He refused any other setbacks. The leg healed remarkably quickly this time without the piece of shot. Darius was strong and healthy now, never having taken a fever or an infection from this recent surgery. Recuperation was swift, surprising even the medicos from the War Office. He was not fit to sit a horse yet, so there was no talk of his rejoining his unit, but he was fit enough to go out and kill someone, though no one spoke of the duel. It was illegal, after all.

Having satisfied the doctors of his health, Darius moved downstairs, where he could get to the rear courtyard to gain strength and proficiency with the crutches. He refused to try the park, where some-one—someone with blond hair and blue eyes, for in-stance—might see him stagger about. Watching from the front windows as she exercised the dog in the square early in the mornings did even more to speed his recovery. Finally he was able to join her.

The crutches were just about the only thing hold-ing Darius back from taking Sonia in his embrace; holding the exuberant dog's collar so he didn't jump was just about all that was keeping Sonia from throwing her arms around the major. Then they re-membered where they were and that nothing had been said between them.

"How nice to see you out and about, Major Con-over, and looking so well."

"And you are looking lovelier than ever, Miss Randolph. Thank you for the basket of fruit and the other treats from your kitchens."

So it went. They compared letters from the chil-dren, the progress of her brother's promotion, the health of Lady Atterbury and Blanche. Small talk, but they were together. They spoke more with their eyes, the briefest of touches when they both petted the dog at once. He came every morning after that and took over Fitz's exercise, to rebuild his own muscles, he said. He threw sticks, played keep-away, and hobbled around and around the square until he graduated from crutches to a cane. Every morning he purchased a posy from the flower girl to tuck in Sonia's bonnet or pin to her gown. Every morning they all shared meat pasties from the pieman, who was growing wealthy on the little entourage. Sonia was still escorted by her maid and footman, and Conover's batman, Robb, came along, too, at first to make sure his master didn't overdo, then to enjoy the company. Maisie Holbrook often went home with a posy in *her* mobcap, too. And Fitz invariably wolfed his pie down so fast, then looked so piteously hungry, that the major usually bought him another. Then they all went to sit with the admiral for a bit, Darius content just to watch Sonia as she told the old gentleman about this party or that play.

Darius never knew such peace. He tried to convince himself that this was enough, if he never had more. He didn't believe himself for a minute.

Sonia felt she merely existed for most of her day and night. She really came alive only for the two hours in the morning. "Do you think you might be up to a picnic?" she asked hesitantly, fearful he might refuse.

He knew he should. Nothing was changed; she should not be with him.

"I went on a lovely picnic to Richmond last week. The gardens were beautiful."

He knew all about it, having heard from one officer how exquisite she looked in a teal blue hussar-style riding habit. "You know, the kind with braid and trim up and down." The fellow used his hands to show where the trim went. He was lucky he could still use a fork. Darius was treated by another gentleman to an account of how Miss Randolph sat her roan mare as if she were born there, which she nearly was, according to Hugh: "M'mother was a notable horsewoman. The only thing she and the governor had in common, besides us, of course."

Darius could almost picture Sonia on horseback, wind tousling her golden curls and bringing a flush to her cheeks. Then again, he could picture other ways for her hair to be tousled and her cheeks to be flushed. No, he really should not be around her. Not if he hoped to maintain any sanity whatsoever.

"The physicians have forbidden me to ride yet," he said with both relief and regret.

"Then we could take the carriage," she hurried on. "And we don't have to go as far as Richmond, so your leg won't be jostled. We could just take the coach to a grassy place off the carriage path in Hyde Park."

He was tempted. Oh, how he was tempted. Sonia on a blanket in the sun, away from prying eyes and wagging tongues . . .

"And we'll invite Hugh and Blanche to come along for propriety's sake," she pressed, determined to have more time with him, one way or another.

Thud, thud, tap. That was two legs and a cane coming back to earth. "And I suppose the dog, too? Very well, as long as he doesn't dunk me in the Serpentine."

The day set for the picnic was not ideal. Hugh thought it might shower. Blanche thought it might be buggy. Robb thought the ground might be too damp for the major to sit on. Sonia and Darius were going, period.

They took two carriages. To Hugh's delight, he got to drive the major's curricle, with the highbred bays. Blanche sat with Hugh, and Robb stood at the back as tiger and guardian of the beloved matched pair. Sonia and Darius followed in the dowager's open landaulet, with Maisie and Fitz and the picnic basket. Ian rode with the driver.

Because the ton didn't parade at such an unfashionable hour, they had the park nearly to themselves. Nursemaids and governesses found the day too dismal to linger with their charges. Sonia didn't notice the overcast skies, and Darius was pleased the gabble-grinders would not have Sonia's name to chew. Hugh found a spot where the tanbark dipped close to the river, and a little knoll and some trees made a pretty vista. They took a short walk while the servants tethered the horses and spread blankets and pillows and enough food to feed twice their number. Or half their number and Fitz.

They passed one other couple, Sir Wesley Norbert and Mrs. Quentin-Jones, who were less likely to run to the tattle-baskets than most, so Darius was able to relax. He was grateful, in fact, to sink down onto the blankets with his back propped against a tree and a cushion under his leg, after their brief stroll. He wasn't used to carriage rides or uneven ground. Besides, sitting down, he didn't have to concentrate on where he was putting his feet. He could stare at Sonia to his heart's content, drinking in the sight of her in nile green jaconet, with clusters of yellow rosebuds and ribbons strewn around. Who cared if the sun did not shine? She was springtime to him.

The servants had a blanket and basket of their own, so Sonia got to fuss over Darius, heaping his plate, filling his glass, asking at least once a minute if he was comfortable. "You don't have to try so hard, sweet Sonia," he whispered. "I am content just being with you." Neither Blanche nor Hugh commented on Sonia's blushes or shy, answering smile. Blanche was discovering that Hugh's war stories were even more exciting than her romance novels, and he was feeling less a Sunday soldier with a nice young girl hanging on his every word. Sonia and Darius could have been in another world for all they cared.

The food was gone too soon, and the ground *was* beginning to feel damp through the blankets, yet no one wanted to go home. There was still a bit of wine left and some lemonade, so they gave themselves another few moments.

Then a group of horsemen rode along on the path. Instead of passing by, they dismounted and tied their horses to bushes and branches, before approaching the little group under the tree. There were five of them, one with a cherry-striped waistcoat, one with canary trousers, and one with a satisfied smirk on his face. Ansel Berke.

Cry "Havoc!" and let slip the dogs of war.

Chapter Seventeen

$\mathcal{T}$rust the bloodthirsty Romans to come up with a cheery turn of phrase like that. They really did have dogs of war, you know, whole packs of huge canines that they let loose before their invading armies, to soften up the enemy lines, as it were.

Do you know how they got those dogs to fight like that? They starved them! That's right. They did throw them the occasional arm or leg, to teach them that people were food.

I can see an army of bees. Geese maybe, but dogs? If they were not starving or protecting someone they love, they'd be stopping off at every bush. And I'm sorry to say this, but we have been known to fight over the same bone. Then again, one bitch in heat and your whole battalion goes to the dogs!

Why would dogs go to war anyway? Do you think the *perros* of Spain care whether it's the French or the British who overrun their country, decimating the fields and forests? Between them they take every *pollo* and rabbit, leaving *nada* for man or *mousito*. Peon and pup will starve either way. *Madre de gatos*, war is hell on the hounds, too!

Then again, some wars are inevitable.

"We have some unfinished business, Conover," Berke announced when he was a few yards away. Hugh and the girls scrambled to their feet, and the servants hurried over, forming a protective ring around the blanket. Darius stayed where he was, reclining against the tree trunk.

"Not in front of the ladies, I think" was his only reply.

"He's right," one of the baron's companions said. Sonia recognized him as one of Rosellen's foppish court. "Not good ton, old man. Mustn't sully delicate ears and all that."

Berke scowled at the pomaded dandy. He'd only brought the pack of useless caper-merchants along because he did not want to confront Warebourne alone. The skirter was too eager to use his fists. And Berke had to get this settled soon. Conare had paid his most pressing debts, on the condition that Berke bring matters to a head. As soon as he'd received word from Sir Norbert that Warebourne was in the park, Berke knew he had to act today. Besides, he thought his bravado would make him look nobler in Miss Randolph's eyes. Or Lady Blanche's, if it came to that.

He bowed to Sonia, then to Blanche. He threw his chest out, in a new plum satin waistcoat printed with pink cabbage roses, and announced, "My apologies, ladies, but I dare not let the dastard get away." He turned back to his hand-picked audience. "I'm afraid he'll find another reason to cry off. First he hid behind his brother, then his uniform. Next he found a dog to make his excuses." He paused while the men around him laughed. "Now he hides behind a woman's skirts."

Darius was still comfortably propped against the

tree, an insultingly casual reaction to Berke's cock-of-the-walk swagger. "I don't consider a picnic in Hyde Park in broad daylight to be precisely hiding, Baron. I just find you de trop at this moment."

Berke started to get red in the face. "I don't care what you think, you makebait. I've been waiting and waiting for you to stick your nose outside. If you can stand, you can duel."

"He can't," Sonia put in before Darius could answer. "We came in the carriages"— she waved to show how close they were parked —"and all the servants helped."

Darius frowned. "Hugh, take the ladies away."

"Dash it, Major, you said I could be your second. How can I make the arrangements if I'm off nursemaiding two chits?"

"That was not a request, Lieutenant," Darius stated in a voice used to being obeyed, and instantly.

"Don't you dare pull rank on my brother at a picnic, Darius Conover, because you cannot order me around anyway. I am not leaving." Sonia was in her usual try-to-stop-me mode: arms crossed, feet firmly planted, a look of determination in her blue eyes that could have stopped Boney in his tracks.

Darius shook his head. Someone really had to take that chit in hand one of these days. He smiled, thinking about being the one. Then he turned to the dog, who was wagging his tail next to him. He put one hand on Fitz's back to pull himself up. "It's the least you can do, old son. Now sit, sir." He reached down for his cane. "And stay. There has been enough interference from you willful Randolphs. The dog should obey me, at least." He took two steps nearer Berke. "As you can see, I can walk."

"Aha! What did I tell you?" Berke crowed to his cronies. "The pudding-heart was just stalling!"

"Sonia, sweetheart," Darius said, looking right

153

at Berke, "pour me a glass of wine, will you, my dear?"

Hugh's mouth fell open, and one of the men behind Berke snickered. "Dutch courage, eh?"

Sonia bit her lip to keep from laughing, but Berke worked himself into a rage at the endearments, as Darius knew he would.

"Why, you miserable mawworm, to be insulting a gently bred female with familiarity like that! Dueling is too good for you. You ought to be horsewhipped!"

Sonia, meanwhile, poured the last of the wine into a glass and handed it to Darius. "Here, darling." She smiled and batted her lashes at him.

The major's lips twitched as he took the glass and went another few steps closer to Berke. When only a foot or two separated them, he told the baron, "Very few things in this world will give me as much satisfaction as putting a bullet through you. Perhaps this is one of them." With which he tossed the contents of his glass in Berke's face. He watched as the red wine dripped down the baron's chin and onto his starched cravat. "There, now your neckcloth matches your waistcoat. Perhaps you'll start a new fashion." He turned his back on the peer and carefully wiped his fingers on a napkin Sonia thoughtfully provided. "Thank you, my dear. Oh yes," he tossed back over his shoulder. "Consider yourself challenged. If you'll be so good as to name your seconds, I'm sure my enthusiastic young friend here shall be delighted to call."

"No!" Berke raged. "We'll settle the details now in case you decide to run off to the army again. Let everyone see the thing was done right. You challenged, so I get the choice of weapons."

One of the Tulips lisped, "But you mustn't pick swords, Baron. Not when the fellow's practically a cripple. Noblesse oblige and all that."

"*Au contraire, mes amis.*" Darius twisted the top of his cane. The sheath fell away and he suddenly held a long, thin rapier in his hand. Before Berke's horrified eyes, the blade swished through the air, whistled past his ear, and sliced off, not one, but two of the buttons on his waistcoat. "Go ahead. Choose swords."

"Pistols," Berke croaked. "Pistols."

"Excellent. Shall we say two days hence? That should give you enough time to find a surgeon, for do not fool yourself into believing I mean to delope. Unless, of course, you wish to retract your statements concerning a certain card game now, in front of these witnesses."

"Never!"

Darius held the sword to Berke's neck. "I do not believe we need to trouble the ladies further with the time and place, do you?"

"No, no. As long as it's settled."

"It's settled, all right. I wouldn't miss it for the world."

The drizzle started when the subdued group was packing the baskets and blankets. Darius insisted Blanche and Maisie ride with Sonia in the landaulet, its cover drawn, while he rode in the open curricle with Hugh.

"Don't argue, for once," the major told Sonia when she protested. "Hugh and I have things to discuss. This will save time. And I have been out in far worse. I am not like to expire from an inflammation of the lungs in the next two days."

Sonia was not amused. She climbed stiffly into the carriage and did not speak to Blanche or her maid on the ride home. She did clutch the damp dog to her side, oblivious to the damage to her gown.

Blanche's aunt's residence was closest, so they dropped her off first. A sober-faced Hugh got down to walk Blanche to her door, after she hugged Sonia good-bye.

Ian handed Miss Randolph out at Atterbury House. Marston started down the steps with a large black umbrella, until he saw the glum expressions on all the faces. He marched back up, umbrella and all. Bad enough he had to face disgrace in the hallway; he didn't have to go outside looking for it.

Darius climbed down from the curricle and caught up with Sonia under the portico's shelter. He was breathing hard from the exertion, and he looked back to see Hugh hunched over at the ribbons, sitting in the rain waiting for him. Robb was at the horses' heads, stroking them. "Damn and blast!" Darius muttered. "This isn't the way—"

Sonia put her hand on his sleeve. "I know, you mustn't keep the horses standing."

"I shan't be in the park tomorrow morning, you know. There are too many things needing to be done."

Sonia thought of how he must hire carriages and book passages, in case he had to flee. He needed to see his solicitor and his man of business and his bank. She nodded.

"It's better this way," he said, putting his hand over hers, then bringing her hand to his lips.

"Better for whom?"

"Just better. I hate good-byes. And we had today, didn't we?"

"Yes, it was lovely." She tried to smile for him.

"There's my brave girl," he said, still holding her hand. "I'd tell you not to worry, but—"

"But that would be foolish, like telling me not to breathe. I'll pray for you."

"I know you will. And trust me, Sunny." He brushed a damp curl back under her bonnet. "I—no, just trust me."

"I do. Now go before Hugh takes a chill and misses his big chance, and before you see I am not so brave at all."

"No good-byes?"

She shook her head. "No good-byes, just Godspeed."

He kissed her hand again and then bent toward

her and quickly brushed his lips over hers. He turned and started down the stairs.

"Darius, wait!" Sonia ripped one of the sodden yellow rosebuds off her gown and tossed it to him. Darius caught the bit of silk in his hand, carefully placed it inside his coat, next to his heart, and bowed. Then he left without looking back.

Everyone in London knew of the duel. Berke made sure of that, especially since the location remained a secret so the authorities couldn't interfere. Lady Atterbury closed the house to callers. If anyone was laying this pottage in her dish, she didn't want to know about it. Uneasily she felt she might have done something to avoid the imbroglio, spoken to Rosellen or sent Sonia out of town. Deuce take it, she was just a tired old lady. She decided to have palpitations instead of pangs of remorse.

Marston was grateful. With no visitors, he didn't have to dart into the butler's pantry for a nip. He kept a flask of the old duke's port right in his tail-coat.

Bigelow declared the whole household was going to hell in a handcart, then out of boredom she picked up one of the discarded novels. "Trash," she declared. "Moral turpitude." Then, "Oh my."

So there was no one to insist Sonia keep her appointments, or keep her head up despite the gossip making the rounds. Which was a good thing, since Miss Randolph just stayed in her rooms. She didn't read, wouldn't see Blanche or Hugh, never opened her father's latest letter. She did not eat much, and she even sent Fitz out with Ian for the dog's exercise. Strange, Ian commented to Maisie, the dog's coat was usually damper before his walk than after.

Swans mate for life.

Chapter Eighteen

*M*ore men than women remarry after the death of their spouse. Men are more conscious of a need for an heir; they are also more helpless. The men are used to having someone pamper them, or miss having a person around who cannot quit if she dislikes the position.

Women, conversely, remarry less, especially if they find themselves well off, like Lady Atterbury and her friends. For the first time in their lives they have a modicum of freedom and independence, with no father or husband as overlord. They have friends, entertainments, the willing paramour or two. For some women, one taste of married life is enough to convince them they do not need second helpings.

Of course, there are some women who wear black for the rest of their lives out of fondness for their departed husbands. Some of them just hang the crepe in their heart and never find another man they could love so well.

Miss Sonia is loyal. She never forgets her old friends; she never kept another "pet." Her

mare, Dilly, does not count; that's transporta-
tion. She writes to her father every week, never
speaks ill of George's wife, Jennifer, does not
buy French lace. She is true-blue. I taught her
well.

It took Miss Sonia eighteen years to settle on
Darius Conover. I did not have another eighteen years to wait for her to find another mate.
Her heart broken, she might go back to Berkshire to mourn. I'd already tried my luck there
at finding her a father for her children. Worst
of all, by King Arthur's Clavall, she might decide never to marry!

Besides, I like the major.

So it looks like I'm going to have to play
Canis ex machina again. I'm ready, I just cannot see my way clear.

I cannot use the same technique as last time.
The major is too downy a cove to fall for the
same trick twice. And his legs are much
stronger. I could knock the baron down, but
there is no guarantee he'd break his leg, and
they'd just go at it later. These two are determined to commit mayhem on each other.

I am preparing myself to make the ultimate
sacrifice. I'll leap between the major and the
bullet if I have to. My father would face a horde
of wolves to protect his lambs, if there were
still wolves in England. My mother would fight
to the death any threat to her pups. I could do
no less. I was ready.

The gathering of gentlemen, mostly officers, at
Ware House lasted well past midnight, with songs
and laughter and fine wines and food. In the usual
way of soldiers before battle, everything was spoken of except the duel. Conover's friends left with
hearty backslaps and calls of "See you tomorrow,"
or "Remember that mill on Saturday next."

After they left, Darius sent Hugh up to bed and

told Robb to get some sleep, too. He opened the door for Fitz to go across the square, but the cork-brained mutt stayed sprawled by the fire. "Stay, then. I'll send you home later."

Darius went back to his study for a final check that everything had been taken care of. When he threw another log on the fire, the dog followed him, collapsing in front of the hearth with a sigh, as though the effort were too much. The major smiled and turned to his desk and the lists he'd spent two days making. Things had been so much easier when he only had to face death at the hands of the French. He had no property then, no dependents. Robb would see to his horse and personal possessions; Milo would look after everything else.

Thinking of Milo, Darius touched the letters left on his desk, one for each of his brother's daughters. He drew the family signet ring off his finger and placed it on the letter for Benice, the eldest. Then he tenderly took Milo's watch out of his own pocket and centered it atop Gen's letter. On little Tina's he put one of his own treasures, which he carried with him on all the marches and transports: a silver-framed miniature of his own mother, with two dark-haired little boys gazing up at her.

There was an envelope with *Miss Randolph* inscribed on it, but the envelope was empty. He sharpened a quill to try again, and took her little yellow rose out of his pocket for inspiration. Words just did not come. He had no right to say what was in his heart. Finally he picked up the carved sandalwood box filled with medals Robb had removed from his uniform, to make Darius less a target. He put that on top of the empty envelope. Then he stared at the fire until it was time to wake Robb and Hugh.

"What are we doing up so early?" Hugh asked as he staggered into the morning room, wiping his eyes. "We don't have to be at the Oaks for hours."

"Breakfast, my boy, breakfast."

Hugh's face took on a greenish cast when he saw the mounds of food on Conover's plate. The night's revelries hadn't set well with him, nor did the idea of facing his sister if things did not go the way she wished. "How can you eat at a time like this?"

"Easiest thing in the world," the major answered around a nearly raw beefsteak. "You better get used to it. A soldier has to eat when there's food. You never know when the next opportunity will come. Right, Robb?"

"Yes, sir. Many's the time we had naught but what were in our pockets, and no way of knowing how long it had to last. 'Sides, no sense in dying on an empty stomach." Having served the major, Robb was standing by the sideboard, picking out his own breakfast of kippers and cutlets.

Hugh's coloring turned even more bilious.

"At least have some coffee, Lieutenant. Settle your nerves."

When Hugh was seated, trying to avoid the sight of all that food, he noticed the dog. "What's old Fitz doing here? I thought he always went home when the company left."

Darius shrugged. "He wouldn't leave. And let me tell you, if the condemned man got one last wish for company, it wouldn't be Fitz. He snores."

Reminded of the duel, Hugh swallowed hard and said, "Don't joke."

Robb just shook his head. Young cawker's tender sensibilities wouldn't last long at the front. He poured out an ale for Major Conover.

"Uh, Major," Hugh asked, "you going out in your uniform? I mean, shouldn't you be wearing black or something?"

"Black is for funerals, Randolph. If the French didn't manage to kill me all these years despite my being as easy to spot as a peacock in the snow, then I'll just take my chances with Berke. I can't think he'll have trouble seeing me at twenty paces, no matter what I wear. Robb did remove the medals over my heart, if that makes you feel better."

Hugh noted how the uniform jacket was a tight fit over Conover's broad chest, now that he'd regained his weight and perhaps a little extra. Hugh eyed the major's plate again. "Maybe you'd do better to remove the coat anyway, free your arm up better."

Darius continued cutting his steak and chewing. "Mm. I'll think about it, if it's warm enough."

Hugh nodded, but was still troubled. "Some of the, uh, gentlemen last night were a bit above par."

Robb snorted. "Castaway, more like."

"I saw no reason not to open my brother's cellars, Hugh. If I'm around, I'll replace the bottles. If not, Cousin Preston doesn't deserve that fine old brandy half as much as my fellow officers. At least they stood by me."

"Zeus, didn't mean to find fault with your hospitality, sir! No, it's just that some of the men's tongues were loosened a bit—in their cups, don't you know—and, well, m'sister's name was mentioned more than once in connection with the duel."

Darius put his fork down, forcibly. "Your sister is not involved in the duel. Her name is blameless, and don't you let anyone convince you otherwise. Next thing we know, you'll be issuing challenges like Berke, and making Sonia's name a byword for real. The talk will die down after today, you'll see, so don't do anything harebrained. Do you understand, Lieutenant?"

When the major used that tone of voice, Hugh did. "Then the whole thing really is about a game of cards?"

"Don't be a nodcock. I wouldn't give the time of day to Berke or Preston. Do you think I'd sit down to a hand with them? I walked into the room, saw the two of them, and left. The whole thing was a farrago of nonsense."

Hugh was skeptical. "Then why? Mean to say, a

fellow hates you, so he avoids you. No need to start a brouhaha. That's why everyone's looking for deeper reasons. Couldn't still be that old rapper about Berke's sister. As you say, he's got nothing to gain by shaking the skeletons out of his own closet."

Darius swirled the liquid around in his glass. "I don't know about that. I might be wrong, and there's no way to prove I'm right, but I think Berke has a lot to gain. You do know he's nearly always below hatches from gaming?"

"Everyone knows that. He's at the clubs every night."

"As long as you realize he's a basket-scrambler and don't let him near your sister."

"Sunny? She's too downy a bird for that! She tolerates him for Lady Atterbury's sake, but just barely."

"Good. Anyway, I had my man do some checking to see where Berke gets his income. It's not from his lands; he bled them dry years ago. They are mortgaged to the hilt. And he's not even a particularly successful gambler. Yet he always seems to come about, at least enough to maintain his standing on the town. My cousin Preston, on the other hand, has more money from his mother's family than he knows what to do with, and keeps winning more."

Hugh digested that. "You mean Preston is backing Berke?"

"Something like that, and Preston could be calling in his markers. As I say, I could be wrong and Preston could be supporting his wife's brother out of the goodness of his heart. Then again, pigs could fly. I cannot think of anyone else who will benefit by my demise."

"Lud, why didn't you ever say so?"

"What for? It's just conjecture. Milo always stood between me and the title, and I thought I'd die a hero anyway. Much better than taking one of

Berke's bullets over some lightskirt. He always was a crack shot, you know. That's why it was so easy for him to make the challenge. He never believed he could lose. I thought at the time that if I met him and lost, that would be half confessing I knew the girl."

"Uh, are you any good with a gun?" Hugh thought to ask, a trifle late.

Darius smiled. "Passable." He reached for another rasher of ham.

Hugh was still mulling over the information. He was not a quick thinker at the best of times, but before dawn was especially taxing. "Still don't figure about the girl, Berke's sister."

"According to Berke, who I'd trust as far as I could throw, she named me. But what if she said Conover? I know I never laid with her. She was a bran-faced chit with rabbity teeth. Fellow'd remember a thing like that. Preston's a Conover, too; Conare's just a jumped-up title he bought from Prinny. Maybe that's why he's been settling Berke's accounts for all these years."

"And Berke couldn't force him to marry the chit because Preston was already married. Gads, his own sister-in-law!"

"Maybe Berke didn't know or didn't have proof. Or else he was trying to protect his other sister, Rosellen. Maybe he even thought to blackmail Preston. It's possible we'll never know. Once he challenged me and slandered my name, he couldn't back down without looking the fool." He shrugged. "It's all idle speculation now at any rate. At least it will be over soon." He tucked a scrap of yellow silk back into his pocket from where it had lain next to his plate. Then he got up and began filling another dish.

Hugh had to hold a napkin to his mouth. "Lud, you're not going to eat all that, too, are you?"

Darius answered, "No, it's time to leave," as he

selected lamb chops and a sirloin with the bone left in, potatoes and gravy, a muffin or two.

Halfway out the door, Hugh complained, "Well, if you ain't going to have another meal, what in the blazes is that?"

Darius put the plate down on the floor, under Fitz's nose, and smiled as the dog started gobbling. "Insurance."

I wasn't ready.

Chapter Nineteen

*T*hat's it! That's how man, truly just one of us higher species, manages to maintain his domination. No, not by his fancy fingers or use of tools, nor by his convoluted thinking, by Tray! Canis Major, it's pockets!

He can store things. Oh, squirrels bury nuts, and dogs hide their bones, and foxes take food back to their dens all the time, but I mean really store things. Man doesn't have to be worrying about his next meal, so he can keep larger issues in mind. He can even keep two things in mind at once.

While some of us are only recently come to the security of steady meals, human persons have long since gone beyond the drama of mere day-to-day survival (except the very poor, of course, but no one seems to count them). Men have transcended immediacy.

I saw food. I ate it, like my fathers the wolves, like my cousins the jackals. An atavism, that's what I am. I am as stupid as the squirrel who can be tempted into the open with a handful of corn. Squirrel stew. That's me, squirrel stew.

The only times man allows his appetites to overrule his reason are when he's in his cups, or in the act of love. Cat dirt, I should have got him foxed! I could have found him a woman. One waits at the corner every night. No, those would only have been temporary solutions. The major was not likely to forget his purpose, not like me, I am ashamed to admit.

My dreams of being inscribed in the annals of canine glory have been written on the wind. I was going to be a hero, like Aubrey's dog, Dragon, who not only identified the Frenchman who slew his master, but took the varlet on in single combat before the king—and won. I was going to equal Dragon in valor. They would have named a star after me.

Dragon, hah! My full belly is dragging, that's all. My tail between my legs, I go home. Miss Sonia will need me. My place is by her side.

"Well, you picked a fine time to stay out all night," Sonia complained to the dog who drooped next to her chair. "I'm awake all night worrying, and you're out tomcatting! A nice how-do-you-do." The dog looked up at her from under shaggy gold eyebrows, whimpered once, and went back to sleep. Sonia went back to polishing silverware. Technically this was Marston's job, cleaning the fragile heirloom epergnes and candelabra. The butler had grown lax and fumble-fingered; Grandmother should see about pensioning the old fellow off. Sonia didn't mind the chore anyway. It gave her something to do, and the polishing table in the butler's pantry was right beside the front door.

Here it was after ten and she'd received no word. She gave a tiny swan-shaped salt cellar a hard buffing. Her brother had sworn to come to her as soon as there was word. She wanted to throttle him. She nearly rubbed the wings off the poor swan instead. Next she attacked a monstrosity of a centerpiece, with elephants marching around the base, trunk to tail, howdahs on their backs, palm trees overhead, monkeys in the trees, and large, parroty-type birds on top whose open mouths were candle holders. Even Lady Atterbury hated it. The thing was a wedding gift from Great-Aunt Sophrina, so it stayed. Today it was getting the polishing of its life. The palm trees were almost swaying.

Where was that chaw-bacon brother of hers anyway? she fumed, rubbing an elephant until it squeaked. Everyone knew duels were at dawn. If he'd stopped off at the barracks, she'd— What if he was busy with surgeons and things? Darius had said trust him. She did, of course. But she didn't trust Ansel Berke, or the accuracy of dueling pistols, or the skill of some unknown physician. She didn't even trust her heart to keep beating through all this waiting. What would she do if— No, she was not going to think about that. Just let him live, she prayed, even if he flees to America or back to the army. That's all she was asking, for now.

By eleven the monkeys on the centerpiece were screaming for mercy, and Sonia was starting on the parrots. Ian had taken Fitz out and was dragging the reluctant dog up and down the street in front of Atterbury House, watching for the first glimpse of Lieutenant Randolph. The dowager was out of her bedchamber for the first time in days, running Bigelow and Sonia's maid ragged with her demands for possets and potions. Marston stood erect by the front door, magnificent in livery and powdered wig. Only the glazed look in his eye revealed that the dignified butler was as drunk as a lord. Sonia polished.

"He's coming!" Ian finally shouted from the corner, to be echoed a moment later by Marston's stately "Lieutenant Randolph approaches," as he marched across the marbled hall to report to the dowager in the drawing room. Sonia jumped up, sending polishing cloths and powders every which way.

"He's alone!" Ian called.

"The lieutenant appears to be unaccompanied," Marston intoned, crossing the hall again. Sonia clutched the centerpiece to her chest, sending a monkey or two hurtling through the palm trees.

"He's whistling!"

Marston silently slid down the wall to land prostrate on the marble. The centerpiece soon joined him on the floor. Sonia jumped over both to run down the outside stairs and throw herself into Hugh's arms, dirty hands and soiled apron and all, right there on the street.

"Tell me, tell me!" she cried, tugging him back up to the door. "Who won?"

Hugh jingled some coins in his pocket and whistled again. "Why, I did, don't you know. Laid m'last month's pay on the major. Got good odds for Conover's bum leg and Berke's reputation."

"Dash it, Hugh, you know I don't care about your addlepated wagers! What happened?"

Hugh got a glimpse of his grandmother fanning herself in the drawing room, so he pulled back. "Uh, what say we go to the dining room, have a bite to eat, what? Didn't get much of a breakfast, by George."

"You'll get in here this instant, young man, and stop your confounded shilly-shallying," Lady Atterbury demanded. "Warebourne survives, I assume?"

Hugh bowed and nodded.

"And Berke?"

"Him, too," Hugh replied, looking pleadingly at his sister.

Now that she was not on tenterhooks, Sonia could take pity on Hugh. If she couldn't save him from their grandmother's rancor, at least she could feed him. She sent Bigelow and Maisie off to see about a substantial tea for her brother, since ringing for

Marston was going to be useless for some time to come.

Hugh didn't speak while the servants scurried back and forth with trays and platters. He did mention, though, around a thick slab of fresh bread with a chunk of cheese on it, that he hadn't stayed for the postcontest festivities at the Golden Hare. "That's why I'm so sharp-set. Knew you'd be anxious, so I rode back straightaway."

"And Darius, Major Conover, is at the Golden Hare? *Celebrating?*" Sonia asked. He was off enjoying himself while she was in such agony?

"Devil a bit," Hugh answered, making himself another sandwich with some cold meat. "He's on his way to pick up the Warebourne chits in Lyme. Said the coaches were all packed and ready, and he missed the brats. Wanted them near him, he said. Can't imagine why, m'self." He kept eating.

Sonia tossed a napkin at him. "But what happened? You still haven't told us about the duel!"

"Oh, that. Neatest bit of shooting I've ever seen. Quickest golden boys I ever made." Lady Atterbury angrily drummed her fingers on the armrest of her chair. "Uh, better to start at the beginning."

"Finally," the dowager muttered.

Hugh ignored her, preferring his sister's eager smile. " 'Twas foggy. Usually is for this type of thing, early morning, don't you know. Trees look spooky." Lady Atterbury cleared her throat; Hugh rushed on. "Anyway, we were there first. Darius wanted to be early so his men could scour the woods to make sure no sharpshooters were hidden in the trees."

"He never thought Ansel Berke would be so dastardly!" the dowager insisted. "The man's a baron and a prime marksman, from all I hear."

Hugh shrugged. "Darius is a soldier. Said it pays to be careful. His man Robb says the major hasn't led his men into an ambush since he was a green 'un on his first foray out. Besides, that Warebourne title might be worth something to someone else other than Berke."

"Conare," Sonia breathed, her hand to her mouth.

The dowager merely went, "Harumph. Jackanapes doesn't know what he's talking about. Gentlemen like Berke and Conare do not behave like savages. Proceed, sirrah."

"Well, Conare didn't show his face anyway. Berke came along in good time with a parcel of mincing fops, all their high-heeled slippers getting stuck in the grass. At least Berke wore Hessians. He was laughing and carrying on with the coxcombs as if he didn't have a care in the world, comparing snuffboxes of all things! Let me tell you, such confidence drove his odds down."

Hugh sat up straighter with self-importance. "I conferred with his man. He conferred with Berke. I conferred with Conover. Neither man would apologize."

The dowager snorted. "If they were going to apologize, you looby, they needn't have waited six years!"

Affronted, Hugh told her, "My job, don't you know, trying to negotiate a compromise."

"Hush, Grandmama, let Hugh tell the story his own way."

Hugh nodded toward his sister. "Right. We loaded the pistols. Have to admit m'hand wasn't quite steady, all those old fa—fops watching. Then we marked off the paces. The baron and Darius took their places. Berke was all in black, once he buttoned his coat and turned up his collar. Darius stood in his shirt-sleeves. Some old court-card rattled out the call. They paced. They turned. And Darius shot the pistol right out of Berke's hand before the baron even lowered his weapon to fire it!"

Sonia clapped, and Her Grace let out her breath.

"Right. Darius must have been practicing, the way he swiveled on that good leg of his. I've never seen the like. And his shot destroyed one of Manton's prettiest sets. One's no good for dueling, you know. Have to be a matched pair. Well, Berke started crying foul. No one listened, and they were his crowd, all congratulating the major on a deuced fine shot. So Berke screamed louder that Darius fired early. The old gent who was judge looked down his long nose at Berke and declared it a fair fight. Made the baron look a fool, with his hand getting all swollen and red from powder burn. He drove off in a snit."

"And then?"

"Then cool as you please, the major and Robb whip some jugs out of the carriage and set 'em up for target shooting. Sure enough, the sheriff and the magistrate come not five minutes after Berke left. And what do they see? A bunch of gents taking practice. Nothing havey-cavey about that, though some of the shooters were a bit on the go. I won another bundle from the magistrate, betting on Darius. None of the others would take him on, naturally. Anyway, as soon as he could without giving offense, the major sent 'em all off to the Golden Hare, breakfast on him, while he and Robb drove off. I got to bring the curricle home."

"Will the baron be satisfied, do you think?"

"He'll never challenge Darius again, that's for sure. And you can bet none of those other chaps will think to insult the major either, not after the exhibit he put on. My guess is they'll laugh at Berke if he tries to stir up another mare's nest."

"Honor was satisfied," the dowager declared. "Berke knows better than to destroy his own credibility."

"Thank goodness," Sonia said, pouring her brother another cup of coffee, then fussing with the sugar tongs. "And did the major, uh, say when he was coming back?"

"No, but he told me to pass on that he'd call as soon as he returned." Hugh grinned. "And he did ask for Papa's direction. Thought he might stop off in Berkshire on the way. Too bad I had to tell him that the governor is halfway to Scotland. My last letter said Father expected to wait nine months for a grandson, and nine months it would be."

"That inconsiderate imbecile!" Her Grace's displeasure rattled the teacups.

"Darius?"

"The major?"

"No, you blitherers, Elvin Randolph! Disporting himself with a young bride when for once in his life he should be at home with his stinking sheep! Here's a catch for his daughter, and he'll let it slip through our fingers with his cavorting. Yes, cavorting like a cockerel!"

Hugh grinned again. "Somehow I don't think Sunny's bird is going to fly the coop so fast."

"Nothing's been said," she protested, to which Lady Atterbury snorted. Sonia could feel the heat rising in her cheeks, but that only matched the glow in her heart. He was going to speak to Papa. Sooner or later. Then she recalled her grandmother's words. "Does that mean you approve, Your Grace?"

The dowager raised her lorgnette to her nose and stared at Sonia. "I have always liked the boy," she lied. "It was his situation I deplored. Now he is on his way to being a respected member of society, a hero, an earl with at least fifty thousand a year. Have your wits gone begging, girl? Of course I approve."

That afternoon a bouquet of flowers was delivered for Miss Sonia Randolph, eighteen yellow roses. The enclosed card read *Yrs., Warebourne.* Not very loverlike, but considering the interested audience of Lady Atterbury and her cronies, Blanche, and Hugh, Sonia silently thanked him for sparing her further blushes. She was especially grateful when they all felt the flowers and the card required some comment.

"Very proper," one of the old ladies decreed. Another added: "Just the right touch."

Lady Atterbury nodded. "The boy has class. I like that."

Blanche just said, "Very nice." She was patently disappointed the major hadn't made any protestations of undying love. So was Sonia, but she kept that to herself, along with the relevance of the yellow roses.

Only Hugh voiced his discontent. "He signed it Warebourne. Sounds like he's selling out."

"What did you think, you clunch?" Lady Atterbury asked. "He was going to fetch the children so he could take them with him to a war? Or did you suppose he was going to call on your father to buy some hounds so the officers could have a hunt in Portugal? No Harkness granddaughter is going to go following the drum, not while I live and breathe. You really are woolly-headed, Hugh Randolph. Your father should be proud."

"I wouldn't mind traveling with the army, Grandmama," Sonia said, thinking of Blanche and Hugh, and also that she didn't want Darius to give up his career for her.

"No one's asked you, missy."

As a matter of fact, the thought occurred to Sonia—and to everyone else—that no one had asked her anything.

Human beings think too much.

Chapter Twenty

Cogito, ergo sum. I think, therefore I am. Of course you are! What did you suppose, you were the worst nightmare of a herd of beef cattle? Or did you rationalize that since a rock cannot think, a rock does not exist? Descartes should have stuck to mathematics!

Sometimes men are all thought and no action. They dillydally when they should just do it! Now Darius found another impediment not to get on with what Tippy calls "a marriage of true minds." He cannot find Miss Sonia's father! That's true mouse droppings! He thinks, therefore I am at a loss.

What if the first bud of infatuation fades? What if it never blossoms, but withers on the vine? That happens. There has been no offer; there is no ring. Nothing to make crying off a major social disaster. For barking out loud, there is nothing to cry off *from*, except some sighs and longing looks. The pigeons who hang around Almack's for the stale refreshments no one eats say there's many a slip twixt the cup and the lip. In Berkshire we say, don't count your chickens until they hatch. What if all this comes to is an omelette? Those pigeons, the fattest I've ever seen, are full of stories of fickle females and rakish gentlemen who seem to fix their interest, then move on.

And there is adultery, the ultimate in fickleness. Miss Sonia was raised better, but what of the major? I understand that couples often spend this infinity of indecision, then the year's betrothal, go through with saying their vows before man, God, and the licensing bureaus—and break those same sacred vows as easily as eggs for breakfast. If Darius Conover thinks to throw Miss Sonia over, or be unfaithful to her later, better Berke had shot him, by Pluto!

I can't think. I'm too busy worrying.

A single yellow rose was delivered to Atterbury House at three in the afternoon for the next ten days. Sonia kept the roses in a vase beside her bed, then pressed them in her Bible. She kept the notes, which all read *Yrs., Warebourne*, in a drawer with her gloves and handkerchiefs. On the eleventh day, the rose was delivered late, not until dinner, and in a small gold filigree holder with a brooch back. All the previous flowers had been wrapped in tissue with a ribbon, all of which reposed in yet another drawer. The eleventh rose had no note, but was obviously to be worn, and tonight was Wednesday. Everyone knew what that meant.

Sonia spent the next hour selecting a gown to wear to Almack's. She finally settled on an ivory satin that had gold lace trimming at the hem and around the neckline. Sonia had never worn the gown, considering the décolletage too immodest for her taste. Madame Celeste had insisted the dress was much less risqué than that worn by most debutantes, and that Mademoiselle had the figure for it. Bigelow agreed with Sonia that the deep vee was suggestive—"Muslin company"—and suggested Miss Randolph tuck a lace fichu into the neckline: "Some lights are better hidden under a bushel." Sonia thought the filmy lace took away from the gown's classic lines, so she never wore Celeste's creation. Tonight the ivory satin was perfect, with the yellow rose nestled between her breasts. There was no lace fichu.

Lady Atterbury bestirred herself to attend the Marriage Mart that evening, wearing her favorite purple taffeta, with diamonds on her chest and an egg-sized ruby in her turban. Hugh was commandeered as escort.

"What, for stale bread and lemonade? Or the chicken stakes in the card room?"

"Neither. You come to lend your sister countenance."

Hugh grinned. "She'd do better if you lent her a shawl." He tempered his teasing with an affectionate hug, telling Sonia she was in prime twig.

Darius was already in the King Street assembly rooms. He was at Sonia's side before she greeted the hostesses, cutting through the horde of admirers clamoring around her. He signed her card for the opening cotillion and one other set, late in the evening. There was no chance to speak, with Monty Pimford reciting his latest masterpiece and Wolversham requesting a dance so he could explain Coke's newest theory. Darius most likely could not have spoken anyway. He knew how impolite it was not to look a person in the face when addressing him, or her, but he couldn't lift his eyes from Sonia's soft, lush, velvety—rose, he told himself. Look at the rose. No, look at her eyes. He gave up and moved away before embarrassing himself completely.

Sonia followed him with her gaze, as did many another female, both young and old. Darius had chosen to make his first invited entry into the bastion of the haut monde also his first appearance as the Earl of Warebourne. He wore the satin knee smalls that were de rigueur, and the black satin evening coat established as the mode for gentlemen. His waistcoat was white marcella with subtle gold thread embroidery, and his neckcloth was conservative, except for the yellow topaz and diamond stickpin. All in all, he was clothed befitting an earl, and his clothes fitted to perfection. His soldier's build, all hard muscle and broad shoulder, was almost as noticeable in Weston's handiwork as in one of Lord Elgin's Grecian warrior-athletes. Sonia's eyes hardly left him as she absentmindedly conversed with her other acquaintances.

When the music finally started, Sally Jersey was reluctant to part with the most elegant, virile man at Almack's that night. She had no choice. Before she could lay a dainty hand on his sleeve to restrain him, Lord Warebourne was gone.

He bowed to Lady Atterbury, then held his hand out to Sonia, not trusting that his voice wouldn't crack like a boy's. Sonia was nearly as tongue-tied at his magnificence, wondering if such a handsome, sophisticated nobleman could possibly be interested in plain Miss Randolph, now that he had the world and its daughters to choose from. She was too practiced in the social graces, however, to stand mumchance fretting. She knew a lady was supposed to initiate conversation when silence threatened, so she thanked him for all the lovely roses.

Darius swallowed. "I, ah, see you are wearing my token." See? He could hardly look elsewhere or remember whether he was doing the Roger de Cleavage or the bosomlanger. Luckily the dance was a cotillion, so he did not have to change partners.

Sonia smiled. "Of course I am wearing it. You sent it. But tell me, my lord, why eighteen that first day?"

Now he looked directly into her bluebell eyes, which were at about the level of his chin. Just right.

"You are eight and ten years old, your brother said. A rose for each precious year."

"I should have known you'd be even more smooth-tongued as an earl, my lord," Sonia replied with a dimpled grin, pleased beyond measure at his words.

"What, are you about to start 'my-lording' me like everyone else? I won't have it."

"Still giving orders?" she teased. "You shall have to decide which it's to be, my lord earl or major, sir."

"Darius."

"Darius," Sonia repeated, winning a warm smile. "Then I do not have to be stuffy Miss Randolph?"

"I have never met anyone less stuffy. And I think you have been Sunny to me since I heard your brother say it. Even before, but I didn't know the word. Do you mind?"

"Of course not, silly."

"Of course not, *Darius*," he corrected, just so he could see her dimples flash again. "But that's only in private, you realize. For now." At her raised eyebrows, he went on: "You do know I have tried to contact your father? I have sent letters to every inn your brother George mentioned, and half the great houses of Scotland. It appears your esteemed parent wishes to remain undisturbed on his wedding trip. Blast him!"

Sonia giggled, delighted at his evident frustration.

"Minx. Until I have word from your father, I intend to see that not one hint of impropriety touches your name. None of the old tabbies will utter the slightest meow of disapproval."

"But I do not care what they say. I've never been a prunes-and-prisms miss, you know."

"I know it well, and am thankful you're not a pattern card of decorum, else you'd never have given me the time of day. And I never cared what they said about me either. Nevertheless, I find that now I care very much that no blame attaches itself to you from my attentions."

"What, not even one step over the line?" She looked down at the rose at her breast. His eyes followed, as she knew they would.

Darius painfully dragged his gaze to her soft, smiling lips and even teeth, her little pink tongue. "Unprincipled baggage! Not even a smidgen of gossip, so don't tempt me. By Jupiter, if I wasn't determined to do this up proper, do you think I'd be satisfied with two miserly dances? Especially when I know every ramshackle rake in the place will be looking where he's got no business. Let me warn you, my girl, I do not intend to be any complacent . . ."

"Complacent what, my lord?"

"Darius." He bit his tongue. For once in his life he was going to do everything by the book, even if it killed him. If ever he needed to throw something . . . "Just understand that I would ask for every dance, if I could."

"And I would answer yes," Sonia told him, without subterfuge or coy flirtatiousness. Which caused Darius to forget all of his resolutions and raise her hand to his lips, which caused them to miss a step, which caused the couple behind to bump into them, which— So much for resolutions.

Everyone at Almack's that night knew it was a match, even without Lady Atterbury's not so carefully veiled remarks about Elvin Randolph's unfortunate absence. By tacit consent, no one mentioned the old scandal, especially after Blanche let slip a clue or two about Hermione Berke and Preston Conare. Having heard Hugh's suspicions, Blanche decided this was the best plot she'd come upon, surely too delicious not to share, particularly if it could smooth her friend's path. Blanche took extra pleasure in mentioning to that haughty Lady Rosellen that no one held *Darius* Conover to blame. Rosellen ignored Blanche, but then she always did.

Rosellen was too busy to listen to platter-faced

chits and their empty prattle. Like many another
lady there, she was trying to attract the man of the
hour. Rosellen unobtrusively pulled at the already
plunging neckline of her favorite red satin before
moving to stand by Lady Atterbury's chair when
Darius brought the troublesome Miss Randolph
back. The chit was supposed to be Ansel's meal
ticket. The dangerous new earl was supposed to be
fair game to an enterprising female.

"Ah, the prodigal son is returned," Rosellen
quipped when Warebourne bowed in her direction
after Sonia tripped off with some green boy. "And
they are serving up the fatted calf," she suggested
evilly.

Darius merely raised his eyebrows.

"Of course, some men don't like sweet new wine
with their meals," Rosellen went on. "They prefer
a riper vintage, tart and spicy."

"Some older wines turn vinegary," Darius commented.

Watching from her place in the set, Sonia was
making note to inform Lord Warebourne that she,
Sonia Randolph, did not intend to be any complacent whatever either! Then she saw Rosellen scowl
and stomp off. Darius winked at Sonia as if he felt
her pique from across the room and was telling her
there was no need for concern. She would have felt
better if she'd heard what sent Rosellen off in an
angry swirl of draperies: "And some men don't care
for mutton dressed as lamb."

Whoever at Almack's did not know of the unoffi-
cial engagement was quickly apprised when Darius
claimed Sonia's hand for the first waltz. All of his
nobler aims flew by the board when Sonia simply
walked into his arms and said, "I've been waiting
forever for this." Darius recalled, a bit too late for
his expressed objectives, that Miss Randolph did
usually get her way.

* * *

There were other opportunities to dance in the next days, although never enough. They held hands in the shadows at the opera, stayed touching a moment more than necessary when Darius helped Sonia on with her cloak, or up to his curricle for a ride in the park. Where his instincts may have overridden his better intentions, Lady Atterbury's resolve held firm.

"One premature infant in the family is enough," she commanded, rapping his fingers with her lorgnette after they'd lingered overlong on Sonia's waist. Sonia laughed to see the stalwart hero reduced to blushing schoolboy, but she, too, started wishing that her father might grow a little homesick for his lands and dogs, if not his children and new grandson.

The dowager was so intent on keeping decorum—and a good twelve inches—between Sonia and the earl that she exerted herself to attend many evening functions she'd previously considered too fatiguing. How tiring could it be to boast of her granddaughters, one already a marchioness and finally breeding, the other soon to be a countess? Even rackety Hugh seemed to be headed in the right direction, which was wherever Lady Blanche and her title and acreage led him. Unfortunately the featherheaded chit was fixed on following the drum; Lady Almeria thanked her lucky stars she did not have the keeping of that hen-wit.

During the daytime, while the dowager conserved her strength, she still made sure Sonia was adequately chaperoned. Hugh and Blanche went along on every outing, with Sonia's maid, her groom, Ian, and even the impossible mongrel. Lady Atterbury was further reassured when Warebourne brought his man, his nieces, and their new nursemaid. Miss Inwood was a responsible, respectable young miss sent by the children's grandmother to replace the flirtatious Meg Bint. Lady Atterbury would have rested easier if the entire British blockade were along to play dogsberry for her granddaughter and that devilishly handsome lord, but what could happen on a jaunt to Richmond with so many in the party?

What could and did happen was that Ian, always one to appreciate a pretty face, took Miss Inwood and the children off to explore the maze. Hugh and Blanche strolled through the gardens lost in a discussion of military maneuvers, and Sonia's maid, Maisie, was pleased to share her picnic blanket with the major's man, Robb, behind a yew hedge and out of sight. For all intents and purposes, Darius and Sonia were alone on a wool throw, except for one large black dog who insisted on more than his fair share of the blanket. Fitz's usurping sprawl naturally forced the blanket's other two occupants into closer proximity. Neither Darius nor Sonia complained.

As anyone with a ha'penny's worth of sense could have foreseen, Sonia was soon wrapped in Darius's arms, half in his lap, half out of her gown, fully out of breath.

A kingdom may have been lost for a nail, but an ant crawling across Conover's neck saved the day. "No," he vowed, as he returned to his senses. "No." He set Sonia away from him. "And fix your gown," he ordered. "And your hair, and . . . and do something about your mouth. For pity's sake, not that!" he groaned, when she ran her tongue over swollen lips. Sonia gurgled with laughter to see him drag his fingers through his own tumbled locks. She reached out to brush a curl off his forehead, but he firmly pushed her hand away. "None of that, minx, or I am lost. We'll talk."

Sonia thought he was just about the most enchanting sight she'd ever seen, spouting propriety and giving orders with his cravat all rumpled. She kissed his nose and quickly sat back. "Very well, sir. What shall we talk about?"

Darius leaned back on his elbows and smiled. "I spoke to some of the younger party members. They

183

think I can make a difference in Parliament if I take my seat. There are crucial votes for military spending and such coming up."

"Then you won't mind being an earl?"

He looked around: blue skies, flowers, laughing children, and sweet Sonia instead of mud and muck and blood and horror. He laughed out loud. "If this is a taste of civilian life, I'm all for it! There are others in the army who can do my job just as well, and I think I can be of importance to the War Office here. Treatment of veterans, conditions for the enlisted men, just expediting supply deliveries. There is much work to do."

"And you cån help support the bills protecting climbing boys and limiting the hours for children in factories and mines."

"Gads, Sonia, you expect a lot. I know nothing about such measures."

"But I do," she told him with perfect complacence.

"Very well, with your help I can certainly do more for climbing boys and child workers while in Parliament than I could while in Spain. And I have to see about Ware, too. I've been leaving everything to the stewards and estate managers, but I'll have to make some decisions soon, although the devil knows how. I know even less about farming than I do about legislature."

"But I know more. Especially if there are sheep. And Papa will be ecstatic to help; he's worse than Lord Wolversham when it comes to new methods and improved production."

"Will he like me, do you think?"

"Go grouse hunting with him once and he'll adore you, for your aim alone. And if you admire his hounds, his sheep, and perhaps his new wife, Leah, he'll welcome you with open arms. Mostly he'll love you when he sees how happy you make me. You are happy, too, Darius, aren't you? You truly don't mind selling out?"

He had to squeeze her, just once for reassurance. "I doubt I'd make a good officer any longer, Sunny. My heart and mind would be back here with you and the girls."

"And boys."

He grinned. "Sons, too. What more could a fellow ask?" He leaned back again. "I must be the luckiest man alive! Look up. That's how I feel, that I could reach up and touch the sky. No clouds, just sunshine. Sunny and me. There is nothing I cannot do, or be, thanks to you. Everything is perfect!"

"No, Darius. You are perfect."

He reached out and touched her cheek. "If you believe I'm perfect, then I am."

The Greeks had a word for this. They called it *hubris.*

Chapter Twenty-one

$\mathcal{T}$he Greeks did not think this hubris, this pride and self-confidence, was such a good idea. Then again, the Greeks didn't think much of dogs, either.

There's an old story—I know, not another dog story! What did you expect, Puss in Boots?—of Alcibiades, an Athenian statesman and soldier and regular rum touch, if you ask me. One day he went on a tear, rampaging through the city during his wild revels. Then he went out and bought a dog, the prettiest, most expensive greyhound he could buy, for suchamany drachmas. And he cut off the dog's tail. For Spot's sake, he did! When asked why, Alcibiades answered that he did it so the Athenians would remember *that*, rather than his earlier wanton destruction. They didn't. In fact, aside from Plutarch and us dogs, no one remembers the tail at all. Nor, when they hear of Alcibiades, do they recall that he was a famous general or a student of Socrates'. No, what comes to mind first about Alcibiades is best expressed in the schoolboy's taunt: Ace likes lace. The Greeks didn't think much of women either. No wonder their civilization did not last!

Anyway, so much for pride. The Greeks believed that the gods took retribution on men who rose above their station. Things are not so personal anymore. Nowadays people just say, Don't tempt fate, or Knock on wood. Would lifting my leg on a tree do as well?

The major should succeed at politics. I heard no overweening determination to reach the top of government positions, no burning desire to run the country. I agree with the Great Republican: Greed and ambition are not particularly desirable traits in those who hold office. The major had none of those tendencies. Maybe now I can relax.

"Your father, my dear, is a very elusive gentleman. Does he never answer his mail?"

Sonia's cheeks pinkened to match her jaconet walking dress. Her grandmother's sentiments had not been quite as delicately phrased.

"That Elvin Randolph should be strung up by his thumbs," Her Grace declared. "Why, we're the bobbing blocks of the ton. They're all speculating he's been without a woman so long since your mother died that he needs must make up for lost ground. Balderdash! I know all about his convenients in the village, and so I'll tell anyone who asks. We will not even be able to have a fashionable announcement ball if that nodcock stays away much longer. Everyone will be off to Bath or their country properties, hang him."

"He promised George to return for the baby's christening next month, Grandmama, and you know I never wished for a big squeeze anyway."

"Gammon. We've waited this long for Itchy Britches Elvin, we'll not have any hole-in-corner affair. Do you hear me, miss? I finally got my butler sober."

Sonia just nodded and smiled. She was going to let Lady Atterbury throw London's grandest bash for the engagement because Her Grace's heart was so set on it, and because the dowager had put up with so much already. Then, however, Sonia was going to have the wedding of *her* dreams. She'd be married in the Sheltonford chapel, with Vicar Gilcroft officiating, just as he'd officiated nearly every Sunday of her life. All her friends, neighbors, tenants, and staff would come to see her father give her away. Blanche could be maid of honor, and Fitz would wear a bow. Vicar Gilcroft simply had to let Fitz in the church, just this once, without it being the annual blessing of the beasts; there'd have been no wedding, no meeting at all, without Fitz. Sonia also planned on three little flower girls strewing rose petals and orange blossoms. After the wedding they could all go to Ware for the summer instead of on an extended bridal journey. Sonia was anxious to start meeting her new tenants, helping to care for the lands.

Miss Randolph kept busy meantime, but not too busy for her old friends or her little friends. She and Fitz often met the Warebourne girls in Grosvenor Square after their visit with the admiral. Sonia made sure the girls took part in her other activities when possible, like excursions back to Richmond Park or events like an evening at Astley's Amphitheater. She often accompanied the trio on simple outings to Hyde Park to feed the ducks. Fitz learned to leave them alone—the ducks and the bread.

One day Sonia arranged to keep the children company in the park while Darius kept an appointment with the War Office. He was working on getting Hugh transferred to his own cavalry regiment, where, he told Sonia, his former comrades would look after the lad. Hugh would not be made a fool or cannon fodder, and the colonel's wife was sure to take Blanche under her wing if the war dragged on. Leaving Sonia with her servants and the girls, Darius promised his nieces ices at Gunther's later; his eyes promised Sonia at least a stolen kiss or two when he returned to fetch them.

Sonia and the children had a wonderful time, training Fitz to be a circus horse, like the performers at Astley's. They'd brought a hoop along to play with, and taught Fitz—and Baby—to jump through.

Genessa said she was practicing for teaching her new pony, when they returned to Ware for the summer. Benice thought she'd make her kitten a lace tutu, for her to wear when she rode the pony or Fitz.

"I think we shall have to ask the cat, my dear," Sonia told her, "and the pony."

Gen tried to wrest the stuffed dog from Baby's hands, to ride atop Fitz with a hair ribbon as reins. Bettina protested, loudly, so the new nanny, Miss Inwood, sent the older girls off a ways with the hoop, while she held the toddler and the toy on her lap. Bettina was not reconciled.

"Here," Sonia volunteered. "Give me Tiny, Miss Inwood. I haven't had a coze yet today with Mimi."

Sonia looked up from the baby's prattle a few moments later when the older girls stopped their chatter and gathered closer to her skirts. Sonia raised her head and looked around to see what had caught the children's attention, Preston and Rosellen Conover promenading toward them. Sonia stood, still holding Tina, and curtsied. "Come, children, make your bows to your cousins."

Benice made a stiff curtsy and whispered, "Lady Conare, my lord." Gen made the slightest bobble, and the baby threw herself back into Sonia's arms.

"Still as unmannerly as ever, I see," Lord Conare derided, taking out his quizzing glass.

Bettina hid her face in Sonia's shoulder. Sonia almost wished for a big shoulder to lean on herself.

Instead she spoke brightly: "We've been having a lovely day, haven't we, girls? Do you want to show your cousins what you've been teaching Fitz?" Tina clung harder, Gen shook her head no. Even Benice, who could usually be counted on to do the pretty, scuffed her toe in the ground.

"My dear Miss Randolph," Conare drawled, "as sweetly charming as I recall. And foolish. What makes you think we'd possibly enjoy seeing children and dogs frolic about? Why aren't the brats in the classroom anyway? Surely they could be learning something other than how to become common performers."

Miss Inwood was starting to bristle at the slur to her charges and her competence. Sonia intervened. "Why, Miss Inwood has done amazingly well in no time at all. Genessa knows her letters and numbers, don't you, precious? And Benice is halfway through an exquisite sampler. I'd be surprised if she does not become a notable needlewoman, with such patience and dexterity." Sonia chuckled. "Much more than I ever had as a child. They have come along so well, in fact, that we declared this perfect spring day a holiday."

Sonia's effort won a shy smile from Benice, but a sneer from Conare. "I had assumed my nieces were not learning to be sheepherders." He raised his quizzing glass from the now-quaking Benice and fastened his enlarged eyeball on Sonia. "And 'we'? I have not heard any interesting announcement. Perhaps I missed something to account for your inexplicable interference in my young cousins' education."

Rosellen snickered. "And as for patience, the on-dit is that you and Warebourne have none. Be careful, my dear, for nothing is so hard to hook as a fish that's already stolen the bait."

Sonia looked worriedly to the children while Conare added in that affectedly slow voice of his: "I am not sure Milo's children need to learn quite that much of the world at their tender ages."

Miss Inwood put her arms on the older girls' shoulders, and Ian took a step closer to his mistress. Sonia counted to ten before she started to wrap her tongue around a few choice words to blister the supercilious pair's ears. Before she began, however, Fitz ran through his new paces. He jumped through the hoop, which was held loosely in Gen's hands. The hoop got away, rolling across the damp grass, onto the dirt path, and over Lord Conare's shiny Hessians. Preston jumped back, sending the hoop in Rosellen's direction, where it left a muddy ring right across the hemline flounce of her sheer peach-colored muslin.

"Why, you little brat!" she screeched at Gen. "You did that on purpose. I've a good mind to—"

No one found out what, because Rosellen was positively not in mind to confront the large growling dog that stood between her and her intended victim. Rosellen grabbed Preston's sleeve and demanded he escort her home immediately, before anyone noticed her begrimed skirts.

"Cousin Rosellen is a wicked, wicked witch," Gen declared when the pair was out of sight. Sonia did not bother rebuking her. Shaken, she hugged the baby with one hand and smoothed back the dog's bristled ruff with the other. Benice's lip trembled, and Ian and Maisie looked ready to charge after the disappearing couple, so Sonia gathered her composure and said, "Well, we shan't let unpleasant people ruin our pleasant day, relatives or no. I believe I have just the thing in my reticule, a wonderful story of knights and ladies and dragons." She straightened the baby's dark curls, which reminded her of Darius's. "And a lot of pictures. Here, Miss Inwood, you take Tina and I'll find the book."

When Sonia handed over the child, however, Maisie Holbrook exclaimed, "Oh, miss, your silk spencer is all wet. The babe must have drooled all over it."

"Oh dear, I cannot go to Gunther's looking like I'd been under a spigot, and I promised the children a story. I know. Maisie, please return to Atterbury House and fetch my blue spencer. It will match the trim on my gown equally as well as this damp one."

"Of course, Miss Randolph. I'll just hop out of the park and hire a hackney at the gate. I'll be back before the cat can lick her ear."

"Fustian, Ian and the coach are sitting right there doing nothing. He'll drive you."

"Pardon, ma'am, but we couldn't both go off and leave you alone here."

"Nonsense, Maisie. I will not be alone with three children, a nurse, and a dog. Besides, you'll make better time if you don't have to walk to the park gate. At any rate, no one can protect me from insults, which is the worst one can expect in Hyde Park in the afternoon."

An unwanted and unexpected proposal was worse.

Ansel Berke had his driver halt the coach near Sonia's bench. He strolled closer while Sonia was reading the picture book. Fitz sniffed stiff-legged at the baron, who swatted at the dog with his walking stick. Fitz growled and went to investigate the crested, closed carriage.

"A word with you, my dear?" the baron oozed, striking a pose before her bench.

Sonia had not seen Berke for the last sennight or so. He looked more pasty-faced, less polished somehow. His clothes were all the stare, just a trifle awry, as if he'd dressed in haste. Sonia could not judge the condition of his gun hand, not with his gloves on. Injured or not, the baron was not her choice of companion. Even his heavy cologne nagged at the back of her throat. "I am sorry, my lord, but as you can see, I am occupied right now.

Perhaps if you call at Lady Atterbury's in the morning—"

"No, no, just a moment of your time," he urged, rudely pulling the book out of Sonia's hands and thrusting it at Miss Inwood. "The nanny can read. Do come, just a step, my dear."

Sonia did not want the children or Miss Inwood to hear anything else not meant for innocent ears, so she did get up. She walked a few paces away, not toward his carriage, but back along the carriage path, still in sight of Miss Inwood and the girls.

"Do hurry, Lord Berke. I am expecting Dar—Lord Warebourne shortly." She said nothing else, but the baron's color rose.

"Ah yes, Warebourne. That is precisely what I wished to speak of, my dear Miss Randolph. Word has reached my ears that there is a possible understanding—"

"Lord Berke, please do not say another word."

"I must! Please believe I have your interests at heart. You cannot know that scoundrel. Why, my own sister—"

"My lord, I insist you cease this conversation at once. I can only find it distressing and distasteful." She turned back to the children, only to find the baron in her way, on his knees.

"I beg you, my dear, marry me instead. I'd make a far, far better husband. No unsavory past, no sniveling dependents, and I have always been one of your staunchest admirers. You must admit my regard is long-standing."

"I . . . I am honored by your offer, my lord. However, I am already committed to Lord Warebourne, in my heart if not in the record books."

Berke got up and brushed at his knees, frowning. "And I cannot convince you to change your mind, albeit the dastard will play you false?"

"No, my lord. If Darius Conover should walk past right now"—Sonia only wished—"with a demirep

193

on one arm and your sister Rosellen on the other, I would not marry you."

Berke left her in the path. "So be it."

Sonia rejoined the children as his carriage drove off. She shook her head. What an odd afternoon it was!

"Do you wish to finish the story?" Miss Inwood asked.

"No, you continue. I think Fitz and I shall walk back along the path to meet Ian and Maisie. The sooner I am out of this damp garment, the better I'll feel."

Sonia had no intention of going far, just far enough to get the stench of Berke's perfume out of her nose. Around a bend in the path, Fitz flushed a duck, to the surprise of all three of them. The duck quacked, the dog barked, and Sonia laughed as Fitz tore off after the flying fowl. Sonia whistled for him. "Come on back, you clunch-head. You've never caught so much as a fly."

The dog lumbered back, tongue lolling happily as he crashed through the underbrush along the walkway. When his noise abated, Sonia said, "Oh dear, I think I hear Tina crying. We'd better go back." Then she heard Genessa yell, Benice squeal. She started running. "Go, Fitz," she shouted to the dog, sending him ahead faster than she could move in her narrow skirts. "Go see, Fitz, go." Fitz passed her in a black flash, barking.

The dog never heard the thud of a walking stick hitting the back of Sonia's head, nor her scream as a blanket was thrown over her.

Only half-aware from the blow, Sonia struggled as hard as she could when she felt herself being lifted and shoved onto a cushioned seat. A door slammed and a familiar voice called: "Drive on, Jeppers, but not so fast as to arouse suspicion."

"You'll never get away with this," Sonia gasped through the blanket's folds.

"Why not? Who's going to tell, the dog? By the

time they find you, you'll be committed to me, in deed, my dear, if nothing else. I think I'll enjoy that part. And all the money, of course, when you have to marry me."

"Never," Sonia vowed as she slipped into unconsciousness, the cloying scent of Berke's cologne the last memory she had.

Never have I regretted my mixed blood more.

Chapter Twenty-two

*B*on *chien chasse de race.* Breeding tells. Miss Sonia was behind me when I sped to the children. Nurse was on the ground, moaning. Baby was shrieking and turning purple. Gen was screaming, and even quiet Benice was sobbing and trembling, staring at the blood on Miss Inwood's temple. I dashed back to see what was keeping Miss Sonia. Help! I barked. Help! Hurry! Only she was not there. One whiff of the carriage trundling down the roadway told the story: My mistress was kidnapped.

Great Dog Star, what was I to do? My mother's blood raced through my veins with every quickened beat of my heart. The chase, the chase! View Halloo and never let go! Never lose the quarry, even if your heart bursts in your chest. My nose had the scent. My eyes had the sight. My feet itched to be off.

But my father's spirit also suffused my mind. Stand and defend the innocent. Protect the vulnerable, the valuable. Stay with the lambs you were given to guard, no matter that keeping them from harm means giving up your life.

I ran back to the crying, frightened children. Nurse was still on the grass. I ran forward to the path. The coach was rounding a bend. I ran back; I ran forth. There was no answer. So I did the only thing I could do. Tossing aside generations of breeding, I reached inside to my visceral ancestors. I sat down, threw my head back, and howled. Aw-woo. Aw-woo.

"What in the blazes is that ungodly noise?" Darius asked Robb, seated beside him in the curricle. "It sounds like all the hounds of hell are baying at the moon at once."

Hugh called over from where he rode his chestnut alongside the carriage: "Get used to it. That's m'father's favorite sound. In fact, reminds me of his old hound Belle. No other dog ever had a voice like that except—"

"Gads, Fitz!"

Curricle and horse raced down the carriageway, sending strollers fleeing like ninepins.

Ian and Maisie were returning with the Atterbury vehicle at the same time, from the opposite direction. They had, in fact, passed Berke's coach.

They all met in the clearing near the bench and poured onto the greensward, leaving the blowing horses for Robb to tie. Maisie quickly took charge of Miss Inwood, holding her own apron to a bleeding head wound while Ian half carried the nursemaid to the carriage.

Darius knelt by the nearly hysterical children, gathering them all close as he tried to soothe them and find out what happened. Hugh stood by helplessly while Fitz kept up a continuous keening howl.

"Dash it, Hugh, at least get Sonia to shut up the blasted dog!" Hugh looked around at the same moment it occurred to Darius that Sonia was missing.

"Hell and damnation!" Darius tried harder to make sense of the children's garbled tale of circus tricks and runaway hoops.

"Please hush, Gen. Whatever happened could not possibly be your fault. Benice, sweetheart, I am counting on you to be your own levelheaded, sensible self and tell me where Sunny went."

Benice didn't know. Between sobs that turned to hiccups under her uncle's steady confidence, she managed to tell him how Miss Sonia went for a walk, that way, after a man talked to her, some time after Cousin Preston and Lady Rosellen were in the park. "And they said awful things to Sunny, and Fitz growled at them, so they left. Then the other man came."

"Did you know the other man, Benice?"

"I think it was the same mean man we saw at Miss Sonia's house the day we brought Fitz there. Miss Sunny went off with him and got mad. We could tell. But he went away, and Miss Inwood was reading. Then another man came, a bigger man I never saw before, and hit Miss Inwood and then ran into the bushes. We screamed and Gen tried to kick him, but he got away. We yelled and Fitz came, but not Sunny." She started to weep again.

"Don't worry, Benice, we'll find her. And you were very brave, Gen. Now, do you remember anything at all about the man who hit Miss Inwood?"

"No, but the first man had a walking stick. He tried to hit Fitz with it."

"And he had a waistcoat with big green dragonflies on it."

"And he smelled funny."

Darius cursed under his breath. "Berke. It has to be him, and his henchman or such."

"I'll kill him," Hugh swore, but Darius answered first: "You won't find enough pieces of him left." Then he became the complete army officer, organizing his campaign, deploying his troops, giving his orders.

"Ian, you take Maisie, Miss Inwood, and the children to Ware House. The staff can look after Nurse and send for a doctor if needed. Gen, Benice, I am counting on you to be brave and look out for Tina for me so I can go after Sunny."

"I want to go with you, Uncle Darius."

"I know, Gen, but I need you to guard the home front. Do you understand? Robb, you go with Ian to Ware House and get my pistols. Saddle up and go—Deuce take it, I don't know where!" He ran his hands through his hair. "Hugh, where is Berke's country place? We could go haring off in every direction and lose each other *and* the trail."

"I think his seat is in Oxfordshire, but that's crazy. Surely he'll go north to Gretna, so we just have to follow the pike."

"That's if he means to marry her."

Hugh started cursing, softly, for the children's sake.

"No," Darius thought out loud. "He must want to wed her, but she will not be willing. Now, there's an understatement if I know Sonia. He'll have a battle on his hands the whole way to Scotland, so I bet he'll just get her out of town, into a rented lodging or a wayside inn, and keep her there until she agrees."

"That miserable—"

"Yes, but there are a lot of roads out of London, and a lot of inns. We'll have to figure he took his own coach, at least, so he wouldn't need strangers along for the abduction. Someone's bound to remember seeing the markings."

The dog's howling had turned to yelps as Fitz dashed to and fro along the carriageway. Darius studied his movements. "We'll start this way, out of the park. Fitz seems sure. At the gate, you go north, Hugh, in case I am wrong and he is headed for Gretna Green after all. You can go faster on horseback. I'll follow Fitz. Whoever picks up a trail sends a messenger back to Ware House for Ian and Robb. Make sure you leave messages along the way, and I'll do the same. Robb, if you haven't heard from either of us by dusk, go to the Runners. Ian, wait as long as you can before alerting Lady Atterbury."

When the others nodded their agreement, Darius sent the carriage off and watched Hugh use his heels on the chestnut. He climbed into the curricle. Fitz jumped up beside him, whining.

"Yes, I know, old boy. We'll never let her out of our sight again. Now, hang on, Fitz, you're in for the ride of your life."

Sonia awoke to a fierce headache and the rumbling of a carriage. The blanket was on her lap, thank goodness, no longer over her head. Her hands and her legs were tied, and the window shades were drawn on the carriage. Ansel Berke was seated across from her in the gloom with a smug smile on his powdered face, so either she was having the most detailed nightmare of her life, or the pompous ass really was abducting her for her dowry. After he stole her virtue.

She tested the bonds on her wrists under cover of the blanket. The carriage was traveling slowly enough that she could hope to survive a jump from the coach if she could only get her hands free. Sonia thought they must still be in the city, from the lack of speed and the traffic noises she heard, so she ought to be able to find help, once on the street. With the curtains drawn, she had no way of discerning direction or destination. She just knew the sooner she was away from this bedlamite, the better. Unfortunately, although the bonds were not painfully tight, she could not undo the knots.

Sonia decided to try reasoning with the baron again. She did not bother appealing to his sense of honor, justice, or fair play. Sonia never spent her coin on lost causes. Berke had already proved his dearth of scruples by the kidnapping, so her only hope lay in convincing the thatch-gallows that his scheme was doomed to failure.

"It won't work, you know," she told him. "No matter what you do, I'll never be your wife. I'll refuse to make the vows."

"As I said, you'll have no choice, my dear. Your family will insist on the marriage."

"My family will accept my decision no matter what happens."

He cackled. "You truly are an innocent. Lady Atterbury will welcome a leper to Grosvenor Square before a ruined woman. Unless I open them, every door will be closed to you."

"Not my father's," Sonia insisted.

"From what I hear, he doesn't remember *having* a daughter. Do you really think his new young wife wants a tarnished spinster under her roof? I knew Jennifer Corwith during her season. Grasping chit, her dowry was too paltry to put up with her puling. Nevertheless, your brother's wife ain't about to want scandal touching her new position, precarious as it is, with the squire taking her own neglected stepsister to wife. As for your sister in Bath, why, Backhurst is as proud as he can stare. He most likely won't let Catherine even correspond with a fallen woman."

Sonia set her mouth in a determined scowl, especially after she was forced to acknowledge the truth of his arguments, so far. "George's wife and Catherine's husband might place public opinion above family. My papa never will. He'll take care of me, so you'll never get a groat of my portion."

Berke leaned toward her and laughed again, an unpleasant, humorless sound. Even his breath was foul, unconcealed by his stagnating scent. "Your papa will take care of you?" he sniped. "The way he took care of you all your life, letting you run wild about the countryside? Oh yes, my dear, I know all about you and your delightful family. You suit me to a cow's thumb, you see, so I made the effort. The ton is already half-convinced you are no better than you should be. A night or two at a posting house should turn the tide."

"I repeat, never."

No longer amused at her resistance, Berke leaned back on the seat opposite hers. "Your opposition is gallant, my dear, and I do appreciate not being treated to tears and the vapors. However, you waste your breath. You'll marry me if I have to find a Newgate friar. If I have to drug you or knock you senseless. Your consent is not required, Miss Randolph, so save your strength for tonight."

Now, Squire Randolph may have held a loose rein over his youngest daughter, but he never sent her unprotected on her rambles. He made sure she had her dog—and a dirty trick or two. He taught her to use reason first, but when that failed, foul play. Sonia felt she'd tried being reasonable, without getting through to Berke's self-interest, if nothing else. Now she brought her hobbled legs up to seat level and kicked her booted feet forward, right where they were certain to get the baron's undivided attention.

"This way, eh, Fitz?" Darius was regretting Robb's absence. Every time he wanted to get down from the curricle to seek information, he had to find an urchin or an ostler to hold the fractious bays. His leg was starting to ache, and his mood was growing blacker and blacker as the traffic moved slower and slower. His only consolation was knowing that Berke was making no better time through the congested streets. Some blasted victory celebration, Darius cursed.

When they did come to a halt behind a water wagon or whatever, or when they reached a crossroads, Fitz leaped down and sniffed around as often as the major. The dog whined and circled, then jumped back up, barking. Soon Darius took to watching the dog as much as the horses and the other vehicles. Fitz seemed to know what he was doing, and the major's instincts told him to follow the animal. Those same instincts had kept Darius alive for years, so he aimed his cattle where the mongrel's nose pointed.

"I hope you're right, old boy, but I don't know how you can be so sure. They have a good lead on us. Do you think you can find Berke's coach in this mess, huh, Fitz?"

Of course I can. I peed on it, didn't I?

Chapter Twenty-three

Some wag once said that fleas are good for a dog. They keep him from brooding about being a dog. Dogs don't brood. Hens brood. Do you know how little it takes to make a dog happy? A full belly, a soft bed, a kind word are usually enough. Why should we brood?

It's not dogs who are unhappy with their lot. We're not the ones who always want more than we have, more than we need. It's man who is top dog at greed.

Like the baron. Talk about brooding! He should have had so many fleas, he'd have time for nothing but scratching. That might have kept him from wanting more and more and my mistress! He had a title and a tidy competence. They were not enough. Gambling did not increase his wealth, so he tried to steal Miss Sonia's portion, especially, I think, because she was to be Conover's mate. Greed.

Napoleon is greedy. He gambles with whole armies and he kidnaps entire countries. Do complete nations of men share their avarice?

No, that's foolish beyond belief, even for such flea-brains.

Besides, I have to pay more attention now.

The streets are crowded. Many carriages, horses, and pedestrians have passed this way. The noise of a military band a few blocks over saturates my senses, so it is harder to concentrate. Still, I know we are on the right course. If only we could hurry some.

Then the major went off the scent, no matter how I told him different. He told me to hush, that he's cutting through back alleys and side streets to gain back some of Berke's lead. If the baron was on the road ahead, which I knew he was, we might come out ahead of him. A fine military maneuver, if successful. Otherwise we could be dodging through narrow lanes and cluttered alleys, chasing our own tails.

I was ready to jump down. I could make better time on my own, ducking between carriages. Then we intersected the main road at a corner where a sweep was working. The major tossed a coin to a peg-legged man in a tattered uniform. "Can you hold the horses, soldier?" he asked.

The veteran took a bite of the coin in his hand and vowed he'd treat 'em like high-priced whores. Now, *that* should make Caesar and Jupiter relax. I yipped at them as I dashed past. They'd stay put.

Other horses and their drivers cursed at me as I ran between hooves, under carriage beds, circling. Was Berke still ahead of us, getting away, or was he just coming toward the intersection? A night-soil collector had just gone by. I couldn't smell a thing!

The major was standing up on the curricle seat—good thing I told those nags to stand still—looking in both directions. "There he is!" he shouted, vaulting down and running ahead. I was right at his side.

The major stopped by the sweep, threw another coin, and snatched up the lad's broom. The man has gone queer as Dick's hatband, I thought. I ran ahead, closing in. Then the broom sailed over my head, javelin-style. All that practice paid off. The broom finally slowed and flipped end over end, right in front of a crested coach-and-four. Those were four horses who suddenly believed in sorcery. They started bucking and rearing in the traces, looking for the witch and screaming about being turned into Americans or something. The driver had all he could do to keep them from bolting through a dress shop window. Soon every horse on the street was making noise and mayhem, horses being as excitable and subject to suggestion as adolescent girls. The drivers were shouting, nothing was moving on the street. People were pouring out of stores and a corner tavern.

We ran in for the kill. The major pulled the carriage door open, reached inside, dragged Ansel Berke out by his collar. I was his comrade in arms. I was brave. I was brutal. I gave no quarter. My growls rolled across the street like the mighty lion's roar stretched across the great savannah, as I went for Berke's throat. . . .

"Get back, you overgrown dust mop, I knocked him out with the first punch." Darius threw the limp baron to the street like soiled laundry. Fitz immediately jumped onto Berke's chest, slavering into his face. Berke wasn't going anywhere. The major drew the rapier from his cane and brandished it for the sake of the driver. "Don't think of coming to his aid. Don't think of driving off."

"No, guv'nor. I ain't gonna think at all, if you say so. Never liked this job anyways. 'E promised me back wages if I went along, is all."

Darius wasn't listening. He was climbing back inside the carriage for Sonia. He used his sword to cut the bonds at her ankles and wrists, cursing the entire time. "Are you all right, Sonia? Did he hurt you? I'll kill him, by George, if he so much as touched a hair on your head."

When her hands were free, Sonia reached up to feel the back of her skull. She winced.

"He's dead. I don't care if I hang." Darius started to get out of the chaise, murder in his eyes.

"No, Darius. I am fine, truly. I do believe Ansel was coming to see the error of his ways anyway. He suffered much worse than I did, I assure you."

Darius took her in his arms then, right there in the closed carriage, telling Sonia that she was brave and clever, and Berke never stood a chance. His relieved outpourings were lovely, but Sonia began to fear her bones might break from his squeezing so hard. And the noise . . . She managed to loosen his grip enough to raise the curtain over the carriage window. A mob of people were standing around the coach, some angrily knocking on its side.

"Darius, please."

He released his hold on her, but only long enough to slip his arms under her legs and behind her back. He swung her out of the carriage. Some of the spectators applauded when he set Sonia on her feet.

"Coo, it's just loike a fairy tale, ain't it?" a young maid with a serving tray in her hand sighed. "Ain't 'e the 'andsome 'ero an' all."

Sonia winked at Darius and nodded her agreement to the girl.

A burly individual in a leather apron pushed his way to the front. " 'Ere, 'ere, wot's this about some toff runnin' off wit' a gentry mort? Oi'll give 'im a taste a home-brewed, oi will."

Another man in the circle guffawed. "An' that be just like you, you great lummox, t' come on like a bloody Crusader after the war be won. It's the dog wot has the skirter. There be naught for you t' do wit' yer great bloomin' muscles 'cept flex 'em for Polly 'ere."

Some of the other men laughed. The aproned fellow stepped forward angrily, but Darius held his hand up.

"Thank you all, good people," he said, "for coming to our aid. We still have need of your services to restore the lady." He pulled out his purse. "Might someone take a hackney to Ware House in Grosvenor Square to inform my household?"

Darius selected a messenger from the eager volunteers while the serving girl Polly blotted her eyes on a dingy apron. "A real nobleman, 'e be. I cain't wait t' tell me ma."

Darius passed a few more shillings around. "For your help in clearing the street and getting these wagons moving." Angry draymen cheered and returned to their carts and loads. Darius handed a coin to the girl with the tray. "Perhaps I can impose on you to provide some tea for the lady, Miss, ah, Polly? And you"—with a handful of guineas to the aproned bruiser—"if I am not mistaken, own that tavern yonder. Serve a round on me to everyone who has been inconvenienced." Another cheer went up.

"But wot about 'im?" one of the men asked, jerking his head toward where Berke still lay in the gutter, the dog on his chest snarling if Berke made the least move.

"Him?" Darius asked casually, snapping his fingers and whistling the dog away. "Why, he's mine. All mine."

Berke cringed, but maintained enough self-esteem—or stupidity—to get to his feet. He looked down on the muddy pawprints on his fawn breeches, the pulled threads on his dragonfly-embroidered waistcoat, the dog drool on his limpened neckcloth. He sat back down on the cobbles, all confidence and bravery gone together.

Darius was beyond caring whether he had a fair fight or not. Grabbing Berke by the frills of his shirtfront, he dragged the baron to his feet.

"Why, you bastard? Why have you done everything you could to ruin my life? What did I ever do to you?" A fist to Berke's middle punctuated the questions, but did not elicit any answers, so the major tried shaking the smaller man. "Tell me why, if you hope to live until tomorrow."

"L-l-love M-M-Miss R-Randolph," issued forth.

Darius did not like that answer. "You loved her enough to clobber her and kidnap her, and try to force her against her will? Whatever that is, it sure as Hades ain't love. You wanted her money. But you've been snapping at my heels before you ever set eyes on Miss Randolph and her dowry." He shook Berke again, harder. The sawdust calf pads sank to Berke's ankles. "For the last time, why?"

"M-m-my s-sister."

"Gammon. And still not good enough. You know I didn't touch the girl, just like you know I never cheated at cards." He gave another shake. Berke's corset snapped with a loud crack. Then the nipped-in waist of his superfine coat wasn't quite so nipped, buttons popping onto the street.

Berke groaned. "My other sister. Rosellen."

"Ah, finally something of interest." Darius allowed Berke's feet to touch the ground, but he kept hold of the baron's shirt. "Do go on."

"Rosellen wanted to be countess. She tried to bring Milo up to scratch, but he wouldn't have her. He chose Suzannah instead, but Rosellen never forgot. You were just a second son, a soldier, so she wed Preston. Then she found out about him and Hermione."

"So you did know all along."

Berke closed his eyes. "Rosellen couldn't expose her own husband without looking the fool. And she already hated the Warebournes."

"And you went along with her out of brotherly love?"

"Rosellen paid me. My debts."

"And when I came home from the war, she saw

her way clear to winning the title after all." Darius was revolted, not shocked.

"No, that was Preston's idea. He controls the purse strings."

"I'm surprised you dance to his tune. Seems to me you could have played the piper, with your lack of ethics."

Berke mumbled something Darius couldn't quite catch. Neither could the few spectators still standing around them on the side of the road. They moved closer. The tavern wench had fetched Sonia a chair, along with some lemonade, and stood next to it, mouth agape. "Coo, it's better'n a play at Drury Lane. Maybe 'e was too nice to blackmail the other gent. 'E looks too pretty to be so mean."

Sonia rubbed her chafed wrists. "I do not think he's too nice for anything!"

"Nor do I," Darius agreed. He took a firmer hold on Berke's collar. "Preston wanted the title, and Rosellen—well, her motives are best left unsaid. But yours? You were on the lookout for an heiress. Everyone knew that. You could have lined your pockets without challenging me. In fact, you could have sold your information to Milo, then me. I think there's more to this than you have mentioned."

"Preston . . . knew something about me." Berke licked his lips. He looked at Sonia, then away. "A youthful indiscretion, nothing more. But he threatened to go to the authorities, or the scandal sheets." He looked at Warebourne in desperation. "I'd have been thrown out of my clubs!"

Darius shook him one last time for satisfaction, then shoved him away. "So you were content to save your reputation by ruining mine. What was it, the usual hanging offense?"

Berke sank to the ground, staring blankly at his scuffed boots. He merely nodded, gulping back sobs.

"One more question." Darius spoke softly. "Milo and Suzannah's carriage accident?"

"I swear I know nothing about it," Berke babbled. "If Preston did, he never let on. There was no inquiry. But I didn't, I swear. I wouldn't. Please." He raised his hands in supplication.

"Zeus, you disgust me. The world would be a better place without you in it."

The baron's shoulders started shaking on their own. Darius turned his back on the sorry sight to greet Ian and Robb. The reinforcements had arrived, along with six servants in Ware House black and gold livery, on horseback, brandishing pistols.

"Good grief, man," Darius shouted at Robb. "You've armed the underfootmen! Can they shoot?"

"Nary a bit. The guns ain't loaded, except for mine, a course. You thinkin' I should aim it at this muckworm here?"

While Darius was still bemusedly observing his new recruits, Robb chuckled. "Right, sir. Gettin' 'em on horseback was the harder part. But I had to send two of the stable lads out for the lieutenant, and leave another couple of riders behind for carryin' messages. Someone responsible had to stay back with the young 'uns. This is what was left."

"Robb, you deserve a promotion. For now, though, I am afraid you and your troops will have to do escort duty. Baron Berke is leaving the country. You and your stalwarts will make sure he reaches his ship—any ship—safely. First, however, I believe yon innkeep will provide ink and paper. I am also certain Baron Berke will accommodate me by writing down his little tale. His passport, don't you know." He turned to the nobleman. "One-way passport. Is that understood?"

Berke moved his head up and down a fraction.

"But what about Preston and Rosellen?" Sonia wanted to know. "Those two blackhearts can't get away with all they've done to you!" Sonia was so angry, she looked as if she'd take on the miscreants herself.

"Oh, I think we can be forgiving of our cousins . . . from Jamaica. Preston has holdings there. He'll go."

Darius waved an arm at the ring of watchers. "He'll never dare show his face in London again."

" 'Ere, 'ere," echoed from the crowd. "Exile's too good for the likes o' him."

"Yer lettin' this 'un off easy, guv." The circle of spectators was growing larger again, and they did not want a peaceable ending at all. They wanted blood.

Darius was pleased to oblige. He picked the baron up once more, drew back a steel-driven fist, and completed Berke's disarrangement by· repositioning the baron's nose. Then he lifted him bodily and tossed him into the coach. The mob cheered as the carriage drove off with Robb and Ian and its resplendent if reluctant mounted escort. Most of the onlookers dispersed, thinking the show was over.

Darius turned to Sonia, who had been applauding as loudly as the most eager street urchin. "Bloodthirsty wench, aren't you?" he asked.

"Oh no. If I were bloodthirsty, I'd have drawn his claret myself!"

"I bet you would have, my endless delight." Darius laughed out loud and opened his arms to her.

Sonia walked into his embrace like coming home. "I knew you'd come," she told him, ignoring Polly's smiles and the currently unemployed sweep's whistle.

"I'd come through the gates of hell for you, Sonia," Darius whispered in her ear, his hands caressing her back, sending thrills down her spine. "And I would not leave without you, for I'll never let you go again. I cannot wait on your father. I've tried to be patient and do things properly, but I simply don't have that kind of strength. Sonia, you are my sunshine and my heart's song. Please say you'll be mine, forever."

She looked up at him, straight into his soft brown eyes. "Darius, I have been yours, forever." Which required a kiss. The tavern girl wiped her eyes.

"Soon?" Sonia asked when the world stopped spinning.

"The banns or a special license?"

"Can we be remarried later, in Sheltonford chapel, with everyone there?"

"We can be remarried anywhere you want. Once a week. In front of the prince, Parliament, or the Pied Piper. Just soon!"

"Then we need a special license. The banns take three weeks, my lord earl."

"Countess Sonia." He tasted it on his lips, then on her lips. Polly was blubbering. Then Darius sprang back. "My God, Duchess Atterbury. She'll have me boiled in oil!"

Sonia laughed. "Don't tell me the hero of the hour is afraid of one old lady?"

He grinned back. "I'd rather face the Spanish Inquisition any day. But I'll do it, for you!"

This time the kiss lasted so long, the crossing sweep was making book with a knife sharpener, and the serving girl was sobbing.

"Here now, sir. Enough of that. You'll embarrass the lady." The peg-legged man led the horses and curricle over to them.

Darius stepped back. The sweep ran forward with the lord's sword-cane, and Polly retrieved the lady's bonnet. She wiped it tenderly with her tear-dampened apron before reverently handing it to Sonia.

"Quite right, soldier," Darius said while Sonia tied her bonnet's strings. "Thank you for reminding me of my, ah, duty. And the cattle look calm enough, too. The bays won't stand for just anybody. You must have a way with horses. Cavalry?"

"McConnell's Fifth, sir. Private Brown, sir."

"Brave lads, Brown. Talavera?" he asked, gesturing toward the veteran's missing leg.

"Right enough. And your own bum limb, sir?" the man queried back, recognizing a fellow military man.

"Salamanca." Darius looked around when he felt a tug on his sleeve. He couldn't misread Sunny's hopeful expression. "Seems to me—to us—that one of our finest shouldn't be out on the street like this. And I seem to need a groom. You're qualified, Private Brown, except one thing worries me."

Brown's face fell. "That's what they all say, sir. No one thinks I can do an honest day's work with my wooden leg." He turned to leave. Sonia was starting to sputter.

"No, both of you!" Darius stated. "I just worried that Private Brown might be offended if his duties included pony lessons for three little girls."

"Bless you, sir, I nursed enough Johnny Raws through maneuvers. Little girls and ponies'd be sheer heaven."

"Then climb aboard, man; we're off to find a special license. Here, darling, up you go."

Fitz jumped up between Sonia and Darius on the seat. They both gave him a pet before Darius gave the horses the office to start. "Good dog, Fitz."

Good dog, Fitz?

Chapter Twenty-four

That's it? I win the day for them, save the children, sound the alarm, track the coach, subdue the villain. And "Good dog, Fitz" is my reward?

I suppose it's always been this way. Romulus did not name the city Lupa, though he and his twin Remus would be carrion without us. People are born under the sign of the ram, the bull, the crab, even the scorpion. No one is born under the sign of the spaniel, in the house of the harrier, on the cusp of the collie.

It's not just dogs, either, although of all the species, we give man the most love and loyalty. Does anyone remember the name of even one of Hannibal's elephants? Daniel gets all the credit for pulling the thorn out of the lion's paw. For barking out loud, Daniel was going to get eaten! No one congratulates the lion for his forbearance and sense of fair play. I could go on, but whining never brought dinner hour any closer.

And a pat on the head is enough, I suppose,

since I know my job was well done. So they won't name a star after me. I was very, very good. Thanks to me, we now have a house of our own, with tenants to help, villagers to visit, farmers to advise. We have laughter all the time: little-girl giggles and deep-throated rumbles and, yes, even the first gummy, droolly grins of Master Miles Cecil Randolph Conover, Baronet Ware.

Now I have more time to go visit the setter bitch at the game warden's cottage that I met a few months ago. There's one puppy in her new litter that I like to think resembles me. He's black, with my gold eyebrows, and his tail is cocked at just the right angle for a dog, jaunty yet dignified. There's something more about him. You'd recognize the right pup instantly. He's the one who won't stay in the whelping box, no matter that he falls on his nose climbing over the sides. He's the one who has to taste the straw and the grass and the morning dew. He chases sunbeams and growls at shadows. That's the one.

"Darling—"

"My love—" Darius laughed and tucked Sonia's hand back onto his arm. They continued walking on a slow tour of the nearby grounds, admiring the summer flowers. "You go first," he said.

Sonia listened to a bird calling in the woods. "I just wanted to discuss an idea I had about a school in the village, but it can wait. What did you wish to say?"

Darius groaned. "Only that you have to stop employing every waif and wanderer who passes by. The maids are already tripping over each other, and the horses won't have any hair left from all the currying they are getting from the excess of grooms we seem to employ."

"You cannot complain about the stables, my lord,

216

for you hired Brown yourself, and that half regiment he said needed positions. And you did agree that Polly was wasted at the tavern, especially since Maisie and Robb will be setting up their own household. And that poor girl whose family all died in the last influenza outbreak—"

Darius held up a hand in surrender. "But the others, Sunny. And the ones the vicar will mention to you tomorrow. I finally got Lady Atterbury to forgive me for marrying you out of hand. You know she said she'd have my liver and lights if we sent her any more untrained servants with sad stories."

"Oh pooh, that's just Grandmama. She was delighted with Portia Foggarty. Grandmama really did need a companion, and Portia's husband left her in dun territory when he went off to fight in Spain."

"Yes, but—"

Sonia patted his arm. "I know, darling. That's why I think we need a new school."

"We already have a school, Sunny. With two teachers, a maid, and a man-of-all-work. You are going to bankrupt even the Warebourne treasury, my pet."

"Fustian. We are increasing the holdings magnificently, and your investments are profitable beyond even your expectations. Remember, we went over all the accounts together just last week, so don't give me any Banbury tale of impending poverty."

He grinned and kissed her on the nose, where a sprinkle of freckles was starting to make a summer appearance. "You may hire as many unskilled workers as you wish, then, wife." He began to trail kisses down her neck.

Sonia was not to be diverted. "That's the point of the new school, Darius. The one we have is for children, to teach them their letters and such. I want another place where those adults in need can learn a skill. Weaving or fancy needlework, perhaps, or learning to keep accounts. Even cooking and the ways of polishing a gentleman's boots. Anything that might secure someone a position. Then they can earn their own way and need not depend on the parish rolls."

"Clever wife, saving me money in the long run. Have I told you lately that I love you?"

"Not since breakfast," she answered with dimples showing.

"Oh, much too long ago." He proceeded to show her in convincing fashion.

"And have I told you recently how happy you make me?" she asked.

"Never often enough. Come, let's go back to the house while the children are— What's that hen-witted dog done now?"

"Fitz," Sonia ordered. "Put that puppy down! You know it's too young. I told you yesterday and the day before, too. I cannot imagine how the mother permits you to keep scooping it up and taking it away."

Darius knelt. Fitz gently placed the pup in his cupped hands.

"I don't know why Fitz persists in bringing us this same little fellow," Sonia said, stroking the shiny black fur while the puppy wrestled with his lordship's glove.

Darius grinned. "Don't you, my love?"

Now, don't get me wrong, I'm not ready to chase my last cat, but, after all, every dog must have his day.

Now available from
REGENCY ROMANCE

Marry in Haste and Francesca's Rake
by Lynn Kerstan

Together for the first time, two Regency classics star
heroines gambling on love, not knowing if they will
lose their hearts—or win true love.

0-451-21717-9

Miss Clarkson's Classmate
by Sharon Sobel

Emily Clarkson arrives at her new teaching position
expecting her employer to be a gentleman, and she's
shocked to find a brute. He's expecting a somber old
maid. And neither is expecting the passion that soon
overtakes them both.

0-451-21718-7

Lady Emma's Dilemma
by Rhonda Woodward

Once lovers, Lady Emmaline and Baron Devreux have
different points of view concerning their long-ago
tryst. But in an unexpected encounter, the two simply
have too many questions and the answers only come
by moonlight—and with a little mischief.

0-451-21701-2